BOY 39

DEREK HOLSER

Printed in the United States of America.
Edited by Leah Holser, Samantha Blackmer, Esther Keane, Sara Norcott
and Frankie Franklin.
Design by Josh Hill. Logo by The Affari Project.

ISBN 978-0-9882805-0-2
0 9 8 8 2 8 0 5 0 7

*To Leah, who knows everything about me,
And loves me just the same.*

First Printing
October 29, 2012
#191/500

Hannah-Marie,

I wish you all the best in every pursuit that God has placed in your heart. Never surrender and believe for the impossible.

Best Regards,

Derek Hale

- Undoing One thing Always Does Another -

1

"Next," Sentry-5 ordered. He stood at the head of the line, his broad hands pressed against his hips, glaring at the two girls who were at the front of the procession of students. His bushy eyebrows jutted out from his forehead like twisted branches over a brooding abyss. His ominous eyes, dark ovals of simmering rage, declared his violent intentions. One look was enough to scare most kids into submission. His scowl terrified and his physical presence was overwhelming; at 6'6" with doorway-wide shoulders, Sentry-5 was the largest enforcer the students had ever seen.

He wore the usual sentry uniform: a full-body jumpsuit. He looked like an enormous auto mechanic, minus the grease. A flat chrome belt buckle engraved with the silhouette of an evergreen and the words *The Woodlands* separated his brawny torso from his tree trunk legs. A sewn-on red patch with a white number 5 covered the left side of his chest.

"Keep moving!" he bellowed at the two boys circling to the back of the line as they dragged their feet against the mossy ground, kicking pinecones. The misty rain that dripped and rolled off of everyone's edges was no deterrent to his demands, nor was it a hindrance for the students' outdoor activities. Life in the Pacific Northwest was mostly lived against a backdrop of grey skies, tall trees and dampness. Lots of dampness.

The students were lined up along the northernmost wall of the Yard. A rectangular space surrounded by ten-foot high cinder block walls, the Yard was the only exposure to the outdoors at The Woodlands. Electric wires suspended between short black poles ringed the top of the wall, forbidding exit or entry. The Yard was the place where the children at The Woodlands experienced their only independent moments.

They were allowed free time in the Yard twice a day for fifteen minutes during the week, and two one-hour sessions on Saturday and Sunday. The Yard was comprised mostly of twelve horseshoe pits and a mix of dilapidated sporting nets and jungle gyms. The Yard was anchored in the center by a single willow tree framed by an oval bed filled with leafy ferns and barely living wild roses.

A double row of listless seven to twelve-year-olds; the well-trained children waited in silence for their heads to be shaved. They stood in alternating gender pairs, most of them wearing brown or white tunics over tan leggings. The students who were serving work detail or completing punishment assignments wore white shirts under dark blue coveralls. The constant mechanical hum of the clippers, operated by the two sentries who stood between Sentry-5 and the front of the line, provided a monotone soundtrack for the melancholy atmosphere. It was the first day of the month, Shearing Day at The Woodlands.

Every student's head was shaved on Shearing Day. The monthly ritual had been initiated a few years earlier, as a means of reducing potential fraternization between the older boys and girls. All students at The Woodlands were numbered rather than named. It was part of the constant effort to eliminate individuality. Mirrors had been removed long before Shearing Day was instituted, as any focus on physical beauty was wasted energy. In spite of these attempts to eliminate distraction, the hormones of developing adolescents occasionally overpowered the constraints of discipline.

Thirty-Nine stood beside his podmate Thirty-Three, behind the two girls now at the front of the line. Thirty-Three glanced over at Thirty-Nine, who stared straight ahead. Thirty-Three coughed to get Thirty-Nine's attention.

"Silence!" Sentry-5 shouted.

Thirty-Nine looked over at his smirking podmate. As their eyes locked, Thirty-Three arched his eyebrows and pointed at the girl in front of him. He winked, and moved his eyebrows rapidly up and down. Thirty-Nine shook his head in exasperation.

Thirty-Three sure loves to stir up trouble, he thought.

They had been podmates for almost five years. During that time,

Thirty-Three led the entire student body in disciplinary infractions, while Thirty-Nine moved toward the top of the class. Thirty-Nine was a model of consistency while Thirty-Three's only consistency was his near weekly violation of one or more of The Ten Axioms of The Woodlands.

Now Thirty-Three was courting danger with Sentry-5 just to alert Thirty-Nine that Eleven was in front of them. They had been standing behind her and another girl, Fifteen, for at least ten minutes. Yet he chose this moment, standing less than ten feet from Sentry-5, to notify Thirty-Nine of her presence.

Thirty-Nine rolled his eyes and nodded his recognition of Eleven's existence. He understood his friend's interest in her but he hated to indulge Thirty-Three's folly. There was no disputing Eleven's superiority. No matter what human subculture exists in this world, a hierarchy always develops over time. Regardless of geography, history, social customs, or even the definition of beauty, celebrity is always gained by some at the expense of others. In the secluded subculture of ultra-intelligent orphans at The Woodlands, Eleven was preeminent. She was the Head Student.

Thirty-Nine stared at her figure as the clippers buzzed her scalp. Her long legs gave her an advantage in jumping exercises. Her lean arms seemed constantly coiled for action, even when she was writing at her desk. She was older and taller than most of the other students. If he closed his eyes, he could picture her vivid blue eyes and her freckled cheeks. Eleven was twelve years old. She was an early bloomer; it was impossible for any boy older than eight to not notice her.

Fifteen, the girl standing beside Eleven, was an ill-tempered introvert with a slumped frame and a frown to match. Fifteen rarely spoke and she spent most of her free time in the Yard scribbling in a notepad. Two weeks earlier, Thirty-Nine had bumped into her as he sprinted across the Yard, trying to get to the one good swing near the jungle gym. As he stared at the short light brown hairs drifting off the clippers and sticking to her thick neck, he remembered the interaction.

—————————————————————————————————

"Sorry!" He tried to apologize as he untangled his right leg from her left arm. They had fallen to the ground upon colliding, and his foot was pinned under her upper back. As she rolled over, relieving the pressure on his lower leg, he apologized again.

"I'm sorry Fifteen. I shouldn't have been in such a rush."

She sat up and climbed to her feet, pressing her hand into her chubby thigh as she brought her left leg up followed by her right. As he stood up, she looked at him and wheezed, "There's no reason to ever rush around here. Unless you're rushing to die."

Thirty-Nine stared at her. He knew she was an odd girl but he did not expect such a ghoulish response in the Yard, especially in the middle of a rare cloudless day. He still wanted to get to the swing as well. He glanced over her sloped shoulder and saw two boys already climbing onto it.

"Oh well," he muttered, forgetting for the moment that he was still in a conversation with a queen of darkness.

"Oh well?" Fifteen asked, puffing out her pudgy cheeks, annoyed by his lack of concern for her well-being.

"I'm sorry," Thirty-Nine said for the third time. "Are you ok?"

"I'll be ok when I'm free of this ball of dirt." She spit on the ground and looked skyward. "And when I find myself at home among the ancestors of the heavens."

"Sure...of course." Thirty-Nine replied then dashed away to anywhere in the Yard where she wasn't.

He looked up from the recollection as Fifteen and Eleven were getting their last patch of hair shaved away. He and Thirty-Three stood motionless behind them, waiting.

As the last clump was brushed away by the sentries, Sentry-5 barked his command for the boys to move toward the shearers.

"Next."

Thirty-Three stepped forward first, eager to occupy the space exited by Eleven. As Eleven turned to the right, Fifteen turned to the left. Both appeared to be headed to the back of the line, as the students always did until the final head was shorn.

The two girls passed by Thirty-Nine and Thirty-Three, whose fuzzy scalps were entering the first swath of pruning by the clippers.

Suddenly Fifteen yelled, "Now!"

At her shout, Eleven bolted away from the line and began running toward the closest wall, about twenty feet from where the boys stood. Fifteen lumbered straight toward the opposite wall, at least fifty yards away.

A collective gasp rose from the students. The sentries stopped cutting hair to pursue the fleeing girls. Thirty-Nine and Thirty-Three turned to watch the spectacle. It had been two years since the last attempted escape.

As one clipper-wielding sentry pursued Eleven, the other chased Fifteen. Eleven had a good lead and she was the fastest student at The Woodlands. She hurdled the backstop of a horseshoe pit without breaking stride, her momentum propelling her within steps of the wall. The sentry in pursuit was not as agile. As Eleven's hands slapped against the wall, he stumbled over the horseshoe pit and slapped the ground with his face. Several students gasped, and a few muted cheers echoed through the Yard. Sentries began flooding from the double doors into the Yard, whistles blowing as the command "Everyone down!" blared from the intercom speakers mounted throughout the Yard.

Thirty-Three dove to the ground and lay still, ignoring the muck that splattered on his arms and face. He propped his chin on his pudgy hands and continued to watch. Thirty-Nine, more conscientious than his podmate, huffed at the dirty spray now speckled on his legs from Thirty-Three's plop. He avoided getting mud on his face by slowly laying on the small tarp covered with hair clippings.

Eleven feverishly felt for a finger hold in the wall. Her strong hands glided across the blocks until she felt a gash in the concrete. She slipped the first three fingers of her left hand two knuckles deep into that hole and reached with her right hand for a lip created by broken mortar about six feet off the ground. Her eyes focused on the top of the wall as she tensed her legs and dug her feet into the wall, pulling her body up by her fingertips. Like a human spider she paused for a moment suspended, staring at her target.

A gray metal electrical box was affixed to the base of the black pole that supported the multiple strands of electrified wires stretching along the top of the wall. Dust flew out as Eleven tugged against the inside of the crumbling joint compound. She used her two feet and left hand as scattered launching pads, simultaneously applying force with all three, enabling her to reach the top with her right hand. She dangled for a moment by one long arm, while her left hand flung and reaching for the top. Once, twice, she grabbed at it as her weight and momentum pulled her off-balance. Just as her right hand began to drag across the edge, grip weakening, she caught a lip of cinder block with her right foot and stabilized herself.

Thirty-Three sighed in relief as he saw Eleven hook the top of the wall. Both hands gripped the ledge and both feet pushed her up to a comfortable place, her armpits serving as anchor points for her body. She slid her arms between the wires and the top of the wall and hooked her hands on the other side of the wall, the side that faced the rest of the world; the world that no Woodlands student had ever visited.

Thirty-Nine was watching Fifteen. She was huffing and puffing but still had a fifteen-yard lead on the nearest sentry as she approached the end of the Yard. Just before she reached the far wall, she knelt down and dragged the four-shelved horseshoe storage rack against the wall. She stepped into the base of the makeshift ladder and swung her thick leg up to the second shelf while balancing her body by pressing her hands against the wall. As she began climbing, Thirty-Nine noticed an enormous brown blur churning across the ground. It was Sentry-5. He was running full speed, his body rumbling over the earth and shrubs as easily as the clippers had mowed down the hairs on Thirty-Nine's head.

Eleven pulled a rock from under her tunic and banged against the metal box that powered the electric wires strung around the perimeter of the wall, desperately trying to short circuit the remaining barrier to escape. Thirty-Three watched her frenzied hammering through squinted eyes, his body twitching in response each time he heard the ping of stone on metal. As she struck it a fifth time, orange sparks burst from the black pole and a loud pop resounded across the Yard. Thirty-Three clenched his fists as the box exploded. Eleven reached for the now un-electrified wire and began pulling herself to the top of the wall, mere moments from tumbling over the barrier and into freedom.

As she pinned the dead wires under her right leg and hugged the top of the wall, the sentry in pursuit rose to his feet and scrambled near the base of the wall. He reached to his hip for his club but as soon as his fingers felt it he knew it couldn't reach her. His left hand was clenched around a heavy oblong object. *The clippers*, he remembered. He switched the hair cutting device to his right hand and drew back to throw.

Meanwhile, Thirty-Nine had his fists balled up at his side, frightened and enraged by what was unfolding before him. Fifteen reached the top of the horseshoe rack, and somehow hoisted herself to a position near the top of the wall. Her body was still hanging within the confines of the Yard. Her meaty hands and thick wrists reddened under the strain as she pushed against the top of the wall, straightening her arms and lifting her heaving chest against the rim of the wall.

Sentry-5 reached the base of the wall.

"Drop now!" he shouted, flinging the horseshoe rack against the wall for effect. Its metal frame clattered and bent as it collided with the concrete.

Fifteen only pushed harder, scooting her tummy up the wall.

"Drop now or you're going to regret it!"

She refused his command, as her waist now reached the top of the cinder block. Her elbows and armpits were busy wrestling the wires down under her wriggling body.

"I warned you!" he screamed. He reached up with his massive hands and seized her by the ankles. Even a girl as large as Fifteen looked small in comparison to the ogre in the brown jumpsuit. In one rapid motion, he yanked on her legs. She had begun pressing herself upward, but the force of his pull counteracted the power of her push. Her hands slid out and off the top of the wall. She floated for a moment, arms flailing overhead. She could see the forest stretching beyond her for miles, its endless green serenity teasing her with freedom. A butterfly fluttered inches from her face, its yellow and electric blue spots dancing in the wind. And then, everything went black.

Sentry-5 rotated his shoulders with all his might, forcing her to plummet back toward the earth. As he pulled, her chin collided with the top of the wall, shattering her jawbone, spraying broken teeth and blood into the air. Her head slammed backward from the tremendous torque of Sentry-5's wrenching tug on her legs. As Fifteen's stout neck snapped, her body went limp and banged against the wall like a rag doll before crumbling to the ground in a tangled heap of unconsciousness. Thirty-Nine squeezed his eyes closed, hoping that somehow Fifteen would survive.

"Get up. Please get up," he whispered through clenched teeth as he covered his face with his thin fingers.

Eleven sat atop the wall, feet hanging over the edge. She glanced down to survey her landing spot. The earth on the free side of the wall was no different than the ground from which she had just leapt; yet it appeared greener and more alive than anything she had ever seen. Unbeknownst to Eleven, while Thirty-Three watched in silent frenzy, the sentry just below her was about to release his clippers like a baseball player throwing his best fastball.

She pushed off just as he threw the clippers. They flew straight and true, the jagged edges digging into her skull as it slammed against her head with a knockout force. The concussion sent her tumbling into the open space beyond the wall but she never saw her own landing. She was rendered senseless, sprawled in the mossy muck, blood trickling from the back of her head. The other sentries joined the clipper-thrower, and boosted one another over the wall to retrieve Eleven's limp body.

Thirty-Three shuddered and punched the ground, spraying more mud.

"She was so close! She would have been the first!"

Thirty-Nine opened his eyes. Fifteen lay motionless on the grass. Her twisted neck bent at an unnatural angle, causing her head to flop. The top of her head scraped the ground. Her deep blue eyes stared at Thirty-Nine, quivering for help through Sentry-5's wide-legged stance. Dark brown blood puddled under her nose and across her face. She spluttered and coughed, trying to breathe as Sentry-5 stood over her, refusing to provide any assistance.

Sentry-1 rushed to Fifteen and knelt down to clear her airway. A squat block of a man, Sentry-1 was the senior guard at The Woodlands. He was reserved but firm, and in recent years even seemed gentle. At least compared to Sentry-5.

As Sentry-1 reached out to save Fifteen, who was moments from lethal oxygen deprivation, Sentry-5 raised his enormous muddy boot and kicked his fellow guard in his side, lifting him several feet off the ground and fracturing several ribs.

"Don't touch her!" Sentry-5 shouted.

Sentry-1 rose to his feet again, ignoring Sentry-5's command. He surged back toward the barely breathing girl.

"Leave her!" Sentry-5 yelled. He dove at Sentry-1, hitting him across the neck and head. Sentry-1, a human fireplug, ducked under Sentry-5's tall body with ease. Sentry-1 tunneled toward her, clawing at the ground.

Sentry-5 climbed to his feet and yanked his club from its holster. He hurdled Sentry-1's legs and ended the rescue attempt with a powerful whack of his club across the back of Sentry-1's head.

Sentry-1 fell unconscious, just inches from Fifteen.

As the gurgling sound faded and all movement in Fifteen's body ceased, Thirty-Nine couldn't look away. He didn't blink. After another thirty seconds, neither did Fifteen. The desperation in her eyes evaporated as quickly as early morning fog in the summer, replaced by the glassy stare of death.

Sentry-5 tapped her body with the toe of his boot. Satisfied she was gone, he used his heel to roll Fifteen over, face down in the mud. He turned around, and as he did, caught Thirty-Nine's stare. Sentry-5's eyes lit up at the sight of the petrified boy. As the corners of Sentry-5's mouth curled up in a sinister grin, Thirty-Nine turned his head away, grabbing his stomach with one hand, clamping his mouth shut with the other. His body convulsed as he fought the urge to vomit.

Thirty-Three whispered from three feet away, his chubby body splattered with mud, "Are you ok?"

Thirty-Nine shook his head sideways, afraid to open his mouth.

"They were so close. Somebody's going to get out of here one day." Thirty-Three whispered.

"Silence!" A sentry with a bullhorn declared from the middle of the prone children.

"All rise!" He ordered. "Proceed to The Wheel. We have a punishment to distribute."

The children stood to their feet and traipsed away from the scene of the violently thwarted escape. No one spoke as they moved toward the center of the Yard. For a moment, even the birds stopped chirping. The rain began falling harder, pelting the procession of young people, as though Mother Nature herself recognized the injustice of Fifteen's death and wanted to pay her respects.

As they gathered near The Wheel, the ultimate punishment at The Woodlands, Thirty-Nine could see a commotion from the double doors. The sentries had dragged Eleven back through the building, and entered the Yard. Her wrists were lashed together with duct tape and her ankles were shackled with a four-foot chain, forcing her to hop to keep up with her captors.

"We have a foolhardy student who has chosen to violate Axiom 1." The voice of Dr. Nampala, head of The Woodlands roared over the outdoor speakers.

"Students, what is Axiom 1?"

The students were now surrounded by sentries, each one with his club held aloft, ready to bash the skull of any misbehaving child.

"Axiom 1 of The Woodlands," the muted pre-adolescent voices spoke in chorus, "True freedom is found in the mind. True freedom is discovered in surrender to the greater good. The only true freedom is service of The Woodlands."

"Very good, students!" Dr. Nampala's voice directed their attention to The Wheel. "Now, Eleven, our *Head Student*, has chosen to violate Axiom 1 by abandoning her commitment to The Woodlands – to her *family* – to chase some fantasy of the world beyond these walls."

Thirty-Nine stood next to Thirty-Three, their differences highlighted by proximity. Thirty-Nine was lean and a little taller than average, with pale skin and light golden yellow eyes. Thirty-Three was chubby and squat. He had olive skin and dark brown eyes. In addition to their physical differences, their personalities were polar opposites. Thirty-Nine was a dispassionate rule follower with perfect marks in every class; Thirty-three was an emotional bundle of energy who hadn't achieved an error-free month in two years.

"Place Eleven in The Wheel. A reminder to us all."

With that pronouncement, the loudspeakers silenced. The sentries marched Eleven toward The Wheel, a medieval-looking punishment device that was the ultimate physical discipline for students at The Woodlands.

The Wheel, a rough-hewn wooden sphere about ten feet in diameter, was the terror of every student, even Thirty-Three. In its former life, it may have worked as a water wheel at a grain mill. Now, it served to brutally keep children from disobeying The Axioms of The Woodlands. Clumps of tan vomit and dried rivulets of crimson blood from several years of victims stained the splintered device. Students were blindfolded and strapped in, then spun while strange shrieks echoed from speakers overhead. An electric pulse shot through the metal brackets framing their hands and feet. After enough rotations were achieved to induce vomiting, the disobedient student was released and forced with whips to run across gravel while blindfolded.

"Look at the back of her head," Thirty-Three whispered as Eleven was paraded in front of the group. Blood oozed through a six-inch gash halfway down the left backside of her skull. A drying strip of crimson traced the line of her neck, dribbling down onto her tunic, stopping near her left shoulder blade.

"That's a bad cut." Thirty-Nine replied, eyeing the sentry closest to them. The sentry stood gazing across the pack of students. None of the children looked at the sentries; nearly one hundred sets of young eyes stared at Eleven as two sentries lifted her onto the Wheel, which was tilted horizontally to allow for easy placement of her exhausted body. They bracketed her feet into place with metal fetters.

Thirty-Three looked down and scuffed the weeds at their feet, pushing a couple up out of the ground. The exposed roots reminded him of Sentry-5's eyebrows.

"Sentry-5 is evil." He whispered without looking up, fearful of receiving a club to the head from a nearby sentry.

"Yes. Pure evil," Thirty-Nine replied, "as long as he's around, nobody's getting out of here."

"They came close."

"Close to what?" Thirty-Nine's voice started to rise in response to Thirty-Three's foolish insistence that escape was possible. He coughed and lowered his voice. "Fifteen's dead and Eleven's all beat up. I don't get why she did it anyway – she's the Head Student."

They looked up at the Wheel. Eleven was spread-eagle on the wooden disk as it turned upright and began spinning. Eleven's head was not secured and it flopped from side to side until the Wheel turned faster. As it sped up, her body was pinned by centrifugal force, embedding several splinters into the soft tissue of her lower back and legs. Her body shook intermittently from the electric shocks surging through the cuffs around her hands and feet.

"I know why she did it."

Thirty-Nine looked over at Thirty-Three. His eyebrows arched in the middle of his forehead, a pyramid of hair that expressed strong doubt regarding his podmate's comment.

"I do," he whispered through clenched teeth, annoyed that Thirty-Nine didn't believe him.

The Wheel stopped spinning and Eleven was flung to the ground. She crawled a few steps and collapsed in front of the cluster of students. Her imposing athleticism did not come to her rescue. She could barely hold her head up. She tried vainly to stand. As she stumbled and dropped once again, she avoided eye contact with the younger students at the front. Though no one spoke, they all had the same impression, which was Dr. Nampala's intent: If Eleven was unable to break away from The Woodlands, no one could. Six sentries moved into position, surrounding her, leather whips in their hands.

"Time for the Run of Penance!" Sentry-5 barked. He was standing forty yards away, at the end of a faint track of gravel and dirt.

Thirty-Nine looked down. "Ok, why did she do it?" he muttered.

"Because she can't take the rules. She knows there's more to life than 'optimization of the mind', or whatever the Chief is calling the point of his experiments."

"And she nearly died." Thirty-Nine replied, fighting the urge to yell. "Fifteen did die. Was that worth it? No. Where would she go even if she got out? Like it or not, this is our home. We're orphans. Just follow the rules and this stuff won't happen. She didn't follow the rules. Look at her now."

Eleven was tumbling forward on the gravel. Every few feet a hoarse breathless scream escaped from deep in her throat. The crack of the whips against her clothes popped like corn kernels in hot oil. As she neared the end of the track and came closer to Sentry-5's waiting clutches, Thirty-Nine looked at Thirty-Three and finished his comment on living within the confines of The Woodlands.

"I just think it's better -"

"Silence!" Sentry-14 shouted. A rail-thin weasel-like guard with tufts of dark hair curling over the starched edges of his collar and sleeves, he moved closer to the boys. They jerked to attention in response, hands against their sides, eyes looking straight ahead.

"The show is over." Dr. Nampala's voice came through the Yard speakers again. "All students who still require shearing, please remain in the Yard. All other students, free time is cancelled, thanks to Eleven and Fifteen's traitorous behavior. Line up for escort to your pods."

The sentries shepherded the students into two groups. The freshly shaved heads were sent back into the dormitory, through the main double doors. They were led by Sentry-5, who was carrying Eleven over his shoulder like a hundred pound bag of dead fish. With each step, her defeated body flopped against his back. Her hands and legs dangled like loose threads, tapping against his waistline.

"Always remember – The Woodlands is your home. We are family." Dr. Nampala's voice softened as he repeated the final sentence. "We are family."

"I don't like this family." Thirty-Three mumbled as they neared the shearing zone.

Thirty-Nine tried to reign in his companion's emotions. It was a daily chore, trying to console and encourage his podmate to toe the line and abandon fantasies of a life beyond The Woodlands.

"It's the only family we've got, Thirty-Three. We're orphans, remember? Our real parents are dead. Now, one of our sisters is dead, chasing foolish fantasies. No thank you – I know you think it's possible but I would never try to escape." Thirty-Nine whispered.

"Let's go, Thirty-Nine, Thirty-Three." The barber sentries were back in position. The boys stepped into the same spot where just minutes earlier, they had admired the near perfection of Eleven. The whirring sound of the clippers filled the air and the rest of their hair began drifting to the ground, as lifeless as Fifteen.

"Here she is, Dr. Nampala," Sentry-5 tossed Eleven onto the second of three beds in the small recovery room two doors down from the cafeteria. She bounced on the stiff mattress. She moaned as she curled into a wounded ball. Sentry-5 stepped away and stood near the doorway of the windowless room.

The recovery room was used for assessing and treating students with illness or injury. It was a simple square space with three beds and a few carts with gauze and surgical tools. The room also had two wide cabinets along the wall behind the beds; medical supplies were visible through the metal-framed glass doors. Like all rooms at The Woodlands, this one was plain and clean. The tan walls were free of decorations. The white tile floor was mopped twice a day. The shiny floor reflected the lamps stationed in each corner, giving the area a harsh sterile brightness. Each bed was color-coded, like many things at The Woodlands. The green bed was for those projected to have a quick recovery; the orange bed, upon which Eleven lay, was for medium recovery times; and the black bed was reserved for children who were battling to stay alive. At the moment, she was the lone student in the room.

Dr. Nampala sat in a wooden rocking chair in the corner furthest from the doorway. His bony frame was evidence of many skipped meals and sleepless nights. His dark eyes, underlined by even darker circles, stared through tortoise-shell glasses. His shaggy salt and pepper hair hadn't been washed in several weeks. As he curled his untrimmed fingernails through his patchy beard, he slowly rocked.

A diminutive blue-cloaked lady entered and slipped behind Sentry-5's hulking frame. The patch on her jacket pocket was white, embroidered with a red cross and a white number seven. She stepped toward the row of beds, gloved hands ready to assess Eleven's injuries and administer treatment.

Dr. Nampala's melancholy eyes tracked the nurse as she entered. He cast his gaze toward the awaiting sentry. "Thank you Sentry-5. You may go. Please dispose of Fifteen's carcass."

"Yes sir." Sentry-5 replied.

"Nurse-7," Dr. Nampala said as Sentry-5 exited. "Please review Eleven's condition." He pushed himself up from the rocking chair, its back tapping against the drywall as he stood.

"Yes sir." She circled around Eleven's bed, eyeing the unconscious girl.

As Nurse-7 worked through the examination, Dr. Nampala patiently stood at the foot of the bed, nicotine-stained hands clasped behind his back. He leaned against the metal bed frame, his slight hips just below the top bar. His thighs wedged in between the wide set slats. As he stared at Eleven's pointed chin and button nose, he began reminiscing.

"I remember her well. That cool spring day when she was delivered. She was older than most, already a toddler. We learned, after a few of them, not to recruit any students older than nine months. Ah, but she was so precocious."

Nurse-7 lifted Eleven's sinewy arm and commented into her pocket recorder, "Several quarter-sized abrasions on her forearm. Upper arm appears unaffected. All bones are intact."

Dr. Nampala continued his recollection as the nurse moved to examine Eleven's head and neck.

"She has been impressive. Still holds the record for youngest to complete the dialectic praxis, all seven phases. Something has been changing lately, though." His detached monotone narrative was interrupted by Nurse-7's continuing assessment.

"No skull fractures, facial structure is undisturbed." Nurse-7 said into her pocket recorder.

Dr. Nampala stood up straight and looked at the floor. "I guess we've all been changing some. I remember when this all started. I thought we'd be done by now. I guess nothing is ever what you expect. A lot sure has happened since my early days at S'Klohatch."

Nurse-7 looked up, startled by Dr. Nampala's personal comments. He rarely mentioned anything but the work of The Woodlands. Fortunately for the nurse, he was lost in his thoughts and didn't notice her reaction. He stood at the foot of Eleven's bed and reminisced about his life.

The S'Klohatch Reservation was Dr. Nampala's home from birth until he was twelve years old. Located in a heavily forested chunk of virtually unoccupied land on the Kitsap Peninsula, a two hundred square mile claw shaped outpost. Used by white settlers for logging and shipping, Kitsap Peninsula lies between Seattle and the Pacific Ocean. Dr. Nampala's Native American ancestors had inhabited the area for centuries.

In the early 1900's, his people were rounded up and plunked onto a 1,300-acre reservation. Only a tiny portion was inhabited. Even today, only about five hundred live on the reservation. Most people lived and died there, without seeing much of the world.

Dr. Nampala was one of the few who got off the reservation. After being identified as a brilliant student, he was taken from his home and sent to an elite boarding school in Boston. After succeeding and then failing as a government scientist, he had secretly returned to his roots to continue his research at an abandoned weather research facility. He named it The Woodlands.

"Dr. Nampala," Nurse-7 whispered, cautious of disturbing her taskmaster.

"Yes." He replied without looking at her. His mind was still somewhere else, pondering the past decade. He was thinking about the mounting pressure to deliver what he was funded to create. As his top student and greatest hope for success lay battered before him, he wondered if he would do it all over again. All people have regrets. Especially evil people.

"I'm ready to provide my comments on Eleven's condition."

"Just a minute." He returned to the rocking chair, his perpetually bare feet slapping against the cold tile. He reclined in the wooden rocker and crossed his legs. He closed his eyes and pulled off his glasses, revealing deep indentations in the bridge of his large nose.

"Go ahead." Dr. Nampala instructed.

Nurse-7 nervously cleared her throat. Her strong Brazilian accent belied her attempts to sound American. "She is remarkably intact considering the blow to her head and the eight foot fall. It appears as though her right shoulder and side absorbed the contact with the ground. She has a cracked rib and her shoulder will be sore for a week or longer. She does not have any other broken bones. She has multiple abrasions from falling on the penance walk."

"It's the *Run* of Penance, Nurse-7," Dr. Nampala corrected.

"Yes sir." She pressed her clipboard against her chest. "I'm sorry. Shall I continue?"

"Yes."

"She needs stitches in her head. There's a gash that will need about twelve stitches. I think she has a low-grade concussion. My recommended rest time is one week."

Dr. Nampala leaned forward, his bare toes sticking to the tile. He uncrossed his spindly legs and leaned his thin arms over his knees. "Ok, I'll give her two days. And she's lucky she gets that. Stitch her up and leave."

"Yes sir." Nurse-7 replied.

He leaned back in his chair and closed his eyes. He exhaled as though he was pushing the weight of the world off his lungs. Folding his hands in his lap, he could hear Nurse-7 getting her supplies ready. The sound almost reminded him of his childhood, listening to his mother rummaging in the kitchen before dinner. As he rocked, he thought about the journey that had taken him from a boy on the reservation to a scientist overseeing a secret research facility funded by anarchists.

He was named for an explorer of the late 1800's, Joseph Leonard, who had befriended his great grandfather. Of course, he always wondered why his parents chose Leonard instead of Joseph. Leonard Nampala was a frail but bright kid, whose potential for greatness was discovered during a routine examination of students on the S'Klohatch Reservation. During sixth grade standardized testing, his math and science scores were flawless.

Soon after the testing, two men in dark suits showed up at his mother's trailer. His father had left when he was four years old. Now thirteen, he tried to be a man but still felt the urge to sit in his mother's lap on the tough days.

"You know, he can have opportunities no one out here gets." The taller man told Nampala's mother. "We will give him the proper training, nutrition and environment. He could become *somebody*."

"Somebody?" Ms. Nampala asked. "What's that supposed to mean?"

"What he means, ma'am," the stocky dark-suited man next to him said, "Is just that he's not likely to find any way to achieve his potential here. In this place." He waved around their broken down trailer and pointed out the window at the dingy atmosphere of the reservation.

"What do you think, Leonard?" His mother asked.

"If it means leaving you, then my answer is no."

"We don't really take 'no' for an answer." The taller man reached down and grabbed the frail boy by the arm, squeezing tightly and staring into his brown eyes.

"We will take care of you. And we *will take* you." He hissed.

"I don't think so." His mother said, moving toward her only child.

"Yes ma'am. We will." The shorter man grabbed her and pinned her against the wall. "We are in charge. He has the brain we need. He's coming with us."

Little Leonard fought and kicked at the bigger man but he couldn't overpower him. A moment later, he was staring through tears and a dusty rear window of a black sedan. As they sped away from the reservation and left his mother alone, Leonard Nampala cursed under his breath.

"One day I'll come back. And America will regret my return."

He was placed in an elite program at the Institute for Sciences. Obsessed with being the best, he was accelerated in the program and began college courses at age 15. He completed his Ph.D. at age 20.

From the beginning he displayed a ruthless determination to succeed. He was obsessive and stubborn. He refused to tolerate the weak, the lazy or the foolish. His cold opinion was that science brought power. The kind of power he would need to get revenge.

Over time, he demonstrated less and less ethical integrity. He was reprimanded for his willingness to ignore the typical standards of practice and protocol in pursuit of results that proved his theories.

Though he was abrasive and intense, he achieved significant results.

His behavior was tolerated, even overlooked. Because of his brilliance and his voracious appetite for work, he was granted a fellowship to research the interaction between the powers of the brain to influence and even control others.

The US Military funded his research. The ultimate goal was to produce operatives who could use thought projection to control the enemy. He began his research working with expendable primates.

After several years, the newly minted Dr. Nampala was able to identify a cluster of neurons in the brain of young chimpanzees that, when injected with several synthetic hormones, could be focused to create agitation or delight in the behavior of the proximate chimpanzees. The control chimps were affected by the thoughts of the enhanced chimpanzees at distances up to fifty feet. He was most successful replicating his results when the enhanced primates were sleeping, and were in a dream state.

After a year of impressive outcomes, the results began to flatten out. Dr. Nampala believed it was due to the limited capacity of the chimps. He requested the opportunity to experiment with humans.

A few brave Army volunteers were unsuccessfully used for the research. After eighteen months with zero results, he became convinced the failure was due to the age of his subjects. If he had people the same age as the chimpanzees, five to twelve years old, he was certain he would be able to duplicate the mind-activity link. The supple tissues of still-developing brains would provide the platform for revolutionary breakthrough in neurosciences.

He approached the director to request having children replace the adult soldier test subjects. The director's rejected his proposal instantly. A violent confrontation ensued, leaving Dr. Nampala without a fellowship, and for the first time in fifteen years, without a focused purpose for his ingenious amoral mind. It was now time for his revenge.

He began to find a few similarly blacklisted researchers in underground groups that met in shady cafes or weird back rooms of decrepit nightclubs. After one of them provided him with details for a potential funding source to use an abandoned weather laboratory in the Pacific Northwest, Dr. Nampala initiated a series of two-minute telephone conversations with an international anarchy group identified only as The Future. Over the course of two months, those conversations culminated in an agreement for a ten-year project titled <u>Ventriloquism Chaos</u>.

Outside the Electric Slide nightclub late one night in 1988, a husky man driving a nondescript van delivered the contract. The cold air in the alleyway smelled of homelessness and car exhaust. Dr. Nampala shuddered and held his gloved hand over his mouth to heat the frozen air as he inhaled. The driver of the van pulled up and handed him a plain manila envelope. The driver wore a ski mask and never spoke. As he drove away, Dr. Nampala saw a dark rectangle where a license plate should have been. He shuddered, realizing he had officially joined a criminal enterprise. The cold air sunk into his bones. As he peeled open the envelope, the final shred of morality that remained in his soul flaked away and fluttered to the ground like the snow flurries dancing in the glow of the cracked streetlight over his head.

The envelope contained one hundred thousand dollars cash and a single bullet wrapped in a handwritten note that read, "success or death." It also held a contract signed by A. Finley, a two-time felon for arson who had escaped prison in 1985 and built a disjointed network of anarchists into The Future.

The contract provided for the stated outcome of "absolute thought transference manifested by third-party speech". It would be Dr. Nampala's job to provide The Future with the ability to create thought soldiers, young people who could project thoughts into the speech of another person. The Future envisioned unleashing these thought soldiers into a crowd at a political speech. The thought soldiers could treat any country's leader like a wooden dummy, with any words The Future wanted him to speak projected from a young mind in the crowd.

Thought soldiers could be the ultimate weapon. They could incite war and chaos – they could overthrow the world's systems – without de-tection. If Dr. Nampala could achieve this in ten years or less, his payment would be ten million dollars. If he couldn't...well, the bullet and the note made his alternative clear.

Ten years had passed since that cold night in Boston. Now, as Dr. Nampala rocked in the recovery room, his best hope was sitting in the cot in front of him, her stitched head still oozing from the escape attempt.

Dr. Nampala opened his eyes and looked at her. He stood up and walked over to her bed, sliding his glasses back onto his face. He whispered his frustrations to his sleeping prodigy.

"You. Must. Never. Try. To. Escape." He turned and moved along the side of the bed. He peered down at Eleven's peaceful face, dabbed with freckles and scratches. The purplish color of her closed eyelids reminded him of the dark fear of failure, and subsequent death, that he kept trying to push out of his mind. He dragged his fingernails gently along her arm, causing goose bumps to dot her forearm. He leaned over her, his long hair falling within inches of her bruised cheek.

"There's only one reason you're still alive, Eleven," He whispered.

A nearly imperceptible moan slipped through her cracked lips, causing Dr. Nampala to lean back and study her face.

"Are you awake?" He asked.

Eleven gave no response. Her eyes remained closed, her body still.

"We will talk. Later. But, you must know there is only one reason you're still alive. Because I let you live."

"How much time until your next training session?" Thirty-Three was slung across his bed, his face hanging over the side, as he spoke to his pod-mate.

"I don't know." Thirty-Nine paused from tidying up the oval-shaped room, called a "pod". Each pod was an egg-shaped space with beanbag beds rounded into the fat end of the room. The walls were covered with light blue fibrous wallpaper that felt like the skin of a kiwifruit. He looked up at the chrome framed digital clock over the door.

"It's 9:48 am. So, I've got twelve minutes. You could help, you know." Thirty-Nine looked down at Thirty-Three's wide back and thick legs sprawled on the bed.

"You still have your shoes on!"

Thirty-Three rolled over and looked down at his dirty boot-clad feet.

"I guess so." He shrugged. "Saves time. I have to go back to finish some outdoor duty at ten o'clock, anyway."

Thirty-Nine grabbed a wad of socks and tissue that were stuffed into the top drawer of the lone desk in the pod.

He turned to Thirty-Three, "Tell me, how did these get in there?" He pointed to the open drawer that was filled with paper, a couple of books and some pens.

"Sorry." Thirty-Three replied. He hunched his shoulders as he stood.

As his boots hit the floor, dried mud fell on the recently vacuumed throw rug that lay between the beds.

Thirty-Nine tossed the socks at Thirty-Three, and glared at the fresh dirt on the floor.

"Sorry again!" Thirty-Three swung his chubby hand up in an attempt to catch the flying hosiery. The socks bounced off his forehead and fell at his feet.

Thirty-Nine chuckled. "It's ok. But, you probably want to make your sleep sheath." He pointed to the twisted up satin fabric bag lying on Thirty-Three's bed.

Like a form-fitting sleeping bag, the sleep sheath served as every student's bedding. Enriched by bio-nutrient saturated oxygen, the sleep sheaths are color coded for various projects and bio-neurological enhancements. They came in five colors: opaque, white, yellow, orange, and black. The color darkened to coincide with the difficulty and rigor of every child's project. Seven out of the ninety-seven students at The Woodlands had the black sleep sheath. It was a true status symbol. Thirty-Three's sleep sheath was white. Thirty-Nine's was orange with navy blue trim.

Thirty-Three grabbed the sleep sheath and began flattening it out in preparation for folding. As he swiped the shiny white cloth with both hands while kneeling on the corner to hold it still, he remarked over his shoulder to his podmate.

"I still can't believe how close Eleven came to getting out."

Thirty-Nine was organizing folders on top of the dresser they shared, placing them by subject into mesh cubes. He nearly dropped the whole stack at Thirty-Three's comment.

"I thought we agreed not to talk about it."

"I know. We did. But you know me." He shoved his sleep sheath toward the head of his bed and walked over to Thirty-Nine.

"I just can't help myself. I mean, for Eleven to take that chance. What do you think was in her mind?" Thirty-Three leaned against the side of the dresser and rested his big head in his hands, smashing his cheeks up, causing his lips to pucker like a fish. Thirty-Nine turned his head and eyed his friend.

"You're funny. You know that?"

"Yesh," Thirty-Three replied through twisted lips.

"I appreciate you, and we're good friends, right?" Thirty-Nine asked.

"Yesh."

"So," Thirty-Nine looked at the clock. "I don't have much time but I want to make this clear. There has never been a successful escape. There will never be a successful escape."

"Why not?" Thirty-Three whispered.

"Well, for one thing, everyone who has tried has been killed. Except Eleven, and she almost was. Second, we don't have anywhere to go. We are orphans. That means we have no family." His voice elevated like a tent preacher. He pressed himself taller, standing on his tiptoes as he declared the crux of the issue, at least for him.

"We know nothing about where we came from. We know nothing about anything except The Woodlands. This is where we are. This is where we've been. And, this is where we're from."

"Yesh. But," Thirty-Three lifted his face. "It's not where I'm from! I know there's more out there. There has to be somebody like me out there. Someone that knows what happened to my family. Someone that can explain where I came from. And, someone who will help me get where I want to go."

"Go? Where do you want to go, Thirty-Three?"

They stood at the corner of the dresser. Thirty-Nine's lanky frame eclipsed by Thirty-Three's roundness. Thirty-Three looked down.

"Look, I understand your attitude," Thirty-Nine continued. "I know you have different feelings about the outside world. I guess if I felt like there was someone out there looking for me, I might feel differently. I'm sure I would. But the truth is, there's not. There's no family for me to go to. So, this is our life. And it's not terrible, as long as we obey. I know you have visions of a life beyond The Woodlands. I just can't share them."

Thirty-Three moved back a step and excitedly slapped his hands against his legs.

"You're right! I do have feelings about the outside world. I want to explore and experience and be excited, and any other adventure emotion that starts with 'ex'!"

They both laughed. Although they were very different, they enjoyed linguistics, like most of the students at The Woodlands. They were trained to think uniquely, to investigate not only the answers to the questions in their courses, but the phrasing of those questions as well.

In the past, Thirty-Three might not have enjoyed the subtle intellectual humor of the moment. He had changed over the years, but he still chafed at the rigidity of the place. However, the order and the courses and the testing that was life at The Woodlands always matched Thirty-Nine's disposition. He almost felt at home in The Woodlands. Thirty-Three never had.

Thirty-Three was non-compliant. Unlike most of the children, Thirty-Three was sixteen months old when he arrived. It took much longer for him to be de-programmed from the real world. He spent the first month in near isolation, which only accomplished the cementing of his stubborn streak.

"Well, once again, I guess we'll have to agree to disagree." Thirty-Nine replied, after they'd finished chuckling.

"For now. But, I know you'll come around. Eventually." Thirty-Three replied as they both moved to the door to wait for a sentry to come and transport them to their respective places; Thirty-Nine to a dream sequencing session, and Thirty-Three to more physical labor in the Yard.

They stared at the silver door.

"He's running behind today." Thirty-Nine remarked.

"What kind of training are you doing today?" Thirty-Three asked, rubbing his hands on his dark overalls then cracking his knuckles.

"Dream sequencing stuff again. It seems like it's all I've done for the past week." Thirty-Nine replied.

"Up until recently you were all logic and analytics. What's going on with all this dream stuff?"

"I don't know but the Chief wants to do it. So, I do what I'm told."

"You sure do."

"What's wrong with that?" Thirty-Nine asked.

"Nothing, I guess." Thirty-Three turned to his podmate, shrugging his shoulders. He looked up at the clock. "Sentry's late. You would never be late if you were a sentry."

Every student at The Woodlands had a reputation. If they had a yearbook and voted for class characters, Thirty-Nine would be elected Mr. Conscientious. He lived by the book. Everything was "black and white" during the day. But when he fell asleep and began to dream, well, things got a little strange.

Nightly, he sweated through vibrant, color-filled dreams that remain in his heart even after awakening. For the last few months, every dream ended in the same place, with the same people all doing the same thing as the night before. During the last two weeks, Dr. Nampala instructed his researchers to deconstruct this repetitive end of Thirty-Nine's dream.

In the dream, Thirty-Nine walks into a rectangular building with steeples and colorful windows. The building is made of grey and light brown stone, with ornate gables and a small unkempt rectangular courtyard. Thirty-Nine approaches the property by walking on a rough-hewn stone path, now worn smooth from several centuries of foot traffic. He passes under a rounded arch that leads from the path into the courtyard.

The courtyard is sparse and bare. A few vines grow over the sloped and decaying four-foot high boundary wall. An occasional weed sprouts through the cracks in the cobblestone square. The only decorative element is a water fountain featuring a crumbling concrete statue of an unknown angel. Its eyes look toward the earth, and its wings now mere humps protruding above its shoulders.

He walks past the statue and proceeds on to the gigantic wooden doors that serve as a formal barrier to entry. Grasping one of the large elliptical iron handles with both hands, he tugs, pulling the door open just enough and he slips across the dull bronze threshold.

The inside of the building is warm and alive. The clatter of bustling activity echoes from the hallway that feeds into the lobby. An oval room draped with dark wood paneling and small windows, the lobby has the feel of a medieval chapel. Thirty-Nine notices a small wooden lectern upon which rests an ivory paged, gray velvet bound book. The book is always open to the fifth page. He can spy a few signatures on the thick rough-edged stationary; some are simply names, while some contain salutations such as "Best Wishes" or "Congratulations". Thirty-Nine approaches the lectern. Rising on his tiptoes, he reads the third line on the page, every time. Every dream.

To Nicole and Corey: Against all odds, true love remains!
Your friend, Bruce.

After reading the brief message he walks to the dark brown double doors just beyond the lectern. The lilting tones of a string quartet float from inside. As he stands between the book and the interior doors, Thirty-Nine can hear women's voices growing louder from the hallway. He frantically looks for a place to hide, but the lobby is a perfect oval, with no nooks or crannies in which to seek refuge. He scrambles to the far side of the lobby and flattens himself against a section of cherry paneling that holds a stained glass window above his head.

What a terribly poor substitute for hiding, he thinks. Yet no one sees him. Ever.

The lobby newcomers are dressed for the occasion. Two matronly women wearing simple black dresses stand next to two young women in crimson dresses, outlined in white lace. Both of the younger women are holding a bouquet of carnations, lilies and spray roses. All four are whispering words that Thirty-Nine cannot hear, but their facial expressions reveal a common emotion - joy.

The women fuss over each other. They are either oblivious to his presence or they can't see him. He presses his body against the worn wood walls as he watches the procession. After a few last minute primps and a smoothing of the fabric around their ample hips, the two older women open the double doors and enter the sanctuary.

As they do, Thirty-Nine catches a glimpse of the interior. The interior room is bright and gleaming, with stained glass panels stretching from waist high to far above a grown man's reach. Ancient cushion-less wooden benches are positioned in the room from beginning to end. They stretch from side to side, broken by a center walkway outlined by amber grout.

As they walk in, the tap of the women's high-heeled shoes provides a rhythmic back beat, perfectly in time with the violinist's solo. The two younger women walk into the room. They maintain a distance of six paces between each other, striding in a polite feminine march to the front row.

He slinks toward the middle of the room to get a better view of the proceedings, and a new woman enters the lobby. As she walks in, Thirty-Nine catches his breath and freezes along the wall. She is tall and regal, with bright green eyes. Her tanned strong fingers firmly hold a large bouquet of wild flowers so freshly cut they reflect light onto her face. A shimmering white gown wraps her body as tightly as fresh snow hugging the mountain-side after a winter storm.

Unlike the other women, she looks right at Thirty-Nine. She sees him. Her flat cheeks and thin lips serve as the perfect frame for her beautiful smile. Her eyes behold Thirty-Nine with a mixture of adoration and awe. At this point in the dream, Thirty-Nine's body temperature elevates, as though her gaze carries energy across the tranquil lobby.

She moves toward Thirty-Nine and holds out her arm, silently asking him to escort her into the chapel. As Thirty-Nine places his forearm in the crook of her elbow, he feels taller. He looks eye to eye with the stunning lady and she blushes, smiling widely. She nods, still silent, beckoning him to lead her to the doorway. As they cross the threshold into the sanctuary, Thirty-Nine looks down at the thick wooden door casing that separates the lobby from the sanctuary. Faded and splintered, it rises an inch higher than the rest of the floor. No matter how hard he tries to step above it, he always stumbles over this strip of wood. As Thirty-Nine falls, a young man appears on his left, catching him and saving him from complete humiliation.

The young man is wearing a black suit, with a gray and black striped necktie and a dark gray vest. He smiles at Thirty-Nine, and nods toward the beautiful lady. Looking down at Thirty-Nine, he straightens up and winks.

"I'll take it from here, son."

Try as he might, Thirty-Nine can never quite make out the young man's face. He feels the firm grip of a strong hand on his arm as the dark haired rescuer grabs him. By the time Thirty-Nine is steadied and looks toward the man, the newly arrived escort has already turned his head, focused on the walk. They move ahead without him. As the people just noticed by Thirty-Nine in the pews rise, he wakes up. Every time. Every dream.

He reaches up to rub his shaved head, still half-asleep, and the pinch he feels in his right wrist reminds him it was all just a dream. Again.

"Disconnect, please," he commands.

The slight tug of the cable as it slides out of his right forearm always feels like turning a sock inside out. Except it's like the sock is on fire.

Thirty-Nine lay still, waiting for a researcher or a sentry to come remove the straps around his arms, legs and waist. He blinked rapidly to clear his eyes. The ceiling overhead was the same dingy white as always. Rectangular fluorescent light cages hung suspended by thin wires. The aroma of warm electronic devices and the low hum of fluorescent lighting filled the room.

"I couldn't see his face. Again." Thirty-Nine declared, turning his attention from the dingy ceiling to the blank green wall beyond the bank of medical devices lining his cot.

"We know." The answer came from a small metal speaker box mounted above an observation window. The deep voice with clipped pronunciation continued, "We will induce dream tracing sequence 775-A23 tomorrow."

Thirty-Nine was startled by the familiar sound of the stretched out words spoken by that voice. It was the Chief. Like most of the students, he had little direct contact with Dr. Nampala. If the Chief was leading the observation during a research session, it meant that Thirty-Nine was really climbing toward the head of the class.

Thirty-Nine heard a click as the release pin activated under the bed. He sat up and looked down at the cold linoleum floor. He slid off the sterile cot and stood, waiting.

"This one has potential", Thirty-Nine heard someone behind him say. No one had entered the room through the door in front of him. He turned around but saw nothing except the undecorated light green concrete wall. He shook his head, thinking maybe he was still groggy from sleeping in the middle of the day.

"We have to find the activating element for his uncinate fasciculus. His recent scans show dramatic enlargement compared to the other children."

"Even compared to adults", Thirty-Nine heard another voice reply to the first.

Again it sounded like it came from behind him. He glanced over his shoulder. He still saw nothing but the green wall.

Sentry-5 entered, wearing his constant scowl.

"Let's go." He commanded.

Thirty-Nine followed him through the doorway and into the hallway. He stayed about two paces behind his massive escort. The sentries were the enforcers of the rules and, on some occasions, the assistants for medical treatments. They delivered the students to their various classes, research sessions, meals and time in the Yard.

Like the children, they were unnamed. They were not friendly. They were not kind. None of the kids ever talked to the sentries. As they walked toward his pod, Thirty-Nine had no plans to initiate conversation.

"Man, I'm tired." Sentry-5 said.

Thirty-Nine did not reply.

"Got to remember to put in the order for those new belts for the water filtration system. And the pallets in the basement need to be removed. Wonder if Sentry-8 got that done."

Is he talking to me? Thirty-Nine thought.

They took a few silent steps.

Sentry-5 continued talking. "Dr. Nampala put Sentry-13 in the lead officer role for the month. I don't get it. No one works as hard as me."

Thirty-Nine leaned his head to look around the broad body of his chaperon, trying to see if Sentry-5's mouth was moving. He couldn't get a clear view, so he moved a little closer. He looked like a little remora swimming under a shark as he darted nearer to Sentry-5. Thirty-Nine was engulfed in the mammoth man's shadow.

"I don't know what I have to do to get a promotion. Maybe kill some more kids..."

"What!" Thirty-Nine called out; he quickly clapped his hand over his own mouth, shocked by the sound of his voice.

Sentry-5 paused in the hall, about ten feet from Thirty-Nine's pod. He turned and glared down.

"What?" Sentry-5 asked.

Do I respond? Thirty-Nine thought. His stomach quivered as he looked up at the towering presence before him.

Sentry-5 repeated his question as he balled up his right fist, "What did you say, boy?"

"Umm. Were you talking to me?" Thirty-Nine replied.

"Are you trying to get some kind of reprimand today?" His square face reddened with anger as he leaned closer to Thirty-Nine. "If you've got a problem, we can certainly visit The Wheel. Do you have a problem?"

"No sir."

"Are you sure?"

"Yes sir. I'm sure. I'm sorry, it won't happen again!"

Thirty-Nine inched backward, to increase the space between them, and perhaps to give enough for a miss should Sentry-5 decide to do something violent. He knew better than to give this sentry an excuse to inflict punishment, especially after what he'd seen in the Yard a few hours ago. He couldn't believe his mouth had uttered anything.

Sentry-5 continued glaring at Thirty-Nine. A long jagged scar that ran from under Sentry-5's chin and ended near his lower lip turned white as his face flushed with rage at the insolent boy. Just as he was about to speak, his walkie-talkie beeped.

"Sentry-5, do you copy?"

Sentry-5 shook his head at Thirty-Nine. "You're lucky, boy. Get in your pod. But, I'm watching you."

He moved to the side of the hallway and motioned for Thirty-Nine to walk. He reached down to his hip and grabbed for the walkie-talkie.

"Sentry-5 here," he replied into the little black square.

Thirty-Nine walked close to the far wall, edging by the sentry. As he slipped by, Sentry-5 moved out of his peripheral vision.

That was close, he thought. But he thought too soon. As the last hint of Sentry-5's silhouette disappeared behind him, Thirty-Nine felt a driving collision in his left side.

His midsection convulsed as the crunching blow of Sentry-5's giant right fist slammed into Thirty-Nine's lower back. He tumbled to the hard cold floor, placing his hands out to brace for impact. He lay face down for a moment, thankful he hadn't slammed his head on the ground.

"Sentry-5, secure your student and report to the clearing room immediately," the voice over the walkie-talkie ordered.

"Roger. Get up, boy!"

He tapped Thirty-Nine's hip with his heavy boot. Thirty-Nine scrambled to his feet, fearful of another hit from Sentry-5. He brushed his shirt and rapidly finished the walk to his pod.

What a jerk. I hate Sentry-5. Of course, what am I doing talking to him, anyway? Idiot.

Thirty-Nine's internal dialogue bounced back and forth between blaming himself and hating Sentry-5. He remained conflicted as he stepped to the doorway of his pod.

Sentry-5 moved alongside him, gleefully smirking at Thirty-Nine's pain. He pulled out the key card and inserted it into the slot beside the door. A small touch screen glowed in the center of the metal door, and Sentry-5 typed in a lengthy code, and the elaborate security system was deactivated, allowing Thirty-Nine to enter. He pushed Thirty-Nine into the pod.

"Don't ever speak unless spoken to!"

With that warning, Sentry-5 slammed the door shut. The familiar beep of the pod's security system activation and mechanical clink of the deadbolts sliding into place told Thirty-Nine the door was locked. The dissipating sound of the sentry's footfalls told him he was safe from further abuse.

For now.

He slumped to the floor, his back against the door. As the adrenaline faded, he could feel an ache beginning in the spot where Sentry-5 had punched him. He rubbed his hand across his lower back. The silence in the pod told him Thirty-Three was still out on work assignment.

"Oh, man, that hurts."

As he sat on the floor, he looked around the pod. It was dark, the shades drawn on the single large rectangular window directly across from where Thirty-Nine sat. He looked at the beds. He spotted Thirty-Three's sleep sheath, still unzipped and improperly folded.

"Guess I'll fix his bed again. Geez! And Thirty-Three wonders why he's always in trouble."

Thirty-Nine rolled over and pushed up to a kneeling position. He sat on his feet and pulled up his shirt to examine his injured side. With no mirror, he did the best he could to inspect his wounded body. He craned his neck trying to twist his head down to see his side, trying in vain to see if a bruise had formed. He rubbed his bare skin with his palm and returned his hand to his face. There was no blood on his hand, so at least he wasn't cut.

"Small victory, I suppose," he sarcastically grumbled.

He stood and walked over to begin fixing Thirty-Three's bed. He slid the zipper closed on the shiny white fabric and, in the way they'd been instructed, began folding Thirty-Three's sleep sheath into thirds, then in half. He placed it near the top of the beanbag mattress, in the spot where a person from the outside would place a pillow. Pillows weren't included in their bedding, as the Chief had discovered in his first year of work that they disturb the natural flow of ions in the sleeping brain.

Thirty-Nine looked at the neatly folded sleep sheath. "Thirty-Three owes me one." He stepped back from the bed and grinned, "More like one thousand!"

He turned toward the square chrome clock on the wall above the doorframe.

"4:44."

"Sixteen minutes until dinner. Wonder where Thirty-Three is? Maybe he's not finished with the courtyard project."

Just then, Thirty-Nine heard the familiar sound of the click of a sentry's keycard outside his door. He scurried to the desk and sat down, grabbing the Behavior Manual from a small stack of books tucked between a lamp and the beige wardrobe where their uniforms and shoes were stored. Thumbing to page 21, he began reading aloud:

"The purpose of the filtration system is to perpetuate a longer usage life for the entire facility. Weekly cleaning is mandatory and is assigned to each student above age 6 on a rotating basis. The first component..."

The opening door interrupted his impromptu review. Thirty-Three stepped in, the knees of his overalls caked with dirt. His face was covered with brown finger streaks from repeatedly wiping away sweat with his filthy hands.

"Thirty-Three, where were you?" Thirty-Nine asked as he tossed the manual back onto the desk.

"I got an extra two days of Yard duty for spilling my juice at breakfast this morning. It wasn't even my fault. Twelve bumped me while I was walking toward the table."

"Well, at least you didn't get punched today," Thirty-Nine replied, standing up and lifting his shirt to expose his battered side.

Thirty-Three looked at his podmate's side. He whistled as he saw the apple sized purple ring on his back.

"Wow! Thirty-Nine! That's a good bruise buddy. What happened?"

"I'm not really sure. I mean, I know how I got the bruise. Sentry-5 punched me. But, why I got hit? Well, that was strange."

"Sentry-5?"

"Yes."

Thirty-Three moved closer to Thirty-Nine so that both were standing near the corner of the desk. He looked back at the clock.

"We've only got twelve minutes. Can you tell me while we get dressed for dinner? For once, I'd like to avoid trouble."

"I'm with you."

Thirty-Three turned to the wardrobe and opened the door. "Which color are you wearing tonight?"

"Aren't you going to wash your hands?"

Thirty-Three looked down at his stumpy hands. Every fingernail was packed with mud and every knuckle looked like tiny rivers of white in a sea of brown as he opened and closed his fist.

"Good call."

Thirty-Three grabbed a couple packs of sanitary wipes from above the wardrobe and ineffectively dabbed his hands.

"So, what color you want?" He asked as he tossed the wipes on the floor and looked into the wardrobe.

"White, I suppose. I've worn the brown one three nights in a row."

Thirty-Three reached inside and flipped a white tunic over his shoulder to Thirty-Nine. He caught it and placed it on the desk and began unbuttoning his jacket.

"Thanks." He quietly brushed the residue of Thirty-Three's grimy hand from the shoulder of the tunic and continued to tell the story of his crazy day.

"So, I was in the dream sequence room."

"The dream again?" Thirty-Three interrupted.

"Yes. It's weird. This past week, I feel like I'm replaying the dream, searching for something different to happen. The dream really wasn't different. After I woke up, though..." He trailed off as he straightened the white tunic and slid it over his head.

"I'm hearing voices or something...I think. Anyway, it was on the way back to the pod that the really strange thing happened."

Thirty-Three stepped out of his overalls and left them in a clump on the floor. He lifted a brown tunic overhead and slid his arms into the sleeves before wriggling his head through. He stepped over the dirty clothes and asked Thirty-Nine for clarification.

"What are you searching for? And what do you mean you're hearing voices?"

"You know how I have the wedding dream all the time?"

"Yes."

"Well, the Chief keeps putting me to sleep, trying to unlock something - I don't even know what he's looking for - but he asks me every time I'm done if I can see the man's face."

"The groom?"

"Yes. But, I can't. I see his body and feel him catch me, but by the time I look towards his face, he's already walking away."

Thirty-Nine shed his pants and folded them neatly on top of his jacket before placing them in the hamper under the window.

"Pick up your overalls," he ordered Thirty-Three.

"I will. What are you, a sentry?"

"No, but I like a clean pod. You already know this."

"Fine." Thirty-Three snatched his overalls off the floor and tossed them on top of Thirty-Nine's clothes in the small dark blue wicker basket. "We've got five minutes until we have to go."

"Ok. So, today when I woke up, I heard a voice talking about me. Except it didn't come through the speaker in the room. It sounded like someone was in the room. The voice came from behind me. I turned and looked but no one was there."

"Did the researchers use any Loxapine on you?" Thirty-Three was relentless in his research of the various pharmaceutical substances administered to the students. Any time he could see a name on a label or IV bag, he would remember it and look it up in the library. Loxapine, as he had explained to Thirty-Nine many times, was an antipsychotic drug that reduces emotions. He knew it well because he was often under its influence.

"I don't know. I mean, they injected me but they didn't make me take any pills. Who knows for sure?"

"But just because you're hearing voices, why would Sentry-5 hit you?" Thirty-Three rolled his eyes at his own question. "Never mind, that was a really dumb question. Sentry-5 doesn't need a reason to beat us."

"It was after I heard the voices. I was following him back to our pod, and I swear he said something to me."

"They never talk to us." Thirty-Three reached back in the wardrobe and grabbed his slip-on boots. "Unless they are yelling at us or mocking while beating us."

He sat down on his bed and began pulling on his boots. "You better get your shoes on. We've got three minutes."

Thirty-Nine turned to the wardrobe and grabbed his dark brown boots. As he twisted his feet into the firm leather shoes, he finished his story.

"I was surprised that he would say something normal, you know, like a conversation. He said something about replacing belts and getting a promotion. You know, like a normal human would. I blurted out 'what?' because I couldn't believe he was speaking to me. He turned on me, but then he got a call on his walkie-talkie. As I walked by him, he nailed me in the back. Hard. I sure hope I don't have any broken ribs."

"If you had broken ribs, you wouldn't be moving as good as you are. Believe me. I know about broken bones." Thirty-Three held out both arms and pointed at his left thigh, then his nose. He pulled his hand down and pointed at his nose twice more.

"That's true. You've had your share of casts. How many bones so far?"

"Ten. But my nose has been broken three times, so that's thirteen."

Thirty-Nine continued his explanation of the altercation with Sentry-5. "The weird part is he I don't think he said anything out loud. But, we were the only people in the hall, and I heard it as clear as I'm hearing you right now."

"Weird. Well, maybe you're a mind-reader!" Thirty-Three chuckled and knuckle-rubbed Thirty-Nine's fuzzy head. He looked at him, eye-to-eye, with a maniacal stare. "Quick, what am I thinking?"

Thirty-Nine laughed and played along.

"I don't know...um, you're thinking...hold on. Got it!" He snapped his fingers and pointed at his podmate's ample gut.

"You're thinking about how hungry you are!"

"Lucky guess." Thirty-Three laughed. "Let's get to dinner."

They walked to the door as the clock above turned to 4:59. They could hear the approaching sentry's footsteps.

"Well, if you could read minds, that would sure be a big help around here," Thirty-Three whispered as the beeping door alerted them to the sentry's arrival.

"Dinner," Sentry-13 announced, opening the door and waving for them to exit the pod. The boys walked out and followed him down the hall. Thirty-Three was thinking about eating, and Thirty-Nine was thinking about thoughts.

Hearing them, that is.

Only one student was missing from dinner that night. Eleven. She was awake and had been summoned to Dr. Nampala's office. A dark circle of steel and concrete, his office was located at the top of the observations station. A glass dome roof allowed him to observe the skies. A balcony that encompassed the top floor of the station allowed him to observe the students' activity.

He sat alone in one of the rocking chairs in his sparse office, waiting for Eleven to arrive. His hands were folded across his slim midsection. He rocked slowly as he leaned back in his seat, his bare feet on an old Persian throw rug. He looked through a large picture window at the wet treetops below. Summer had ended sooner than usual and though it was September, the air around Port Mashton already had the bite of winter.

Researcher-4 buzzed the door to enter his office.

"Come in," he shouted from the other side of the room.

Researcher-4 walked in, holding a clipboard in her left hand, ushering a limping Eleven with her right. Researcher-4 was a slightly built, serious woman with a bobbed hairdo that framed her apple-shaped face. Her large sparkly blue eyes belied her introverted personality and her cold efficiency. She was consistently trying to discover methods to be quicker and more effective in her research. Although a Napoleon complex is unusual for women; at barely five feet tall, she tried harder than most to prove herself. She was nothing if not earnest. As she stood next to Eleven's bruised but tall body, she looked like a kid sister dressed up as a scientist.

Dr. Nampala continued rocking as they stood near the doorway.

"Come closer, please."

They shuffled nearer to him, past a seating area furnished with threadbare sofa, two stiff leather chairs and a glass-topped coffee table. Researcher-4 spoke up as they neared Dr. Nampala, rocking in front of his desk.

"Dr. Nampala, I know that you want to talk to Eleven but I wanted to let you know –"

"You're right." He cut her off. "I do want to talk to Eleven."

"Yes sir." Researcher-4 stepped back and hung her head as Eleven tried to stand tall. As she pushed her chest out she winced from the pain in her body.

"It's good to see you awake, Eleven." Dr. Nampala remained seated. She stood in front of him, staring down at his angular face. His scraggly beard, as always, was intertwined in his fingers as he spoke.

She did not reply to his greeting. For Eleven, it was not so good to be awake, and it certainly wasn't good to see Dr. Nampala.

"Eleven, I'm going to make this quick. You look like you're having a hard time standing up. I certainly don't want you to be in pain."

She flexed her legs in response to his comment. She stood as straight as she could and tried to mask the hurt. Her face tightened but she didn't make a sound.

"Your escape attempt this morning was completely unacceptable. I'm not going to ask why you tried. I'm not going to ask how you could betray The Woodlands. I'm going to tell you." He stopped and pushed himself to standing against the intricately carved arms of the rocker. As he stood up, the chair bounced back and slowly stopped rocking.

He was barely taller than Eleven and probably lighter. He slid his glasses to the end of his long nose and peered over the swirling brown and black colored frame. His dark eyes tightened as he glared at Eleven. She returned his stare, and in spite of her feelings, did so without displaying emotion.

"I'm going to tell you what you need to do. You need to follow the rules. You need to trust that I am, as I always have been, looking out for you. You could have died today. Truthfully, if you were not the Head Student, I would have let you. You have a lot of potential, Eleven. But, one more stunt like that and you're done. Not done at The Woodlands. Done at life. Do you understand?"

She nodded.

"Let me hear you!" Dr. Nampala abruptly yelled, shattering the stillness, causing Researcher-4 to jump and drop her clipboard. It clattered on the floor.

"Shut up, Researcher-4." He stared at Eleven. "Now, let me hear you."

"Yes sir."

"Good. Now, you have tomorrow to recover. After that, it's back to work. Researcher-4, take Eleven to her pod."

They started walking away. They were near the door when Dr. Nampala called out.

"Researcher-4."

She turned, her face red from the shame of dropping her clipboard. She nearly dropped it again as she hurried to face her boss.

"Yes sir, Dr. Nampala?"

"Give her a couple extra doses of the compliance serum tonight. I don't need any more trouble from her. Especially now."

"Yes sir." Researcher-4 turned back to Eleven, who was standing near the door, waiting for it to be opened.

"Oh, Researcher-4," Dr. Nampala said as he sat back in his rocking chair.

"Yes sir." She turned once again.

"Hold on to your clipboard!"

"Yes sir." She hustled to open the door and lead Eleven back to her pod. Neither said a word as they rode the elevator back down to the dorm area. A sentry appeared as they exited the elevator. He escorted them to the pod and entered the proper code and key to allow the door to be opened. Eleven stumbled into her pod, while Researcher-4 went back to the central control lab to add the compliance serum to Eleven's overnight drug cocktail.

Eleven lay down without changing clothes. She rolled onto her stomach and reached her bruised arm under the bedframe and pulled out a folded up piece of paper.

She gingerly turned onto her back and began reading the simple words scrawled with a red marker:

Dear Eleven,

I know most people here hate me. I understand because I hate myself. I cannot remember a single happy day. I want out so bad, I am going to try to escape. Last month in class, you said if I needed anything you would help me. Well, I want to escape. Will you help me? If you will, meet me by the tree during the evening free time.

Sincerely,

Fifteen

"I'm so sorry Fifteen," Eleven whispered. She folded her hands over the paper and held it against her chest. She closed her eyes and thought about the day. As the Head Student, Eleven was the best at just about everything at The Woodlands. There may have been a few students who excelled in one or two categories of assessment but no one except Eleven was consistently near the top in every category.

Before today's catastrophic adventure, Eleven had been at the top in behavior. Exceptional obedience was a factor in determining the Head Student. She had not violated any Axioms in years; yet for some reason, she had chosen to rebel this morning. Not in a simple thing either, like leaving a bowl on the cafeteria table or cheating at a logic test. She had committed the ultimate crime at The Woodlands. Betrayal. Attempted escape was the absolute worst sin. She was the first ever to survive. The eight students, including Fifteen, who had tried to escape in the past five years, died.

She thought about life at The Woodlands as she lay on her bed, trying to stay as still as possible. The more she moved, the more she could feel the bruises. Everyone was stunned by her action. But everyone didn't know about the old box she uncovered in the area of the library undergoing renovations the same week that Fifteen wrote that note. No one did.

She barely opened her eyes and rolled her head to the side, looking at the middle of her pod through the dark channels formed by her eyelashes. Her line of sight moved over the baby blue rug in the center of the floor and across the glazed concrete that was polished weekly. Her scanning stare stopped at the desk positioned diagonally from where she lay.

The simple white desk had three large built-in box drawers with chunky metal handles. A single sliding envelope drawer hung under the desktop, under which her legs often rested while she worked on an assignment or read the latest test results from her research sessions. In the bottom box drawer, under her binders, she had hidden the contents of that old box she uncovered in a broken section of wall in the library – some files, a notebook, and a really old book. She was the only one who used that desk drawer. Her podmate wouldn't dare open it without permission. It was the safest storage place she had.

Eleven thought about getting up to look at it again. She hadn't even looked through the old book because the information in the files had been so astonishing. As she curled her head up, pain shot through her neck, causing her to lay flat again. *Tomorrow*, she thought, closing her eyes. *Tomorrow, I'll look at everything again.*

As she drifted back to sleep, she had one final thought: *Dr. Nampala has no idea that I know. And I hope he never does.*

"What am I missing?" Dr. Nampala asked himself. Nearly thirty minutes had passed since Eleven left his office. Though he was very frustrated and perplexed by her escape attempt, he had little time for reflection. He rocked a few minutes longer and moved on to reviewing the week's research outcomes.

As he scanned a stack of papers with various colored graphs and charts and obtuse data, he grew increasingly puzzled by Thirty-Nine's results. He had been directly supervising Thirty-Nine's sessions for the last four days and he was even more surprised by the exceptional outcomes. Thirty-Nine was steady and near the top of the program, but in the last few weeks, dramatic changes had unfolded before Dr. Nampala's eyes.

"The child has a remarkable brain structure and his temperament is practically immune to stress. It's beyond any I've seen. Better even than Eleven."

He reached out to a smoldering pipe on the side table.

He sucked deeply on the polished cherry-wood stem and exhaled a cloud of smoke into the cavernous space overhead. Most of the decor in his office was unchanged from the twenty plus years it had served as a research center in the 1960's and 70's. The walls were light grey painted steel. The room was a circle of windows. It was the Chief's thinking area. No one dared enter during his brainstorming sessions unless they had a death wish.

Diagrams of the human brain and the central nervous system hung on most of the walls, covered with the scribbled thoughts and detailed analyses of the obsessed leader of The Woodlands. A chart comparing the distinctions between a human's adolescent brain and an adult brain as well as several primate brains was prominently taped in the center of a movable chalkboard.

Still holding his pipe, he stood from the chair and walked to a single metal locker behind his paper-strewn desk. It had several additional locks built in and its base was bolted to the floor. He bit the pipe, holding it tightly between his yellowed teeth. As the smoldering flame nibbled the remaining tobacco, he twisted the combination tumblers, lining up the correct sequence of numbers until the door was unlocked. He popped it open and stared into his private storage space. A stack of three old cardboard shoeboxes rested on the locker bottom.

He reached down and tugged a single box out from the bottom of the stack. He turned to his desk and set the box on a pile of crinkled data sheets and pulled the lid off to reveal a mirror. Since mirrors were outlawed in the facility, he kept this one securely hidden. He firmly believed any distraction from the work, even personal hygiene, other than routine health maintenance needs, limited the efficiency of the project. Fortunately, his superior mind had long ago vanquished such petty distractions and he only kept the mirror to review how he appeared to the students and staff. As the leader, he felt it was critical to project health and vitality.

Tilting the box in his hands, he stared at his reflection. Dark pupils surrounded by red lightning bolt veins streaking in every direction stared back through tortoise-shell glasses. The sleepless nights had rendered his eyes permanently bloodshot. A cascade of stick straight salt and pepper hair fell on either side of his patchwork beard and rested above his collarbones. His heavily lined forehead camouflaged the briefness of his time on earth. Though he was only 36 years old, without furnishing a birth certificate, no one would believe that he was a day under 50.

He stared at the deep lines in his cinnamon skin as he racked his brain for the solution to the puzzle he'd been trying to solve since he walked away from the government and entered the world of underground human experimentation. As time grew shorter, his patience grew thinner. Even with himself.

"Damn it Leonard. You better figure it out." He hissed.

He definitely needed to figure it out. If he could, he'd be collecting ten million dollars from The Future. If he couldn't, he and everyone else at The Woodlands would end up meeting Fifteen in the afterlife much sooner than anticipated, in less than two months.

He placed the mirror back in the box, and the box into the locker. He shut the door and turned each combination randomly until he was certain the locker's contents were secure.

A buzzing sound interrupted his silent reflection. The leftover beige government issue phone a few feet away on a small circular conference table notified him of a call from his main data analysis room.

He dropped his pipe into a tin mug on his desk and walked over to the phone.

"Dr. Nampala, we have the preliminary results from today's batch of testing on the 9-10 age cohort," the voice of an assistant lab worker announced over the speakerphone.

He jumped right into the pressing questions without taking time for pleasantries. "Is there any improvement in the static activity of the neural overlays? The color resonance markers?"

"The overall group numbers remained the same as the last three trials."

"That's unacceptable. Who is this?" The tributary like veins on either side of his forehead popped out, snaking from his receding hairline to his temples. Each thud of his heart felt like a nail gun against his sternum. As it pounded faster, he reached under the phone table and grabbed a bottle of pills.

"It's Researcher-9," a soft shaky female voice replied.

"Researcher-9, Researcher-9." Dr. Nampala muttered, thinking. "You're from Kiev, right?"

Dr. Nampala tried to remember every detail of the background of his research team, staff and sentries. He used the information to understand how best to coerce them into producing the results he wanted.

"I'm from Minsk."

"Close enough. It's somewhere over there near Poland."

"It's Belarus, sir."

"Fine, Belarus. You've been with us for seven years now, and your parents are still living?"

"They were when I left."

"They still are. I can tell you. That's a fact. And, Researcher-9, I know you'd like to see them. And, I'd like for you to see them. But here's the thing," Dr. Nampala's voice grew shrill as he shouted. "If we can't get the research right, nobody's going home. Ever!"

"Yes sir."

"So, what's the problem?"

"Well, sir, the students..."

"Don't blame the students!" Dr. Nampala shouted over the voice of Researcher-9. "It's your job to figure out what supplementations and enhancements will work to trigger the desired results. It's simple. We must develop a student with the ability to hear thoughts, then to project thoughts. Do better!"

"Yes sir. Dr. Nampala, there is one interesting result from this last round of trials."

"What's that? And don't tell me something about a possible hybrid sequence in the labrum modeling. Researchers 6 and 10 already told me about that idiotic dead end. Tell me something real."

"No sir. Yes sir. I mean, I don't have anything on the labrum modeling. I noticed when charting the students, that Thirty-Nine's patterns during peak REM activity were..."

"Thirty-Nine?"

"Yes sir."

"Do you have that report in front of you?"

"Yes sir."

"Send it up to me. I want to review it myself."

"Of course, sir," the relieved voice of Researcher-9 sounded cheerful as she replied to Dr. Nampala's request.

Dr. Nampala put the bottle of pills back in a small file box under the phone table. He returned to the rocking chair and sat down, eager to receive the report on Thirty-Nine.

"Something is going on with this kid." He nodded slowly as he rocked in the chair, rubbing his hairy chin. "Time to push him further. Time to test the limits. Time to figure him out."

The next day passed without event. Thirty-Three continued his work detail, toiling in the Yard for hours, weeding and repairing the small wooden fence that encircled the flower bed under the tree in the center of the Yard. Thirty-Nine continued to be sequestered in dream sequencing sessions, still unable to visualize the face of the man in his dream. Eleven continued to heal, as well as cautiously read the materials she had discovered in the library.

In the afternoon, she opened the old book. It contained secrets that were beyond her wildest dreams. Secrets that told of a possible escape method she would never – could never – have imagined. She re-read its old worn pages and hoped with all her heart that it was true.

As she read, her heart hurt for Fifteen. In the pages she scanned was a possible escape route that did not require scaling the deadly walls of The Woodlands. If only she had read this before attempting the escape. She could have spared Fifteen's life.

She couldn't pull it off on her own. She wasn't sure even what she was going to pull off, but when thinking about which student might join her adventure, one boy immediately came to mind. There was one kid who would surely be willing to risk it all for a chance to leave The Woodlands. There was only one student who never backed down from a sentry's abuse. The only student who feared nothing: Thirty-Three. At dinner, she would make contact.

The students entered the cafeteria abuzz over Eleven's return to routine. The back of her head was bandaged with white gauze and clear medical tape. Several spots on her arms sported heavy bandaging. Most of the students whispered when she walked by, wondering what had possessed her to risk death to go beyond the walls. No one spoke to her, of course. Rumor was far more entertaining than reality.

Other than the gossip about Eleven, dinner was typical. The trays that evening, like most meals, were filled with pressed food bars and a pulpy juice blend filled with multiple liquid vitamins and minerals. The Woodlands' chefs were nutritional scientists who prepared customized food products for each student. Caloric input and output was regulated and measured daily, along with a multitude of other biological indicators. Each student dutifully ate everything that was served. If they didn't, they would be placed on the Wheel.

After dinner was over, as the students lined up for the transition to evening instruction, Eleven sidled past Thirty-Three.

"I found something amazing in the library. Meet me in the Game Chamber after assembly tonight, at seven o'clock," she whispered in his oversized ear, and kept on walking toward the front of the line.

Thirty-Three nudged Thirty-Nine as he stared at her moving toward the front of the line.

"Why'd you hit me?" Thirty-Nine whispered.

The sentries were moving into position alongside the students. They flanked the rows, in alternating fashion. With one sentry for every four students, it was not easy to have an unguarded moment. This certainly wasn't one.

Thirty-Three turned his eyes away from Eleven and made eye contact with Thirty-Nine. He flit his eyes forward in Eleven's direction then rolled his eyes back to Thirty-Nine.

Thirty-Nine looked ahead, seeing nothing but the backs of other children's heads. He looked at Thirty-Three quizzically, feeling like a repeat of Shearing Day was underway.

Thirty-Three repeated his eye movement, this time tilting his head diagonally, hoping Thirty-Nine would see Eleven, now almost at her place in line.

Thirty-Nine looked up the row, in the direction Thirty-Three had indicated. He recognized all the students, even from behind, but he knew what Eleven looked like from any angle. He spotted the bandage on the back of the left side of her head.

"You sure think about her a lot," Thirty-Nine whispered.

As they were escorted to the assembly room for evening instruction, Thirty-Three couldn't stop smiling. Once they were standing in front of their assigned blue plastic chairs, the screen at the front of the room scrolled down, the projector hummed to life and a recording from the Chief began to play.

"Good evening, family. Let us recite The Woodlands Mantra…"

The students echoed the mission statement of the facility; the same words they had heard and said every morning and night since arriving as infants and toddlers:

"The brain is the new frontier. The mind is a vast, unexplored region filled with endless possibilities. The power of the mind to communicate and control is inevitable. My potential is only discovered in my mind, through the assistance of The Woodlands. I submit my thoughts and desires to this single pursuit: Fulfilling the vision of Dr. Nampala, the supreme mind and worthy leader."

"Well done. Now sit down. Tonight, students, I want to remind you of the importance of each of you fulfilling his or her part in the success of The Woodlands. One day, you will rule the world. One day, you will be sent out into the world beyond these walls and have great influence. Greater than you could ever imagine. In order to achieve success, you must follow my instructions in every detail. There can be no success without obedience. There can be no obedience without trust. I trust you with the mission of fulfilling my life's work. Trust me with the work of fulfilling your life's mission."

After reminding the students of the role each played in success for The Woodlands, he began to give out the weekly recognitions and reprimands. Every student was trained from arrival that they were instruments for the greater good. They were taught that the human body served as a storehouse for the human mind. Children who complied were given a weekly treat, usually extended free time. Children who rebelled were given punishments. Most children complied and in many ways, were even happy.

"Boy-41, you did an excellent job on your logic sequencing strategies Tuesday," Dr. Nampala continued on, praising one of the good students.

Like the bad students, they were usually repeat offenders. Dr. Nampala enjoyed listing the virtues of the obedient children, as he pursued every method of reinforcement to improve student compliance.

Thirty-Three paid little attention to these moments. His stubbornness was awe-inspiring. He seldom failed to disrupt the order of life at The Woodlands. True to form, as Dr. Nampala spoke, he tapped his knee against Thirty-Nine.

Thirty-Nine knew better than to turn his head away from the screen. He tapped Thirty-Three's foot in response.

"Eleven wants to meet me," Thirty-Three muttered under his breath.

"I'm sure," Thirty-Nine replied, trying not to laugh.

"I'm serious. She whispered to me when we were lining up. She wants me to meet her in the Game Chamber after assembly."

"Good for you. She probably just wants to beat you at chess again." Thirty-Nine kept his voice low and even. He certainly didn't want Thirty-Three to know he was jealous. Even if it were only an opportunity to play chess, it would still be interaction with Eleven. Regardless of her intentions, all the older boys would leap at the chance to have uninterrupted time with Eleven. For some of the boys, especially Thirty-Three, her escape attempt had intensified the infatuation. If his attraction for Eleven had been like smoldering embers in a campfire before, it became a raging wildfire the moment he saw her astride the top of the wall. Now, she wanted to meet him in the Game Chamber. Tonight.

The Game Chamber was built shortly after Dr. Nampala arrived at The Woodlands. It was a hexagon with six game rooms. Each game room was a simple square unit, with pitched plexi-glass roofs, arranged around the base of the observation deck. A single long hallway circled the perimeter of the Game Chamber.

Dr. Nampala liked to walk around and view the student's interactions from his perch. He watched their mental abilities but also focused on their competitiveness, social interactions, and emotional response to winning and losing.

The students were able to visit the Game Chamber between seven and nine o'clock at night. The only students who were allowed to go were those who had performed well the previous week and had no restrictions for bad behavior.

"And finally, for the fifteenth week in a row, Thirty-Three has received a reprimand," Dr. Nampala droned on. "Students, what is The Fourth Axiom of The Woodlands?"

"Precision yields greater possibilities," the students replied

"That's right. And Thirty-Three was imprecise with his beverage this week. Sloppy, sloppy, sloppy," Dr. Nampala scolded.

The announcement of his reprimand snapped Thirty-Three out of his daydream, in which Eleven was telling him how great he was.

"Shoot! I can't go to the Game Chamber tonight."

Thirty-Nine pinched his upper lip between his teeth to prevent a smile from spreading across his face.

"Everyone stand," Dr. Nampala ordered. "It's time for the benediction. Eleven, come to the front and lead the class in The Woodlands Chant."

The students rose to their feet. Eleven stepped out of her row, and limped to the front of the assembly. A wave of whispers followed her as she passed each row of students.

"Silence!" The sentries ordered from each corner of the room.

After climbing the metal stairs that led to the platform beneath Dr. Nampala's giant digital image, she turned to face the crowd, her expression carrying a hint of insolence. Before leading the students in the chant, she had to read an apology that a sentry had placed in her lap during dinner. She unfolded the handwritten note prepared by the Chief and read aloud:

"Classmates, Sentries, Dr. Nampala:

I committed a wicked, loathsome betrayal earlier this week. My decision to help Fifteen in an escape attempt was a wretched one. I chose to give aid to a rebellious student who was under obvious psychological strain. Instead of leading by reporting her intentions, I became infected by her fantasies. As the Head Student, I can tell you unequivocally – any thoughts of the outside world without Dr. Nampala's guidance are a fantasy. He is our leader and father. His wisdom sustains us. His concern protects us. I was wrong and I apologize to all members of The Woodlands family for my traitorous action. I will never do such a thing again. You must never do such a thing. The Woodlands family is one of a kind and is to be cherished."

She looked out at the shiny faces staring up at her. She vaguely remembered feeling like the youngest ones, their naivety easy to see in the innocent eyes and placid expressions of the simple-hearted and simple-minded. She also instantly recognized the older students' twisted expressions. The dimness of their tainted eyes, confusion tinged with skepticism filled the furrows formed by their scrunched brows. Each one unique, even with shaved heads and matching tunics. Eleven slowly folded the paper and held it in her left hand.

"Very good Eleven," Dr. Nampala intoned from the screen above her head. "I couldn't have said it better myself. Students, please forgive Eleven, as I have. Proceed, Eleven."

Eleven lowered her head as she saw two sentries approach the platform.

"And now, students, The Woodlands Chant."

She placed her hands firmly on her hips and in a monotone voice, led the other students in the collective ode to the Chief's vision:

The world is danger, the world is unclear,

The power of intellect destroys all fear,

The world is filled with fools. One day all will see,

The power of The Woodlands, the power in me!

The screen over Eleven's head retreated, and the students turned to exit the assembly. Eleven resolutely walked down the steps and passed the rows of chairs, while the students waited in their rows until she reached the back of the room. As the Head Student, she was at the front of the line in every procession. The two sentries that arrived near the platform during her apology flanked her as she walked toward the exit.

Once she reached the back row of seats, the students began filing out into their original positions, two-by-two, with sentries lining up to escort them to their pods.

A soft buzzer sounded and the electronically activated double doors swung open. The students silently marched out of the assembly area and down the main corridor. Eleven led them through the wide space where ninety-five percent of student traffic occurred. Her pace was sure, matching her outlook. Now that she had made contact with her first recruit, she noticed her pain less and she trusted her instincts more.

The same instincts that had carried her to the top of The Woodlands might help carry her out of The Woodlands. A lot depended on her instincts regarding Thirty-Three. He was a wildcard, and she was counting on him to show up in a big way.

"I can't meet her," Thirty-Three said as soon as the door was sealed behind them in their pod.

"I know. In trouble again, huh?" Thirty-Nine replied.

Thirty-Three flopped onto his bed, kicking his boots off, flinging them against the door.

Thirty-Nine, still near the door, ducked to avoid the flying shoes.

"Do you have to always throw your stuff around the pod?"

"Sorry."

Thirty-Three rolled onto his stomach and propped his head up with his hands under his chin. He kicked at his sleep sheath while returning to conversation with Thirty-Nine.

"Do you think she likes me?"

"What do you mean?"

"Well," Thirty-Three paused, searching for the right words. He didn't know how to describe his interest in Eleven. It was different from his feelings for anyone else.

"Do you mean does she think you are biologically attractive?" Thirty-Nine interjected, attempting to help end the awkward silence.

"I guess. Yeah, do you think she finds me biologically attractive?"

"That would not be a reasonable determination on her part."

"What's that supposed to mean?"

Thirty-Three was used to Thirty-Nine's dispassionate interpretation of the world. He couldn't be too offended by Thirty-Nine's potentially insulting response since he knew that Thirty-Nine was only analyzing the situation using objective comparisons.

"Well," Thirty-Nine responded, moving over to his bed and sitting down. He untied his shoes and continued, "She is nearly flawless. Her scores are always at the top of her cohort. She is physically and emotionally superior in every way."

"Like how?" Thirty-Three shot back, rolling over onto his right side, staring directly at Thirty-Nine.

"Are you sure you want to know?"

"Yes, I'm sure."

"Ok. She is tall and athletic with lean, muscular legs and a flat mid-section. You are short, not very athletic and not at all lean. She has engaging blue eyes. You have dull brown eyes. Her skin is aglow with health and vitality; your skin is coarse and dry. You are ornery and temperamental. She is composed and deliberate. Your ears are too big for your head..."

"That's enough," Thirty-Three interrupted Thirty-Nine's laundry list of his negative features. "It's not like you're some kind of super attractive person, either. You are just, umm, well, I guess I'd say, you are just regular. Your face is plain, your skin is pale, and your nose is small. You look pretty regular. Except your eyes, of course."

Everyone commented on Thirty-Nine's eyes. Even Thirty-Three begrudgingly admitted they were remarkable. They were a soft golden yellow, like miniature sunsets. His eyes almost seemed to glow during the rare moments when Thirty-Nine became emotionally engaged. Since none of the students ever saw themselves, their fascination and even obsession with appearance was actually heightened. Even the windows were slightly backlit to prevent them from being used as a mirror. Thirty-Three never left the pod (if he could help it) without Thirty-Nine giving him a description of how he looked, and vice versa.

"Ok, so what if I'm not the most beautiful student?" Thirty-Three continued talking, focusing on his concerns. "I understand that on the outside she may have some features that are better than mine, but what about the other parts of me? The part that isn't all wrapped up in brainwaves and mental abilities?"

"You have plenty of those parts. You are the only kid here who seems to have your " He paused to come up with the right words to describe Thirty-Three's mercurial nature.

"...emotional range. It seems a terrible waste to me. All those outbursts and reprimands, physical punishments. You allow your weaker feelings to overwhelm the primary role of your brain. It's stupid. It doesn't make any sense."

"Those weaker feelings are a part of me. I think you have them too, you just don't know it. Anyway, maybe Eleven likes those parts of me. But it doesn't matter now. She'll be at the game center..." He looked at the clock. "She'll be at the game center in about fifteen minutes," he continued, "and I won't be there."

"What, exactly, did she say when she told you to meet her?"

"She said she found something exciting in the library, and she wanted me to meet her at seven o'clock."

"I don't mean to lessen your excitement but that doesn't sound like she has a biological attraction. I think she just wants to tell you about what she found in the library."

"Or," Thirty-Three stood and rubbed his hands together excitedly; "she is pretending she found something at the library so she can meet me!"

"Or not." Thirty-Nine mumbled.

Thirty-Three paced in the middle of the pod. He glanced up at the clock again. 6:50 PM.

"I know!" Thirty-Three turned and pointed his pudgy index finger at Thirty-Nine.

"What?" Thirty-Nine asked, standing as if beckoned by Thirty-Three.

"You go instead of me. Call for a sentry. You can meet her and see what she says."

"Are you sure?" Thirty-Nine felt a strange sensation as he pretended not to be excited about a rendezvous with Eleven. It was like a rumbling vibration was engaging his central nervous system through his internal organs. His stomach suddenly felt hollow and his heart raced.

"Yes, I'm sure. It's not like you are going to do anything to mess up my chance to be the boy she likes the most, anyway. You don't have any problems with those weaker feelings. Go on, buzz for a sentry."

Thirty-Nine walked over to the intercom box on the wall near the foot of his bed. His finger shook slightly as he pressed the black plastic button and requested a sentry for escort to the Game Chamber.

Maybe I should tell Thirty-Three I think Eleven is biologically attractive too, he thought.

He turned to Thirty-Three, who was still pacing in the middle of the pod.

"How do I look?"

Thirty-Three turned to his friend, surprised by a smile on Thirty-Nine's face.

"You're expressing happiness. Why are you smiling?"

Maybe not, he thought, trying to calm down.

"Oh, I'm just excited to play chess against the best player. You know how much I would like to beat her." Thirty-Nine said.

"Oh, ok. You look fine. Like always."

The sound of the sentry opening the door stopped their conversation.

"Thirty-Nine, you are granted thirty minutes in the Game Chamber. Let's go."

"Good luck!" Thirty-Three called out as Thirty-Nine walked out of the pod.

Good luck, Thirty-Nine thought. *It's going to take more than luck for Eleven to find me biologically attractive.*

It's going to take a miracle.

The lighting seemed dimmer than usual. Shadows of elongated triangles formed by the industrial sconces that illuminated the hallway appeared every eight feet. Thirty-Nine began counting the four-foot square tiles in his head as he followed the sentry toward the Game Chamber.

Twelve, thirteen, fourteen, fifteen...

"I better get that shipment of 30 millimeter vials in tonight," the sentry said, interrupting the monotonous numbering of floor panels.

Thirty-Nine heard him. Unlike yesterday, he held his tongue. He quickened his pace to edge up alongside the sentry. It was Sentry-7, a man of no particular reputation and no distinguishing physical characteristic. He was another big goon who prodded and poked the students like a rancher moving cattle from one grazing field to another.

Sentry-7 looked down and to his right, puzzled by Thirty-Nine's movement. Thirty-Nine grimaced sheepishly and bounced his head sideways.

Sentry-7 scowled briefly but said nothing. They continued walking, side by side, Thirty-Nine trying to peek at the sentry's face without staring. As he looked forward, he saw Sentry-1 approaching them.

"The Woodlands forever," the sentries declared to one another, the customary greeting among the workers. As Sentry-1 passed by, Thirty-Nine heard Sentry-1 add, "Forever is a long time. Especially when you're all alone."

Sentry-7 didn't respond. Thirty-Nine's head jerked around to look at Sentry-1. The stocky senior sentry was proceeding down the hallway. Thirty-Nine was dumbstruck by the sentimentality of what he thought he heard Sentry-1 say. He slapped his head, hoping to clear his thoughts as he continued following Sentry-7 to the Game Chamber.

They rounded the corner, and were a few hundred feet from their destination when Thirty-Nine heard his sentry:

"He probably still hasn't finished the transfer paperwork."

Thirty-Nine looked as discreetly as he could at Sentry-7's mouth. He stared as they walked.

"What a tool."

His lips did not move.

"Ok," the sentry said, turning to Thirty-Nine, "we're here. Be at this door in 31 minutes for your return."

"Y-y-yes s-s-sir," Thirty-Nine stuttered.

He walked from the dormitory corridor into the Game Chamber hallway. Before entering, Thirty-Nine paused to set the timer on his digital pocket timer for twenty-nine minutes. He slid it back into the side pocket of his tunic. In the corner of Room One, two students were playing a game of Connect Ten.

He moved quickly to Room Two. The four LCD screens on the left wall were filled with rapidly alternating geometric patterns. Two students sat below each screen, game controllers in hand, matching patterns for points. The goal was to increase subliminal awareness skills. Thirty-Nine had always been exceptional at that game, though recently he had grown bored with the limited challenge it presented.

Thirty-Nine entered Room Three, the chess center. After hearing Sentry-7 "speak" in the hallway, he was distracted. He was still wrestling with whether he was losing his mind, was simply hearing things, or had developed some new ability to perceive sentries' thoughts. He walked by Eleven without seeing her, seated alone in a rocking chair next to a small bookshelf filled with manuals for improving spatial reasoning skills.

He meandered between the empty chess tables, looking at the different styles of the sets. He stopped in front of a table with carved wooden pieces that were shaped like wild cats. The king was a lion, the queen a lioness, the bishops were panthers. He picked up a bobcat pawn and turned it over, feeling the felt on the base.

Feels like my head two weeks after Shearing Day, he thought, rubbing his head. He rested his hand on his scalp a moment, reflecting on the events of the week.

Wonder what's out there, he thought, looking up at the glass ceiling overhead. *Maybe Thirty-Three has a point. It is a pretty big world, after all.*

Far above, a greenish blue wispy streak split the night sky. Thirty-Nine stared for a moment, pondering the world outside, his thumb still massaging the base of the bobcat pawn.

That kind of thinking leads only to trouble. Poor Fifteen, he thought, shuddering at the memory of her crumpled body on the ground. The thought shook him, and he looked back down at the chess table. He remembered his purpose for going to the Game Chamber.

"Eleven," he whispered to himself.

"Yes," came a response from across the room.

He spun around, still holding the bobcat pawn in his hand. There she stood. Thirty-Nine exhaled as he stared at Eleven, arrested yet again by her beauty and poise.

Thirty-Nine reached behind to set the chess piece on the table, and as he did, his arm knocked half of the pieces clattering to the floor. His face reddened as he crouched down, grabbing the various three or four-inch sculptures in his left hand and placing them in the shelf created by pressing his right arm against his side. Reaching out to grab the white lion king, he sensed another body nearby. He looked to his right, arm full of chess pieces, and there was Eleven. She held out a mountain lion rook piece.

"I think you dropped this," she said in a singsong voice, mocking his clumsiness as she plunked it onto the jumble of statuettes in the crook of his arm.

"Thanks." Thirty-Nine's red face was now merely rosy as he squashed his emotional responses. He stood upright and placed the chess pieces on the table.

"Thirty-Three told me you asked him to come here."

Now it was Eleven's turn to experience a flushed face. She stepped back, her cheeks aglow.

"He told you?" she whispered.

"Yes."

"Is he not coming?"

"No. He's got restrictions. The Chief announced it in assembly. Thirty-Three sent me on his behalf."

"You're not Thirty-Three."

"True. I can give him your message though."

"I don't think so." Eleven turned to walk away.

"Hey," Thirty-Nine said loudly.

"Yes." She turned to face him again.

He didn't want to lose the opportunity to spend time with Eleven. And he was curious about her intentions for the meeting. Maybe he could appeal to her competitive streak.

"Do you want to play? I think I can take you this time." Thirty-Nine pointed at the chess pieces he had set on the table. Eleven was highly competitive. At the core of The Woodlands mission was placing the children in an environment that constantly emphasized competition and rewarded success, even in trivial games. Dr. Nampala taught that no challenge was insignificant, for all challenges revealed a weakness to be purged. Though she was disappointed that Thirty-Three was absent and still very sore from her injuries, Eleven couldn't resist Thirty-Nine's invitation.

She looked at her counterpart. His bright eyes smiled as she held his gaze. His eyes were such a golden yellow they reminded her of the pictures she'd seen in the geography book of the endless wheat fields of America's Great Plains. For a moment, she imagined they were there. Standing near a barn, staring out the waving tops of wheat, like an ocean of gold. An ocean of sun-kissed gold.

An ocean of sun-kissed gold, Eleven thought.

"Eleven?" Thirty-Nine asked, interrupting her thoughts.

She grimaced and stepped closer to Thirty-Nine, still annoyed that Thirty-Three had gotten in trouble. The very attribute that led her to select him kept him from attending.

"What did you say?" Thirty-Nine was no longer smiling.

"Nothing. Sorry, I was just thinking. Sure, let's play." She winced as she reached out to pull on the back of a chair. Thirty-Nine rushed to help. He grabbed the chair and in the process, felt the soft firmness of her arm against his as their hands touched momentarily. She instantly let go and allowed him to move the chair.

No other students were in the room, nor had there been any since Thirty-Nine walked in. He had played Eleven a dozen times in the past few months, and his record was ten losses and two stalemates. Not good. They silently went about setting the pieces in the proper locations. Thirty-Nine didn't speak because he was afraid she might leave if he said something stupid. Eleven didn't speak because she was in pain and frustrated by Thirty-Three's absence.

As she placed her hand on a white bobcat pawn, Eleven thought about Thirty-Three and remarked aloud, "That kid is such a mess."

Thirty-Nine turned his eyes away from the chess pieces and looked at Eleven. Her typical demeanor could best be described as disaffected. Though she was competitive and the Head Student, her natural grace and composure made it seem like she was simply passing time but never fully committed to anything. Or anyone. Tonight, however, though she was sullen, she was focused. Her intent, though still unknown, was palpable.

She slid White Pawn 4 out two paces.

"Your turn."

Thirty-Nine looked at the board. He moved Black Pawn 3 one pace. Eleven reached out, and set her panther Knight in front of her.

Now I have to wait two days. Not good.

"Wait for what?" Thirty-Nine asked.

"What?" Eleven replied, staring at Thirty-Nine.

"You said you have to wait two days."

"I didn't say anything. I thought it."

Like the edge of a rainstorm, her words poured out the answer to Thirty-Nine's strange week. The voices when he woke up from dream sequencing and Sentry-5 "talking" and then hitting him in the hallway. Sentry-1's comments on the way to the Game Chamber...and now her. Her response rolled across the table into Thirty-Nine, and both of them realized what was happening to him. In him.

You hear thoughts, Eleven thought.

He stared at her intentionally closed lips. He nodded slowly, and lifted his eyes up until their gaze met. Thirty-Nine's hand trembled slightly as he moved Pawn 4 two paces. Their eyes remained fixed on one another.

Unbeknownst to them, far overhead, Dr. Nampala was leaning against the railing on the observation deck. He held the report from Researcher-9 in his hand while he stared down at his two top students playing chess.

"It just started yesterday," Thirty-Nine whispered. He looked around the room. Though they were alone, the revelation of his extraordinary talent made it feel like he should whisper, as though they were in the middle of a religious ceremony.

Eleven moved her knight diagonally four spaces and looked down at the board, analyzing the situation.

If Thirty-Nine can read thoughts, he might replace me at the top of the class.

"You're still the best student," Thirty-Nine mumbled. "But," he replied with a grin, "that was an illegal move."

Flustered, Eleven looked down at the board. "Oh, right."

Thirty-Nine's confidence was growing as he realized that his joking with Thirty-Three about hearing thoughts was not a joke. Hearing thoughts was a game changer. And he had discovered it in the Game Chamber.

"Ha ha."

"What's so funny?" Eleven asked, moving her knight back in place.

"Oh, I made a pun in my head. A really bad one."

Eleven slid Pawn 7 two spaces. She was no longer focused on the game. She was thinking through how to react to this revelation. She had always been ambivalent to Thirty-Nine. He was a good student. He was always compliant, and sometimes even supportive, of The Woodlands. She needed someone like Thirty-Three to share her discovery with, for it was a discovery that would certainly be confiscated by the Chief if she were caught.

She needed a student who didn't mind trouble. Or better yet, a student who enjoyed it. Thirty-Three fit the bill. She stared at the chess pieces aligned on the table. The regimented row of the unmoved pieces provided a contrast to the couple pawns and knights that stood alone, unprotected, in the middle of the board.

She looked at her competitor until he made eye contact. She stared into his eyes, trying to discern his allegiance.

Would he tell the Chief?

Showing Eleven that he was willing to take a risk, Thirty-Nine reached out and moved his queen into the center of the board.

"You can trust me," he whispered, unexpectedly sensing nervousness as he spoke. His insides were agitated. He wondered if his pupils were expanding. The gurgles in his stomach assured him that his parasympathetic nervous system was on full alert. He had secretly desired time with Eleven and now here he sat, face-to-face with her, in the Game Chamber, hoping to be let in on a secret. All while internalizing the truth that he was in possession of a supernatural power. He was, to say the least, not his usual self at the moment.

"I can trust Thirty-Three," she whispered, sliding Pawn 4 diagonally, capturing his queen, flicking away his uncharacteristic attempt at spontaneity.

Thirty-Three. His podmate. His friend. A small flicker of guilt entered Thirty-Nine's consciousness. Thirty-Three would be upset if he knew of Thirty-Nine's intentions. If he knew that Thirty-Nine was equally enamored with Eleven and at the moment, was doing everything he could to endear himself to her.

"Ok. I tell you what. I will take an oath. A pledge. Nothing you tell me will be shared with anyone but Thirty-Three."

He moved his bishop, taking her Pawn 4.

"Fifteen minutes," a voice in the hallway announced.

She turned her head. Thirty-Nine looked up over her well-defined shoulder. There stood a sentry, in the entrance area. They instinctively stiffened and looked back at the table. Neither dared speak.

Can you hear me? She thought.

Thirty-Nine slowly nodded his head twice, then rolled his head and hunched his shoulders, as if his neck was sore. He glanced back up. The sentry remained.

Maybe you hearing my thoughts is confirmation that I'm supposed to trust you. Her eyes stared down at the board but her mind was focused entirely on her would-be conspirator.

I would never have considered telling you before. But, maybe this is a three-person job. Or more. I don't know. But I'm going to tell you. We don't have time to be choosy.

Thirty-Nine's eyes never strayed from staring at the table but his heart ran laps inside his abdomen as he sensed Eleven was beginning to trust him.

But you can never tell a soul. Except Thirty-Three. Got it?

Thirty-Nine nodded.

"Your move," he whispered, pointing to the board.

She had completely forgotten about the game. She studied the arrangement. She moved her queen diagonally into the first row beyond the pawns and continued thinking to Thirty-Nine.

I was in the library. In the back cabinets of reference materials, where they are renovating to put in the secondary psych lab. I was looking for some more information on the history of the indigenous population of North America. I thought I could make a good impression on the Chief. I was near the demolished wall in the very back corner. As I thumbed through some binders looking for details on the native tribes, I spotted something shiny in the broken drywall and splintered wood on the ground. It was a silver briefcase reflecting sunlight through the window. No one was around, so I dug it out. As I knelt down and looked inside, I found some really old notebooks and papers. I read them yesterday.

"Are you serious?" Thirty-Nine whispered. He moved another pawn two spaces forward.

I'm very serious. I've never been more serious. Nothing is what we think. And none of us should be here. I discovered a way to escape without going over the walls. We can get out of here.

Her eyes narrowed as she looked dead at Thirty-Nine.

Everything we've been taught is a lie. The Chief is a criminal. It's all in the stuff I found. Here's the deal. If the Chief is successful, we'll be con-

trolled by some group called The Future. We'll be their slaves! If he fails, in just a few weeks, we'll all be killed. Either way, we can't stay. I'm getting out of here. But I need help to do it.

"Are you serious? We're going to be slaves? Or killed?"

Eleven nodded her head. The fire in her eyes was unmistakable. She wasn't joking and she was going to break out. Now, Thirty-Nine was faced with the biggest decision of his life: Join the rebellion or remain a silent complicit child with little hope of ever doing anything but following the orders of evil men.

Thirty-Nine gulped. Every student who had attempted escape was conspicuously buried in the Yard. Every escape attempt had been a variation on a theme – scaling the walls. There were no tools available to dig a tunnel under it. It encircled the entire compound and was topped with electrified wires. In reality, all previous escape attempts had been suicide missions.

Maybe it was the human spirit's desire for freedom because even though Thirty-Nine never thought of escape - it simply wasn't rational - as Eleven continued, his weaker feelings, or "emotional parts" as Thirty-Three described, were ablaze with excitement. Every element of the evening had exceeded his expectations. It was exhilarating and frightening.

She shared the big details about what she had found in the books. One file contained correspondence between Dr. Nampala and a group of murdering anarchist thugs called The Future. But, most importantly she told him about the old book and how it described a way to escape that didn't require anyone trying to get beyond the walls.

Time travel.

"Time travel," Thirty-Nine whispered. "That's not real." He mumbled quietly to avoid being heard by the sentry that hovered in the hallway.

It's worth a shot, she thought. *Just wait until you read the book before deciding, ok?*

"Ok."

She didn't share any more details about the book. She told him via her thoughts how she had snuck the books out in the un-hemmed trim of her tunic that she had pulled apart to create a pocket.

During the entire thought conversation, both of them continued playing chess, as if on autopilot. The rest of the game was a blur of inconsistent decisions and uncharacteristic moves. For the first time in his memory, Thirty-Nine didn't care about winning a game.

Dr. Nampala was puzzled as he continued to watch from above. "Strange. They are playing very amateur chess. Why would he surrender his second bishop without using his rook to take out her bishop?"

He studied the charts from Thirty-Nine's recent testing again. "According to this, his abilities should be heightened. Yet his game play is very unfocused, as if he's regressing." He stared at the two children, their every move visible through the specially designed and lit roof. After a minute, he walked back into his office.

"Time to have a conversation with that boy." Dr. Nampala walked back into his office, escaping the cool evening air. As he stepped through the sliding doorway, he flipped on the overhead lighting and moved to his desk.

Beep. Beep. Beep. Thirty-Nine's pocket timer notified him that his time was almost up.

Tell Thirty-Three everything. After his restrictions are lifted, we will meet again. Eleven stood up from the table, the game unfinished, and walked toward the sentry.

Thirty-Nine sat still for a moment. He closed his eyes.

Eleven wants to escape. Time travel? The Chief is a criminal?

Through his closed eyes, he could sense lights flickering, telling him time was up. Before opening his eyes and getting up, he remembered the most significant part of the whole night.

I can hear thoughts. How does this work? How can I control it? Can I control it? Fear and doubt, awe and confusion rushed through his mind. As he opened his eyes, he saw Sentry-1 standing on the other side of the table.

"Time to go," the flat-faced guard demanded. Sentry-1 was the longest tenured enforcer at The Woodlands. He was shorter than every other sentry but his sledgehammer fists and his telephone pole legs showcased his brute strength. He was reserved in manner and far less violent than Sentry-5 but his loyalty to Dr. Nampala was without question.

During the early days at The Woodlands, he had been responsible for training the students in physical exercises and still presided over the monthly conditioning exams. He was the oldest enforcer and as time passed, he had grown less rigid. His attempt to rescue Fifteen from Sentry-5's brutality was the most compassionate by any sentry since the founding of The Woodlands. Rumor was he was once married but when his wife died he devoted his entire being to The Woodlands.

"Thirty-Nine, did you hear me? Come with me. Now. Dr. Nampala has ordered your delivery to his office."

Thirty-Nine stood up. Nampala? His office? He had never been to the Chief's office. The only kid he knew that went there was Thirty-Three, and that was not a good thing. He hadn't done anything wrong. Had he?

"Let's go. Stand up!" The sentry barked, moving closer to Thirty-Nine.

"Yes sir." Thirty-Nine rubbed his suddenly sweaty palms on his thighs and pushed his chair back. He followed the sentry up to Dr. Nampala's office. He fretted the entire way, trying to guess why he was being summoned. He was so preoccupied with the potential trouble looming in the Chief's office he didn't even notice Sentry-1's thoughts.

If he had, he would have discovered that Sentry-1 was not just the original guard at The Woodlands. He also provided the very first student at The Woodlands.

Sentry-1 was Fifteen's father.

"Have a seat, Thirty-Nine." Dr. Nampala instructed, pointing to a leather chair positioned next to a small loveseat and coffee table arrangement.

He turned to Thirty-Nine's silent escort. "Thank you Sentry-1. I'll buzz for you when we're finished."

Sentry-1 exited without responding. He stumbled through the door and sat on the entryway floor. He leaned against the cold wall and tilted his head back. As he closed his eyes, images of Fifteen flickered through his mind. His barrel chest heaved as he sighed. He was still committed to The Woodlands and he knew losing Fifteen was always a possibility. He just didn't know losing her would make it so hard to breathe. He looked down at the faded white trim along the wall. It had been a long time since he first painted that. It had been a long time since he came to The Woodlands.

He remembered how Dr. Nampala had consoled him when his wife died. How he brought him in with his baby girl and gave them a fresh start at The Woodlands.

"I really appreciate your help, Leonard," he told Dr. Nampala one night before the new children began arriving. They were fixing up the place, cleaning and painting the dusty old rooms. It was exciting and new, and he was happy to support his good friend's dream of scientific breakthrough.

"No problem, Tom. I'm glad you are able to help. I guess we met back there at the DOD project for a reason, after all. I'm sorry about your loss. I know Clara was a great woman."

"Yes." He couldn't say anything else, so he picked up the wide brush and continued painting the baseboard along the hallway leading to the main office.

"Tom, I'm going to remove names for purposes of confidentiality. So, I'm going to call you Sentry-1. You'll be the first of many guards and staff people. I want you to lead them."

"It would be my honor."

"And little Denise. Your baby girl. What does she weigh these days?"

"Fifteen pounds yesterday." Sentry-1 smiled and looked at her asleep in a playpen in the corner. Through the mesh netting of the playpen, he could see her pudgy fists balled up under her delicate round face.

"Fifteen." Dr. Nampala repeated. "We'll call her Fifteen. For confidentiality. You'll need to call her Fifteen also. You understand. I don't want the other children or the workers to know she's your daughter. She's technically not even supposed to be part of the project. But, I've made an exception for you."

"Sure." Sentry-1 nodded and kept painting, thinking little of the request. Dr. Nampala had rescued him from despair. He would do just about anything for his genius scientist friend.

Sentry-1 sighed and slowly stood to his feet. It wouldn't be good for someone to see him on the floor. He gathered himself and returned to the customary position in front of the closed door.

In the office on the other side of that closed door, Thirty-Nine sat down in the chair and looked up cautiously at Dr. Nampala.

"Thirty-Nine. You're really growing up, son." The Chief walked over and sat in the loveseat. He propped his bare feet up on the coffee table, nudging a few old books to the side with his calloused heel. Thirty-Nine had never been this close to the Chief. He was smaller than expected. As Dr. Nampala clasped his hands together, his needed-to-be-trimmed fingernails drew Thirty-Nine's attention. His eyes traced down his bony knuckles to the hairless skin on his hands and forearms. The rest of the Chief's body was covered in rumpled loose clothing, like a slack mainsail on a windless day.

"I remember when you first joined us. You displayed some potential. You were usually in the top quartile in your class." He stared at Thirty-Nine, gauging his reaction. Thirty-Nine looked down briefly, uncomfortable with the Chief's positive affirmations.

"Thank you, sir," he mumbled.

"Which is why I'm puzzled by recent events."

Thirty-Nine stared at the light colored nicks in the wooden legs of the coffee table. He wasn't sure what the recent events were and he was not going to volunteer a comment unless asked.

"Can you recite Axiom 2?" Dr. Nampala asked.

Thirty-Nine raised his head, looking at his leader.

"Yes sir."

The Chief extended his arm and beckoned with his open hand. He nodded his pointy chin, motioning for Thirty-Nine to say the Axiom.

"Great physical health supports great mental health. Great mental health equals perfect decisions."

"That's right. Now," the Chief unfolded his hands and dropped his feet from the table. He sat on the edge of the table and leaned close to Thirty-Nine. A strong odor of cigarette smoke and deli meat assaulted the boy's nostrils. Thirty-Nine recoiled at the Chief's aroma.

"Don't be afraid, son. I just want to talk. According to your file," he pointed to a black legal folder resting on the desk a few feet away. "You have always consumed the proper nutrition. And you get your exercise. But, I couldn't help noticing your game against Eleven tonight. Would you say you were making perfect decisions?"

"I was trying to, sir. Maybe I was nervous because I was playing against Eleven? She is the Head Student, after all."

Dr. Nampala lurched back, slapping his hands on his thighs. His shoulder length hair shook as he laughed.

"Nervous?" he asked incredulously. "You completed Emotional Detoxification Treatments I, II, III, & IV before you were six years old! Why would you experience nervousness?"

Thirty-Nine scrambled to come up with a cogent response. As he frantically searched his mind for a good answer, Dr. Nampala pulled a notepad and a pen out of his shirt pocket.

"I mean - what I meant to say - is I had trouble getting focused on the game. Perhaps I was just tired from the dream sequencing work. You know, like Axiom 5 says..."

"I know what Axiom 5 says. Well," Dr. Nampala looked intently at Thirty-Nine. "You do look a little pale. How's your heart rate?"

Thirty-Nine placed his fingers against his neck and closed his eyes. He counted for fifteen seconds. "Fine, sir, seventy-four beats per minute."

This kid is not being honest with me. There's something changing in him. I should beat him, but he will likely withdraw further if I engage with force.

Thirty-Nine heard the Chief's thought and gulped. His skin tightened and his heart jumped to ninety beats a minute.

"Tell me," Dr. Nampala questioned, changing the subject. "What do you think of Eleven?"

"I think she's very good. She's the best in The Woodlands."

"I know that. What do you think of her appearance?"

"I don't." Thirty-Nine lied. "I don't think appearance is a relevant measure of human value. All worth is discovered only in the power of the mind."

"Good answer." Dr. Nampala began writing on his notepad, every thought flowing straight to Thirty-Nine's brain as clearly as if the Chief were speaking.

Seems rational. Perhaps the recent abnormal brain development is the cause of his poor game play. I can't torture him, though. Need him at full strength. Diet and activity levels are satisfactory.

"Have you had any stomach troubles?"

"No sir." Thirty-Nine was struggling to sit still. He pulled his foot under his opposite knee and grabbed his shin with his hands. The old leather chair squeaked as he moved.

"Are you comfortable?"

"Yes sir."

Fidgety. Annoying behavior. Focus, Leonard. The matter at hand. Check recent psychological profile results.

Dr. Nampala continued to jot on his notepad, his head down, his hair covering most of his face. All that Thirty-Nine could see was the underside of the Chief's glasses and his sizeable nose sticking through a coarse mop of black and gray.

"Tell me, Thirty-Nine, did you witness Fifteen and Eleven's attempted escape?"

"Yes sir."

"How did it make you feel?"

Thirty-Nine paused before answering. He had experienced a visceral reaction but he didn't want to give the Chief any idea that emotions were a part of his processing. He summoned his self-control and slid his foot back down to the floor. He sat up straight and replied.

"I am not sure what you mean by feel. The students violated the rules and they were punished accordingly."

He responds appropriately. But his physical movements are suspicious. He controls emotions well, but not enough to fool me.

Dr. Nampala looked at Thirty-Nine. This slight tall boy seated before him was a puzzle. Thirty-Nine's exposed ankles and lower leg told him a growth spurt had occurred. The indented leather armrest and the white tips of his fingernails told him Thirty-Nine was holding on to that chair tightly, as if he were holding in information by squeezing the arms of the chair. Thirty-Nine looked directly at Dr. Nampala through rapidly blinking eyelids.

Those bright yellow eyes, Dr. Nampala thought, looking back at his notepad. He bit his lower lip as he scribbled his final thoughts.

What about his heredity? Review the boy's mother's file. She was one of the few local targets. Assign Specialist-3 to identify Thirty-Nine's mother's whereabouts and obtain current health records. She may shed some light on the recent changes in the boy.

Thirty-Nine's hold on the leather went from nervously tight to death grip. He looked down at the floor, fearful that the Chief might see his wide eyes and his trembling chin, not to mention the likely change in skin tone as he felt a rush of heat through his cheeks. His knee began bouncing with agitation. The sound of his shaking leg against the edge of the chair interrupted Dr. Nampala's writing.

He looked over his notepad at Thirty-Nine, whose head was now lowered and whose foot was tapping on the floor like a starving woodpecker against a hickory tree.

"What is wrong with you? What is going on in your head?"

Thirty-Nine looked up. He couldn't stop his foot. He had never experienced any sensation like this. He was always in control. He took a deep breath, grateful that at least his face didn't feel too flushed.

"Yes sir. I think I'm just really tired, sir." He was desperate to get out of the office.

I have a mother! A real live mother. Not an orphan. She's alive! A mom. A family. Thirty-Nine's thoughts slammed around his head, making it nearly impossible to reply to Dr. Nampala.

"Maybe if I could get a little rest..." his throat went desert dry as he struggled to speak.

Maybe I have been pushing him. But, what choice do I have? Dr. Nampala thought. *Still...maybe a break...*

"Ok. Take a day off. But be ready to go to work the next day."

"Yes sir." Thirty-Nine stood up in a daze.

"*Mother's whereabouts and current health*," Dr. Nampala's thoughts ping-ponged in Thirty-Nine's precocious mind.

"I've got big plans for you, Thirty-Nine. We just need to do some fine tuning." Dr. Nampala pulled out his walkie-talkie from his pocket. "Sentry-1!"

"Thank you sir," Thirty-Nine numbly mumbled. He walked to the door to wait for Sentry-1. As soon as the door opened, Thirty-Nine stepped through. His heart was pounding and his body was perspiring. He did not know how to assimilate the night's events. In one short hour, he had received more life-altering information than most people do in a decade.

He robotically followed Sentry-1 through the facility. Both of their faces were blank but each mind was consumed with a single thought about a family member:

My daughter is dead, echoed in Sentry-1's brain.

An eerily opposite refrain repeated not just in Thirty-Nine's head but also, for the first time ever, in his heart:

My mother is alive.

"Where were you?" Thirty-Three accosted him mere seconds after the pod door closed.

"Did they give you extra game time because you're so good?"

"Huh?" Thirty-Nine looked at his podmate, whose eyes were blazing with the fire of anticipation. Thirty-Nine rubbed his face with his hands. "Oh. No. I need to sit down."

"What's wrong? Did Eleven show up? What happened? What did she say?" Thirty-Three's rapid fire questioning might as well have been foam bullets peppering a steel wall, for they had no chance of penetrating the fog of thoughts clouding Thirty-Nine's mind. He staggered to his bed and flopped onto it, burying his face in the smooth fabric of his folded sleep sheath.

His reaction was nothing like the response Thirty-Three was expecting. He had been waiting for over an hour for some exciting details of the meeting with Eleven. He walked closer to Thirty-Nine's bed and continued his vigorous interrogation.

"Hey! Thirty-Nine! Hello? What happened?"

Thirty-Nine felt like a journalist trying to choose the morning headline. He had three powerfully compelling stories to choose from. As he lay on his stomach, eyes closed, his rational nature reappeared to help figure out what to tell Thirty-Three about first. Knowing his audience, he realized he only had one choice. Lead with Eleven.

"Here goes," his muffled voice announced as he pushed himself up. He swung his legs around and sat up, his still-shoed feet brushing the fringe of the carpet on the tile floor.

Thirty-Three dragged the desk chair over and swung it backwards, plopping down. He straddled the chair and grinned in expectation of the story to come.

"Eleven was in the library, near the area where they are rebuilding."

"Where's that?" Thirty-Three interrupted.

"The library."

"Duh. I mean, where in the library?" Thirty-Three hadn't been to the library in about four months. When the other students were in library sessions he was usually repairing desks or painting walls.

"It's not important," Thirty-Nine snapped. "Just let me tell you what happened, ok?"

Something about the tone in his friend's voice told Thirty-Three to shut up. His smile evaporated and he stiffened in his chair.   "Ok. Sorry."

"Sorry to be rude." Thirty-Nine felt shame over this new failure to control his emotions.

"I forgive you. Now, what did she say?"

"She found a notebook in the rubble where the room in the back is getting rebuilt. It's a really old diary of a kid from a couple hundred years ago. This kid was traveling with his dad on a Northwest expedition and became friends with some of the local Indians."

"So?" Thirty-Three bounced in the chair.

"So, this diary has a section in it - she didn't show me - that talks about a spot where the natives used to be able to pass through a corridor in time. A spot that opens every ten years and only lasts two days. You can go back exactly ten years from the day he entered the corridor. It was mostly used by the elders of the Indian tribes to go back and leave messages for the future, like where to plant crops, when a disaster might happen, et cetera. The leaders kept it very secret. They used it to demonstrate supposedly supernatural powers to the common people."

"Crazy! That's nuts!" Thirty-Three slapped his forehead.

"Yes, that's what I thought. So, Eleven thinks that we - you- can find the spot and go back in time and try to figure out a way to get us out of here. Problem is, it takes you back exactly ten years, before The Woodlands existed. It's not like we could go tell someone - if there is anyone to tell - to come rescue us because, ten years ago, there's no "us" to rescue."

"Wow." Thirty-Three tilted back, holding on to the frame of the chair to keep from falling over.

"I know."

"What else did she say?"

"What do you mean, 'what else'? Isn't that enough?"

"I mean, did she say she anything about me?"

"You're such a child. No. She was very serious about her discovery. She didn't have the interest or the time to let me know if she finds you bio-logically attractive."

"Ok. Well, do you think it's true? I've never heard you talk seriously about escape. Yesterday you told me it was crazy to think about it."

Thirty-Nine stood up and scratched his head. "I don't know," he replied, placing his hands on his hips. "But this book is actually not even the craziest thing that happened tonight." He sat back down and looked into Thirty-Three's dark brown eyes.

"What do you mean?"

"I mean bizarre stuff is happening, right? But the more I think about it, I believe it's all connected. Remember how I told you about the sentry hit-ting me? And you joked about me hearing your thoughts?"

"Yes."

"I can."

"You can what?" Thirty-Three leaned closer, placing his hands on top of the back of the chair, his chin on top of his hands.

"I can hear thoughts. I did it when I met Eleven. And, I did it when I was summoned upstairs to the Chief's office."

"You had to go to the Chief's office?' Thirty-Three pushed the chair back and jumped up, steamrolling over the notion that Thirty-Nine could read thoughts.

"Yes."

"He smells like bologna and cigarettes, huh?" Thirty-Three laughed.

"Ha! Yes, it's gross. He's always talking about our health, what a hypocrite..."

"What did he have you up there for? Last time I went up, he threatened me with three days straight on The Wheel."

"I didn't get threatened with The Wheel. I don't know exactly why he brought me up. He asked about my chess game with Eleven. He asked about my health. When he did, he started scribbling notes that I heard through his thoughts."

"How can you hear thoughts?"

"I don't know - yet. It happened with the sentry twice and with Eleven and with the Chief. Practically all day long. Since I woke up from the dream sequencing. We can figure it out later. But that's still not the craziest thing. You won't believe this."

"Believe what?"

Thirty-Nine rose from the bed and walked closer to his podmate. He placed his hands on Thirty-Three's shoulders and looked intently into his soul. "My mother's alive."

Thirty-Three's eyes widened. His head rocked from side to side, as if to silently say "No." The fantasy of a parent out there, who was real and who cared, was something even Thirty-Three tried not to think about. It was too painful.

"It's true. The Chief wrote down, Assign Specialist-3 to identify mother's whereabouts and current health. He was writing about my mother. Whereabouts? Current health? What else could it mean?"

Thirty-Three slipped out of Thirty-Nine's grasp. He turned his back and shuffled toward the door.

"Don't you believe me?" Thirty-Nine implored, unsure of whether to approach Thirty-Three.

Silence.

For the longest time, Thirty-Three had wrestled with his inability to fully fit in at The Woodlands. He wanted to be able to go through the day without any rebelling actions, without any sarcastic comments that always led to a restriction or a physical reprimand. To be able, like Thirty-Nine, to coldly and rationally analyze a situation and reach objective conclusions. But no matter how hard he tried he could not shut off the emotional spirit inside. The silent tears in the night confirmed that he was different. That he did not belong. He turned to face Thirty-Nine, his eyes damp and reddened, his chin quivering.

"I believe you." As he spoke those words, a flood of tears cascaded down his plump cheeks. His voice cracked as he tried to continue speaking. "I - I – I," he stuttered, as his ability to speak was restrained by his hysterical breathing.

"I'm sorry." Thirty-Nine said, moving closer. "What's wrong?"

Thirty-Three clenched his fists and grit his teeth, trying to stem the tide of emotions.

"I - I - I believe you," he stammered. His breathing was stabilizing, though interrupted every few seconds by the staccato inhalation that always accompanies a sobbing episode.

"Just relax." Thirty-Nine sat down cross-legged on the small rug near the door. He patted the floor gently, inviting Thirty-Three to sit beside him. Thirty-Three sunk to the floor and folded his legs up, clutching his knees to his chest. They sat for a few minutes, each staring at the bare floor around them.

"You – you – you're telling me to relax." Thirty-Three snorted and sniffled; a large bubble of mucous peeked out of his nostril and then disappeared as he inhaled. "You're the one whose mother is alive!"

The warning bell announcing ten minutes until lights out sounded its ominous growl. The sound jolted each boy from his trance. Thirty-Three continued speaking.

"I believe you. I have always believed. I didn't know why but no matter how I tried I have never been able to feel at home in this place. You know why?"

"Why?" Thirty-Nine replied. Both of them were still seated, staring straight ahead in a daze, their eyes blankly scanning the bare wall and window shade across the pod.

"Because this isn't my home. Because I have a home. Out there. If your mother is alive, then it's possible mine is too. It's possible all the students' moms are still alive."

"You're right. Theoretically, there's no reason other parents aren't alive. It seems now that everything about The Woodlands is in question."

"Of course it is," Thirty-Three stood, animated by anger. "This place isn't a home or even a school. It's a prison."

"Settle down." Thirty-Nine rose to his feet. "We have to get ready for bed." His rational mind began pushing to the fore.

"Even if it's true, we can't allow our emotion to overwhelm us. We have to behave as if nothing has changed. If we - if you - can't keep it under control, then we don't have a chance at escape or rescue or whatever. Of course, that's if Eleven's book is true."

"Ok." Thirty-Three composed himself. "Of course. The night sentry will be here any minute. Let's go to bed and tomorrow, we will meet Eleven."

"Ok."

The boys silently took off their clothing and put on their night suits. They climbed into their beds, slid into their sleep sheaths, and closed their eyes.

Long after the lights were out and the night sentry had come and gone; after their hearts were settled and the half conscious state of early sleep had begun, Thirty-Three whispered,

"I believe. I believe it all."

Thirty-Nine's mind heard but his voice did not respond. His eyes were still wide open, staring at the dark ceiling. The blank blackness above him might as well have been the edge of the entire universe for all the newness of possibility that lay before him.

His mother was alive.

He could hear thoughts.

They could escape from The Woodlands without climbing the walls.

His mind was open to attempting something he never would have considered. More importantly, after today, his heart was as well.

It was well after midnight when he finally fell asleep. As he drifted off, he thought of only his mother.

Where is she? What does she look like? What is she doing?

"...Happy Birthday dear Nicole, Happy Birthday to you!" Mr. Douglas warbled joyfully, completely out of tune.

He set a small chocolate cupcake with a single lit candle on the counter where she was completing the inventory spreadsheet. Her kind-hearted boss had remembered. It had been eight years since she started working at the general store, though she told him she was only going to work long enough to save up for bus fare to a big city and a few months' living expenses.

"Thank you, Mr. Douglas." She smiled. The creases in her forehead and the lines streaking from the corners of her eyes said she was in her late thirties, though today was only birthday number twenty-seven. In spite of the tough road of the past decade, her green eyes still smiled with the hope that life would be better one day.

"Go on," he urged, his gray eyes bulging behind his thick eyeglasses. "Make a wish!"

"Don't be silly," she retorted, waving her hand to shoo him away. But he remained, and shuffled even closer, leaning on his walker with a trembling but firm grip.

"You don't know how many times you'll have this chance. I should know." He winked and patted himself in the middle of his chest.

"You've got lots of time left. Doc says you'll probably live forever with that new pacemaker." She could see he wasn't going to leave, so she closed her eyes.

All she could think to wish for was the same thing she'd prayed for every night since that horrible week when Aunt Rita died and Jake disappeared.

"I wish to find my Jake and hold him again." She whispered, beginning to cry. The years had done nothing to diminish her passion to find her son. She puckered her lips to blow but couldn't manage to hold her mouth still, as a tear rolled down into her open lips. She clapped her hand over her face and sprinted toward the employee restroom in the back.

"I'm sorry Mr. Douglas." She called over her shoulder.

The old shop owner puffed and blew the candle out, his spirit deflating as the wisp of smoke rose to the ceiling. He leaned on the counter, tears forming in his recently cataract-free eyes.

Nicole splashed cold water from the large mop sink - the only sink in the former broom closet. Mr. Douglas had converted it into a ladies room a few months after hiring Nicole. A small vase of dusty plastic flowers sat on the corner of the glass shelf that underlined the mirror. Nicole gripped the sides of the sink and looked at her splotchy face in the mirror. Her bright green pupils practically glowed in the center of her reddened eyes.

"Oh Jake, my baby. I just can't let you go. Jesus! Where could he be?"

She had replayed the week he disappeared so many times; she sometimes confused it with the current day. As she stepped back from the sink and turned into the toilet stall to grab some tissue, she hit the play button in her memory one more time.

She was seventeen years old then, and any hint of self-confidence she had then had long since been shamed out of her. Coming home pregnant to an unforgiving father will not only leave you homeless, it'll leave you hopeless. Her mom had died when she was a toddler, so her dad's reaction left her with nowhere to turn. After two nights sleeping under a roof made of dumpster lids tilted back against a shopping center wall, Aunt Rita had found her and brought her in from the dark.

Though they weren't related, Aunt Rita became everything to Nicole. Sister. Mother. Best friend. Aunt Rita was in her late 70's but seemed stronger than most teenagers. She had worked most of her life in the old mill at the head of Mashton Bay, and was the only lady to last in that rough business. The mill had closed a few years back. These days, she got by on a small pension and frugal living.

She had very little but she shared it all with Nicole. As important as food and shelter were, of even greater value was the wisdom of a woman who had survived for decades in a harsh world. Homesteading in a small camper with no telephone and a propane tank for heat and cooking, Aunt Rita lived like most of the 300 or so people who grew up and chose to stay in Port Mashton - simply. After Jake was born, Aunt Rita took care of him while Nicole worked to provide for all three of them. They might have only had each other, but that was enough.

The day everything changed was ending like the day before. Nicole was walking home from work, another slow day at the little coffee shop in the two streets that made up the town. Since the mill closed, the shop barely had enough customers to break even. Sometimes only a half dozen people would visit during an entire day. Nicole felt like she was nothing more than sympathy hire.

It was a two-mile walk from the coffee shop to the camper. Though the day had rendered her nearly comatose, after a few minutes in the fresh air, she had a skip in her step. As she continued down the dirt path, she breathed in the revitalizing air of the unpopulated terrain. It was late spring, and the sky was as clear as the glacier streams that ribboned the forest floor.

Her plain brown hair was French-braided, thanks to Aunt Rita. As she scampered home, she had an old funky bumper sticker-covered backpack slung over her shoulder. It had song lyrics scribbled on the large pouch that held her change purse, headphones, and Jake's diapers. Still very much a girl; now forced to be a woman. She worked hard and prayed even harder.

As Nicole approached their home, she could see Jake holding a silver toy airplane. He circled it around and around through the air, making a whooshing sound.

"Shhheeeewwww," he shouted, as he held the toy higher and then spun it in a descending maneuver.

What a sweetie, Nicole thought. *Life's not so bad, after all. Not with him to come home to everyday.*

She could see Aunt Rita sitting in the homemade tire swing that hung from the old pine tree, her long grey hair pulled back in a simple po-nytail. She casually waved at Nicole, her curved fingers showing the effects of age and arthritis. In a world of empty promises, one thing Nicole could depend on was Aunt Rita's love. She treated Nicole like the daughter she never had and she doted on Jake as though he was her own grandchild.

"Hey, Aunt Rita," Nicole called as she drew closer to the front of the camper. The grass was moist, and a few blossoms were popping on the cherry trees.

Aunt Rita looked up and smiled, "Hello sweetie, your little Jakey is becoming quite a pilot."

At the sound of Nicole's voice, Jake had turned toward her. He recently starting trying to walk, and his teetering frame made Nicole want to run and pick him up. She sprinted the last few yards, backpack caroming off her body. As she reached her little boy, she lifted Jake high over her head.

"You're my little airplane, Jakey!" Nicole laughed. Her chubby nine month old was still clutching his toy airplane. As she spun him around, he smiled and giggled, his bright golden yellow eyes sparkling like champagne bubbles in a crystal flute.

Aunt Rita wriggled out of the tire swing.

"That little boy is the smartest kid I've ever seen. Nine months and he's already saying a few words. Earlier today, I swear he winked at me!"

"He's a special boy." Nicole answered. "Maybe he's a genius like Einstein? Maybe he could be a scientist?" She squeezed him close. He cooed in response.

"He's a little genius allright." Aunt Rita stepped over and planted a kiss on his fuzzy little head. Her stomach growled.

"Say, are you hungry, Nicole?" Aunt Rita said.

"Yes, I could eat something."

Aunt Rita trudged into the camper, leaving Nicole holding baby Jake. She swung him around until she got dizzy. She set him down and laughed, her head spinning.

"What would I do without you, little boy?"

Jake smiled and pointed to a small stack of pebbles.

"Oh, did you build that? Maybe you're a little engineer?" Nicole asked. He nodded in response.

Aunt Rita entered the camper feeling strange. Her shallow breathing caused her to feel lightheaded. She looked down and massaged her forehead with her weathered hands. The cheap linoleum hexagon-patterned flooring started spinning.

"I better sit down. Nicole!" Aunt Rita called out as her eyes closed and her body slumped to the floor, rocking the camper.

Nicole was giggling with Jake when she heard the clatter of dangling chains against the tow hitch as the camper rattled from Aunt Rita's collapsing body.

"Aahh...Gaaa...Uhhh." A terrible sound came from inside the camper.

"Aunt Rita!" Nicole dumped Jake in the faded blue lawn chair next to the black metal steps. "Stay here Jakey!" She rushed inside the camper.

"Aunt Rita!"

Her elderly guardian was laying face up on the floor near the kitchenette sink. Her lungs strained to pull in air, and her body trembled. Nicole rushed to her side and put her arms around Aunt Rita's waist.

"Let's sit down for a minute, you'll be all right", Nicole said in a hush as she helped her to the bench sofa bed along the back wall. Aunt Rita slumped against the back wall, her head ricocheting off the cheap faux wood paneling.

"Your skin is so pale. Rita! What is happening?" Nicole knelt down in front of Aunt Rita, pushing her knees apart and wedging herself close to Aunt Rita's chest. She grabbed her head under her chin and looked at her face. She tried to look into her eyes but Aunt Rita's eyelids were fluttering so rapidly it was impossible.

"Do you hurt, Aunt Rita? Are you in pain?"

"I - I - can't br-bre-breathe. M-my ch-ch-chest," she stammered. Her normally tan face was the color of fireplace ash.

Nicole stood up and reached above the shelf bed for the cardboard box labeled "Medicine" in red marker. She rummaged through it frantically searching for aspirin. She held up a small plastic white bottle and read its label. Jake crawled out of the chair and up the stairs. He lifted himself over the threshold into the camper and continued to crawl over toward Aunt Rita.

"Does ibuprofen help with heart attacks? Crap!"

"Ee-ta? Ee-ta?" Jake was at Aunt Rita's feet, tugging on her pants' loose polyester fabric.

Nicole turned toward them both. Aunt Rita's head was slumped over on her chest, her eyes closed. Nicole stepped toward her, simultaneously using her shin to slide Jake away from Rita and toward the camper door. He tumbled backward and started to cry. His whimper heightened Nicole's anxiety.

"Jake, don't cry!" She snapped.

Her stern tone didn't stop the crying. In fact, he howled as if he'd been kicked by a horse. Nicole didn't have time to tend to him. She moved closer to her fading friend.

"Aunt Rita?"

She grabbed Rita's hand and squeezed. The blankness of her body told Nicole no response would be coming. Still, she refused to accept that Aunt Rita was gone.

"Aunt Rita? Aunt Rita?" Her voice rose until she screamed, "Aunt Rita!"

She turned to the doorway of the camper and banged her fist against the flimsy wall.

"No way! No way! Oh God, oh God!" She crumpled like a house of playing cards, knees and elbows jutting out and banging the side of the bench seat as she fell. There was no phone. There was no one within at least two miles. Only the birds could hear her screams. The hunger she had felt moments before was replaced by a plummeting sensation as she started to sob.

"Ma...ee...eee." Jake's faint whimper pierced Nicole's suffocating veil of agony.

She turned to her little boy, who had crawled back to Aunt Rita's lifeless feet. His tiny fingers were intertwined in her shoelaces. Nicole scooted over to him and slid her hands under his armpits, dragging him into her lap. For the next twenty minutes, she squeezed him and wept.

Her composure slowly returned as she held Jake close.

"No one to call. What can I do?" She whispered to her little boy. No answer came except the occasional squirm and whine to be let outside to play.

"Jake, let's go outside." She picked him up and walked out into the fading daylight, leaving Aunt Rita's dead body untouched on the bench. They walked in the grass, she clutching him close, he making baby noises.

"We can't go back in there. I don't know where to go. I don't know who to go to. What am I going to do? I don't want to just leave her."

Jake began squirming in her arms, fidgeting to get free.

"Here, play with your pebbles." She set him down but took no steps, because remaining next to him would keep her mind right. She looked down at his little body, as he sat in second-hand denim overalls, the outline of his full diaper rolling up around his thighs as he stretched to reach some more rocks.

"Do you know what to do, Jakey? Of course you don't." Nicole shook her head at herself, still staring blankly down at her child.

"I don't know what to do. Now it's just you and me. We're going to have to walk into town and tell somebody to get the doctor or the police. What am I going to do?"

She went back near the camper but didn't go in. She couldn't. Her backpack had some snacks and diapers for Jake. She had no appetite. Locking the door, she grabbed her backpack and picked up Jake. As she staggered toward the village, she clung to Jake like a dazed prizefighter clings to the body of his opponent, hoping against hope to prevent the knockout blow.

Two days later, she'd be down for the count.

Down, but not out.

Mr. Douglas was getting worried about Nicole. She had been in the bathroom for at least twenty minutes. He started inching his walker around her workstation and down the aisle toward the ladies room. The inventory at his shop was minimal but they did a decent business in beef jerky, peanut butter, bread, potato chips and soda. Most of the customers were truck drivers, oilmen, prospectors or crabbers headed north. They didn't really have regulars, but they had each other.

"Nicole?" he hollered as he shuffled closer to the door.

"I'll be right out," she quickly replied through the cheap pressboard door. Best to respond right away or he'd shout even louder.

"Get it together," she instructed herself as she sat on the toilet lid. She stared at the random scratches and smudges that had accumulated on the tacky orange wallpaper three feet away. The faded white vinyl strip at the base of the wall was peppered with black streaks, zigzags left behind by the comings and goings of customers and employees over the seasons. As she regained her composure, she prayed that one day her life would quit bouncing along the bottom and actually gain traction toward something more. Something better.

"Ok." Mr. Douglas yelled, his hearing aids barely operational. "I'll be at the entrance bench. Don't think we'll have any more shoppers today. Don't forget to eat your cupcake!"

She grinned. "Eat your cupcake," she repeated. "Old Mr. Douglas.

He's the first decent man I ever knew." She stood up, smeared her nose with the back of her hand and walked to the sink. She looked at herself, the tip of her nose red and swollen.

"He may be decent, but he isn't going to be a husband, Nicole." She laughed at herself. "That's gross."

Mr. Douglas was about two-thirds toward the front of the store when she finally exited the bathroom.

"Mr. Douglas." She said.

He continued scooting down the aisle, passing the magazine rack. *TV Guide*, *Reader's Digest*, and *Weekly World News*.

"We ain't having that Cosmo crap!" Mr. Douglas had told Nicole during her early days on the job.

"Mr. Douglas. Mr. Douglas!"

Finally, he heard her and turned around. He stood near the small rack of tightly rolled cigarette sized horoscopes and colorful packs of gum. He pivoted slowly to his left and peered over the rumpled collar of his thirty-year old cardigan.

"Yes, Nicole? Are you alright?"

"Yes, Mr. Douglas." She walked through the small section of office supplies. It consisted of two boxes of privacy envelopes, four packs of pens and two rolls of packing tape.

"Good."

As she reached him, she couldn't help smiling. Like Aunt Rita years ago, he had rescued her from a very bleak situation. His tender generosity had given her new life when she was inclined to give up on living.

"Leave your walker. Walk with me instead." Nicole put his left arm over her right, and dragged his walker away with her left hand. They hobbled along, toward his bench near the front door.

"Thank you for my birthday cake."

"You're welcome dear."

"Mr. Douglas?" Nicole asked as they turned toward the final leg of their journey, just beyond a few cords of firewood that were taken in on consignment from the few teenage boys who lived on the reservation. "Do you think I should give up?"

He exhaled heavily but said nothing. They continued making their way to the bench. He stayed quiet. As they approached the white and lime green vinyl-covered seat, Mr. Douglas, began to speak as only a thrice-divorced man nearly eighty years old could.

"Nicole," he began as she gingerly aided his move from standing to sitting. He patted the seat cushion. "Sit down, dear."

Nicole sat to his right. They stared at the 3,200 square foot space before them. The configuration of the aisles and the main register hadn't changed in forty years. At the end of the nearest check stand a torn and faded lottery sign hung by a couple rusty staples.

"Nicole, I've been around a while. And I still don't know much." He cocked his head and looked at her profile. Her button nose and thin eyebrows sandwiched her deep-set eyes. She returned his glance, her greens staring at his grays.

"But, I do know a few things about women. Of course, whole lot of good it did me!" He snorted as he laughed at his romantic misfortunes.

"Oh, Mr. Douglas, I can't believe that. You were a great husband, I bet." She patted his knee. As she did, the quiver of his Parkinson's surprised her. She quickly pulled her hand away.

"I made plenty of mistakes. But, you know, some people live and learn; other people just live. I hope I learned. What I'm trying to say is this. I've been through some rough patches. I've been through an earthquake or two, took a bullet in the war and came home to see my wife with another man. And I have to say, through all that, I don't think I've ever met any force on earth quite as powerful as a momma who won't give up."

Nicole's eyes started to well up. She inhaled deeply. "Even after nearly ten years?"

Mr. Douglas uncrossed his arms and slid his shaky right arm over her shoulder, giving her a slight squeeze. "Even after one hundred years."

"The police told me to let it go. They said the best thing is for me to accept that Jake's dead. Even suggested I have a memorial service." She slapped the bench in frustration. "I think I'm the only person who believes that he's still alive. That he's still out there."

"Nicole, let me tell you something my daddy told me when I was just a little boy."

"What's that?" she shifted, turning to look directly at him.

"It only takes one person believing to make it so."

Nicole placed her hand back on Mr. Douglas's trembling knee. He placed his hand on hers. They sat together, an old, worn-out man and a young, worn-out woman. A few minutes passed, silent except for the overly loud tick of the clock mounted on the wall near the umbrella stand in the corner.

"And, you know what?" Mr. Douglas asked.

"What?"

"It must be so." He squeezed her hand and smiled. "Because in this case, there's two people that believe."

Thirty-Three woke up first, even before the campus alarm. "Today is the day. I can't wait to see Eleven." He unzipped his sleep sheath and sat up. He hopped to the floor and reached out to shake his podmate.

"Thirty-Nine," he whispered. "Wake up. Big day today!"

Thirty-Nine slowly rolled over, ignoring his friend's request. He had slept little during the night as he wrestled with the realization that his mother was alive and nearby.

"Come on," Thirty-Three said loudly, "Get up!"

"Fine, fine," a lethargic response came from Thirty-Nine's sleep sheath. He forced his eyes open and unzipped his sheath.

"Do you realize my mother is alive?"

"Yes. And do you realize that Eleven is the answer to you finding her?"

Thirty-Three walked over to the white square touch screen calendar. It resembled an electronic thermostat panel.

"It's Thursday. I've only got one more day of restriction." As he looked at the digital device, a new alert popped on the screen.

"All student assembly before breakfast," he announced as he turned to Thirty-Nine.

"Strange," his no longer groggy friend replied, "we just had assembly last night. The Chief rarely deviates from the schedule."

"I need to shower first," Thirty-Three said, poking his nose near his armpit and taking a sniff. He walked into the phone booth sized metal stall near the end of his bed.

Just seconds after Thirty-Three began his shower, the door to their pod opened.

"Thirty-Nine." It was Researcher-9.

"Yes." He stood abruptly.

"Come with me. You will have breakfast at Dr. Nampala's office."

"But - the assembly."

"No concern. You have permission. We have an important meeting with Dr. Nampala."

"With Dr. Nampala? I'm not even dressed."

"Hurry up. I will be right outside the door. Be ready in three minutes." As she opened the door to walk into the hall, he noticed two sentries standing at attention, their backs pressed against the corridor wall.

As soon as the door closed, Thirty-Nine moved straight to the door of the shower and knocked.

"Just a minute!" Thirty-Three hollered over the noise of cascading water.

"Open up, I got to talk to you. Now!" Thirty-Nine whisper-shouted, hoping that Researcher-9 and the sentries couldn't hear him. He knocked again to demonstrate the urgency of the moment.

"Hang on." Thirty-Three opened the door, water still running and splashing all over the floor around the stall. "What is it?"

Thirty-Nine jumped back from the splattering water. "Turn it off, you're going to get a new punishment for making a mess!"

Thirty-Three turned the knob as Thirty-Nine tossed him the towel that was on the shelf beside the stall.

"I have to go. Researcher-9 came to pick me up and take me back to Dr. Nampala's office."

"What for?" Thirty-Three asked as he swabbed at his still-shampooed hair with the towel.

"I don't know. But I have to go. You need to talk to Eleven about everything at breakfast, ok?"

"Ok. I'll see you after morning exercises?"

"I hope so. I've got to hurry. Make sure you talk to Eleven. And don't forget to mop up the water." Thirty-Nine rushed to his clothes closet and quickly changed into his freshly laundered white tunic. As he walked to the front door, he turned to Thirty-Three, who was still naked, dabbing up the water off the tile floor.

"Good luck."

"You too."

"And Thirty-Three..."

"Yes?"

"Put some clothes on!" Both boys laughed as Thirty-Nine waited for Thirty-Three to jump back in the shower before he opened the door to join Researcher-9. He turned the knob and announced, "Ok, I'm ready."

Sentry-1 led Researcher-9 and Thirty-Nine down the hall. The other sentry remained in the hall outside the boys' pod.

"You've had some very interesting cerebral activity during the last few dream sequencing sessions, Thirty-Nine," Researcher-9 said as they neared the elevator.

"I have?"

"Yes. Have you had anything unusual happen this week? Any headaches? Any weird sensations? Deja vu?"

If she had asked those questions just two days earlier, Thirty-Nine would have told her about hearing people's thoughts. He might have even told her about the book that Eleven found. But knowing his mother was alive changed everything. He rubbed his head slowly.

"No. I can't think of anything," he replied as the elevator doors opened.

"After you," Researcher-9 said, motioning for Thirty-Nine to enter. She paused and held her foot against the door. She turned to look down the hall in the other direction. "We'll wait," she said to someone in the hall.

Thirty-Nine stood toward the back of the elevator, staring up at the recessed lighting framed within the metallic ceiling. He looked around the cabin. The walls were covered in dark brown fabric and the control panel was a simple white square with backlit Bakelite buttons. Thirty-Nine's gaze moved down from the ceiling to immediately in front of him as the others walked in.

"Eleven," he practically gasped. "Umm, hi there," he added, hoping no one else noticed his surprise at her appearance.

"Hello," she coolly replied.

Researcher-4 joined Researcher-9 and followed Eleven into the elevator. Most of the researchers that Thirty-Nine had seen were bespectacled older men with somber expressions. The two researchers escorting them today were both twenty-something females in navy blue lab coats.

"Thank you Sentry-1, Sentry-13," Researcher-9 said, pressing the button marked "3".

No one spoke as they ascended to Dr. Nampala's office. Thirty-Nine stared at the threadbare carpet under his feet the entire time. The researchers stood in front of him and faced the door; Eleven was beside him. She reached her slender fingers out and brushed his forearm.

Can you hear me? She thought.

Thirty-Nine nodded.

Do you think we're in trouble? Do you think the Chief knows about the book?

Thirty-Nine shrugged his shoulders. The elevator stopped.

"Let's go," Researcher-4 said, turning to beckon them out of the elevator. The researchers led them toward the swinging double doors that led to Dr. Nampala's office. They walked up to the keypad near the corner, swiped a card and entered a code. The doors swung open, inviting them in.

Only twelve hours earlier, in this same room, Thirty-Nine had discovered his mother was alive. What would he discover today?

Dr. Nampala was standing, like a restaurant maître d', to the left of the small entryway between the hall and the office.

"Welcome Eleven, welcome back Thirty-Nine, are you hungry?"

Neither of them had seen Dr. Nampala behave this kindly. He wasn't always mean, but he was never friendly. Rumor around The Woodlands was that he was physically incapable of smiling. Neither was prepared for his welcome.

"Yes sir," Eleven finally replied for both of them.

"Wonderful. Follow me. Researchers, please excuse yourselves. You can return in thirty minutes. I'd like to have a private breakfast with these two star students."

The researchers walked out, and Eleven and Thirty-Nine followed Dr. Nampala to a table set for a full breakfast.

Star students, Thirty-Nine thought.

17

Dr. Nampala led them to a dark wooden table draped with a white linen runner. Its polished cherry slab was shockingly formal for The Woodlands. It looked as though it had been imported from a two hundred year old mansion. Two large crystal candlesticks stood in the center of the table, holding dark blue unlit candles. A small arrangement of white, purple and blue hydrangeas sat on either side of the candlesticks. The table was arranged to seat nine, with one head chair and four on either side. Every place was set with light blue china resting on white linen placemats.

"Please find your name and be seated," Dr. Nampala instructed.

As he motioned for them to sit down, Thirty-Nine noticed that three settings had little tent name cards. The head seat was reserved for Dr. Nampala. Eleven saw hers and sat first, on Dr. Nampala's right. An empty unnamed place setting was between hers and the Chief's. Thirty-Nine walked around the table to the other seat with a name card, directly across from Eleven. He pulled out the high-backed wooden chair and sat on its tan suede cushion.

Eleven looked down at her place setting. She counted two forks on her left and one above her plate, along with a small spoon. She scanned her area, noticing the intricate basket weave pattern on the handle of all the silverware. Thirty-nine looked in the direction of Dr. Nampala's seat, waiting for him to speak.

Dr. Nampala walked to the head seat and stood behind it, arms folded. He stared at his two pupils. Thirty-Nine stared back briefly, then joined Eleven in looking down at the table.

This better work. These kids better come through or I'm screwed. We're all screwed. Thirty-Nine heard the Chief thinking.

"Eleven and Thirty-Nine," he began, causing them both to raise their buzzed heads. "The Woodlands has been pursuing the challenge of isolating and maximizing the power of the mind for nearly ten years. We've had some minor breakthroughs, but we need more."

He moved to his right, stepping into the rays of sunlight that streamed from the window behind him, illuminating dust particles in the air and highlighting the gray patches in his uncombed hair. His hair fascinated all of the students. As young students, Dr. Nampala explained that one day, when they were as powerful as him, they could grow their hair.

"Long hair is external evidence of the internal strength of your mind," Eleven remembered him saying. Now as he moved closer to her, she questioned whether his mind was powerful enough to deserve such long tresses.

"I have never been this direct with any other students," Dr. Nampala announced, now standing directly to Eleven's left. She turned her body in her chair and looked up at him. Thirty-Nine held his gaze steady, looking at the Chief's face but not directly into his eyes.

"But," he continued, "you are the best. And when you're the best, you receive preferential treatment." He leaned toward Eleven and placed his scrawny hand on her shoulder. "Preferential treatment may be given but it is also expected." He stepped back and snapped his fingers.

"Where are my manners?" He laughed, his wheezy laugh sounding like a broken vacuum cleaner battling to keep suction. "Let's have breakfast. While you eat, I will tell you about preferential treatment and its companion, heightened expectations."

He turned his back to them as he walked back to the head of the table. Their eyes met for a moment, both wondering what would happen next. Eleven quickly tapped the side of her head and pointed at Thirty-Nine.

Don't say anything about last night, ok? She thought.

Thirty-Nine rolled his eyes.

Dr. Nampala sat down and smiled. "Breakfast!" he ordered, to no one in particular. At his command, three sentries, each pushing wheeled carts, appeared from a door behind Thirty-Nine. They rolled the carts to the end of the table opposite Dr. Nampala and removed the covering black cloth, revealing an array of unprocessed whole foods. Unpeeled and un-blended apples, bananas and oranges were on one tray. Chocolate waffles on another. Finally, fried eggs, with perfectly bulbous, unbroken yolks atop crispy whites sat on the last tray.

"You may serve us." Dr. Nampala instructed.

The sentries moved deliberately, as though they had rehearsed. Each one walked swiftly to one of the three diners, delivering one piece of each type of fruit, two chocolate waffles and two fried eggs, until all three were served. As they rolled away, a fourth sentry appeared, filling the stu-dents' glasses with water, and Dr. Nampala's with coffee.

Thirty-Nine and Eleven were dumbfounded. They had only ever seen this kind of food in books. They were confused. Dr. Nampala preached the power of the nutrition that they received. Their meals were the height of science and nutrition. Every bar, powdered drink and pill was formulated to help them achieve maximum brainpower.

"I know what you're thinking," Dr. Nampala said through the rising steam from his eggs and waffles.

Does he? Eleven thought, jerking her head to look at Thirty-Nine.

"I don't th…" Thirty-Nine abruptly said aloud, responding to Eleven. He stopped himself and bit his lower lip in response.

"What's that?" the Chief asked.

"Nothing, sir."

"It wasn't *nothing*. What were you going to say?"

Thirty-Nine fidgeted in his chair. "I don't think. I mean…I don't know what to think. I don't know how to reconcile this meal."

Eleven looked over at him, wishing she had longer legs so she could kick him under the table.

You're too transparent. We'll never escape, she thought.

Thirty-Nine heard her. She was right. He had to become smoother in his interactions with the Chief or they'd be found out. He'd never get out of The Woodlands. He'd never see his mother.

"I know, Thirty-Nine," Dr. Nampala replied. "It doesn't fit the proto-col. But, wait until you taste it. You'll see. This is my demonstration to you both that I believe you deserve to be treated differently. You are *elite*. Go ahead, take a bite of this first." He pointed to the chocolate waffle.

Like Thirty-Three, Eleven had come to The Woodlands as a toddler. She had some latent memories of real food. She was first to react, grabbing the warm waffle with her hand. She held it up and studied it briefly – it was a large light brown square filled with small square pits, riddled throughout with chocolate chips.

"Ok," she said, bringing the waffle toward her mouth. As she bit into it, the sensation of crunching the crisp edges faded into a moist sweetness. The pockets of chocolate exploded along her tongue. In every way, this new food was extraordinary. No grainy texture. No bland greenness.

"Wow! That's good!"

Dr. Nampala smiled. "I knew you'd like it."

Eleven continued eating. Thirty-Nine watched her. Either she was a great pretender or she was genuinely enjoying it. A few small dribbles of chocolate rolled out the corner of her mouth, onto her narrow chin as she finished the first waffle. As she reached for the second, Dr. Nampala stopped her.

"Slow down, Eleven. Take your time. Your system is not used to this delicious food. You don't want to overdo it. Drink some of your water. Thirty-Nine, you haven't tried yours yet. Go ahead."

Thirty-Nine grabbed the waffle and took a bite. He chewed slowly, allowing every texture and taste to make its way around his mouth.

"That's really good," he gurgled, not waiting to finish chewing be-fore speaking.

"I'm glad. We will continue eating, but now," Dr. Nampala leaned over his plate and pointed at them both with his fork, "I need something from you."

Both children sat up straighter.

"I have spent considerable time thinking about you both, and then last night, as I watched you play chess, I had an idea." He leaned to his right and yelled, "Researchers!"

The two researchers who escorted them to the office entered from the same door as the sentries.

"Eleven. Thirty-Nine. I have been working with Researcher-4 and Researcher-9 on a new experimental program. You are to be the first students to be enlisted. The researchers are going to be your personal managers. They will explain the plan." He stood to emphasize his final comment.

"At the end of four weeks, we will know if Eleven remains at the head of the class, or," he turned to look directly at Thirty-Nine, "if the boy can surpass her." He grabbed the white coffee cup from his place and walked toward his desk. He sat down in his rocking chair, shuffling it around to face the dining table. He waved his hand in the air dramatically.

"Researchers, please explain."

Both of the researchers lugged a stack of blue folders thicker and nearly as heavy as a cinder block, clipped together in various places by silver metal clasps. They remained standing at the end of the table. Researcher-9 spoke first.

"Thank you, Dr. Nampala," she began, as she set her stack on the corner of the table. "Thirty-Nine, you are my responsibility. Researcher-4 will be in charge of Eleven." As she spoke, her voice quivered slightly. Thirty-Nine studied her face. She had shallow-set pale blue eyes. As she spoke, she looked at the children with a hint of kindness. Her hair was pulled back and held in place by a cluster of navy elastic bands. A small but noticeable jagged scar underlined her left cheekbone.

"We will begin this afternoon with daily sessions. We will meet every morning in this same manner..."

"With the same breakfast," Dr. Nampala interjected, almost cheerful at his motivational genius.

"Yes, with the same breakfast. You will still be expected to complete your chores and your assignments. However, you will no longer be in the afternoon experiments that you've been in. Researcher-4, please explain the afternoon schedule."

"Yes. I will retrieve both of you after lunch cleanup," Researcher-4 responded, her narrow nostrils flaring as she spoke. She was not as biologically attractive as Researcher-9. She was short and plain looking, and spoke with a clinical vocabulary. Her round face was highlighted by streaking wisps of hair that ran far past the front of her ears. She spoke with the overly earnest manner of a person trying to prove herself. "I will transport you to our

work center below this office. Dr. Nampala will be observing and occasionally directing, but for the most part, Researcher-9 and I will be instructing
you and analyzing the results from your testing."

Thirty-Nine, Eleven thought. *Look at the label on the bottom folders
in Researcher-9's stack.*

Thirty-Nine looked down at the collection of folders in front of Re-
searcher-9.

"The testing will include some new enhancements and a new cross-
cerebral collaboration device," Researcher-4 continued.

All Thirty-Nine could see was the front corner of the folders. He
angled his head and arched his eyebrows, hopefully not enough to draw
attention but enough to let Eleven know he couldn't read the labels. She
understood.

*One of the folders is labeled "Procurement and Delivery Report -
Boy Thirty-Nine".*

"And," Researcher-9 spoke, causing Eleven and Thirty-Nine to focus
on the instructions. "We expect you both to excel by pushing each other to
improve. Your attention must be precise and intense. If this works, you may
be responsible for the greatest discovery in the history of biology and psy-
chology combined." She seemed to smile as she finished the last sentence.

"Thank you researchers," Dr. Nampala stood up, sipped his coffee
and walked over to the table. "Are you ready for this project?"

"Yes sir," the researchers replied in unison.

They turned and walked to a small cabinet along the bare wall. Re-
searcher-9 opened the double metal doors and pulled out two black nylon
briefcases. She handed one to Researcher-4 and they walked back to the
table. Dr. Nampala joined them now, and stood between the two researchers.

"Eleven and Thirty-Nine," he announced, "these cases contain a
two-week supply of supplements for brain enhancement. The pills are to be
taken at precisely ten o'clock every night." He nodded to each researcher.

The researchers set the bags on the table, and unzipped each one.
They simultaneously pulled out a card that pictured the combination of pills
to be taken. Then they pulled out plastic earmuffs attached to a pair of sun-
glasses. It looked like a fighter pilot's helmet, minus the covering for the top

of the head. Dr. Nampala took Researcher-4's and held it in front of his face.

"This is the ultimate full brain improvement mechanism. I call it The Mind Cocoon. Your brain enters it as a caterpillar, and awakens a butterfly; ready to do things it has never done before." He slipped it over his face, and pressed the earpieces firmly against his head. "You simply put it on, and press the button here." He pointed to a small red oval in the white plastic that rested on the bridge of his nose. He pulled the device off and handed it back to Researcher-4.

"You will keep them in your pod. They must be plugged in to re-charge during the day. Every night, you must sleep in The Mind Cocoon. It charges your brain and maximizes performance. It improves recall. By maximizing your brain," he paused to let the words impress Eleven and Thirty-Nine, "and improving your connectivity and speed, I believe The Mind Cocoon will be the key to unlock what I've been searching for since we opened The Woodlands. Isn't that exciting?"

Thirty-Nine looked at Dr. Nampala. His stress-lined face was smooth-er. The researchers, especially Researcher-9, looked like a couple of children who were given a new puppy on Christmas morning.

"Yes sir, that's exciting," Thirty-Nine replied.

"What do you think, Eleven?" Dr. Nampala asked.

"It's really great, sir. We are thrilled to be chosen. And I will still be number one." She glared at Thirty-Nine as she finished her reply.

"Well, good. The researchers will take you back to your pods. I look forward to seeing you both in action later today." Dr. Nampala walked away from the table, down the hallway they had entered through, and disap-peared.

"Let's return to your pods." Researcher-4 packed The Mind Cocoon back in its case. "You will need to carry these." Researcher-9 walked over to Thirty-Nine and set it on the table for him. Researcher-4 zipped up the case in her hand and placed it on the table for Eleven. The researchers re-turned to collect the stack of folders at the corner.

"Let's go."

As they stood to go Eleven lingered. She slowly placed her bag over her shoulder. She looked at Thirty-Nine.

When I knock the papers on the floor in the elevator, grab your file.

Thirty-Nine smiled as he picked up the Mind Cocoon case. He nodded his agreement with Eleven's plan.

Maybe she is starting to trust me, he thought as they followed Researcher-9 and Researcher-4 back to the elevator.

Thirty-Three had looked all over the cafeteria for Eleven. He waited until everyone else had been served then stood up and scanned every table, risking additional punishment by doing so. She was nowhere to be seen.

Now he sat in his pod, finishing the week's personal reinforcement exercise. He had to write the 10 Axioms of The Woodlands thirty times each. He was in the middle of writing Axiom 9 – *The brain is the storehouse for the soul; the soul can only be perceived and fulfilled by the optimized brain* – for the fifteenth time when the door opened, revealing Thirty-Nine and Researcher-9 standing in the hallway.

"Sorry again for Eleven's clumsiness," Thirty-Nine said to his escort as he entered the pod.

"It's ok," Researcher-9 replied. "Remember to charge your Mind Cocoon." She pointed to the bag in his hand.

"I will collect you after lunch."

"Ok."

The door closed. Thirty-Nine waited a moment before approaching Thirty-Three. Thirty-Three did not wait at all. He jumped to his feet and rushed to Thirty-Nine, nearly bowling him over with his uncontrollable energy.

"Eleven wasn't at breakfast! I didn't get to ask her about the escape corridor. Or anything else. I didn't even get to see her beautiful face."

"I know - she was with me."

"She was?"

"Yes. I have much to tell you but first," Thirty-Nine held the black bag aloft. "I have something we have to read."

"What is it?" Thirty-Three crowded against his taller podmate, nearly knocking him over.

"Relax! Let's read it over there." He led Thirty-Three to the desk where a stack of handwritten pages rested underneath a worn pencil. "What is all this?"

"It's the last of my reinforcement exercises for this week."

"Don't you have the Axiom memorization certificate?"

"I did. But on the last review session, I flubbed Axiom 9."

"Come on. You've been here how long? Nine years? And you're one of the oldest."

"I know. It's just hard to say stuff I don't believe. Never mind that, what's in the bag? Where'd you get it?"

Thirty-Nine set the bag in the chair and scooped up the papers. He held them loosely in his hand and tapped them on the desk, aligning the tops of the pages neatly. He glanced at the scrawled letters as he placed the stack in a gray wire basket on the right side of the desk.

"This bag was given to me by the Chief. It's got a Mind Cocoon that I have to wear at night. How'd you mess up Axiom Nine? You're still working on optimization?"

"Sure, whatever."

"Well, I guess we're about to find out if the Chief is right. Will the soul be fulfilled by the optimized brain? How's your soul feeling, Thirty-Three?"

"Honestly?" Thirty-Three rubbed his buzzed scalp and looked at the floor. He noticed his pinky toe's nearly invisible and completely useless nail. This observation caused him to wiggle all the digits on his feet. He looked back at Thirty-Nine.

"My soul feels confused. Maybe annoyed? Definitely frustrated."

"I'd say it sounds like you're ready for a potentially dangerous adventure." Thirty-Nine smiled. His sense that they could find independence from The Woodlands' system was strengthening with each passing hour. He lifted the bag onto the desk. "Let's see what this file says."

He un-velcroed a pouch on the side of the bag and tugged out a blue folder. He laid it flat on the desk.

"What's that? Where did you get it?" Thirty-Three excitedly asked, bumping into Thirty-Nine's left side.

"Settle down. I think it tells how I ended up here. Eleven banged into the researchers this morning and knocked a bunch of papers on the floor. When we picked everything up, I snuck this into my bag."

"Eleven? Researchers?"

"Yes. Eleven was in Dr. Nampala's office with me this morning." He turned to face Thirty-Three. "I will explain what happened in a minute. I am dying to read what's inside this folder, ok?"

"Ok." He turned back to the folder. As his butterball podmate scrunched beside him, Thirty-Nine reached down with a shaky hand and opened the folder.

The folder had a single divider with dark brown prongs atop each section, holding two-hole-punched pages in place. The left tab held a single white page that appeared to be some type of government document. It was pre-printed with a series of rectangular boxes that contained check marks and brief sentences or questions.

Thirty-Nine read aloud as Thirty-Three silently scanned the page:

**Sex: Male.   Race: White.   Length: 73.7 Cm.
Weight: 10.7 Kg.**

DOB: 11/14/88 Hair: Brown.   Eyes: Hazel.

Current ID: Trafston, Jake

Distinguishing marks: None.

Source: Single female, WA, USA.   **Extractor: Agent 1412.**

Delivery Date: 05/26/89

Facility Signature: *L. Nampala*

"Whoa. Insane." Thirty-Three nudged his podmate's ribcage. "That's you!"

"I know." Thirty-Nine was in gathering mode now, and would analyze later. He turned the blank divider over and found several pages tabbed to the inside of the back cover. He continued reading:

Extraction Report: 05/26/89.   Start Time: 10:13.
End Time: 17:22

HQ received detail of prospective student from Agent 1150, operating as paramedic on rural outpost 47, Northwest Region. Agent 1150 reported responding to emergency call placed near Sandbar Point Park. Emergency call identified a single mother, Nicole Trafston, reporting death of her child's caretaker. Upon completion of interview with mother, Agent 1150 identified all three prerequisites for extraction:

1. Extreme poverty

2. No immediate family or social support network

3. Healthy child with demonstrable giftedness

Review of Agent 1150's report led to authorization for Extraction Thirty-Nine.

Agent 1412 was assigned and, per protocol, given 24 hours to retrieve and deliver student to The Woodlands.

Agent 1412's report is found on page 4 of this Extraction Re-

port."

Thirty-Nine fumbled with the binder, trying to turn to page four. His shaky hands were now practically convulsing, as his emotions were winning the tug-of-war with his logical mind.

"Let me help," Thirty-Three reached around Thirty-Nine. He lifted the folder and flipped to page four. He laid it back down, pinning the first three pages between the back cover and the desktop. He stepped back to give Thirty-Nine space. He realized that this was not a random mystery. This was not a trivial moment. They were reading the true story of how Thirty-Nine ended up at The Woodlands. Likely this was the story for most, maybe all, of the children at The Woodlands.

Thirty-Nine focused on the page. It was different from the others. It was pink, and appeared to be part of a triplicate form. It had no boxes. It was a lined sheet of paper with handwriting on all but the last three lines.

Extraction Thirty-Nine: Agent 1412 Detail
05/26/89

At 10:13, I entered the approximately 350-meter drive that led to the Sandbar Point Park Lodge, the reported location of the prospective student. Surveillance photographs from 08:00 showed one vehicle parked on the left side of the main building, a 8 X 14 meter rectangular wooden structure with three entry points: a double door at the center front of the building, and two single doors, approximately 2/3 toward the rear of the building, one on either side. I secured my vehicle about fifty meters into the woods just after entering the drive.

After picking my way through dense trees and brush for the first fifty meters, I reached a hiking path. At 10:20, I entered the path and began slowly walking toward the building, pausing every 15–20 meters to listen via electronic ears for any unusual activity.

The sky was clear. Some precipitation had fallen the night before, and the trail was damp but not muddy. Progress to the main building was unimpeded and incident-free.

As I approached the mouth of the trail, I moved into the trees. I climbed into the lower branches of a dense alder tree. I sawed two branches out of my line of sight. Through my binoculars, I could see the interior of the building. Two adults were near the front of the building. I could not get a visual of the target. I monitored the adults. They were engaged in animated conversation. Post-mission transcripts produced from the digital recording made by the electronic ears revealed a discussion about a solution for the target's childcare. The success of Extraction Thirty-Nine resolved that problem.

Thirty-Nine turned the page, barely noticing the stamped "Recipient's Copy" underneath the last line.

I waited in the tree for approximately forty-five minutes. I had not yet gained a visual on the target. At 11:18, the male left the building and drove away in the park vehicle. At 11:25, the female exited the building, carrying the target.

They walked to a small patch of sand approximately 30 meters from my perch. I recorded their activity for one minute using the hand-held video recording device. The target exhibited robust health and strength. He repeatedly walked a few paces before tumbling. I could hear his squeals of laughter without any audio enhancement.

I secured all surveillance devices in my pack and slipped to the ground. The female was pacing on the concrete walkway that lined the outside of the building. The target was approximately 5-10 meters from her. I placed my full-face covering over my head and prepared to extract. There was no option for shelter or hiding between my location and the target. I waited for the female to begin pacing away again, her back to the target, and I sprinted to the target. As I secured him in the pouch strapped to my midsection, his back against my chest and his head facing out, the female screamed. I did not turn to see her but could hear her running toward me. I sprinted into the woods. I circled through the trees until I got out of her line of sight.

I sealed the target's mouth with tape and waited for her get closer to my position. I climbed a few feet up the closest tree and sat silently. The target began crying, so I had to inject him with the tranquil‐izer. At 11:51, she entered the space beneath me. I dropped behind her and neutralized her with a blow to the back of the head. I then dragged her back to the front of the building and exited the scene. I did not see the male return, nor did I witness his vehicle at any point in my drive to The Woodlands.

The target was delivered at 12:22. Further detail (audio and video recordings) can be obtained through the archives, by contacting your Extractions, Inc. representative.

Thirty-Nine pulled the pages back into place, closed the binder and stared at Thirty-Three. They stood in silence together for a few minutes. Their hearts were pounding and their minds were

accepting the revelation that the children in The Woodlands were not or‐phans. They were kidnap victims.

"I don't know what to say."

"It's ok, Thirty-Nine, we don't have to say anything right now. Just rest for a bit. We have lunch soon, and I have to finish the Axioms so I can be removed from restriction tomorrow."

Thirty-Nine didn't reply. He placed the folder back in the pouch of the bag. He walked over to his bed and sat down. Staring at the floor, he replayed everything in his mind.

As much as the events of the preceding twenty-four hours had begun convincing Thirty-Nine to accept Thirty-Three's perception of The Woodlands as a bad place, the contents of the folder cemented his agree‐ment. He believed The Woodlands was a criminal enterprise, and he was prepared to stop it and rescue the other children, by any means necessary.

Eleven dutifully charged her Mind Cocoon in her pod, while waiting to go to lunch. Her podmate, Seventeen, a quiet artistic nine year old, was in a lesson, which meant Eleven would be uninterrupted for the next few minutes, until it was time for lunch. She dropped to her knees and reached under her bed. She felt between the mattress and the support beams for the book. Her fingers felt its worn leather as she slid it out and rolled onto her bed.

She held it close to her face and studied it once again. Browned, uneven pages bound in beige canvas. The spine was taped and re-sealed with a dark rubber-like substance. She rubbed the binding. The spine felt gummy and stiff, like an aged pencil eraser. The body of the book was still intact.

Eleven turned it over in her hands. On the front, in flowing letters, were the words: ***Wesley Kenton - Notes in Time***. The title appeared handwritten. It was certainly not part of The Woodlands curriculum. Eleven grimaced as she flipped it over. She wished she had opened it before agreeing to help Fifteen try to escape.

The back cover had no writing. The rough canvas was worn but not broken. She looked closely at the back and saw a faint but discernible shape in the lower right corner of the back cover. It was the impression of a key.

"Hmmm. That's different." She rubbed it slowly, her finger nudging along every jut and jag in the shape. It felt solid. She opened the back page, and there, resting for a century or more in a small saddle-stitched pocket, were two keys. Eleven slipped her thumb and forefinger into the pocket and pulled them out.

The keys were identical. About two inches long, with grooves etched both along the edge and within the solid handle. The carvings were symmetrical and clear, like letters in an alphabet, but they were not a language with which Eleven was familiar. Yet, as she felt the key's terrain like a blind man feeling Braille, it spoke to her. It felt like she was holding the keys to the doorway home.

"Home." She smiled. "A home somewhere in time. This is crazy. But maybe crazy's all we got left."

She squeezed the keys in her fist and looked around for a place to stash them. There wasn't much to hide anything under, even two small keys. Seventeen kept things tidy. The shared desk was neatly divided between them, a small strip of white tape splitting the dark brown top. Eleven's half contained two composition notebooks leaned against a crystal globe. The metal base supporting the globe was etched, "The Woodlands - 1997 - Head Student". She remembered how excited she had been to win that award. She rose from her bed and walked across the pod. She picked up the globe, allowing the notebooks to topple. Pulling open the large drawer below the desktop, she dropped the globe onto the socks that rested inside.

She glanced at the clock above her door. 11:48 am. Ten minutes until lunch.

She turned to the Mind Cocoon bag, resting on the small bookshelf above the desk. She pulled it down and unzipped the empty side pocket and tucked the keys inside. In her other hand, she still held Wesley Kenton's book. The interesting pages were about halfway through the book. Skimming through wildlife sketches and half a dozen juvenile love poems, she arrived at the pages that had completely altered her expectations about her future: indeed about the future of all the children at The Woodlands:

October 14, 1808. It's been two months since I joined Father here. Mother is not pleased. After he finished Jefferson's expedition, he turned down the commission offered by Captain Lewis. Instead, he decided to chase rumors of gold in the bleak Northwest. She says we could have made a good life, but Father says a good life is a waste when a great life can be had. We haven't seen any gold, or a good meal, in three weeks. I reckon I better write stuff down in case we don't survive the winter. At least Mother will know we were working hard.

<u>October 17, 1808</u>. Rain's been falling hard for nearly four days straight. It's good to loosen up the mud for prospecting but it's miserable for sleeping. Rattling on the roof of the shanty all night. Plus the wolves howling. This is not a fit situation for rest. Father did find a small nugget today. Once the rain lets up, he's going to head into the main camp to make a trade for some warmer blankets and some provisions.

<u>October 23, 1808</u>. I stayed to work the claim while Father went to get the provisions four days ago. He still has not returned. I fear he may have been ambushed. The savages south of us are not friendly. There are a couple of Indian families nearby who have befriended us. I expect to see Otak-Tay, the teenage boy savage, tomorrow. Maybe he will bring news of Father.

<u>October 24, 1808</u>. Father is dead. Otak-Tay told me this afternoon. I will miss him. I cannot spare time for mourning, unless I want to join him in the afterlife. I cannot even go retrieve his body for a proper burial, as Otak-Tay told me three warriors killed Father for stealing some bread from that makeshift store near Tex Johnson's claim. If I try to go down there, they will probably try to kill me too. Father was so irresponsible. I cannot attempt to go back to St. Louis. The winter season would kill me. Otak-Tay's family will share meat, if they can kill an elk in the next couple weeks. Meantime, I will forage and pray for my fortunes to turn.

<u>November 3, 1808</u>. It's been a hard week. Several days I ate nothing. Otak-Tay got word to Tex Johnson that I was alone. There's only four white men left in the main camp down there. Everyone else left for the Northwest Territories or California a week ago. Tex sent me a few small bags of flour and salt. Enough to make cakes for about a month.

<u>November 10, 1808</u>. Otak-Tay brought some venison today. It tasted so great. We talked for a long time. I laughed for the first time in months. He told me of a legend that he heard from his father. He told me that he knew about us coming before we did because the elders foretold it. The elders knew because they lived it already.

Otak-Tay says there is a Hallowed Hallway that is an open corridor through time. It opens every ten years for exactly two days. Forty-eight hours. He pulled out a wooden key and said it goes in the side of the holy willow tree in the center of their village. He wants to try going back. He wants me to go with him. I don't really know how it works, or if it works but I'm going to find out. Otak-Tay and I will meet in three days,

when the corridor opens. We're going to slip out before dawn.

November 20, 1808. We had to hire extra warriors to serve as guards to the main claim entrance. Father says that we will be able to build Mother two mansions, right by the Great River, if that's what she wants. Tex Johnson, who works for Father, says we got more gold than King Solomon. Otak-Tay was right about the Hallowed Hallway. Too bad a couple elders died. Too bad I have to wait another ten years to go back.

The door opened, surprising Eleven. She bolted up in her chair and closed the book, sliding it under her thigh.

"Hello," Seventeen said, "what are you doing?"

"Nothing much, just thinking." Eleven studied her podmate's expression. *Had she seen the book?*

Seventeen walked past Eleven and over to her small shoe rack against the wall, between the bed and the night table. She slipped off her loafers and sat on her bed to put on her athletic shoes.

"Well, you better get ready - we've got the fitness exam after lunch today. Of course, I'll finish almost last again. At least I'll beat Fifty-Two."

"Yeah, I better get ready." Eleven slid the book out from under her leg. She palmed it against her hip as she walked over to her bed to return it to its hiding place.

"What's that?"

"What's what?"

"The thing in your hand." Seventeen was quiet but she paid attention to everything.

"Oh, just a book I got in the library. It's nothing." Eleven stopped before her bed and opened the clothes closet. She set the book on the top inside shelf.

"What's it about?"

"It's a history book." Eleven needed to change the subject. Seventeen was not the kind of student that kept a secret. She even told on herself when a sentry couldn't identify who had left a couple clean napkins on the lunch table last week. She ended up with three consecutive days of

Yard duty. Waste was not acceptable at The Woodlands.

"I went to the Chief's office this morning."

"You did!" Seventeen stood up, straightening her tunic.

"Yes. I'm going to be on a special assignment for a few weeks. I'm not sure what it actually is, but I have to wear that every night."

She pointed at the Mind Cocoon, charging on the shelf above the desk along the wall on Seventeen's side of the pod.

Seventeen liked gadgets. She walked to the desk.

"Cool," she whispered reverently, "may I touch it?"

"Sure. I guess. I don't see why not." Eleven had eliminated Seventeen's interest in the book. As Seventeen held the device up, inspecting every inch, Eleven placed some clothing on top of the book and shut the wardrobe door.

"What do you think this thing does?" Seventeen had slipped the Mind Cocoon over her eyes and peered at Eleven. She looked like an ear surgery patient with light sensitivity issues. Eleven chuckled.

"What's so funny?"

"The way that thing makes you look. Ha ha! I'm glad I only have to wear it at night!"

Seventeen jerked it off her face. "You don't have to laugh at me. I just thought it looked neat."

"I'm sorry. It is neat."

"Well." Seventeen placed the Mind Cocoon back on the shelf. "Not everyone can be superior like you."

"Seventeen. I am sorry." Eleven walked over to her. "You're really great at lots of stuff, you know."

"Yeah right. I'm stuck in the middle of the pack in all the mental skills and I know I don't have any physical attractiveness."

"Yes, you do. And, anyway, appearance doesn't matter."

"Said by someone who can take beauty for granted. Don't pretend we don't notice each other's looks. We might be the Chief's robots but we're still human." Seventeen turned away from Eleven and headed for the door.

"Forget it; our sentry will be here in a few seconds."

Eleven didn't want to forget it. She couldn't afford to have any enemies right now, however minor the contention.

"Seriously, Seventeen, you are really exceptional. And you are physically symmetrical, which is a key element of beauty."

Seventeen stood in front of the door, her bony hands folded in front of her waist. She was three years younger and almost 10 inches shorter than Eleven. She stared back at Eleven through big doe eyes. Her thick pink lips fought to remain sealed, ineffectively trying to cover her too-large front teeth.

"It's ok Eleven. I know you didn't mean to laugh at me."

"I didn't." Eleven walked over to her. "I think you're great." She touched Seventeen on the shoulder briefly, causing Seventeen to blush.

"At least I don't have to wear the weird glasses!"

"That's true. That's true." Eleven placed her fingers in the shape of an "O" and wrapped them around her eyes. "How's this for being physically attractive?" she asked, emphasizing the look by sticking out her tongue.

Seventeen laughed. "Can you hold that look through lunch?"

They both giggled as the door beeped.

"Time for lunch," the sentry ordered, opening the door and motioning them into the hall.

As they headed down the hall, Eleven felt better. Maybe she could trust Seventeen.

Maybe.

I can't believe all this stuff is real, Thirty-Nine thought, as he and Eleven were escorted into the new room that would become their center of experimentation for the next few weeks.

The space wasn't large but it was full. Two elevated cots were positioned in the center of the room, surrounded by multiple monitors, cords and metal-bracketed consoles. Two blue signs with "THIRTY-NINE" and "ELEVEN" printed in white letters hung, one per cot, at the head of the mattresses.

Two sentries flanked the doors through which they had entered. Dr. Nampala held court with several researchers behind a large window that faced the end of the beds. Researcher 4 and Researcher 9, clipboards in hand, stood with Eleven and Thirty-Nine, respectively.

"We will begin with a cross-cerebral dream sequence. Every aspect of the next two hours will be recorded and analyzed. Our goal is to determine if the capability exists to enhance and possibly multiply the individual power of your respective minds by creating a connection during REM sleep. You will feel nothing different, but please alert us to any unusual sensations, images or thoughts."

Eleven and Thirty-Nine stood shoulder to chin, he being several inches shorter, awaiting the typical series of injections that accompanied all dream sequencing sessions.

"In order to establish a baseline for the new procedure, no injections will be given." Dr. Nampala declared through the metal speaker above the window. "Please lay on your corresponding cot."

They climbed onto the narrow, thin-mattressed beds. Eleven placed her hands along the side of her body, her third and fourth fingers dangling over the edge of the mattress. Thirty-Nine folded his arms over his stomach and stared down at his ribcage, slowly moving up and down with each measured breath.

Researcher 4 and Researcher 9 moved into action, attaching a large latex suction cup with tiny metal prongs around the edge to the back of each of the student's heads. A thick black cable snapped onto the end of each suction cup, joining the two. As the splinter-sized metal prongs dug into their scalp, Eleven and Thirty-Three flinched. Eleven rumpled the thin sheet atop the mattress with her hand.

Thirty-Nine glanced to his right. Eleven lay there, looking upward. Her snubby nose was a cute bump in her profile. Her face, even from the side, appeared tight. Determined. Thirty-Nine liked her cool indifference more than anything.

"Researchers, are you ready to begin?" Dr. Nampala asked.

Thirty-Nine was so busy thinking about Eleven he hadn't noticed the Researchers had inserted two more smaller suction pads at the base of his neck and the usual positive reduction cable in his right forearm. He looked at the ceiling, anticipating the warm sensation of the anesthesia that would soon fill his body and send him to sleep.

"Two minutes to begin sequencing," Researcher-9 replied, standing directly behind Thirty-Nine's head.

"Ok. Eleven and Thirty-Nine, listen carefully." Dr. Nampala had entered and was now standing at the foot of their beds.

"Don't sit up. Just listen." Eleven relaxed her neck. "You will enter your sleep in two minutes. Your mission today is different than any you've experienced at The Woodlands. I want you to focus on trying to enter each other's dream. Eleven, you are looking for a small old chapel. Thirty-Nine will be there. After you find him, you are to finish his sequence with him."

"One minute," Researcher-4 called out.

"Thirty-Nine, after your sequence, if time remains, you are to follow Eleven to the bus stop. Try to help her open the door of the second bus. We will be recording every element. This may seem like a small experiment but," he paused and touched both students' feet, "this is historic. By the end of the month, your minds will help us develop revolutionary breakthroughs in brainwave activity technology."

"Twenty seconds," Researcher-1 announced.

"Good night Eleven. Good night Thirty-Nine. We'll be watching." As he spoke, Dr. Nampala smiled.

Eleven drifted off first, eager to accomplish the mission. As much as she wasn't interested in the experiment, she was fascinated by the idea of entering another person's dream.

She found herself standing in an open field surrounded by low rolling hills. A split-rail fence lined the right side of her view, as far as she could see. A few squirrels scurried up and down two mammoth oak trees to her left. She turned around, seeing the same scenery regardless of the direction she faced.

Dr. Nampala said to look for a chapel. Better start walking. But which way?

She shielded her eyes with her hand and peered into the distance. *Was that a steeple or a tree?*

Since there was only one spot on the horizon that was pierced by a cylindrical shape, she started hiking toward it. The knee-high grass and the occasional wild flower was her only companion for the next half hour.

Thirty-Nine looked around. He was in a dark forest. A small building that looked like a large cabin was about sixty yards away. A woman was standing in front of the door staring back at him. Thirty-Nine walked toward her. With each step, he got no closer to her. He started walking faster. Still, she remained, along with the building, no closer to him. He looked down as he began jogging. The ground was changing below him, as though he was moving. He looked to the side. He was passing trees and bushes. He looked ahead. She remained the same distance away.

"Where are you Thirty-Nine?" he heard. It sounded like Eleven.

He tried to call out "Eleven", but his mouth wouldn't open. His lips were stuck. He couldn't separate them. He stopped running. He twisted and contorted his face, trying to call out but his mouth wouldn't cooperate.

"Remember, it's a dream. The answer is always within the dream." Dr. Nampala's voice entered his mind.

He looked around. The woman was still standing in the distance. The trees around him were thin and tall with leaves beginning far above the ground. The earth below was filled with a variety of sprawling vines and shrubs. The ground was muddy. Several swallows chirped overhead. A hummingbird hovered to his right, darting in and out of several large blossoms.

"Thirty-Nine!"

The call of his name sounded like it was coming from the building. He started walking again but still got no closer. The hummingbird followed him, bouncing along, all the while drawing closer to him. It flitted up toward his face as he trudged along.

Its feathers were iridescent blue and its beak was dark brown. It held its place, hovering just below eye level, as Thirty-Nine tried again to speak. His lips remained locked. He looked at the hummingbird. It seemed to be holding its right claw out, as if offering something.

"Thirty-Nine!"

At the cry of his name, the hummingbird fluttered closer to his hands, which were dangling as his arms rested over his bent knees. It brushed Thirty-Nine's hand. Puzzled, Thirty-Nine leaned closer. The hummingbird was now a few inches from his face. It brushed his hand again and popped up to Thirty-Nine's face and held out its right claw, beckoning him to open his hand.

Ok. This is a dream, after all. Thirty-Nine opened his hand and extended his palm. The hummingbird quickly landed on his outstretched hand and quickly flew away, leaving a black pea-sized bead in Thirty-Nine's hand. The hummingbird was gone.

"Thirty-Nine! We need to hurry up!"

He rose. He glanced over his shoulder briefly, at the building and the woman he couldn't approach. She waved goodbye and turned and walked into the building. She seemed so familiar. He feebly waved his hand and fought the urge to chase after her as she disappeared into the cabin. He had to find Eleven.

He walked toward the sound of his name. He looked down at the small bead in his hand. He rolled it between his thumb and forefinger, raising it up to his eyes. It looked like a piece of caviar, dark with a translucent shell, though this bead was completely dry and firm. He held it to his mouth. As soon as the tiny orb made contact with his lips, a small explosion happened. The bead was gone and Thirty-Nine's mouth popped open.

"Wow. Crazy." He laughed. "Dreams. You never know what's going to happen!"

Thirty-Nine started walking again and noticed the ground felt different. The trees were gone. He was standing in a field of tall grass. He looked behind him. No trees anywhere. No building. No woman.

"There you are!" Eleven shouted, running over to him from a few dozen yards away. "Where were you?"

"I was coming through the woods."

"What woods?" She asked as her eyebrows rose in disbelief.

Researcher-9 jotted on her notepad as she watched the rapid eye movements of both Eleven and Thirty-Nine. Their bodies were motionless, but their face muscles twitched frequently. The monitors were displaying multiple lines across various graphs, tracking the brain activity of both students.

"One hour elapsed." She announced. "The connective activity scans just spiked."

"Yes," Dr. Nampala replied, watching a hand-held monitor that worked like a homing device. It displayed a series of dots on a grid. Two red dots side-by-side lit up, representing the two students in proximity to each other.

"They are in a shared dream sequence. Look at Thirty-Nine's face."

"The woods that used to be right there. Never mind. This is a dream, after all."

"We're supposed to go to a chapel. Do you know how to find it?"

Thirty-Nine looked around. They were standing in the field where Eleven had been walking since she entered her dream sequence. It was unfamiliar to him.

"Usually, I just stumble upon it. But I've never had a shared dream before. Let's walk this way." Thirty-Nine pointed toward the left.

"Why?"

"I don't know. It's just what I feel like doing."

Eleven was all business. She was annoyed at how long she had spent walking in a field. That, coupled with Thirty-Nine's apparent inability to direct his dream, caused her to want to take control.

Thirty-Nine sensed her frustrations as she refused to walk; apparently Eleven needed more specific reasoning for the path he had recommended they take. He looked toward his left and squinted.

"Oh, I know why. There's the dark patch in the field. Out there." He pointed again to his left, motioning for Eleven to look.

"I don't see anything."

"It's there. I can see it," he lied. "C'mon, follow me."

They started walking. Eleven was disgruntled but remained silent as they moved in the direction Thirty-Nine selected. After a few feet, the hummingbird appeared again, darting between them.

"There's that bird again," Thirty-Nine noted aloud.

"Is it part of your dream?" Eleven asked.

"No. At least it never has been before."

The hummingbird circled above them, buzzard-like, as they continued to walk. Eleven looked up.

Strange behavior for a hummingbird.

"I know, right?" Thirty-Nine said, responding to her thought.

As he spoke, the hummingbird dove straight down, heading for their heads. Eleven and Thirty-Nine instinctively put their arms over their heads to shield themselves. They crouched together as it plummeted towards them, lurching to the side just before it collided with Thirty-Nine. He looked in the direction where the hummingbird had flown.

A bus was approaching them! He looked down. The field had suddenly turned into a freeway.

"Look out!" Thirty-Nine screamed. He turned to push Eleven out of the way but his footing slipped. The bus was roaring toward them, horn blaring.

Thirty-Nine stood to tackle Eleven out of the way. As he did, a familiar voice said, "I'll take it from here, son."

Thirty-Nine looked up. It was the man from his dream. The familiar shape, once again his face obscured as he whisked Eleven into his arms and jumped into the shoulder of the road.

Thirty-Nine scrambled as fast as he could. A rush of wind and gravel pelted him as the bus flew by, missing him by inches.

Eleven stood up and looked across at Thirty-Nine.

"Where'd he come from?!" She shouted.

"How do I know?"

"Where'd he go?" She asked.

Thirty-Nine looked around. The man was gone.

Eleven shielded her eyes and looked down the road. The man was gone but she could see the back of the large white mass transit bus that had nearly killed them. She fell back to the ground.

"I'm having trouble breathing!"

Thirty-Nine dodged several cars as he ran to her side. He helped her walk into the grass median. They tumbled to the ground as she continued to gasp for air.

In the research room, Eleven's body convulsed for a few seconds. The muscles in her arms rippled as a small seizure erupted within her. "Eleven's in great discomfort," Researcher-4 announced. "Should we disrupt the sequence and bring her back to full consciousness?"

"No. She's fine." Dr. Nampala replied.

Eleven's head shook from side to side. Researcher-9 looked over from her post alongside Thirty-Nine's bed.

"Her heart rate is over 150" she called out, noticing the small monitor affixed to the side of Eleven's bed.

"You tend to Thirty-Nine." Dr. Nampala snapped.

Thirty-Nine's body was relatively still. His heart rate was rapid but not dangerous.

"160 beats," Researcher-9 called out, demonstrating to Dr. Nampala that she was doing her job.

Eleven's legs were now shaking so violently the bed was rattling. The suction device connecting the students was jerking Thirty-Nine's head as Eleven's body convulsed.

"Dr. Nampala. We need to bring them out!" Researcher-9 declared.

"Don't tell me how to run my experiment!" Dr. Nampala shouted.

Researcher-4 remained silent during the confrontation. She watched Eleven's heart rate climbing.

"175 beats," she announced, growing nervous.

"She's fine," Dr. Nampala told her, ignoring the clatter caused by her convulsing body, her flushed twitching face and dramatically elevated heart rate.

Researcher-9 couldn't take it.

"Dr. Nampala," she lowered her voice, hoping a passionless tone would enable her to convince him to stop. "If we don't consider ending this session, permanent damage or even death may occur."

Dr. Nampala stepped closer to Researcher-9.

"Who do you think you are?" He bellowed. His face grew purple as he shouted. "I run The Woodlands, not you. If she dies, she is too weak for my program!"

He slammed his monitor to the floor and turned to Researcher-4. His body trembled with rage as he confronted her.

"What do you think? Are you a sympathetic scientist like her?" He pointed at Researcher-9, who had stepped back to the far side of Thirty-Nine's bed to avoid a potential slap, or worse from Dr. Nampala.

"I am a pragmatist, Dr. Nampala," came Researcher-4's monotone response. She never displayed any emotions. "However, as a pragmatist, I would encourage you to consider the value of Eleven. She has performed remarkably and if the potential of her combination with Thirty-Nine brings the breakthrough we seek, we should consider pausing today's session."

Her words had some effect. Dr. Nampala looked at Eleven. Her eyes were flickering rapidly, her flushed face was a mass of twitching muscles and her body was thumping up and down on the cot.

"190 beats," Researcher-4 announced.

"Fine." They were too close to a breakthrough. He couldn't afford to be reckless at this moment.

"Stop the session." He bent over to pick up his broken monitor.

He turned to both researchers, "If this fails, it's on you. And you sure as hell don't want a failure on your watch!"

He stormed out of the room as Researcher-4 and Researcher-9 frantically placed a mask over Eleven's mouth and nose, releasing the fumes that brought dreams to an end. They hurriedly decoupled the devices attached to Eleven's body, ignoring Thirty-Nine for the moment.

―――――――――――――――――――――――――――――――

Thirty-Nine rolled over in the grass median. "Can you breathe... Eleven?" He sat up and looked around. Eleven was gone. He stood up and looked side to side. The freeway was gone. He was back in the field.

What happened to Eleven?

"Eleven is going to need a recovery day." Researcher-9 told him as he sat up on his bed and looked at her empty cot. "Researcher-4 took Eleven back to her pod."

"We are going to supplement her diet and her oxygen mixture in her sleep sheath to see if we can improve the outcome."

"What happened?" Thirty-Nine slipped to the floor and stood facing Researcher-9. No one else was in the room. Thirty-Nine noticed that he was almost as tall as Researcher-9. He didn't feel intimidated or fearful in her presence.

"Eleven had an episode." Researcher-9 looked directly at him. Her light blue eyes twinkled as she continued, "we hope - I hope - that things change. Soon." She turned her back to collect her notepad and assorted binders that were resting on the rolling tray at the head of Eleven's bed.

"Is she going to be ok?"

Researcher-9 clutched her work materials in her right hand. She stepped to the wall and pressed the button for a sentry. She looked over her shoulder at Thirty-Nine and replied.

"She'll recover. How do you feel?"

"I'm fine. We never finished the dream, though."

"I know. We had to suspend it."

"Why?"

"Don't worry about it."

Thirty-Nine couldn't help worrying about it. Eleven had the book for their escape and her health was crucial for breaking out.

A sentry walked through the doorway opposite Eleven's empty bed. Researcher-9 kept talking to him as the sentry stared at both of them, silently waiting to guide them back to the boy's pod.

"We should resume on the day after tomorrow. Let's go to your pod now. Oh, and Dr. Nampala has elevated you to Head Student."

"Are you serious?"

"Yes. He decided you have earned it. Congratulations."

She walked over to him and nudged him to go before her. They walked around the beds and the monitor stands and out the open door. The sentry closed it behind them and followed just a few paces back.

Nothing was said the rest of the way back to Thirty-Nine's pod. They reached his door and waited for the sentry to scan and enter the code for deactivation of the lock. As he did, Researcher-9 tapped Thirty-Nine on the shoulder.

He turned to see her outstretched hand holding a folded piece of paper.

"Take these notes," she said as the sentry opened the door. "And study for tomorrow. This will help you improve in the experiment."

Thirty-Nine grabbed the paper and walked toward his pod.

"I will follow up with you tomorrow afternoon," Researcher-9 concluded as Thirty-Nine stood in the doorway. "Don't forget to take your pills and wear your Mind Cocoon tonight."

The sentry pulled the door shut after Thirty-Nine nodded and walked into his pod.

His podmate was still gone. He looked up at the clock. It was only 2:20. The dream sequencing had only lasted a little over an hour, instead of the usual two. He unfolded the note from Researcher-9 and began to read the few scribbled lines:

I expect to collect the file you stole tomorrow afternoon. I know you have it and it must be returned. All files are inventoried weekly. If I do not have it, I will be destroyed.

Now you know where you came from. You have a mother. We ALL do. If it helps, know that you are not alone. When the moment arises for freedom to be won, I will be with you. I have no doubt you are the one to lead us. Your experiment results confirm this. Do not fear. We will succeed.

You have been chosen.

Thirty-Nine read the note twice. "You have been chosen." He read the last line aloud, as he paced beside his bed. He held the single sheet of paper in his hand, peering at it like a person who needs reading glasses. He turned it over. Nothing was on the backside, but he could see the outline of the dark blue ink letters from the front of the page. He sat down on his bed.

"Do I tell Thirty-Three? What about Eleven?" He whispered to himself as he folded the paper and held it tightly between his hands. He continued thinking about the implications of Researcher-9.

If one of the insiders at The Woodlands had expressed a mutinous sentiment, were there others? What about the sentries? Why was the Chief doing all of this? Where did all of the equipment and food and clothes come from? So many things that had been simply accepted were now undergoing an inquisition in his mind. He looked around the pod. Thirty-Three's rumpled sleep sheath lay unfolded at the foot of his bed. The gray walls. The utilitarian feel of everything. This place was all he had known.

Maybe Thirty-Three was right. Maybe it was a prison. Maybe not. When something is familiar, it becomes acceptable, even if it's wrong. Life at The Woodlands was predictable. Three days ago, he wouldn't entertain the thought of escape. Yet, now he held a note from Researcher-9 that encouraged him to be the one that would lead an uprising.

Thirty-Nine stood up and turned to his left. He opened the doors to the wardrobe and looked for a hiding place for the note.

Maybe I should destroy it.

No. Keep it.

The inside of the wardrobe had a horizontal wooden pole upon which the few items of clothing he and Thirty-Three wore hung. On the lower right were two built-in boxes that could be used to store socks or underwear. Thirty-Nine knelt down and peered into the dark square. Thirty-Three's dirty socks lay wadded up on the bottom of the lowest one. The second box contained a pair of Thirty-Nine's underwear. He backed away from the cabinet.

"I need more than a pair of underwear to hide this." He scanned the pod, and his sight landed on the desk.

"Of course!" he snapped his fingers as he exclaimed. "The Mind Cocoon bag."

He walked over to the desk. The bag was the size and shape of a professional photographer's camera bag. He tugged open the side pocket that held his file and paused. He read the note one last time.

"You have been chosen." He repeated the last line then folded the paper and tucked it into the side pocket. He sealed the velcro closure and turned away.

Thirty-Nine rested on his bed and awaited Thirty-Three's return. As he lay there, he pondered the remarkable situation in which he found himself. He thought about the words on Researcher-9's note.

"If I have been chosen, it's a strange choice. Thirty-Three has the bravery, Eleven has the superior ability. I can hear thoughts, sometimes. I'm not exactly the ideal guy to lead a rebellion."

He laughed a brief nervous chuckle.

"At least I'll have the element of surprise on my side. I wish I could say the same for Thirty-Three."

Thirty-Three returned and went straight to his bed. He started folding his sleep sheath before getting ready for dinner. Thirty-Nine rolled over and stared at his podmate's chubby figure tugging at the nylon.

"Better late than never, huh?"

"I'm not taking any chances. Tonight is my last night of restriction. What if a sentry happens to see it when he picks us up for dinner and he's in a bad mood?"

"Where was that thought process at breakfast pick-up?" Thirty-Nine hopped out of bed and went to the wardrobe. He pulled out the button-down formal dress shirt. Each boy was assigned one; it was only worn on special occasions like Award Night or The Super Brain Banquet.

"I was still half asleep this morning. It didn't occur to me. Why are you picking on me?" Thirty-Three shot back. He stood up from folding the sleep sheath and looked at Thirty-Nine. "Whoa! You're wearing your ceremony shirt?"

Most of the time, the students wore tunics in the building and overalls when working or playing in the Yard. Thirty-Nine's was a shimmering silver silk top with thick white buttons.

"Yes. My tunic is not clean."

"Your tunic isn't clean? That's no reason to wear your ceremony shirt! You're going to get in trouble!"

"Other students have done it before."

"Like who? The only time is when they were being honored or had achieved something great in testing. You would never wear it unless..." Thirty-Three's voice changed from frustrated to suspicious.

"Unless - did you earn recognition today? Did you do something amazing at the dream sequencing?" He hopped over to Thirty-Nine and pestered him good-naturedly. "Did you? Did you?"

Thirty-Nine shrugged, his lower lip popping out.

"Maybe."

"Tell me!" Thirty-Three punched his podmate in the upper arm.

"Ow!" Thirty-Nine rubbed his shoulder. "Why'd you do that?"

"Sorry - I'm just excited for you. What kind of recognition are you getting? What happened? Come on, you can tell me."

The door started beeping, alerting the boys that the sentry was there for dinner. Thirty-Nine hurriedly tucked his shirt into his pants. "I guess you'll have to wait and see, just like all the other students."

Thirty-Three raised his hand to punch Thirty-Nine again. "You stinker!"

"Dinner," the sentry announced as he opened the door. He looked at them. Thirty-Nine had his hand halfway into his waistband straightening his shirt. Thirty-Three had his right fist drawn back.

"Is everything ok?" the sentry sternly questioned.

Thirty-Three rotated his right arm and rubbed his shoulder with his left hand. "Yes sir. I had a stiff shoulder from earlier today."

"Everything is just fine, sir." Thirty-Nine added.

"Ok. Let's go. Thirty-Nine, you are to sit in Seat 1."

Thirty-Three's eyes widened. *Seat 1*!

As they walked down the hall, following the sentry, other students were exiting their pods into the long corridor. As they saw Thirty-Nine in his formal shirt, they glanced at each other, wondering what was going to happen. By the time they arrived at the dining hall, a trail of titillated students and shushing sentries had formed behind Thirty-Three and Thirty-Nine.

Thirty-Nine followed the sentry to Seat 1. The square dining hall was filled with long dark picnic tables. The tables formed a "U" in the center of the white walled room. Each bench held between 30-35 students. In the middle top of the U sat a small round table with three padded leather armchairs. A pristine white linen cloth graced the top of the table. In the center of the table sat a large laminated card. The card was white with a single black number one.

Thirteen months and four days had passed since Eleven was promoted to Head Student. As Thirty-Nine left Thirty-Three with the masses and followed the sentry toward the private table, he couldn't help thinking what a big deal this would have been a week ago. Now, he chuckled at the hype. After the revelations of the last few days, this promotion was meaningless.

"Sit here." The sentry pulled out the chair directly facing the rest of the students, who were quietly taking their places on the benches.

Thirty-Nine sat down. The sentry pushed the chair in behind him and handed him a cloth napkin. Thirty-Nine placed it in his lap and looked up. A sea of shaved heads looked back at him.

Lucky Thirty-Nine.

I should be number one.

Wonder what he did?

What happened to Eleven?

Thirty-Nine was hearing the student's thoughts. So far, it had only been one-on-one, in isolated instances. Now, a flood of voices was swamping his mind. He looked down at the table. The voices stopped. He looked up again.

I beat him at horseshoes last month, now he's head student?

He looked down. The only thoughts in his mind were his own. This time, as he raised his head, he searched for Thirty-Three. After a few moments, he spotted him. His pudgy, slightly off-kilter sidekick had always been loyal. Their eyes met. Thirty-Three's twinkling with delight; Thirty-Nine's blinking with apprehension.

Way to go podmate. It's all lining up for our escape.

Thirty-Nine opened his eyes widely and shook his head, as if to say "No." Even thinking the word escape in the open seemed dangerous to him. As he continued to focus on Thirty-Three, however, no other student's thoughts entered his mind.

Don't you feel it? Thirty-Three stared hard at Thirty-Nine, who never broke the stare but fidgeted with the silverware in front of him.

Everything is coming together for us. We will be the ones. We will not fail. We will find the way out.

As he listened to Thirty-Three's thoughts, a new sense of resolve settled in his heart. Resolve to try to escape. How it would happen remained a mystery.

"Good evening, students." Dr. Nampala's voice filled the hall, his image displayed on the bare wall behind Thirty-Nine's table.

"Good evening Dr. Nampala," a chorus of mostly high-pitched voices replied.

"Tonight," he continued, "we have a tremendous recognition. As you can see, Thirty-Nine has achieved the highest honor granted at The Woodlands. He is the fifth Head Student in our history. His discipline, facilitated by my leadership, has produced exceptional results. Students, please rise and honor your new student leader."

The sound of scuffling shoes and shifting bodies filled the hall as the students stood and applauded. Thirty-Nine sat there, staring at the table. A warm, tingling sensation filled his body. He closed his eyes.

"Thirty-Nine," Dr. Nampala ordered, "stand before your compatriots."

He slowly pushed his chair back and rose. The students clapped more vigorously as he stood. A few students whistled and stomped. Fearful of making eye contact and being bombarded by thoughts, Thirty-Nine kept his eyes closed and bowed slightly.

"Now students, please follow protocol. Thirty-Nine will lead all assemblies. Aspire to gain his level of excellence in all you do. The Woodlands forever!"

"The Woodlands forever!" The students replied.

"Let us recite the Woodlands Mantra…"

As Thirty-Nine stood there, his head bowed and eyes closed, the students began:

"The brain is the new frontier. The mind is a vast, unexplored region filled with endless possibilities. My potential…"

He did not join them. He held his tongue as he listened to his friends chanting Dr. Nampala's propaganda.

No choice, he thought. Not one of the students had a choice about their life. They probably had real families, like he did. Maybe they had real brothers and sisters. As their voices merged into one sound, he felt the weight of responsibility. He felt the certainty of the moment. This was not a dinner; it was a coronation. He would lead them. He would lead them to a new home. Their real homes.

Eleven's book about time travel, Researcher-9's support, Thirty-Three's daring. He could hear thoughts. Now he was Head Student. This was more than coincidence. The week's collision of extraordinary talent and deadly circumstances filled Thirty-Nine with boldness.

"Be seated. Eat." With that command, Dr. Nampala's image disappeared from the screen. The students sat and the sentries entered, push-carts laden with the pressed food bars and cups of various specially formulated juice-like drinks. As they wheeled around the room, depositing each student's meal, a sentry carrying a single platter approached Thirty-Nine's table.

The sentry held a pair of tongs in his left hand. He stood next to the newly minted Head Student's left shoulder. Without speaking, he plucked two light brown bars and a quartered orange off the tray and placed them on the plate. He turned and walked away. A second sentry walked up, holding a clear jug filled with a plum colored beverage. He poured it into Thirty-Nine's glass and set the jug on the table.

"Will that be all?" he said.

"Yes. Thank you." Thirty-Nine stared at his plate. It was the usual meal. Nothing special.

Where was all the fancy food? Is the Chief messing with me?

He had a hard time finishing his meal, though he knew it was required. He chewed slowly, thoughtfully. He could feel the gaze of the other students but he dared not look up. The separation from the other students and the isolated meal were affecting his disposition. Those "weaker feelings" that Thirty-Three allowed to drive his life were beginning to infect Thirty-Nine's formerly impregnable mind.

He took a drink. He was thirsty. He took another drink. As the thick fluid trickled down his throat, he raised his head, looking directly at where he remembered Thirty-Three sitting. He wasn't there. He looked to the right. No student was there. He scanned the room. Every student had finished eating. No one was left at the tables. He looked beyond the tables. The students stood, silently in a single file line, waiting for him to finish.

He caught Thirty-Three's eyes as he scanned the line. This time only one thought came through. Maybe it was only Thirty-Three's thought but it felt like dozens of voices entered his head, all saying the same thing:

We're waiting for you.

Thirty-Nine gulped down the rest of the food bars and chugged his beverage. He wiped his mouth with the back of his hand and stood to his feet.

They're waiting for me.

He walked toward the line of students, and took his place at the front. For the first time in his life, Thirty-Nine felt ready to lead.

Sleeping was difficult that night. The uncomfortable Mind Cocoon, coupled with the excitement of knowing tomorrow ended Thirty-Three's restriction, caused both boys to toss and turn throughout the night.

When the alarm sounded, Thirty-Nine was quick to rise. He slipped off the Mind Cocoon and unzipped his sleep sheath.

"Morning, Thirty-Three."

"Yes it is."

"Can I shower first?"

"Sure. Wake me up when you're done." Thirty-Three rolled over against the wall and closed his eyes.

Thirty-Nine, though tired from the restless night, had the power of adrenaline to thank for his morning energy. As he showered he thought about the happenings of the week. Much had been discovered. Much remained to be planned. He hoped Eleven would be at breakfast. She still hadn't shown them the book.

He dried off and stepped out of the shower.

"Thirty-Three, get up!" He shouted.

"I'm getting up, I'm getting up," his podmate replied through his fog of partial sleep.

Thirty-Three entered the shower hoping that the steam and heat of the water would rouse him.

Thirty-Nine went to his desk and plugged in the Mind Cocoon. He pulled out the file from the bag and held it, unopened, in his hands.

"Nicole, Mother..." As he vocalized the reality of his mother's existence, his voice cracked and a lump caught in his throat. *What is this feeling?* He cleared his throat and continued.

"Nicole, Mother. I will try to find you." He did not open the file. Placing it back in the side pocket of the Mind Cocoon bag, he sat down at the desk and spun the chair around, just as Thirty-Three was finishing his shower.

"You ready for today?" Thirty-Three asked as he pulled on his tunic.

"What do you mean?" Thirty-Nine leaned back in the desk chair and folded his hands across the back of his head. He rubbed his fuzzy scalp.

"I mean, are you ready to plan the esca...?"

"Shh!" Thirty-Nine cut him off. "Don't say the word, ok? Let's come up with a code word."

"A code word?"

"Yes, like something that means what we want to do, but is a word that isn't connected to breaking out. You know?"

"I see what you mean. Any ideas?"

Thirty-Nine leaned forward and rested his arms on his knees.

"How about sunshine?"

"Sunshine?" Thirty-Three walked over to his bed, to the left of the desk. He sat down and began to put on his shoes, all the while maintaining eye contact with Thirty-Nine.

"I don't know. I just don't even want to hint at the E-word."

"Sure. No problem. So, are you ready to plan the sunshine?" Thirty-Three laughed as he said it.

Thirty-Nine smiled. "It does sound silly. How about *the show*?" Thirty-Nine stood up and held his hands out to his side, palms up, and announced,

"Get ready for the show!"

Thirty-Three stood up. "I like it. I'm ready for the show. I've been ready for the show for a long time."

"I'm ready too. Let's do it."

Thirty-Three wrapped his arms around his podmate, squeezing him with enthusiastic affection. Thirty-Nine slowly moved his arms around his portly pal's back.

Suddenly, the door beeped and opened. Once again, a sentry discovered them in an awkward position. They quickly let go of each other.

"Just helping each other do some stretches, sir." Thirty-Three announced.

"Shut up and start walking!"

"Yes sir."

Breakfast was served as dinner had been. Thirty-Nine sat alone again but this morning he was not bombarded by the other student's thoughts. The other children had adjusted quickly to his new position. He scanned the room more freely, without any interruption by the noise of other's thoughts.

How does this thought hearing thing work? Let's see, he nibbled on his bar and allowed his eyes to drift around.

It seems like I can hear thoughts when I make eye contact. He thought back through all the situations where he had experienced it. *Maybe it only works when people are thinking about me. No. Not all of the students' thoughts were about me.*

As Thirty-Nine pondered his inconsistent supernatural ability, he continued to look at the row of students around him. As his eyes passed along the right corner of the room, he locked eyes momentarily with a younger female student. She did not look away but continued to stare at him. Thirty-Nine looked down, took a drink, and looked up again. She stared.

Thirty-Nine, I have something for you, she thought.

Thirty-Nine blinked but held his gaze. As he looked at her thin, lightly freckled face and her dark, hollow eyes, he thought back to an incident in the Yard about three months earlier, when he and Thirty-Three had been playing.

"You can't run in this area." A younger female student told them as they hurried past, causing them to stop.

"What do you mean?" Thirty-Three replied, breathing heavily. Thirty-Nine stood with him, hands on his hips.

"The new rule requires that you walk between the track section and the swing set. It was announced yesterday." She emphasized the word yesterday, implying that he had been given plenty of time to adjust his behavior.

"You're not even on student patrol. What's the big deal if I run?"

"The big deal? It's a rule! That's all there is to it." She crossed her arms and took a step closer, positioning herself between them and their desired destination.

"Fine. I'll walk. What's your name again?" Thirty-Three asked.

"I'm Seventeen. Why?'

"Just wondered."

Seventeen! That's her name. Why would she have something for me?

The tables and benches, the faces of other students and the sentries all grew fuzzy as he stared across the room into her dark brown eyes.

Meet me in the Yard after breakfast. I have something for you, from Eleven.

Eleven, Thirty-Nine thought as he nodded his agreement with her proposal. She promptly broke the stare and returned to her meal.

Why would Eleven include Seventeen in things? Seventeen is even more of a rule follower than me. Has Eleven told anyone else? Where is Eleven anyway?

He quickly finished his breakfast and stood, signaling that the other students had one minute to complete their meal. Thirty-Nine looked over at Seventeen but her head was down.

Seventeen is now in the mix, he thought.

Maybe this will turn into a show after all.

Boy 39

The students were granted fifteen minutes of free time in the Yard. Every barrier was topped with the electric fence that Eleven had short-circuited during her failed escape.

They dispersed into the Yard during the interlude between breakfast and chores or classes and depending on the day's assignment and the level of the students' abilities, the usual cliques convened in their respective sections of the grounds.

Most of the students aged five to eight (the last new infant was delivered to the Woodlands four years earlier) stayed in several small jungle gym and sand box areas, supervised by multiple sentries. Most of the students were between nine and twelve years old. They were given more open space to play traditional schoolyard games. Kickball, tetherball and rubber horseshoes were popular.

Thirty-Nine watched the students scurry about like ants running to abandoned candy. After a minute standing by the doorway, he made his way toward one of the seven horseshoe pits. Thirty-Three was already there, along with one of the quietest kids at The Woodlands, Forty-One.

"Forty-One and I will play against you and someone else," Thirty-Three declared, surprisingly able to control his excitement about the show. His demeanor was unusually placid.

"Ok." Thirty-Nine grabbed two black steel horseshoes from the rack behind the wooden framed pit. He looked around and saw Seventeen nervously approaching. She stopped about ten feet away and stood there.

"I'll play with her." He pointed to Seventeen.

"Seventeen," Thirty-Three laughed. "Sure, if you want to lose. She probably isn't even strong enough to toss the horseshoe!"

"It's ok. She'll be fine." Thirty-Nine motioned to Seventeen to join them. She slowly walked over.

"If you say so." Thirty-Three turned to Forty-One. "Let's get ready to win."

Thirty-Nine, can you hear me? Seventeen thought, now just a couple feet away and staring at him with the biggest bug-eyes he'd ever seen.

"Yes."

"Eleven was right. She told me last night."

"What did Eleven tell you?" Thirty-Three spun around, overhearing Seventeen's comment. He stepped closer to Thirty-Nine and Seventeen. Forty-One stood a few steps away, swinging his arms in preparation for the game.

"She told me about *him*." Seventeen pointed to Thirty-Nine. Her tone was listless and flat, the vocal equivalent of a deflated balloon.

"What about him?"

"Don't worry about it." Thirty-Nine cut off the conversation, elbowing Thirty-Three and nodding toward Forty-One.

"We don't need any more students involved in the show."

Thirty-Three looked at Seventeen. "Does she know?"

"You can ask *me*." Seventeen replied.

Forty-One had shuffled over, still silently holding his horseshoes. Thirty-Nine sensed the animosity between Thirty-Three and Seventeen. He needed to settle them down.

"Let's play horseshoes, ok?" He glared at his podmate, hoping that he would get the hint to not discuss anything around Forty-One.

"Yeah, let's play." Thirty-Three finally replied, grabbing Forty-One by the elbow.

"We'll go to the other end. Good luck!"

"TEN MINUTES REMAINING," a sentry's voice announced over the loudspeakers mounted on poles throughout the Yard.

"You go first," Thirty-Nine called out across the pits.

As Forty-One's first toss plunked into the sand, Seventeen began talking to Thirty-Nine.

"How can you hear thoughts?"

"I'm not sure. But that's not important right now. Where was Eleven this morning? What do you have for me?"

Forty-One's second throw banged against the metal stake and flipped out of the pit.

"She suffered some kind of seizure during your dream sequencing session yesterday. She should get better, but she is definitely sore and tired. She wanted to come to dinner last night to tell you but Researcher-4 ordered her to pod rest. I didn't tell her that you were now the Head Student."

"Hey! It's your turn!" Thirty-Three yelled.

"Sorry!" Thirty-Nine replied. "You go first, Seventeen."

She gripped the horseshoe, its weight pulling at her shoulder joint as she wound up to throw. She flung it as hard as she could, nearly lifting her feet off the ground. The shoe wobbled through the air and bounced three times before coming to a stop a couple feet shy of the stake.

"Not bad for a little girl!" Thirty-Three teased.

"Why is he so mean?" She muttered through clenched teeth.

"He's not mean. He's just not in control of his emotions." Thirty-Nine answered, handing her a second horseshoe.

"Here - show him up."

Seventeen stepped back a few paces. She swung the shoe back and began running forward, releasing the horseshoe as she approached the back of the pit. The horseshoe flipped, end over end, high into the air. It sailed toward Thirty-Three and Forty-One, and began to lose altitude in a perfect arc. It was as though a magnetic field sucked it in as it approached the pit. It tumbled to earth and caught the top of the stake and rattled all the way down, resting in a puff of dust, completely wrapped around its target.

"Take that!" Thirty-Nine shouted as Seventeen actually jumped into the air with excitement.

Embarrassed by her reaction, she straightened her tunic and meekly uttered, "Yea. Take that."

"Nice shot." Thirty-Three begrudgingly responded.

"You didn't tell her I was Head Student?" Thirty-Nine resumed the conversation as Thirty-Three began swinging his arm at the other end of the pits.

"No. She really likes being the Head Student. I don't know how she'll respond."

"I hope she won't be upset with me. The Chief is the one that made it happen. What did she ask you to give to me?"

"Watch out!" Thirty-Three's shout interrupted them. Thirty-Nine looked up in time to see the horseshoe somersaulting through the air toward his head. He dove to the side, barely avoiding the **overshot by his podmate.**

"Sorry!"

Thirty-Nine stood up, dusting off his shirt and running his hand over his head, knocking small bits of dirt and grass to the ground. He was too interested in Seventeen's delivery to be upset with Thirty-Three.

"Settle down, huh?"

"I guess I don't know my own strength." Thirty-Three shouted, flexing his arms.

"FIVE MINUTES!" the announcement echoed through the playground.

"We don't have much time. What do you have from Eleven?"

"It's in my inside hem. It's the history book she told you about in the Game Chamber." She looked around. The nearest sentry was at least fifty yards away, beating two students who got in an argument over a game of hide-n-seek.

"I'm going to kneel down and put it under the horseshoe rack."

"Here comes a ringer!" Thirty-Three shouted, flinging his second horseshoe toward the stake.

Thirty-Nine turned and pitched his horseshoes toward the small metal rack where the horseshoes were stored.

"Oops. Seventeen, can you pick those up for me while I see if Thirty-Three scored?"

The clang of Thirty-Three's toss against the stake told them he'd nailed it. Seventeen stepped over and knelt down. Thirty-Nine leaned over the pit where his opponent's horseshoes now lay. As he counted out their points, Seventeen's heart was pounding. She shook the book loose from inside her tunic hem. It flopped onto the grass and lay there for a moment, a brown leather patch in a circle of green. She nudged it under the rack with her shaking hands. The moist grass tickled her arm.

"Two points." Thirty-Nine announced as he stood upright and turned to Seventeen. "Thanks for getting those shoes."

Seventeen snatched the two horseshoes, one in each hand, from the grass and stood. She tapped the book with her heel to make sure it was completely hidden under the rack.

"TWO MINUTES."

The sound of the time remaining announcement jarred her as she stepped toward Thirty-Nine, causing her to drop the horseshoe in her left hand.

"I'm sorry," she apologized as she reached down to pick it up.

"It's ok," Thirty-Nine replied, kneeling down, his hand reaching it before hers. "I've got it."

She stopped mid-reach and looked at him, her nerves still unsettled. She handed him the other shoe as he stood up. They faced each other for a moment, eyes locked.

"Do you think it's real? Do you think we can?" she paused and looked over his shoulder. She lowered her voice, "I mean, you know. Can we break out?"

Her eyes brightened as she whispered. Her eyebrows arched in the center of her face. Her chin was lifted, as if her entire head was pushing upward.

What is that look? Thirty-Nine thought, switching the horseshoes in his hand. I've never seen that look before. He replied the only way he knew.

"I don't know. Honestly."

"Throw your shoe!" Thirty-Three shouted. "We've only got a couple minutes!"

He turned from Seventeen and tossed the first one. It landed at least ten feet away from the target.

"Ha! Nice toss!" came the taunt from Thirty-Three.

"Thirty-Nine." Seventeen's quiet voice called from behind him.

"Yes?" He turned slightly, and looked at her over his right shoulder.

"I believe you can do it."

"Well, I'll try to throw a ringer. Thanks for the encouragement."

Not throw a ringer, she thought. *Break out of here. I believe you can. I hope.*

Thirty-Nine gulped. He turned back to the pits. Hope. That was the unfamiliar expression on her face.

I hope so, too, Thirty-Nine thought as he tossed the horseshoe into the air. It, like the first one, fell short of the stake.

"Tie game!"

"ONE MINUTE, TIME TO ASSEMBLE AT THE ENTRYWAY."

"I guess we'll have to have a rematch!" Thirty-Three called across the pits. He turned to his teammate. "We'll win the next one."

Forty-One silently stared.

"Ok, well, if you ever want to talk, just let me know." Thirty-Three turned to the pit and began picking up the horseshoes.

"I'll get these." Thirty-Nine told Seventeen. "You go ahead and get in line."

As Seventeen skipped off, he quickly grabbed the four shoes and walked to the rack. He set three on the top shelf and dropped the last one. He knelt down and palmed the book with his right hand then grabbed the fallen horseshoe. As he stood, Thirty-Nine dropped the horseshoe in the rack and tucked the book into the elastic waistband of his pants. He smoothed his tunic flat over the front of his legs and turned to walk toward the main building.

Most of the students were already in line along the wall. A few stragglers, trailed by club-wielding sentries, were crossing the Yard as Thirty-Nine passed by the circular flowerbed in the middle of everything. A single large willow tree anchored the space, its long, mop-like branches bending toward the earth. As he walked by he felt a strange compulsion to climb the tree.

He looked beyond the circle toward the row of children. He marched to the front of the line and waited for the sentry to open the door. He led the students back into the building and down the hall. Thirty-Nine led the students as they silently walked to their pods to change or await their pick-up for the morning's chores or lessons.

He pressed his hand against the top of his leg, feeling the book, still securely held by the elastic in his pants.

That was easy.

Maybe too easy.

Thirty-Nine's pod was near the end of the main hall, around the corner from the elevator to Dr. Nampala's offices. As they approached his pod, he saw someone standing in front of his door.

Sentry-1 halted the procession.

He walked to Thirty-Nine's doorway and entered into a conversation with the unidentified person. He turned and walked halfway back toward Thirty-Nine and motioned for him to approach.

As he drew nearer, he could identify the individual who parked outside his pod. It was Researcher-9. She was holding three half-inch thick notebooks.

"You are to go with her." Sentry-1 declared. He opened the door to Thirty-Nine's pod and walked back to lead the remaining students to their pods.

Researcher-9 stepped into the doorway of his pod and beckoned for Thirty-Nine to enter. She closed the door behind them and whispered.

"Get the file - quick."

Thirty-Nine hustled over to the desk and grabbed the bag. He turned and began walking toward Researcher-9, pulling open the side pocket as he walked. He reached inside and pulled out the "Procurement and Delivery Report - Boy Thirty-Nine" file and handed it to his escort.

"Here you go."

The door beeped. She snatched the file and tucked it between the binders she was carrying. The door swung open, and Thirty-Three entered. He was surprised to see a researcher standing in the pod.

"Ummm. Hello."

"Hello Thirty-Three. We were just leaving." She stepped back and placed her hand in the middle of Thirty Nine's back, nudging him forward.

"Let's go. Your assignment is waiting."

She pushed him forward, causing him to bump into Thirty-Three, who was still standing near the doorway. Thirty-Nine could feel the book slipping out of his waistband and slapped his hand against the inside of his thigh, pinning it against his leg. He stopped, his body now slightly hunched over, and looked at Thirty-Three, who had stepped to the side when they collided.

"Ok, well I guess I'll see you at lunch."

"Yea."

Thirty-Nine didn't walk forward. He stood still, inching the book up his thigh, trying to push it back into a secure position within his waistband.

"Let's go." Researcher-9 insisted, returning her hand to the middle of his back.

The tightness of his waistband prevented him from slipping the book into place. He quickly reached with his left hand, plucked his waist-band out and shifted the book into place.

"That was close", Thirty-Three muttered.

"What was close?" Researcher-9 replied, looking at Thirty-Three, her hand still resting on Thirty-Nine's back.

"Oh, umm, I thought I was going to fall."

Researcher-9 unexpectedly chuckled.

"Really? You are a different breed, aren't you?" She looked at Thirty-Three's chubby frame. "Maybe your balance is off because of your weight distribution."

Thirty-Three looked down at his midsection and rubbed his belly. He looked back at Researcher-9 and smiled, his hands still petting his gut as he replied.

"Maybe, maybe not. You'd be surprised how this little guy comes in handy."

"If you say so. Let's go, Thirty-Nine."

Thirty-Nine pulled the door open, the book now secured in his waistband, and walked into the hall. Researcher-9 followed him out.

"Where's the sentry?"

"We don't need one right now. Since Eleven was unable to participate in any activities today, I received permission from Dr. Nampala to do some individual testing. Just you and me. This way."

She led him in the opposite direction of Dr. Nampala's office. They walked past the dining hall and continued on to the circular staircase at the northern end of the main building.

"Are we going to the library?"

"Sort of."

Researcher-9 continued walking, down the staircase, her soft-soled slip-on shoes barely registering on the tiled steps. She was rushing through the hallway and implored him to do the same.

"Hurry up now. Let's go."

When they got to the bottom of the steps, instead of walking straight to the main doors for the library, she turned left. A few of the fluorescent bulbs in the ceiling were burned out.

"Almost there."

"Almost where?"

Thirty-Nine couldn't see anywhere to go. The hall ended in a few steps and the bathroom was not what he was expecting for a testing room. Researcher-9 stood to the right of the bathroom door and pressed a keycard against one of the tiles. As she did, the wall at the far end slid open, revealing another hallway.

"Here," she said, answering Thirty-Nine. "Come this way."
They walked through the opening where the wall had just been. As they crossed into the newly revealed hallway, Researcher-9 again pressed her keycard against a tile in the wall. The wall/door closed behind them.

"Ok. Understand that this is not part of The Woodlands protocol."

She said.

She turned to a simple wooden door on her right, twisting the knob and pushing it inward. They walked into a small room, not much bigger than a closet. The contents of the room consisted of two metal-framed chairs with blue plastic seats, placed on either side of an old wooden workbench, and a reading lamp. As the door closed behind them, she switched on the lamp. She placed her small stack of binders, with his file, on the corner of the workbench.

"Have a seat."

Thirty-Nine sat down as she took her place opposite him. As he did, he felt the book in his waistband bending. He pushed his right leg out straight, trying to prevent damage to the book.

He looked around the space. There were no screens, no machines, no monitors or wires in the room. Nothing. They sat silently for several moments as she pulled his file out and placed it in the center of the bench between them. She opened it and turned to the extraction report. She read it silently for a minute. Thirty-Nine slid the book up toward his midsection and slid his leg back under his seat.

"Did you read my note?" she finally asked, looking up from the file.

"Yes."

"We don't have much time. If my calculations are correct, we have about a month or so before you are sent out as a thought soldier, or this place is shut down and we are all exterminated."

"Thought soldier? Exterminated?" Thirty-Nine sat up straight. "What are you talking about?"

"This entire operation is funded by an anarchist organization known as The Future." She laughed and rubbed her chin.

"Sorry, it's not funny at all, I just think it's odd that anarchists create an organization. It's like the opposite of their philosophy. What's that word? Oxymoron. You know what an oxymoron is?"

He thought for a second. "Yes. It's like two opposites put together. I think we talked about it in language development. An example would be the phrase, 'deafening silence'."

"Correct." She smiled as she looked at him. "You are such a bright student. I can see why you'd be the one."

"What do you mean? What is The Future?"

"The Future is an offshoot of several terrorist groups. They desire, truly and utterly, chaos among mankind. It's not necessary to understand why, because you can't. The founder, A. Finley, also has huge Investments in weapon manufacturing companies. He uses anarchists to help build his business. He is delusional but he is wealthy. How The Woodlands came to be is for two reasons: The Future has money, and Dr. Nampala has brains.

Dr. Nampala's research is illegal. He knows this area well and when it was discovered that this facility was remote and abandoned, it was a dream come true for him. The holy grail of his research is creating a way to control another person's speech through thought transference. His mission is to turn you – and the other students – into *thought soldiers*. If he can develop this ability in you, you will be sent out to political meetings and speeches. You will be used to make world leaders speak inflammatory words, beginning with the President of the United States. The Future wants this so that the world will engage in big wars. And of course, war leads to chaos. The Future will get what it wants, the overthrow of world order. And Dr. Nampala will get what he wants, revenge against the United States government. And lots of money."

"That's crazy." Thirty-Nine sat up straight, amazed by the revelation.

"Yes. But, for a scientist, sometimes the breakthrough is worth breaking the rules. Dr. Nampala has about 30 days left in a ten-year agreement. The Future has paid for all of this, for all of the students. The food. The workers. Everything. Dr. Nampala has not produced the results they want. The results they've paid for. If he doesn't produce them in the next few weeks, we will all be destroyed."

Thirty-Nine hugged his waist and slowly rocked back and forth in the chair.

"One month to escape or die," he whispered.

"Or become a thought soldier." She added. "Which is why I wrote you the note. I do believe you are the student with the greatest probability of success. I have been assigned to your file for almost 2 years. About a month ago, I started noticing unique mutations in your brain physiology, as well as much higher levels of several proteins in your post-dream sequence blood samples. I have a suspicion that you are developing..."

She paused and leaned on the bench, resting her chin in her hands.

She stared at him intently as though her eyes were magnets pulling intimate information from within his body.

"Look at me."

Thirty-Nine stopped rocking and leaned forward.

"Tell me, Thirty-Nine."

"Yes?"

"Have you experienced thought transference? Have you sensed other's thoughts?"

He hesitated to answer. She seemed kind. She also seemed kind of desperate. She seemed different than the other workers at The Woodlands. It was like the rest of them were robots. She radiated warmth. Humanity.

If I tell her, I have to trust her. This group is growing. First Seventeen, now Researcher-9. But, it would be a big help to have an insider. A grown-up. Time is running out. We'll die if I do nothing.

"Yes. Yes, I have heard thoughts. But I don't know how to control the ability. I'm trying to figure it out." His body relaxed as he spoke. He sat tall in his chair.

"I thought so! Dr. Nampala doesn't yet suspect it, because I haven't notified him of my thoughts, but he knows something is changing. His plan to harness you and Eleven together is his final attempt to discover the answer and keep his research going. What he doesn't know is the appearance of the man in both your dreams signifies to me that he is a part of the plan. Part of the potential escape. He saved Eleven from the bus. He always catches you before you fall. I don't know exactly, but I'm going to figure out what his place is in this situation. Hopefully Eleven recovers quickly and we can identify him."

"What happened to her?" Thirty-Nine asked.

"I'm not sure. The stress of entering your dream caused her physical body to experience a mild seizure, along with other unintended consequences. It's good that we have this day, however. Otherwise, I'm not sure we could have this conversation."

"But," Thirty-Nine leaned back, "hearing thoughts doesn't get us out of here. No one has ever escaped. Ever."

"It might not get us out. But, it may help you discover an exit no one knows about." Researcher-9 rested her hand on her chin.

"We may have already discovered an exit no one knows about. Well, except for Eleven, because she told me. And Thirty-Three, since he's my podmate." He reached down for the book.

"Oh, and Seventeen." He added. "But that's it. So, I guess four people know about it."

He lifted his tunic slightly and pulled out the small leather-bound volume.

"What is that?" Researcher-9 asked as she reached to touch it.

"Eleven says it tells how to time travel. I don't really know yet because she's the only one who's read it." Thirty-Nine set it in the middle of the table. Researcher-9 felt the worn leather, and thumbed the pages without picking it up.

"Time travel?" she asked.

"Yea."

She scooped up the book.

"May I?"

"Sure. It's probably better for a scientist to read it anyway."

"Oh, I don't know about that. You're a very smart boy. Come here; we can read it together."

Thirty-Nine stood up and walked around the bench. He placed his hand on the table, leaning over Researcher-9's shoulder. She slowly flicked through the pages until she reached a dog-eared section. At the top of the first page, written in fresh ink by Eleven, were the following words:

This is the answer. This is our way home.

27

"It's about time to go home." Mr. Douglas whispered to Nicole. They had been sitting on the bench at the front of the general store for at least thirty minutes.

"It's not quite closing time."

"I guess you're right. Still, it'd be nice to go home early."

"You're getting soft, Mr. Douglas." She replied, patting him on the back. She stared at the faded tile flooring beneath their feet. It reminded Nicole of the basement in her parent's home when she was a little girl.

"It would be nice to have a place to really call home." She whispered.

Mr. Douglas leaned forward, rocking himself to try and stand up. Nicole jumped to her feet and grabbed his arm to serve as leverage as he shakily hoisted himself upright.

"Thank you." He grinned. His moist eyes brightened as he looked at her.

"Not sure where I'd be without you, Nicole. I know it's not what you hope for, but I hope you call this place home."

She grinned.

"Yeah it's not the same. But I do consider you home."

"Nicole?"

"Yes?"

"What happened? I mean, how did you come to be alone? I don't mean to pry, but we've been working together for a long time. I don't understand how a sweetheart like you ended up in such a tough spot."

She looked at Mr. Douglas. The sincerity in his eyes caused her to start to cry. He genuinely cared. When he asked 'How's it going?' he really wanted to know. Finally, she was going to really tell somebody everything. How it all happened.

"We better sit down again."

"You sit. After you get me my walker." He pointed toward the middle of the store, where they had parked his walker.

She grabbed it for him and slid it back to his waiting, trembling hands. As he secured himself and she dropped onto the padded bench, she began thinking about that afternoon she'd sat on an unpadded bench over ten years ago.

"Well, Mr. Douglas. Here goes. The story of my terrible life. Speaking of home, that was my biggest question when I found out I was pregnant with little Jake. Would I have a home? It all began when I met Brian.

Brian was older than Nicole, and he was confident. He had shown up in the area, looking for a place to "find himself" after finishing college.

Maybe it was his maturity that drew her to him, but it was his fun-loving sense of humor that kept her close. In hindsight, Nicole thought, maybe it was her father's emotional distance that made Brian seem so great. Their age gap wasn't large enough to qualify Brian as a cradle robber, but he definitely took advantage of a young girl's imaginations. From the very start, the relationship was never between equals.

Brian was tall and vigorous. He was athletic and friendly. His light brown hair was neatly trimmed, and his perpetual three-day beard made him seem casually cool. Brian was the type of guy who didn't have to try to be popular, it was just part of his personality, like a quick wit or a genuine smile. Brian was great at math, and Nicole both envied and admired his brilliance.

The first two months with Brian had been great, even though Nicole wished they could be together more often. They usually went out for a nice long drive through the forest. Driving back, sleepy and infatuated, Nicole laid her head on Brian's knee and sang along with the songs on the radio. She loved these moments. As time passed, however, those moments decreased, and the dates began to be less romantic.

About two months into the relationship, Brian started asking her to come over to his trailer in the woods. At first, he made it seem romantic. He was going to cook for her. It sounded nice, but after four straight meals of some variation on chicken and rice, the dates devolved into sandwiches and small talk before making out until their lips were sore. Eventually, she grew tired of pushing him off and he got tired of waiting.

Six weeks later, as she held a small stick in the bathroom with a purple "plus" symbol, she knew everything had changed. She was about to tell Brian she was expecting as they reached the entrance to the park where they spent most Saturday afternoons.

"Things have changed for me." Brian said. He was tossing pebbles in the grass as they sat on the support poles for the swinging arm gate at the entrance to the park. The sky was overcast and most of the morning had been drizzling.

"What do you mean?"

"Well, I've been thinking. You know, my parents paid for me to go to college and I probably should be a little more responsible. It's not like I can stay up here forever."

"I know that." Nicole slipped to the ground and walked over to him. He sat there, perched about shoulder high, swinging his lower legs, kicking the post with his heel. She stood beside the post and cautiously touched his foot.

"What are you going to do?" she asked skittishly.

"I don't know," he hopped down and stood half-facing her, half-staring out into the forest behind them. "I thought I'd figure that out up here."

"You can stay until you do?" She half-asked.

He turned completely to face the forest, his back to her, his hands tapping the top of the post.

"I don't know. I don't know what I thought I'd figure out up here.

But, whatever it is, I guess it's not here."

Nicole stared at his shoulders. She stared at the back of his head. He looked like the silhouettes she'd seen on her dad's rifle targets.

She wanted to shoot him, or at least hit him. Instead she asked a question she regretted even as it tumbled out of her mouth. Like some kind of instinctual prehistoric response to a member leaving the clan, she uttered,

"Maybe I can go with you?"

For a moment, he said nothing. He tapped the post once more and then slapped its side.

"Dang it!" He turned to Nicole, his eyes reddening. "I am sorry. I'm not that guy. I think you're great. But..."

The dark sky began to drip. Nicole looked down as large raindrops disappeared into the already damp soil beneath her boots.

What do I say? She thought, digging into the earth with the heel of her boot. *Do I tell him about the baby?*

Cut it off quick. Stop the bleeding. That was dad's advice when things were going south. This time she listened to him.

"Don't bother. Don't pretend. Don't tell me how good or pretty I am. Just go."

The rain fell harder. Nicole's hair was plastered to her head. Her nose dripped rain and the color of her cotton jacket had changed from light blue to navy. Brian looked up at the sky.

"It's not going to stop raining."

"Yeah. Maybe you should just drive me home."

Brian eagerly jumped at the change to get out of the rain - and to stop talking about the relationship ending.

"Ok, wait here, I'll run down and drive back up."

As she stood there, a small soaked slumping silhouette against the majestic wilderness, she began bemoaning the loss of her innocence.

"Well, I guess Dad was right about Brian after all." Her tears joined the torrent of rain, flowing to the ground. "I hope he doesn't say 'I told you so'. Or worse – he doesn't say anything at all."

As they silently drove back to her dad's cabin, she shivered. Brian dropped her off and sped away. She stood under the awning of the small porch, clutching herself, knowing she'd never see him again.

▬▬▬▬▬▬▬▬▬▬▬▬▬▬▬▬▬▬▬▬▬▬▬

"That's terrible." Mr. Douglas whispered. "I'm so sorry."

"It's not your fault," Nicole replied. "A few months after Brian left, I couldn't hide from dad. When I told him, he kicked me out. Another guy I couldn't count on." She half-smiled and looked at the old man beside her. "That's why I say you're my guy. You're the only one who's lasted."

"Thanks sweetie. But I bet there's another guy out there you can count on. Somewhere out there is that little boy of yours. We'll find him. I know we will." Mr. Douglas placed his shaking hand on her knee.

"Do you think this book is true? Do you think time travel is possible?" Thirty-Nine asked Researcher-9.

"It appears genuine." She stuck her finger in the spot where they were reading and turned the book over. "This binding is definitely old enough to be original. Where did Eleven say she found it?"

"In the library. In a section where the room was being remodeled."

"It's not like anything I've seen here before. I wonder if it was buried in the ground under the building?" Researcher-9 opened the book.

"Let's continue reading. We've only got a few more minutes before we need to get to the lab. I told Dr. Nampala I'd do some general attention conditioning exercises with you today."

They turned back to the book and finished reading the final entry in Wesley Kenton's diary:

<u>November 10, 1868</u>. Otak-Tay died last year, and won't be joining me this trip. I am 84 years old now. I never married. I have no children. I've enjoyed many pleasures but none were permanent. The diligence required to maintain this secret has isolated me beyond all expectations. Otak-Tay's friendship made it tolerable. During the early years, we thought it was the greatest gift. Being able to go back and undo things. Being able to set up the future. The money. The treasures. Now I sit with piles of gold around me and no one to talk to. I will be going back this week and I won't return. I want to be with Otak-Tay until I

die. This way, I get nine more years with him. My one friend.

For whoever finds this book, and the keys, please be careful. Altering reality always has unintended consequences. Somehow, I do believe this was meant to be used, for why else would it exist? I digress. As my father said, "Don't ramble. Speak plainly." Here, for whoever uncovers this book, is the plain explanation, as I have experienced it every decade since I was a fourteen-year-old boy.

There is a doorway that opens a corridor that can transport a person into the past. This doorway only opens once every ten years, and it remains open for only two days. You can come and go as many times as you like, but at the end of forty-eight hours it's permanently closed for the next decade.

It opens, by the dates of the American calendar, on November 13. It closes on November 14. I had befriended Otak-Tay, a local savage boy, after moving to the area with my father, who was prospecting for gold. Otak-Tay was the son of an elder in his tribe. Otak-Tay created a handmade copy of the key, taking on a great personal risk, so that I could go back in time and prevent my father's murder. Unfortunately, that event led to other men dying, and Otak-Tay and I became outcasts. Fortunately, we knew of some of the great gold mines and were able to go back and lay claim. The great wealth we horded enabled us to be fortified from vengeance by the families of the men who were killed. It's a brutal thing, murder. Even self-defense is hard when you know that you just caused another man's heart to stop beating.

Undoing one thing always does another.

We later made a second copy of the key, so both Otak-Tay and I had one. Both keys are enclosed. I have made a third copy for my final trip back.

The corridor through time is located in the great willow tree that stands alone. It is easy to identify because there is a perfect circle of open space that surrounds it. From the tree, a man can walk in any direction exactly 500 paces before reaching another tree or bush.

The key fits into a knot in the trunk of the tree, about waist-high on a grown man. Upon placing the key in the knot, a dark hallway will appear to the right side of the tree. Walk into the hallway.

You will find yourself in the same spot, except it will be ten years earlier. Time passes at the same rate. One hour in the past is one hour today.

Perhaps this will never be found. Perhaps it will. To the finder, if such finding happens, be careful. Be discreet. Use the access for good and not evil. It bears repeating:

Undoing one thing always does another.

Sincerely,

WESLEY KENTON

"Does it say where the keys are?" Thirty-Nine whispered.

"No."

She thumbed through the book, looking for any clue as to the keys' whereabouts. Her fingers moved from page to page, her eyes scanning the words for a hint. She kept turning, and Thirty-Nine kept watching, until she reached the back of the book. They both saw the outline of the key at the bottom of the cover.

"That's it!" Thirty-Nine erupted.

Researcher-9 turned the cover over, looking at the inside. She reached into the pocket. It was empty.

"Any keys there?" Thirty-Nine begged, his voice rising with expectation.

"No."

"Well, without a key, we're not going to be able to go."

"Be patient, Thirty-Nine. If Eleven read this, and if there are keys, she probably hid them. She's no dummy."

Her conviction helped him relax. Throughout their conversation, the conviction of her belief that they could escape The Woodlands impressed him and increased his willingness to entertain the reality of the show.

"Ok. Let's say we can find the keys, or figure out a way to make one - Is it possible that's the tree in our Yard?" Thirty-Nine whispered.

"I believe so. The physical description – the open space between it and any other trees - there's a lot to consider." She looked at her watch. "But we are out of time. I've got to get you back up to the main unit for the attention exercises."

Thirty-Nine stepped back from the table. Researcher-9 closed the book and stood also. She held the book as she slid the chairs back into place.

"What day is it?" Thirty-Nine asked as she collected her notebooks and his file and walked around the bench to stand by the door, signaling that it was time to leave.

"It's Friday. You know that." She placed her hand on the knob and twisted, pushing the door and stepping through the doorway.

"I mean," Thirty-Nine replied, following her into the hall. "What day, like the month and year?"

"Oh, sorry." She handed the diary back to him.

"It's November 11, 1998."

As they walked past the library entrance, the halls were empty. There was usually a sentry or two monitoring the corridors. The traffic, other than at meal times, was typically minimal, but rarely nonexistent. Thirty-Nine felt the book against his hip. The urgency of the moment made him extraordinarily sensitive to the book's presence and preventing its detection by anyone.

"Can we stop at my pod before we go to the lab?" he asked, as they climbed the stairs from the lower floor into the main artery of the building.

"Of course."

Thirty-Nine studied Researcher-9 as they walked. She was different from the others. Why? What was her life like before The Woodlands? She spoke with an accent, though Thirty-Nine couldn't place it. Almost every worker spoke with an accent at The Woodlands. Everyone was from a different spot in the world. Homogeny did not exist, at least not in skin color and language. Homogeny did exist: in clothing, the student's haircuts and the doctrine and dogma of The Woodlands.

She carried herself more purposefully than the other workers. Most seemed like automatons, just workers fulfilling orders. She had an intensity she brought to her conversations and Thirty-Nine supposed, to her research as well, that led him to believe she not only knew what she was doing but why she was doing it.

"Where did you grow up?"

They were nearing the main entrance to the dining hall, which meant his pod was about fifteen doors away. Not a sound came from the dining hall. They had not seen a soul during the return trip.

Researcher-9 stopped walking and turned to him. Their eyes met. Hers were moist. A tear dribbled down her right cheek. She looked back down the corridor. It remained empty.

Can you hear me? She thought.

Thirty-Nine nodded.

I am from Belarus, near the border of Ukraine. It has forests like here but no mountains. The people are generous. It was a hard life but simple.

As they moved down the hall, Researcher-9's deliberate pace slowed Thirty-Nine's naturally swifter movement.

"How did you get here?"

During the months after our independence from Russia, I followed some other science students to Minsk, the capital. We heard rumors of American companies pouring in to hire people with high math and science proficiencies. It turned out to be a small job fair, hosted by some United Nations group. I ended up being hired by what I thought was a research & development arm of a pharmaceutical company. Obviously, The Woodlands isn't that.

As they approached his pod, she realized she didn't have the key-card or the code for opening his door.

"I need to buzz for a sentry," she said.

As she reached in her pocket for the paging device to call the sentry, a figure appeared at the corner of the hall.

"That's not necessary."

They both looked up, startled. Two sentries approached them. Thirty-Nine thought how dull-faced they appeared, especially after spending time with Researcher-9.

"Dr. Nampala wants to see you."

"Ok." Researcher-9 replied. She turned to Thirty-Nine.

"We'll pick up your studies after I finish my meeting with Dr. Nampala." Researcher-9 said. She turned to the guard. "Sentry-2, can you open the student's door?"

"No. Dr. Nampala wants to see both of you."

The book, Thirty-Nine thought. He broke protocol.

"Umm, can I please go in and use the restroom real quick?" He pressed his legs together to reinforce the emergency.

The sentries looked at each other. Sentry-2 seemed to be in charge. He looked at Thirty-Nine, his unibrow highlighting his dark, deep-set eyes.

"No. You'll have to wait. Dr. Nampala wants to see both of you. Now."

The sentries moved into formation. The shorter one took the lead, with Sentry-2 walking behind Thirty-Nine and Researcher-9.

"I really need to go." Thirty-Nine pleaded.

"Show some restraint. Don't speak of it again!" Sentry-2 commanded, slapping Thirty-Nine on the back of the head.

He grunted in response to the surprise and slight pain of the slap. The smack angered him but he held his tongue.

The reached the end of the hall. The elevator doors opened, and they shuffled in.

As the doors closed, Researcher-9 thought, *Slip me the book when we walk out. I can keep it hidden in the binders.*

Thirty-Nine slowly prodded the book up and out of his waistband. The second floor passed and the elevator slowed to a stop. The last light over the door illuminated and a muted metallic ding announced the arrival at Floor 3. He held the book under his tunic. It was pinned against his ribs with his upper arm. He clasped his hands in front of his waist to avoid appearing stiff.

The doors slid open, and even the sentries seemed shocked at Dr. Nampala's presence. He was at the entrance to the elevator.

Hold on to the book, Researcher-9 thought.

"Hello, Head Student." He nodded to the group. "Researcher-9." Dr. Nampala's tone was intense. He focused on Thirty-Nine.

"I trust you've had a good first day as the top pupil of The Woodlands."

The sentries stood inside the elevator as Thirty-Nine and Researcher-9 walked out.

"Yes sir. I have." Thirty-Nine could feel a rush through his skin. His face tinged red. All he could think about was the book.

"Your face looks flushed. Are you feeling well?" They paused in the hall outside the elevator. Dr. Nampala, fortunately, was on Thirty-Nine's left side. The Chief touched him on the left shoulder and looked in Thirty-Nine's yellowish eyes like a physician beginning a routine physical exam.

"I'm feeling ok. I really need to use the restroom, though."

"Are you sure that's all?"

"Yes sir." He rocked from side to side and pressed his legs together to emphasize the point.

"Well, let's go." He turned toward the elevator. "Sentries, you may return to your rounds." Dr. Nampala was wearing a blue lab coat, with the sleeves pushed up, exposing his wiry arms. He lifted his arms with a flourish and pointed down the hall.

"After you!"

Thirty-Nine stepped forward, sweat forming around the edges of his hair line as he tried to move fluidly while keeping the book pinned to his side. Researcher-9 came to his rescue, for the first time – to his knowledge – but certainly not the last.

"Dr. Nampala." She moved between Thirty-Nine and Nampala, turning her back to Thirty-Nine.

"Yes?"

As she began speaking to Dr. Nampala, Thirty-Nine took advantage of the distraction. He quickly slid his left hand under his tunic and worked the book back into the waistband of his pants.

"I was in the process of taking Thirty-Nine to the lab for the conditioning exercises you ordered."

"So you were." He rubbed his narrow bearded chin. Its scraggliness and general unclean appearance made Thirty-Nine feel like a rodent was close by.

"But, I decided this morning that we can proceed with the work we began yesterday. I've relocated the equipment to my office. I want to be intimately involved in the development of this project. And so, when Thirty-Nine returns from the restroom, we will begin. Now, let's go. Researcher-9, go into my office. Researcher-4 is already in there with Eleven."

"Eleven?" Researcher-9 asked the question that Thirty-Nine thought.

"Yes, she's had enough rest. She didn't even have to do any chores last night or this morning." His voice slowed and became deeper. He glared at Researcher-9, remembering yesterday's disagreement. "She's fine. Do you have a problem with this assignment?"

Researcher-9 looked down briefly. She composed herself and stared back at his bespectacled eyes. "No sir."

"Good, then get going." He turned to Thirty-Nine. "The restroom is right there." He extended his bony index finger and pointed to a pewter-colored windowless door a few steps down the hall. "I'll wait here for you."

"Yes sir." Thirty-Nine and Researcher-9 walked in opposite directions away from the elevator entrance.

Ditch the book, she thought.

He pushed the metal door inward and walked into a small wash-room. He pulled the book out of his pants and scanned the room for a hiding place. The painted cinder-block walls were bare of any decoration. The floor was clean white tile with gray grout. A single porcelain sink was located immediately inside the door, to the right. The ceiling was made of simple two feet square fiberglass tiles, held in place by an aluminum criss-cross frame. Two circular recessed lights illuminated the entire space.

He walked four steps to the other side of the room. A single metal toilet was installed in the left corner, with no barrier of any kind between it and the rest of the room.

There is no place to stash this. He slapped the dark leather cover with his hand in frustration. *Dr. Nampala's waiting. I'm not good at deviant activity. Thirty-Three would instinctively know how to hide this book. What would Thirty-Three do?*

No answer came and time was passing. If he stayed in there much longer, Dr. Nampala might become concerned; or worse, suspicious. He looked behind the toilet. Just empty space. He looked back up at the ceiling. *Of course. It's the only logical choice.*

The ceiling was far too high to reach. He stepped up on the toilet seat and balanced himself, touching the wall lightly with his right hand. He still held the book in his left hand. Stretching as high as he could, he quickly realized he was still far from being able to touch the ceiling tiles.

The sink. It was the only other potential ladder in the room. Thirty-Nine hopped down and rushed over to the sink. He wedged the book between the faucet and the wall.

The sink hung from the wall just below his chest. He clutched at the inside edge and pulled, lifting his feet off the floor. His legs swung under the sink. As his feet collided with the wall, he pushed hard against it, forcing his body higher. As his waist crossed the edge of sink frame, he rolled over and was now seated crossway on the sink. He grabbed the spigot with his left hand and pushed himself upright. Standing on the sink, he felt a brief rush of excitement.

I can do sneaky things, too!

Thirty-Nine grabbed the book and pushed up the ceiling tile above the sink. He couldn't reach high enough to see into the area above the ceiling, so he tucked the book onto the tile next to the opening, and slid the open tile back almost completely into place. A small sliver of open space between the tile and the frame remained unnoticed by Thirty-Nine.

He hopped down, brushed his clothes and walked into the hallway.

Dr. Nampala was waiting. "Everything ok, boy?"

"Yes sir."

"Let's go. You're my Head Student. Don't let me down."

"Yes sir."

As he followed Dr. Nampala into the office, he noticed things were different from the special morning breakfast he had shared with Eleven. The long table was gone; in its place was a bank of monitors and control equipment. The space was full of shimmering screens blinking with a variety of information, black dials and knobs in chrome frames.

Several long wooden poles with leather straps nailed to the end were leaned in the corner between the wall and the row of monitors. He stared at them for a moment. Each pole had six leather straps, each about four feet long, drilled into the end. He had heard about the whips from Thirty-Three but had never experienced their sting.

"Let's get started," Dr. Nampala announced from behind him. "Researcher-9, are you ready?"

"Yes sir." Researcher-9 was standing to the left. Behind her on an elevated bed, Eleven was strapped in. The bed was elevated and tilted allowing Thirty-Nine could see her face and body. He gasped audibly in response to her appearance.

Her left cheek had a two-finger width bruise that covered her face from the bridge of her nose all the way to her earlobe. Her right eye was swollen and her lower lip was cut in several places, the newly formed scab still moist.

"Something wrong, Thirty-Nine?" Dr. Nampala asked.

"Sir?" He turned to his left, facing Dr. Nampala. The look in Dr. Nampala's eyes was threatening, almost as though he was hoping Thirty-Nine would answer incorrectly.

"I said," Dr. Nampala drew closer to Thirty-Nine, accosting his nostrils with the odor of a freshly smoked cigarette. "Is something wrong?"

As much as he wanted to tell the Chief how upset he was at Eleven's condition, now was not the time to pick a fight. He crinkled his nose and blinked. "No sir. Nothing's wrong."

"Good. It's good to know that my new Head Student -" he paused and repeated himself, projecting his voice toward Eleven's bed, "my new Head Student doesn't have a problem with minor injuries." He looked down at Thirty-Nine. "Or major injuries, either."

Thirty-Nine nodded, his insides boiling with fear and anger.

He walked over to his cot, positioned beside Eleven's. As he approached her, she grabbed the edge of the bed as if to strengthen her resolve. She struggled to open her eyes fully, especially her right eye, with its puffed out eyebrow. She looked directly at him though, and her gaze communicated determination.

"Hello, Head Student," she said in a whispered, cracking voice. Her lower lip oozed blood as she spoke.

"I'm sorry." Thirty-Nine replied, feeling an impulse to wrap his arms around her. Until this week, he would never have thought to give someone a hug. His emotional side's influence was growing with each passing moment.

"Get into position," Dr. Nampala commanded, still standing near the center of the room.

Researcher-9 stood on the outside edge of the setup, waiting for Thirty-Nine to climb into his bed. Researcher-4 was seated at the foot of Eleven's bed with a small electronic device on her lap. A stack of papers sat on a small metal table beside her.

Thirty-Nine climbed onto the bed and lay on his back. While Researcher-9 secured the straps across his legs, arms and midsection, he stared through the glass ceiling at the clouds overhead. It was mid-morning yet the sky's subdued light appeared like it was dusk. The gray had already settled in for the fall season, and sustained sunlight wouldn't return until June of the following year. By then, they'd either be free or dead.

"Student secure."

The whispering whirr of the bed's motor alerted Thirty-Nine that he was about to be moved. The bed tilted him up to the same position as Eleven. As it halted its progression, he was brought into Dr. Nampala's line of sight.

"Begin sequence." Dr. Nampala ordered, still stationed midway across the room. He stood, arms crossed, eyes fixed on the two students. Thirty-Nine looked at him. He had always seen the Chief as sort of a benevolent dictator. Thirty-Nine always assumed that the students who were punished got what they deserved. His impression of Dr. Nampala had changed. He was not benevolent. He was just a dictator. Their eyes met. Thirty-Nine tried to avoid conveying any emotion. He stared blankly at Dr. Nampala. Dr. Nampala stared back, shifting his hands to his chin, rubbing that scraggly beard again.

Let's see how far Thirty-Nine can be pushed. His mind is strong. The genetic report from Specialist-3 on his mother was clear. No health concerns. It's good she's local. Saved time, which we don't have much of. What should I use to accelerate the dream sequence?

That's the Chief's voice, he thought, his eyes opening wider at Dr. Nampala's thoughts, which coincided with the discomfort of the injections. He counted, like always. *First shot, right forearm; second shot, left shoulder; third shot, neck.*

"Add chlorpromazine to their injections. I want to deepen the dream state."

The suction cup latched onto the back of Thirty-Nine's head, the weight of the cable between his and Eleven's head tugged slightly, causing the metal brackets to dig more deeply into his fuzzy scalp.

"Yes sir," answered Researcher-4.

My mother's local. She's close by, Thirty-Nine thought, his mind quickly becoming as cloudy as the sky overhead. Fifteen seconds later, he was fully sedated.

"Are you here?" Eleven was standing near an old church courtyard. The top of a short, broken-down stone wall mirrored the undulations of the earth, preventing her from entering the open square. There had been no open field this time. No wandering about, searching for Thirty-Nine. No bus hurtling toward her. Not yet, anyway.

Thirty-Nine opened his eyes. The sky was always bright blue in his dreams. He stood still for a moment, gaining his bearings. He scanned the area around him. The church was a few hundred feet away, to his left.

Easy so far, he thought.

Eleven leaned against the wall, picking at the crumbling mortar. She rolled bits of it into powder between her fingers. "I'll just wait for him. I'm in the right place. I think."

Thirty-Nine walked across the open grass. Within a dozen steps, he spotted Eleven, slouched against the wall.

"Eleven!" he started running toward her.

She stood up straight. "Over here!" she called out unnecessarily.

As Thirty-Nine reached her, his breathing labored, he waited a minute to speak.

"You need more exercise!" She laughed as he stood beside her, hands on his knees, trying to catch his breath.

He straightened up, hands on his hips. He exhaled and inhaled a few more times before speaking. Finally, he responded.

"You seem to be in good spirits. Are you ok?"

"I'm banged up a bit. But I'll be fine."

She looked great. No bruise, no swollen eye, no bloody lip.

"Dreams sure do bring out the best in appearance." Thirty-Nine said, reminded again of her natural beauty. "You look great."

"Thanks, Head Student. Enough small talk. Let's get in the building and see if I can get a visual on the man in your dream."

————————————————————————————————

"All activity is stable," Researcher-4 declared.

"Good. The additional minerals and pharmaceutical enhancements are working." Dr. Nampala now stood near the beds, between Researcher-4 and Researcher-9, both seated at the foot of their respective students' bed.

"Researcher-9," he continued, "have you been able to get the interface enabled for full transcription?"

"Not yet, sir. I have two technicians working full time on it. We are able to recreate imagery. But actual conversation is still not available. We are finally able to create a sort of silent movie of today's dreams. By next week, though, we should be able to add the student's conversation with each other, and introduce the additional dream characters."

"Ok." For once this week, Dr. Nampala did not seem upset or annoyed with Researcher-9. It surprised her a little, especially since she was already on edge, hoping no one would discover her decision to help the students try to escape.

"What's the turnaround time for producing the movie of today's dream?"

"Less than twelve hours, sir."

"So, I can watch it late tonight?"

"Yes sir."

"Ok. I'm going to review some data at my desk. Continue this dream sequence for the full two hours. Regardless of student discomfort."

"Yes sir."

He turned and began walking away then stopped a few feet from them. "Oh, Researcher-9, do you have Thirty-Nine's acquisition file with you?"

"Yes sir. I have it."

"I need it – I've got an update to add to the file. Specialist-3 collected some genetic data and photographs from Thirty-Nine's mother."

Thirty-Nine's mother? Researcher-9 froze. *He is one of the only locally extracted students. Could she still be in the area?*

"Researcher-9!"

"Yes sir?"

"The file." Dr. Nampala turned toward her, reaching out his slender soft hand.

"Sorry. Yes sir." She fumbled with the notebooks on the table beside her. She pulled out the slim folder that contained all that she knew about Thirty-Nine's past and gave it to Dr. Nampala.

He walked away from the two researchers. They diligently continued to monitor their students' vital signs, as well as various charts and figures that appeared every so often on the screens around them.

Researcher-9 stared at the heart rate monitor above Thirty-Nine's head. Its methodical peak and valley rhythm made her think of the mountains around them. She liked to stand in the Yard during her breaks and stare at the snow-capped peaks, when the sky was clear. She wondered what might be out there, and what might happen if they actually were able to break free from The Woodlands iron grip.

Thirty-Nine led Eleven silently over to the arch that served as the entrance to the courtyard. They stepped through and he approached the statue near the center of the courtyard, as always. Eleven followed closely behind him. Neither was sure about the rules, having never shared a dream with anyone. Could they change the outcome by acting differently?

Thirty-Nine was content to operate as he always had. After so many repeats of this dream, he really wanted to see the man who always took the lady down the aisle. He rested his hand on the chest of the angel statue that served as the frame for the small fountain that collected rainwater.

He looked up. He motioned for Eleven to follow him, without looking at her. They approached the large wooden doors together: he feeling anxious for the possibility of discovery to follow, she feeling ambivalent about the task and eager to get to her dream.

They walked up a couple small stone steps and Thirty-Nine, as always, reached out for the large oval iron handles that hung on the thick wooden door. He tugged on it, but unlike every other time, the door did not open. It didn't budge.

"That's strange." He grabbed it again, with both hands, and jerked. All he got in return was a strained shoulder. "Ouch," he rubbed his shoulder and stepped back from the door. He stared at it as he continued to massage his upper arm.

Eleven stood beside him, looking at the door.

"Maybe it's locked?" she offered.

He looked over at her. Then back at the door. "It's never been locked before." He looked below the handle. The outline of a small key was etched into the dark wood.

"I have the key." Eleven said matter-of-factly.

Thirty-Nine was confused. "There's never been a key needed. That shape was never there before."

"I have the key." Eleven ignored his confusion and approached the door. She pulled a key out of her pocket and held it up for Thirty-Nine to see. "I said I have the key. See?"

As she held it up, it blocked the sunlight shining from behind Eleven. It glowed as the rays flickered around it, reaching for Thirty-Nine's eyes. He squinted as he looked at it. It was the same color as the door, made of wood. It appeared hand-carved.

"Ok, go ahead, I guess."

Eleven reached out and pressed the key into the outline in the door. As she did, they both heard the sound of wind rushing through the courtyard. The door disappeared momentarily, and a long hallway appeared. At the far end stood the lady who had been in front of the building from yesterday's dream. Next to her stood the man who'd saved Eleven from the bus. They both waved at the students.

And then, as quickly as it appeared, the hallway was gone and the door was before them.

"Did you see them?" Thirty-Nine asked.

"Yes."

— —

"Both heart rates just spiked." Researcher-4 said.

"I saw." Researcher-9 replied. "How's Eleven doing today?"

"Focus on Thirty-Nine. I'll take care of Eleven." Researcher-4 replied, turning her back to Researcher-9.

"Fine. But, if you let her die..."

"What?" Researcher-4 spun around on her stool. "What are you going to do? Tell someone? Why don't you do your research like the rest of us? Do you think you're better than everyone else because you're nice to the students?"

"No."

"Then just do your work. Or, I can tell someone" – she motioned to Dr. Nampala's desk – "that you are a potential violator of The Woodlands strict no fraternization policies."

"Ok, ok. I'm trying to preserve the work, that's all. I'd hate to lose a student when we're this close to a possible breakthrough."

—————————————————————————————————

Thirty-Nine and Eleven pulled the door open together, their hands overlapping as they grabbed the wrought iron handle. As they stepped inside the lobby, Thirty-Nine held the door open. Eleven looked at the marble floors and the alabaster walls.

"It looks like the medieval castles from our history class." She spoke in a reverent whisper.

"Yes, it does," Thirty-Nine answered over his shoulder, still holding the door ajar as he stared at the space below the outside handle. He rubbed the worn wood with his small fingers, searching for an indentation.

"The key is gone. The hole where the key went is gone."

Eleven turned back to him and looked at his hand, which was now scrubbing the door, as if the friction would make the key appear.

"So it is. But, I already told you." She stepped closer to him, and began pushing the door closed. He yanked his hand away to avoid getting pinched. As the door sealed behind them, she leaned against it, crossing her feet and folding her arms.

"I already told you." She smiled slightly. "I have the key. Actually, two of them. Not just for this door, but for the other door."

"Oh. The *key*." Thirty-Nine nodded as he slowly repeated the words.

"Is everyone ready?" The voice of an older woman echoed from down a hallway into the space where they stood, still next to the front door.

"The ladies are coming!" Thirty-Nine grabbed Eleven's arm and dragged her across to the second entrance, near the wooden stand on which the velvet book rested.

He pushed her flat against the wall. "Stay here."

He quickly stood on his toes and read the third line on the page of the open book.

To Nicole and Corey: Against all odds, true love remains!
Your friend, Bruce.

"What am I doing?" Eleven whispered.

"Stay there. When the ladies go in, follow them, but stay on the right side. You should be able to see the man."

Thirty-Nine scrambled furiously to the far left of the lobby. He flattened himself against a small section of paneling that framed a small stained-glass window above his head.

Sure enough, four women entered through the hallway across the lobby from where he is standing: two heavy-set older women wearing simple black dresses, followed by two young women in crimson dresses, outlined in white lace. Each of the younger women is holding a bouquet of carnations, lilies and spray roses.

The two older ladies begin to walk toward the entrance to the chapel. The younger women stand single file in the lobby, waiting.

Eleven kneels on one leg, crouching with her arm slung over her bent knee, like a cat waiting to pounce. The wooden lectern is a poor shelter from the eyes of the ladies in the lobby, yet no one sees her. As the two plump gray-haired ladies solemnly pull open the doors and fix them open with a hook and eye mechanism bolted to the wall, Eleven holds her breath.

As the door is being propped open, Eleven could practically touch the lady closest to her. The smell of her over-sprayed perfume fills Eleven's nostrils, causing a near-sneeze. She quickly covered her nose and mouth with her hand, her long fingers extending beyond her cheekbone as she pinched her nose shut with her thumb and the base of her first finger. She glances over at Thirty-Nine.

He waits for the beautiful bride. As they reunite for what feels like the thousandth time, she smiles again and Thirty-Nine feels elevated. He approaches the entryway with her, arm-in-arm, and looks at Eleven.

Eleven is calmly squatting, waiting for the arrival of the man.

As Thirty-Nine steps and tumbles over the threshold, Eleven sees the man appear. Like a ghost, the man is instantly there. He did not walk up. Eleven gasps.

She watches Thirty-Nine fall and the man grab him. As the man steadies Thirty-Nine, Eleven stares at his face. He is older than them, but he is young. His brown eyes are kind and his smile is sincere. He has short-cropped hair, parted on one side. Eleven's eyes trace his face from his narrow forehead around his cheeks to the line of his cleft chin.

He's handsome, she thinks. She blinks and his back is turned, leading the woman down the aisle.

Thirty-Nine looks up as they walk away.

"I saw him!" Eleven exclaimed.

Thirty-Three was restless. He had been waiting for this day for nearly a week. Finally relieved of his restrictions, he was desperate to talk to Thirty-Nine and Eleven about everything they had discovered. About what they might be able to do. About the show.

Instead, they were Dr. Nampala's new pet project and he was stuck using his free time between the morning's logic accentuation class and lunch in his pod doing nothing. He laid on the floor between his bed and Thirty-Nine's, lobbing a rubber ball against the ceiling, catching it as it caromed back to him.

"Wonder what they are doing?"

He was engaged in a running monologue. Dr. Nampala had once told Thirty-Three that he was a verbal thinker, which meant his analysis benefited from speaking through a problem. Right now his biggest problem was a lack of information. Not knowing made him as neurotic as a hypochondriac with an empty medicine cabinet.

"I don't have to know everything. Just enough to know we are actually going to go through with the show." He tossed the ball halfway toward the ceiling. "I hate waiting. This is ridiculous." He stood up in disgust and slammed the ball to the ground. It ricocheted back harder than he expected, smacking him in the chin. As the ball hit his jaw, his teeth snapped shut, biting his tongue.

"Owww!" He grabbed his mouth. "Dang it!" He slid a couple fingers into his mouth and pulled them out. A small streak of bloody saliva greeted him as he stared at his chubby fingers.

"Great. This is Thirty-Nine's fault. If he was here I wouldn't be wasting time bouncing a ball." He looked up at the clock over the door. "11:37. He should be here soon."

He looked down at the ball. It was on the rug under his feet, its seams forming a crooked smile, as if mocking him. He kicked it under his bed.

"Stupid ball."

He walked over to the desk and sat in the small chair. "What would I do if we did get out of here?" He leaned back and closed his eyes, imagining the pictures he'd seen in some of the books on civilizations.

"The zigg – oh, what was that thing called? A ziggurat? Yes, I think so," he answered himself and then continued plotting his future. "I'd build a ziggurat. It would be a mighty brick tower that reached the sky. The only people allowed in would be my friends."

He stood back up and began pacing the area between the desk and the shower stall, near the doorway. "Forget the ziggurat. I want to go on an airplane. That's the first thing I want to do. Fly. Fly high and free to a place where no one could tell me what to do. A place where there were no restrictions! I wonder if there is such a place?"

As he continued to visualize the potential opportunities that might come his way should they escape The Woodlands, an announcement echoed through the halls:

"TEN MINUTES TO LUNCH"

"Ten minutes." Thirty-Three repeated. "Thirty-Nine should be here by now." He started to worry. After yesterday's session, Eleven hadn't been at any meals. Now Thirty-Nine was late.

What if something happened to Thirty-Nine?
He walked back to the desk. He stared at the Mind Cocoon bag. He rubbed its shiny nylon exterior.

"Thirty-Nine can't be hurt. He's too important for the show. He's got all the brains." He looked down at his hefty midsection. "And, I've got all the brawn." He smiled as he patted his sides with both hands and then flexed his right arm, rubbing it with his left.

"Yes sir; I've got the brawn."

The door beeped and opened, revealing a self-adulating Thirty-Three to a sentry and Thirty-Nine.

"What are you doing?"

Thirty-Three turned around and saw his podmate.

"Eight minutes until lunch departure," the sentry said as the door closed behind Thirty-Nine.

Thirty-Three ran to Thirty-Nine, hugging him. After an extended embrace, he stepped back and looked him over. "You're ok? You're not hurt?"

"I'm fine. Other than my ribs you just crushed." He held out his arms. "You want to inspect me for damage?"

Thirty-Three laughed. "No, I believe you. I was worried, that's all. It seemed like you would never get back here. Where have you been? What have you been doing? Where is Eleven? Can we still plan the show?"

The barrage of questions made Thirty-Nine feel like he was getting pounded in the face by a thundering waterfall.

"Relax," he said, walking over to his bed. "I've only been awake for ten minutes. Things are still a little foggy up here." He pointed to his head and flopped onto the bed. He lay sideways, propping his head against the wall, his feet dangling off the side of the bed.

"Ok, I'll try to relax," Thirty-Three replied, following him over to the bed. He stood between Thirty-Nine's feet. "But, I've been waiting. What happened this morning? I don't know what's going on."

"Just give me a second." He scowled at Thirty-Three, who was stationed between his knees, practically leaning over him. "And give me some room to breathe. Please." He closed his eyes and took deep breaths, every exhale purging his brain of the haze of medicated sleep.

"Sorry." Thirty-Three moved back and stood in between the two beds. He waited as long as he could. He looked up at the clock. It was 11:54. They would be leaving for lunch in a few minutes. He couldn't wait any longer.

"Please. Tell me what's happening."

Thirty-Nine opened his eyes and slowly sat up on the bed. His feet hit the floor and he tilted forward, placing his hands on his knees.

"Ok. Sit." He ordered Thirty-Three, who promptly sat down on the edge of his own bed.

"A lot of stuff happened today. Researcher-9 is supportive of our plan to esca... I mean our plan for the show."

Thirty-Three's eyes bugged out. He slapped his mattress. "Researcher-9! Are you serious?"

"Yes. Seventeen gave me the book from Eleven and I read it with Researcher-9 in a secret passage near the library."

"Secret passage?"

"We have to go to lunch in a couple minutes. I'll tell you the main points."

"Ok." Thirty-Three leaned forward, his face in his hands, eagerly anticipating the news.

"The book is real. The time corridor is real. It will be opening in two days. It will stay open for only two days. It's complicated but Eleven has the keys to gain access. She told me in the dream sequence today. And Researcher-9 thinks, and so do I, that the access point is the willow tree in the center of the Yard."

"Wow. Unbelievable." Thirty-Three stood and started pacing toward the door.

"That's not all." Thirty-Nine continued.

The alarm bell sounded, notifying them that it was time to go to lunch.

"What else?" Thirty-Three asked, turning to face his podmate.

Thirty-Nine stepped closer to him, and lowered his voice. "Researcher-9 says if we don't get out of here, we're either going to be slaves to some criminals or; more likely, because the Chief can't get his experiments to work right, everyone at The Woodlands will be killed."

"Unbelievable! I knew this place wasn't our home!"

"The final piece of the puzzle," Thirty-Nine continued, "is the man in my dream – in Eleven's dream. After today's session, Researcher-9 told me she is going to print the images of both the lady in my dream and the man in our dreams. It might turn out that he's not just the man in our dreams, but the man of our dreams."

"I didn't know you were such a romantic." Thirty-Three laughed.

"We'll see if I'm right. Either way, it's time to start the show."

November Thirteen, Nineteen-**EIGHTY**-Eight

9:18 AM

"How are you feeling, Nicole?" Aunt Rita stepped inside the camper door and held it open with one arm. She set a small cardboard box on the floor beside Nicole's bed, and began shaking the sleet off her ragged red plaid overcoat, trying to brush the dampness out into the morning mist. She unwound the thick brown scarf Nicole had knitted for her a month earlier, when the days started getting noticeably shorter.

"Tired." Nicole rolled over to face Aunt Rita.

"Well, you should be. You must have gotten up to pee a dozen times last night." She closed the door and dropped her coat and scarf onto the back of the bench seat. She picked up the cardboard box and stepped to the small sink along the back wall.

"I'm sorry. Did I wake you up?"

"It's alright darling. You can't help it."

Nicole looked down at the enormous hump under her patchwork quilt caused by her pregnant stomach. She reached under her fleece jacket, the two hand-me-down men's t-shirts, and felt the stretched skin of her midsection.

"This baby's got to come soon."

"He will. When he's ready." Aunt Rita said opening the box, and pulling out two jars of peanut butter, a box of saltines, half a dozen cans of tuna fish and three bruised apples. "I got the next few days' groceries from the food pantry at the Methodist church."

Nicole sat up quickly. "Aunt Rita, that's four miles away!"

"Well, I was awake – so I thought I'd get an early start." She reached into the dark stained wooden cabinet overhead and pulled out a quarter loaf of bread. "Peanut butter sandwich?"

"What time did you leave?"

"Oh, about 4:30." She stepped toward Nicole, handing her the plastic jar of peanut butter. "Can you open this? My arthritis…" She massaged her weathered hands and looked down at Nicole. "Besides, it's a good thing I got there early. There wasn't much left from yesterday's collection. The minister said four more families moved to the city last week. There's barely enough churchgoers left to keep having services, much less pay for basic church bills and the minister's salary."

"We should move to the city." Nicole stood up and handed her the opened peanut butter jar. She stumbled past Aunt Rita, and squeezed into the broom closet-sized bathroom. She didn't bother shutting the door as she sat on the beige plastic toilet.

Aunt Rita glanced toward her, seeing nothing but bent knees and bare legs, swaddled at the feet by the rumpled fabric of grey P.E. issued sweatpants.

"We don't need to move to the city. That place is chaos. It's so peaceful here."

"Well, I'm not staying here forever. Just so you know." Nicole grunted as she stretched for the single-ply toilet paper.

Rita turned back to the bread and peanut butter. She spread it thickly on one slice, thinly on another. She pulled a Swiss-army knife out of her pocket and cut one apple in quarters. She placed three quarters on the scratched blue plastic plate that held the thick peanut buttered-slice of bread.

"Your breakfast is ready, dear," she announced, choosing to ignore the topic of Nicole leaving Port Mashton. She grabbed the flower-patterned dish that held her slice of bread and put her quarter of the apple on it. She set both plates on the pressboard fold out table that was no wider than two ironing boards.

Nicole walked out of the bathroom as Rita walked out of the camper to get a fresh jug of filtered rainwater from the tank in the field behind them.

"I don't want to go without you." Nicole called after her. She scooted sideways into the small bench under the table. She looked down and picked one apple quarter off her plate.

"Aunt Rita," she said to herself softly, placing the quarter on Rita's plate, "always looking out for me. Like the mom I never had. Like the dad I never had, too."

She propped her elbows on the table and rested her face in her hands, peeking through the metal slats that lined the screened window to her left. She could see Aunt Rita, walking in the mushy grass and moss toward the clever water collection tank Rita had built.

Looking back at her bulging stomach, she whispered, "I hope I can look out for you as well as she looks out for me."

November Thirteen, Nineteen-**EIGHTY**-Eight

10:00 AM

Thirty-Three was standing in the Yard. The show had begun. Almost every student was in class. He'd volunteered to help the twenty or so eight-year-olds with the monthly yard weeding so he could get near the tree. The show producers, Researcher-9, Eleven and Thirty-Nine, had agreed he was the logical choice as the one to go back. Eleven and Thirty-Nine were in the middle of twice-daily dream sequencing sessions with Dr. Nampala. Plus, he was the most adventurous and quick-thinking student in the whole place.

Thirty-Three was going back in time to find either Thirty-Nine's mother or the guy in his dream. The guy who'd rescued Eleven from death and rescued Thirty-Nine from falling might be the one to rescue them all from Dr. Nampala. At least that was Researcher-9's theory. It was an outlandish idea, but it was all they had. And he only had two days to make it happen.

He couldn't go to the police ten years in the past to report Dr. Nampala because there wouldn't be any crime to report, yet. The Woodlands wouldn't open for another month.

He waited until the sentry was on the other side of the Yard. He walked to the willow tree.

He felt the key that Eleven had given him in his pudgy hand. The other key would remain in her bag for safe-keeping. He began to sweat as he slipped under the dangling branches and felt the trunk for the space to slip in the key. He found it and lined up the edges. He pressed it in and a dark corridor appeared.

"Oh my gosh." He whispered. He looked over his shoulder at the leaves behind him. He was completely hidden from view.

"Let's hope I don't die." He whispered. He took a step and found himself standing in the Yard.

"That didn't work." He looked around. "I didn't feel anything. But something feels different." He rubbed his buzzed head and knelt down. He looked out at the Yard.

The other kids weren't there. He stepped through the branches. The sentries weren't there. No one was there.

"Did it work?" He stepped back under the branches and pulled on the wooden key. It easily slipped out of the trunk and into his stubby fingers. He stood alone, holding a wooden key, in an overgrown yard beside the abandoned weather observation center that would become The Woodlands.

He rubbed it and stared at it, his chewed down nails lined with dirt from the morning's work.

"It worked." He looked around. The squishy ground was bare of vegetation and covered with pinecones and small boulders. "It worked!" He shouted and waved his arms overhead. His body jiggled as he jumped up and down.

"It worked! It worked! It worked!"

He ran in circles, bounding across the field as his shoes tramped over the sloshy earth below, spraying wet dirt onto the pinecones and patches of field grass. The key remained clenched in his hand, which was lifted high overhead as he slowed his circling. Out of breath, he bent over and clutched the legs of his pants.

He looked at the ground below him, which minutes before had been filled with wood chips beneath a large iron swingset.

"Wow," he panted. "The book was right." He stood up and looked at the key. "I better put you in a safe place. I've got two hours to do some scouting and get back."

He unzipped a small pocket in the center of his overalls and deposited the key. As he zipped it closed, he heard the sound of crinkling paper. *The pictures!* He reached into the larger open pocket behind the zipper pocket and pulled out two folded squares of paper. He unfolded the pages, revealing two photographs.

The first page held two pictures that looked like mug shots. A simple head-on close up and a profile picture of a frazzled young woman. Her shoulder-length hair was wavy and absent of shine. Her expression was bemused, her eyes full of skepticism, as though she was a celebrity and the photographer was a polite member of the paparazzi. Thirty-Three studied her face, memorizing her square chin, her deep-set brown eyes. She had a mole near the outside edge of her right eyebrow. "That's a good mark to look for," he noted.

"Ok, Nicole Trafston," he declared holding the other page up alongside it, "and, and...unnamed guy, it's time to find you – either of you!"

Thirty-Three studied the picture of the unnamed man. "Green eyes, sandy brown hair. Looks to be in his early twenties, about the same age as Researcher-9. But what's his distinctive mark?"

Thirty-Three held the picture closer and scanned the image, trying to identify a unique feature that would help him locate Thirty-Nine's potential stepfather. "Looks like a small scar across his cheek. Not much of a mark, though."

The small timer in his pants pocket beeped, alerting him that he'd already been in the past for five minutes, and only had one hour and fifty minutes remaining. With luck, the sentries wouldn't notice his absence, and he'd be able to scout the area for a return trip in the afternoon.

"I better get going." He stuffed the pictures back into his pocket and started walking away from the weather observation station. Based on Researcher-9's investigation, he was about two miles west of a small community called Port Mashton, Washington. Built on a point that juts out into Puget Sound, during the early and mid 1900's, it had been a bustling logging town. When the mill closed in 1975, most of the people left. A few hundred remained, and Thirty-Three hoped, for the sake of nearly one hundred stolen children and their families, that the young man in the picture was one of them.

As he walked closer to the overgrown driveway that would lead him out to the road to Port Mashton, he paused. He looked back at the Yard. He stared at the empty, run-down building that had been his home for as long as he could remember. "Right about here is the fence line. My whole life, I've never been able to walk any further." He jumped over the spot and started running, the wind rushing by his face, the trees a blur. Tears of joy flowed down his puffy cheeks.

"Never again, Dr. Nampala, never again!" he shouted, echoing the joy of freedom through the woods.

November Thirteen, Nineteen-**EIGHTY**-Eight

10:30 AM

"I've got to get down to the coffee shop, my shift starts at eleven today." Nicole was struggling to pull on her boots. Every time she bent over, her lungs squished like a sponge under the pressure of her baby-filled stomach.

"Let me help you with that, dear." Aunt Rita knelt down gingerly, her arthritic knee reluctantly yielding to her brain's command.

"Thank you." Nicole exhaled and lifted her foot.

Aunt Rita tugged the first boot on as Nicole twisted her foot into the tight leather.

"There." Rita wiped her hands as she finished with the second boot.

Nicole looked at Aunt Rita, who winced as she pulled herself to standing. Nicole grabbed the side of the table and the back of her seat. She rocked herself twice to build momentum and pulled herself up, her back arching like a crescent moon.

"I'm sorry to be such a burden."

"You're not a burden, dear." Rita put her arm around Nicole's shoulder. They stood side-by-side, filling the open area near the door of the camper. "We're in this together. You're not a burden, you're a blessing."

"I don't see how."

"You bring me joy and purpose. I'm an old woman now, and without children of my own, well..." She stopped talking and looked at the analog clock over the doorframe. "We better get going. I'll walk with you to work. Two miles is a long way in your condition."

She pushed the door open and they headed down the quarter-mile path to the main road.

"You sure have treated me like one of your own. Better than my own parents treated me." Nicole sadly commented halfway down the dirt path.

"Everyone makes mistakes, Nicole. I pray one day you and your daddy will be reunited."

"He's long gone. I think losing Mom chipped away at him pretty hard. When I told him I was pregnant, he cracked."

"Well dear," Aunt Rita slid her arm around Nicole's back, "You never know what a day may bring. That's why I like to keep it simple. Maybe he'll come back. Maybe you'll go to him. For now, let's not worry about any men except the little one growing inside you."

"Sounds like a plan, Rita. Sounds like a plan." Nicole smiled as they turned onto the main road. "You know what? I think it's going to be a great day!"

November Thirteen, Nineteen-**EIGHTY**-Eight

11:00 AM

The timer beeped three times. An hour had passed. Thirty-Three had about twenty minutes to scope out the village before heading back to The Woodlands. He had been circling the southern area for half an hour, bouncing along the border of the woods. Everything Researcher-9 said was correct, including the likelihood of a bald eagle sighting.

He leaned against a sycamore tree, rubbing its bark against the space between his shoulder blades.

"Ah, that feels good." He recounted what he had seen, rehearsing for his meeting later with Thirty-Nine and Eleven.

"So far, it looks like there are two roads that meet on a point at the waterfront. There are a couple side streets also, but I have not explored them. I counted twelve houses on each side of the east-west road, and ten houses on each side of the north-south. There are a couple antique shops, a coffee shop and a pub. I saw a sign for a drugstore and a medical clinic but the sign said they were four miles away, in Franklin."

He stepped nearer to the road, his heart racing. His only human interaction had been at The Woodlands. He had never entered a store. He had never entered a home; at least he had no memory of doing so. He pulled out the pictures once again. As he studied the faces of the man and woman who might rescue them, his typical bravado began to diminish. Ten years old, completely out of his element, with the fate of a hundred kids on his shoulders.

"This isn't going to be easy." He exhaled and tucked the pictures away. He could close his eyes and see their faces. "At least I know who I'm looking for..."

He toed the dirt beneath him. A crowd of ants scurried around the exposed roots of the sycamore tree, some of them carrying the remains of a dead fly.

"Ants sure have a simple life. Must be nice."

"Don't mistake simple for easy, son."

Thirty-Three jumped at the voice behind him.

"Relax, young fellow. Don't worry, I won't hurt you."

Thirty-Three was nearly hyperventilating as he turned to see an older man standing just a few feet away. He had been so focused on the mission, he hadn't heard or seen him through the thinning trees that separated him from the parking area a hundred feet to his right.

"Breathe, boy. Don't want you to pass out! You running from the law or something?" The old man chuckled, his eyes disappearing behind plump, white-stubble-covered cheeks.

Thirty-Three hunched over, gasping for breath. He held up his fleshy palm, silently asking the old man to wait.

"It's alright, boy. I ain't going nowhere."

Thirty-Three stood up straight. "No. I'm not running from the law." He had spent so much time memorizing the pictures and reveling in the freedom from The Woodlands, he hadn't spent much time thinking about what he might say to people. For that matter, the show producers hadn't really mentioned it either.

"I like your taste in clothing," the old man said, causing Thirty-Three to relax a little and look down at his overalls. They did look good, except the mud-splattered fabric below his knees.

The old man noticed. "Looks like you've been swamping! I'm Ben Douglas, by the way," he continued, his thumbs tucked in the straps of his overalls, which were nearly the same color as Thirty-Three's. "I run the general store down the street." He had a tan long-sleeve flannel shirt under his overalls, which covered his solid frame. His light brown work boots were dusty and worn. His eyes were gentle and kind, inviting Thirty-Three to trust him.

"Hi."

"Hi to you. What's your name?"

"Thirt –" Thirty-Three paused, realizing another flaw in the plan. Nobody had thought about real names. "Umm..."

Mr. Douglas eased him out of the awkwardness.

"Thirt? Well, that's a different name. I'm guessing you're not from around here, are you?"

"I'm not from that far away. Well, at least in distance." Thirty-Three's wit was returning as he became more comfortable with the friendly stranger.

He studied Thirty-Three for a minute. His deep gray eyes were barely visible through his squinting inspection.

"Well," he evaluated, "your clothes are fairly clean – for a boy. Like me," he patted his midsection, "you don't seem to be hurting for food. I guess I could have missed seeing you around. But not likely."

He stepped closer to Thirty-Three and tilted his head, peering at him through half-closed eyes. "I've been here nearly my whole life and there ain't but about two hundred folks total, and most of them buy their groceries from me."

"Well, I guess I haven't been to your store."

"Ok. We'll leave it alone for now." He stepped back. "It's pretty chilly today. You want a hot chocolate?"

Thirty-Three didn't know what a hot chocolate was, but the way Ben asked made him think it was a good thing. It was obvious this man wasn't going to leave him alone.

"Yes sir."

"You don't need to 'sir' me, son. Ben's all right with me, though most of the folks call me Mr. Douglas. Probably because I've been here longer than some of these trees."

"Ok, Mr. Douglas," Thirty-Three replied. He followed him out of the patch of trees onto the pavement.

"We only got one place to buy it, Cloudy's Coffee, down the street." As they crossed the empty street and strolled down the narrow sidewalk, Thirty-Three breathed deeply, his confidence buoyed slightly by the sense he had navigated that encounter without completely failing.

"What can I get for you all today?" the girl behind the narrow dark green laminate countertop asked as they stepped through the crooked screen door and onto the creaking wooden floor.

"Me and my friend, Thirt," he turned to Thirty-Three, who was trailing, "Thirt, right?" He didn't wait for a response. He chuckled and looked back at the waitress.

"Me and my friend Thirt are going to have some hot chocolate."

"Hot chocolate. All right, you want whipped cream on that?"

"I know I do." Old Ben answered with a childlike grin.

The girl walked to the end of the counter, meeting them as they climbed onto a couple of diner-style stools. She looked at Thirty-Three, his round red face capped by hair that was as short as baby goose down.

"How about you? You want whipped cream, Thirt?" She rubbed his head and glanced toward Mr. Douglas.

"Thirt? Are you sure that's his name?"

"That's what he said. I think he's trying to keep a low profile. He's a kid, so I'm sure he likes whipped cream."

That's her. Oh my gosh, that's her! Thirty-Three looked into her eyes as she patted his head. In the space between the metal-trimmed edge of the countertop and a stack of cardboard boxes, he saw her red apron stretched to its breaking point around her very pregnant stomach.

"That's Thirty-Nine!" Thirty-Three blurted out.

"What?" Nicole asked.

"I think he said you're thirty-nine. That's not true. Or kind." Mr. Douglas looked down at the boy. Thirty-Three blushed.

"I'm sorry." He whispered.

"You going to have that baby soon?" Mr. Douglas asked, changing the subject.

"That's not polite either," Nicole jokingly scolded as she turned her back to them to prepare their drinks.

"I'm sorry. I'm not doing any better than you, son. That's probably why the most recent Mrs. Douglas left me a couple years ago." He turned to Thirty-Three. "You'd think after three wives, I'd have learned how to talk to them. Women! I tell you boy, now there's a mystery! You don't have a girl-friend do you, Thirt?"

As soon as the word "girlfriend" was said, Thirty-Three thought about Eleven. *Wish she was here. She'd be so much more dignified than me. Guess I should have paid attention in the Manners Programming Class.*

"No sir", he replied.

The clock in Thirty-Three's pocket beeped four times. He had thirty minutes to get back to the willow tree.

"What was that?" Nicole asked as she turned to them, her hands holding two large brown mugs, each topped by a precariously balanced tower of thick white foam.

"Umm. I got to get going." Thirty-Three jumped down from the stool and started walking to the door.

"What about your hot chocolate?"

"I'll be back. Probably this afternoon. Thanks!" Thirty-Three sped up as he opened the door and headed to the sidewalk. By the time he got to the edge of the street, he was sprinting. Two minutes later, he was back in the woods, jogging toward the willow tree. Jogging back to captivity.

"Well, ain't that something?" Mr. Douglas said, staring at the door-way.

"Wonder where that kid is from?" Nicole asked, a motherly concern in her voice.

He faced Nicole and grabbed the mug closest to him. "I'm not sure. But, I'm going to keep my eye out for him. Seems a little too young to be in this part of the country all alone. He's certainly not open to talking about himself, though."

He buried his face in the pile of whipped cream, trying to sip the hot chocolate. He laughed as he pulled the mug away, his nose and mouth covered in the sweet froth.

"You don't happen to have a straw, do you?"

"Sure thing." Nicole reached into a small glass box on the shelf against the wall. "Here ya go."

Mr. Douglas looked around the empty room. "Well, there's no one else here. You might as well join me." He pointed to Thirty-Three's untouched hot chocolate.

Nicole smiled. "Why not? After all, I am eating for two!"

"And you'll need your energy – you might have a decent lunch crowd today. Did you hear the news?"

"What news?"

"Well, there's talk that a big Canadian lumber company is going to restart the mill. Some guys flew in last night and are staying at the Cooper's farm. Or maybe it was Josie's Bed N Breakfast in Franklin. I can't remember details. Anyway, they will probably be here for lunch, since the pub doesn't open until four. And if they get the mill to full strength, you'll probably quadruple your customer base!"

"My boss would be happy with a regular customer base, never mind quadrupling. If this winter is like last year, I'm probably going to have to shorten my hours. With the baby coming, that's the last thing I need."

"I understand. If I can help, let me know. I still can't believe your father left you in July, with nothing."

"Yeah, well, I've learned plenty about men this year. No offense, but I don't think I'll be trusting any of your kind for a long time."

He didn't reply. They finished their hot chocolates in silence.

"Well," he stood up. "I better get back to the store. Maybe those guys from the lumber company will need something from my place."

"I hope so. See you later, Mr. Douglas."

"See you later, Nicole."

November Thirteen, Nineteen-**NINETY**-Eight

11:55 AM

"Here goes." Thirty-Three stood in front of the tree. Unlike his exit from the coffee shop, his return trip had been smooth. He pulled the key out of his overalls pocket and lined it up with the outline in the middle of the trunk. He pressed it in and everything around him faded. A shaded opening appeared beside the tree. He stepped into what looked like a dark hallway and after two steps he was standing beside two girls spreading a small bag of mulch near his feet.

"Watch out, Thirty-Three," they said in unison.

"Sorry." He jumped back a couple steps, banging his foot against the low metal fence that lined the perimeter of the flowerbed.

"Ouch!" He reached down and rubbed his heel.

"What's the problem?" Sentry-5 appeared near them.

"Nothing." Thirty-Three quickly replied. "I just tripped a little."

"Where were you working?" Sentry-5 walked closer to him, scowling more intensely with each step.

"I was helping with the flowerbed." Thirty-Three pointed over his shoulder at the two girls spreading mulch.

He reached Thirty-Three and pulled out his club. He patted it against his open palm several times. "Are you sure? I haven't seen you and I've been in this area for the last ten minutes."

"I've been here. Honest."

"Fifty-One, Fifty-Eight," Sentry-5 called to the girls. They turned their heads but kept their hands moving, mindful of their work quota.

"Yes sir?"

"Has Thirty-Three been working with you?"

Please say yes, Thirty-Three prayed as he tried to make eye contact with them.

They paused. Fifty-Eight looked at the sentry and then at Thirty-Three. His eyes begged her to cover for him. His shoulders hunched and his eyes bulged, willing her to say yes.

After what seemed like several minutes, during which the smack of the sentry's club against his hand got louder and louder, finally Fifty-Eight replied, her high-pitched voice lifting Thirty-Three's spirits.

"Yes. He's been helping us."

"Are you sure?"

Fifty-One chimed in, smiling as her white teeth radiated in contrast to her ebony skin. "Yes."

"Ok. Five minutes to finish your work. And you," he turned to Thirty-Three, "you better be on your best behavior." He whacked Thirty-Three across the back with the club.

"That's a reminder – don't mess with me."

Thirty-Three crumpled to the ground, twisting and reaching for the middle of his back. Sentry-5 walked away to check on other students in the Yard.

"Thank you," Thirty-Three gasped, now on all fours.

"You're welcome," Fifty-One replied. "He beat our friend yesterday. I didn't want to see that happen to you."

"But," Fifty-Eight interjected, "where were you, exactly?"

Thirty-Three sat up and rocked back, resting on his heels with his hands on the ground. He looked at the tree. The key. It was still in the tree, like a chiseled knotty bump. Fortunately, it was well camouflaged and neither girl noticed.

He stood up and grimaced as he straightened his back. He casually walked toward the tree, placing himself between the girls and its trunk. He leaned against it, sliding his hand down, feeling for the key. He palmed it and closed his fist.

"I was just checking some things out." He finally replied to Fifty-Eight's question.

"Checking some things out?" Fifty-Eight stood up. Her skinny shoulders supported the straps of her billowy overalls – the same overalls that fit snugly on Thirty-Three. "If you want us to lie for you again," she whistled through the gap in her front teeth, "you're going to have to tell us the truth."

"ONE MINUTE. TIME TO ASSEMBLE AT THE ENTRYWAY."

The announcement prevented the conversation from continuing.

"Ok," Thirty-Three mumbled, for once not escalating a confrontation. He kept the key in his closed hand. "I will tell you later. I promise. All I can say is we might not have to live at The Woodlands forever."

"Seriously?" Fifty-One, who was only 7 years old and a head shorter than Fifty-Eight, asked with wonder in her eyes.

"Don't lie to her or I'll beat you myself," Fifty-Eight stood tall and close to Thirty-Three.

"It's the truth. But we have to get in line. Be patient and keep quiet. I'll tell you more, soon. I promise. Let's go. After you, ladies." He motioned for them to lead the way to line up for lunch.

As they turned their backs and began walking, he slid the key into his smaller pocket and quickly zipped it closed.

"Thirty-Three!"

He looked around as he neared the line of students. No one was returning his gaze.

"Over here, Thirty-Three!"

He turned to his left and saw the Sentry-5, standing with another sentry. The second sentry had a clipboard in his hand and was scribbling on it. He was the Yard supervisor that week.

His stomach lurched and his heart sank. He knew what was coming.

"Thirty-Three," the second sentry said, "Sentry-5 tells me you were disruptive today."

He knew better than to refute the charge. Better to be as apologetic as possible. He couldn't afford to be restricted from the Yard on the first day of the show.

"I'm sorry, sir."

"What's the problem, Thirty-Three?" the second sentry continued. Sentry-5 stood menacingly next to him, his hands clutching his club like a baseball bat.

"Nothing sir."

"You realize you are close to the top of our reprimand list every month?"

"Yes sir."

"Well, Sentry-5 wants to give you a physical reprimand. Ten blows to the backside. I think an afternoon and evening of interior cleaning would help remind you how to behave."

The buzz of students whispering as they stood in line along the wall distracted the Yard supervisor.

"Quiet!" He yelled over Thirty-Three, who stared at the bulging veins in the guard's neck. He was a barrel-chested man with bushy hair and eyebrows. He was as strong as an ox, like all the sentries. Unlike most sentries, he was sometimes lenient. With the noise of the other students enraging him, Thirty-Three felt his chances for clemency diminish.

The Yard fell silent except for a few chirping birds. The longer Thirty-Three stood still, under the thick expanse of the fir trees, the chillier he felt from the cool damp air. He rubbed his arms, trying to warm himself.

"Look at me, Thirty-Three." The Yard supervisor instructed, the redness fading from his face.

Thirty-Three looked up at the beastly man before him. The Yard supervisor looked at the pages clipped to the board in his hand. He thumbed through them for a few seconds and then made eye contact with the young student, staring directly into Thirty-Three's dark brown eyes with his own equally dark brown eyes.

"Tell you what, Thirty-Three. I'm going to give you the choice. What do you think would be a better punishment for you? Ten strikes from Sentry-5? Or spending the rest of the day cleaning in the building?"

Thirty-Three looked at Sentry-5, who was smirking with delight, anticipating the opportunity to beat him.

"I'll take the ten blows, sir."

"That's what I thought you'd say," the Yard supervisor

replied, jotting on the paper. "Which means, much to Sentry-5's dismay, you will be cleaning inside the building the rest of the day. Sentry-5 will be your boss. After the twenty-minute post lunch break, he will retrieve you from the Yard and take you to your work detail. Now get in line."

"And if you don't do exactly what I say, you'll get the beating as well." Sentry-5 added, glaring at the Yard supervisor.

Thirty-Three had to use all his restraint to keep from kicking the ground. He was angry. But, he kept his emotions in check. He didn't want to compound the punishment. He stiffened up and looked at the supervisor.

"Yes sir." He retreated to join the other students in line.

He squeezed into his spot in line, his head hanging

as the students started walking into the building. As they moved forward, Thirty-Three's mind was deluged with the thought of the consequences of this complication.

Great. First day of the show and we're already cancelled for the day. I've lost the rest of the day. Every trip counts. Thirty-Nine's going to kill me. Eleven's going to be so upset. I wish they had gone back instead of me. I suck. Now how am I going to find the guy in Thirty-Nine's dream?

November Thirteen, Nineteen-**EIGHTY**-Eight

12:10 PM

"This place is going to take a lot of work to bring back online." Bruce Newton, the 52-year-old vice president of McIntyre Lumber said, as he stood in the bowels of the mill with Corey McIntyre, son of the founder and CEO.

"Yes, but the head saw has a ton of life and the drying kilns were rebuilt just a few years before it closed." Corey replied. He had graduated college six months earlier, finishing his bachelor's degree in business administration in three years. Like most everything he did, he rushed through college to please his dad. He was assigned to shadow Bruce for the first year, learning about the business. This was their second trip together. Corey had four months of work under his belt.

"That's a good point." Bruce had the look of a low level executive. His clothing of choice was a cotton short-sleeve oxford shirt, flat front khaki pants, and on important days, a striped tie.

Corey, on the other hand, was perpetually underdressed. He struggled to feel comfortable even in business casual. His preferred outfit was a guide shirt, hip waders and a light rain shell with a hood. He would fly fish at a moment's notice. He kept his tackle in his truck in hopes that he'd come upon a river while scouting areas for new timber. He didn't just enjoy it; he was good at it. Several of his dad's friends had hired him to help guide them during his college years. It was the most rewarding work he'd ever done. But fly-fishing wasn't part of his father's plan. Finding trees and processing wood was the only plan.

"I'm hungry, Bruce, how about you?" Corey asked, glancing at his dark green digital wristwatch. "It's lunchtime."

"I could eat." Bruce replied. "Let me go out to the car and grab the bagged lunch I got from the motel this morning."

"Bagged lunch? Are you serious?" Corey asked.

"Yes. Nothing wrong with it. We've got work to do."

"I saw a little coffee shop on our way through Port Mashton. It's not far. We could walk there." Corey replied.

"I'm not walking anywhere over a few hundred yards." Bruce rubbed his right leg. "You know my knee still isn't fully recovered from our company softball game."

"That was two months ago!" Corey looked at his heavy-set colleague as they started walking out of the mill. "Did a doctor look at that?"

"No. Been traveling so much. Your dad wants to get three new mills open in the next eighteen months."

"I know."

"Which is why we're brown-bagging it for lunch today. Your dad said this is a quick in-n-out project. We don't have time for leisurely meals." Bruce turned and limped up the stairs to the main platform and walked to the large double doors that had been propped open with a couple small logs. The entrance was wet and a steady rain was falling on the gravel outside.

"It better not be egg salad!" Corey shouted. He stared at the abandoned logging equipment strewn all over the warehouse like building. "This looks like a lot more than a quick in-n-out project."

"You're used to his high expectations!" Bruce yelled from the top of the stairs. He grinned and held up two paper sacks. "You're in luck. Chicken salad sandwiches, potato chips. And there's a nice apple turnover for desert!"

"Fine." Corey moped. "It's still not warm food and coffee." He shivered and rubbed his arms. "It's not like this place has central heating."

"I know." Bruce winced as he descended the stairs. "Here," he tossed a bag at Corey.

"Thanks!" Corey caught the bag and walked to meet Bruce at the bottom of the stairs. They sat together and stared out at the expanse of run-down machinery before them.

"This place reminds me of the first one your dad took over. We were both barely adults. Learned a lot of lessons with that one." Bruce paused and pulled out his sandwich. He unwrapped it and took a bite. "Some hard lessons," he said as he chewed.

"I know you all have done a lot. You've built a great business." Corey replied, grabbing the apple pie first. He wolfed it down in four bites. "That was good. You going to eat yours?"

"Why yes I am!" Bruce laughed. He looked down at his sizeable midsection. "Are you my wife?"

"No sir." Corey replied.

They ate in silence for the next few minutes. Finally, Bruce returned to the same conversation they'd had several times in the past few months.

"You know he wants you to run a mill one day. This would be a good one. You ready for that?"

Corey chewed a bite of chicken salad. He gulped. "I don't know. Not really. But you know, it's whatever Dad wants."

"You'll need to have a better answer than that if you're going to last in this business. Give it time, you'll find your way."

"I guess I'm not really sure I want to do this." Corey wadded up the plastic wrap that had covered his sandwich. "Did you bring anything to drink?"

"I've got a couple root beers." Bruce pulled out two cans of soda. He held one out to Corey. "But let's not change the subject. You know this is your future, right?"

Corey took the root beer and popped the lid. "I'm sorry Bruce, I just don't think I want to run this mill. We're in the middle of nowhere. There's no fly fishing here, either."

"Well, maybe not this one, but..."

Corey cut him off. "I don't want to run any mill."

"Give it time, Corey. You may find that you love it. Your dad..."

"My dad is my dad. I'm not." Corey stood up. "You said he wouldn't want us taking a leisurely lunch, right? I'm going back to work." He stomped off to the far corner of the main floor.

"Another fun day with daddy's boy." Bruce muttered. He lurched back and forth and pulled himself up. "Oh well, it's my job."

November Thirteen, Nineteen-**NINETY**-Eight

1:05 PM

"We've only got twenty minutes until we have to return to the lab in Dr. Nampala's office." Thirty-Nine's voice carried fatigue as he talked with Thirty-Three and Eleven near the horseshoe pits. The rhythmic clinking of the games was soothing. It had become a ritual over the past few days, meeting every day after lunch to further the plan for the show. Now, the show was in its opening day and evaluation of act one was underway.

Thirty-Three had not been able to speak to Thirty-Nine or Eleven during lunch. He only had ten minutes until Sentry-5 would come to get him for his work punishment. He knew he had to tell them about it but he was worried about their reaction. First things first, he thought.

"I made contact with your mother." He reported.

His words jolted Thirty-Nine. Until now, everything had been hypothetical. Even though he had read the report and believed she was out there, their planned escape was shaky at best. His logical mind had been reminding him all week of the desperation of the whole notion.

As Thirty-Three confirmed that the time corridor worked, only Thirty-Nine's fatigue prevented an exuberant reaction. Fortunately for the schemers, his voice was constrained by weariness, or he may have shouted for joy and attracted unwanted attention from the sentries.

"You met my mother?" his raspy whisper was barely audible.

"Yes. She's nice. She made me hot chocolate. Have you ever heard of hot chocolate? It's a drink made out of chocolate. I didn't get to drink it though, because I had to get back here." Thirty-Nine was listening closely to Thirty-Three's words. Eleven was not. Eleven stared at Thirty-Three blankly, her eyes dull and hollow.

"You all look exhausted," Thirty-Three pronounced.

They looked exhausted because they were. Dr. Nampala had ramped up the dream sessions to three times a day, which meant they were "asleep" during six hours of the day. Normal nights were now impossible and had been nearly sleepless for both of them.

"Do you need to sit down?" Thirty-Three asked Eleven, motioning to the ground beside the horseshoe storage rack. She silently stared at him. Her vulnerable countenance softened her typically strong aura, which made him all the more attracted to her. And all the more angry at Dr. Nampala.

"Eleven? Eleven?"

Thirty-Nine turned to her as well. "Eleven? Are you ok?" They each grabbed her by the upper arm, their bodies forming a triangle as they tried to rouse Eleven.

"Thirty-Three, you need to find the man," she finally replied.

Thirty-Three arched one eyebrow as he let go of her arm. "You mean the young guy from your dreams?"

Thirty-Nine scanned the Yard as he waited for her answer. Two sentries were stationed at the far end of the horseshoe pits. She failed to respond, so he answered Thirty-Three's question.

"Yes." Thirty-Nine continued for her. "Researcher-9 is convinced he's the one to contact. The one who can save us."

"Why? I found your mother. Shouldn't I contact her?" Thirty-Three grabbed a horseshoe and fidgeted with it in his hand. "Let's not press our luck."

"I don't know. I just know that's what Researcher-9 said," Thirty-Nine replied.

"Just get us out of here." Eleven whispered.

They both looked at Eleven, whose lethargic slouch had worsened.

Thirty-Three's eyes turned down and he folded his hands behind his back. He didn't respond to Thirty-Nine or Eleven.

"What's the matter?" Thirty-Nine whispered.

"I can't go back today."

"What? Why?"

"I got in trouble with Sentry-5 when I came back. I honestly didn't do anything wrong. He just has it in for me. For all of us."

Eleven spoke up. For the first time since the conversation began, she was engaged. Her eyes gleamed with anger.

"You always say you are innocent. What did you do?" She pressed closer and looked down at him, emphasizing his short, stocky frame by stretching her lithe body to its full height.

He hated disappointing her. They had been so busy planning; he'd had little time to think about his affections for her. Now, as she stood so close, though she was scolding him, he felt nothing but an internal quaking awkwardness and a noticeable increase in his body temperature. During the past year, he would have given anything to stand so closely, to be in her space. Now, regardless of her demeanor, he could only think about how attractive she was.

"I'm so sorry Eleven." He looked up at her captivating eyes, her freckled cheeks and her full pink lips.

"You're so beautiful," he blurted out.

"What?" She stepped back.

He slapped his hands over his mouth. His insides felt like they dropped to his feet. He shut his eyes tight.

Thirty-Nine interjected, nearly as stunned as Eleven. "Thirty-Three, what are you talking about?"

"I'm sorry." His entire body felt like his face – red and flushed. That awkward sensation that elementary school boys in the real world felt every Valentine's Day rushed through him like a surge of electric shame.

"I'm just a mess right now. I thought I would...I thought I would be able..." he stammered, "I don't know what I thought. I don't know why I thought I could do anything special." His throat started to thicken, his sinuses filled with moistness. As his eyes reddened, he looked away.

Don't cry, he thought, *Don't cry*!

Thirty-Nine, ever the dutiful friend, tried to bail out his podmate.

"Eleven." He turned to her, and stood with half of his body shielding Thirty-Three from her view. "We're all under great stress. So, Thirty-Three messed up a little. Tomorrow, he'll go back and make contact. Let's not get rattled. Let's not get..."

"THIRTY-THREE, REPORT TO THE MAIN DOOR."

"Sentry-5!" Thirty-Three sputtered. "I have to go." He looked over Thirty-Nine's shoulder at Eleven. "I'm really sorry Eleven. I promise I'll fix things tomorrow. I promise!" He jogged away, holding back tears, wiping his nose with his shirt sleeve.

"Well, that went differently." Thirty-Nine joked, trying to reduce the tension.

"I don't know, Thirty-Nine. Are we being foolish? I mean, maybe I shouldn't have brought up the book. We would have never tried to escape." Eleven replied.

"Shhh!" Thirty-Nine whispered. "Don't say that. It's the show, remember?"

"Sorry." Eleven sheepishly replied. "But, I'd rather die here than die out there."

"I'd rather not die at all." Thirty-Nine looked at her. "You're just worn out. We will escape – I mean – we will pull off the show. Do you trust me?"

Eleven nodded.

They both turned and watched as Thirty-Three approached the entrance to the main building. Sentry-5 stood in front of the doors waiting, wearing a menacing scowl and holding two large mop buckets.

November Thirteen, Nineteen-**EIGHTY**-Eight

5:30 PM

"How was work today?" Aunt Rita asked as Nicole dragged herself through the screen door. She didn't take off her coat as she slumped into the seat across from Aunt Rita in the kitchenette. Hot tea steamed in the oversized dark green mug in front of her. She reached for the carton of half-n-half and dribbled some into her drink while she replied.

"It was work. Ha. It was slow. Like it has been since the summer ended." She slid the mug slowly back and forth, swirling the cream until it dissolved. She took a sip and continued talking.

"Something weird happened today, though. A strange boy showed up in the café – Mr. Douglas found him in the area. Really goofy kid. His head was shaved. He was probably ten or eleven years old. Said his name was Thirt."

"Thirt?" Aunt Rita peered over her glasses.

"Yeah. Weird, huh?"

"Yes. Did you talk to him? Find out where he was from?"

"Not really. He took off right after they came in." She took another sip and tried to shiver off the chill she felt from the effects of pregnancy exhaustion and her trip home in the cold air.

"That's strange. Hope he's all right," remarked Aunt Rita.

They both stared out the narrow window above the table for a few minutes. The light rainfall bubbled on the glass, creating a misty lens through which they viewed the darkening area between the camper and the woods a few hundred yards away.

"Feels like the calm before the storm." Nicole remarked, still gazing at the ever-dimming sky. She took another sip of the tea, then another. After a couple more sips, she tipped her head back and gulped the rest of the tea down without stopping. She slammed the empty mug on the table and stood up.

"Is something wrong dear?" Aunt Rita asked.

"I don't know." She was anxious about the baby. Aunt Rita had convinced her to have a home delivery. It didn't take much convincing since she didn't have health insurance. Still, Nicole was a modern girl, who had grown accustomed to modern medical conveniences. She was unsure about how to express her feelings. She trusted Aunt Rita, but she also trusted her gut. And her gut was about as settled as a blue jay's screeching cries in the early morning mist.

"I know you're nervous about the baby. But, millions of women have done it, and you're a strong girl."

Nicole held her tongue. She didn't want to offend Aunt Rita but she couldn't shake the fearful feeling creeping through her. It had been building all week. When she was working it subsided; but now, sitting in the quiet camper, it plagued her mind.

Aunt Rita stood and took a couple steps closer to Nicole.

"I've got all the stuff we need in the back." She pointed to the far end of the camper, where a large plastic tub held a variety of amateur medical supplies: latex gloves, washcloths, brush, tubes of lubricant, cotton balls, gauze, syringes, diapers, cups, straws, small irrigation bottles, homeopathic pain medicine, baby blankets and other essentials for pre- and post-delivery care of both baby and mom.

Nicole looked toward the container and then at Aunt Rita. She tried to relax. After all, Aunt Rita had been her lifeline. She had rescued Nicole from homelessness. More importantly, she had rescued Nicole from family-lessness.

"I know. I've always imagined it would be different. I never would have dreamed a year ago I'd be in this position. I guess it was stupid, but I planned on the fairy tale life. Like all little girls, huh? You know, I pictured the knight on the white horse, the castle, the whole thing."

"You're not the only one, Nicole. You already know this but life doesn't stick to the script. It's a wild, dangerous, wonderful thing. I've already seen so much strength in you. You're going to survive this and go on. And you're going to have a family."

She put her arm around Nicole's shoulder and pressed her cheek against Nicole's neck.

"You already do." She whispered as Nicole rubbed her swollen stomach.

"You already do."

November Fourteen, Nineteen-**NINETY**-Eight

6:38 AM

Dr. Nampala paced across the balcony outside his office in the pre-dawn darkness. He hadn't slept soundly in over two weeks, and the wrinkled piece of paper in his hand was the source of his insomnia. It was the first non-digital correspondence he had received since he began his relationship with The Future nearly ten years earlier. Across the top of the page, in all capital letters, it read "SIX WEEK NOTICE." The rest of the page explained that he had six weeks to produce a legitimate, tested, reproducible way to create thought transference and speech control. If not, The Woodlands, and all its residents, would be obliterated. Escape was not an option.

He stopped walking and leaned against the railing, looking down at the dark yard below. The breeze of a coming storm gusted and pushed his wispy, scraggly beard against the upturned collar of his coat. The air was as damp as the underside of a pile of leaves. He shivered as he stared at the trees around him. Towering all around The Woodlands, the dense branches of the old-growth firs layered together provided a natural shield from the world outside. Though the air was placid, save the early morning cackles of the usual birds, Nampala knew that no forest fortress could shield him against the intentions of his funders if he failed to deliver.

The Future's probably watching somehow, he thought as he gazed up into the thick green canopy. *Maybe satellites.* The wind blew harder.

"Too cold out here." He said.

He turned back into his office, shoving open the sliding glass door, pushing harder when it caught in several rust-stained spots. Shedding his coat, he tossed it onto the stool near the cots where Eleven and Thirty-Nine had spent most of the week. Two lamps lit the room.

He walked toward the cone-shaped electric heater that stood beside his desk. Rubbing his hands over it, he remarked, "I guess I have to turn up the heat even more."

His desk was strewn with paper. A small television played an animated re-creation of Eleven & Thirty-Nine's dreams from the day before in an endless loop. Dr. Nampala sat down and placed his hands atop his head. He tilted back in his chair and stared at the screen.

In the scene he was watching, Thirty-Nine and Eleven walked along the side of a narrow tree-lined road. The road curved along the bottom contours of the TV and continued off screen, ending somewhere in the corridors of the students' brains. Tightly bunched trees filled the space across the middle of the screen. An old barn in an overgrown clearing appeared in the upper right. As they approached the viewer, Thirty-Nine sporadically nodded. As they grew larger in the screen, Thirty-Nine shook his head, as if to say "no".

Dr. Nampala leaned forward and pressed the pause button. He stared at the figures before him. His best students and his life's work – his very life itself – was now reduced to shadowy images on a small TV set in the middle of nowhere. He pressed the rewind button, watching the students move spasmodically backward.

"Why is he moving his head?" He pressed play as he pondered his question. His squinty eyes narrowed further as he peered at the screen, his gaunt face mere inches from the glowing device. Over and over, he rewound and re-watched the scene. With each passing turn, the seed of a thought in the corner of his mind grew larger. After the fifth or sixth review, it was clear that Thirty-Nine was not arbitrarily moving his head. And Eleven's mouth was definitely not moving. Yet they were communicating.

Dr. Nampala stopped the video and pushed back from his desk. He rummaged through the tower of file folders on the white oak credenza. Half of the stack tumbled onto the floor as he muttered angrily to himself.

He knelt down and furiously picked through the binders and note-pads, casting each one aside almost as quickly as he touched it, reading the labels aloud. "Twenty-Seven: Redundancy Recognition", "Six: Opaque Extraction Results", "Forty-Two: Cerebral Tolerance Density" On and on he scanned the assorted files until his hands found the hard dusty floor be-tween his desk and credenza. He stood up.

"Where in the hell is that file from Researcher-9?" There was no re-sponse. The room had brightened since he first entered. The clouds turned a lighter shade of gray as the sun rose somewhere on the other side of the dense heavenly shroud. He hadn't actually seen the sun in nearly a week.

Dr. Nampala walked over to the file cabinets in the brightest part of the room, hoping to find the initial file that had prompted him to promote Thirty-Nine to Head Student. The dark metal boxes held a carefully collected assortment of documentation on each student. The files were kept in nu-merical order and inventoried weekly. He tugged open the third drawer from the top and began counting in his head. *Thirty-one, Thirty-two, Thirty-Three.* He thumbed across the labeled tabs as he looked deeper into the drawer. *Thirty-seven, Thirty-eight, Forty...*

"No file for Thirty-Nine!" He shouted and slammed the drawer, pinching his left hand in the process.

"Damn it!" Shaking his hand as he rushed over to his telephone, he hit the intercom button for Researcher-9.

After two prolonged beeps, a groggy voice responded.

"Hello?"

"Researcher-9!" Nampala shouted into the speaker.

"Yes sir."

"Get to my office immediately!"

"Yes sir."

As he waited for her arrival, Dr. Nampala stood in the middle of the room, pondering the potential that he believed existed in Thirty-Nine.

As he stood in the middle of the room, fuming about the missing file, a series of horns sounded throughout the facility. It was seven o'clock in the morning, which meant the day was officially beginning. The noise distracted him from his anger, and set him to thinking about the schedule.

"Where is the sentry with my coffee?"

As if to answer, the door at the far end of the room opened, ushering in a sentry with a small cart upon which sat two coffee pots, two mugs and saucers, and a silver creamer and sugar set.

"What's the delay?" Nampala fussed as the sentry hurriedly set the mugs and saucers on the main table.

"Sorry, Dr. Nampala. Would you like your usual?" The sentry laid a yellow linen napkin to the side of each mug, arranging them kitty-corner on the end of the table. He polished two spoons with a hand towel before placing each one atop a napkin.

"Yes."

As the sentry poured the steaming liquid caffeine into the mug, the double doors at the main entrance opened. Standing in the opening was Researcher-9. The left side of her face was etched with pillowcase lines and her hurriedly pony-tailed hair left multiple stray wisps dangling on either side of her face and neck. Dr. Nampala's tone clearly conveyed the need for her to hustle.

"There you are, Researcher-9," Dr. Nampala called out as he looked up. He had grabbed the mug from the sentry and was quickly stirring in artificial sweetener.

"You're dismissed," he nodded to the sentry.

As the sentry exited through the side door, Nampala began a solemn march toward the entryway. He paused every few steps and sipped his coffee. His eyes remained focused on Researcher-9, as he maneuvered around the various items in the room using only his peripheral vision as a guide. She felt his withering stare searing through her skin, causing her heart to bang on the inside of her chest like a spastic drummer.

"Researcher-9, Researcher-9," he was now standing in front of the small loveseat where Thirty-Nine had discovered his mother was still alive. "Come here. Have a seat." Nampala motioned to the cushions, worn and flat from the many nights he'd fallen asleep studying charts and reports. As she timidly entered the seating area, he leaned back into the rocking chair. She sat down.

Dr. Nampala sipped from his mug and slowly exhaled. He tipped back and forth in the chair, his bare feet pushing and pulling against a thinning patch of carpet. She looked down at her hands, which were clutching the front edge of the cushion in fear, wadding it up like a sponge. She relaxed her hands. As the padding returned to its natural shape, she looked up at her boss. His eyes narrowed into slits each time he took a sip.

"We talked a couple weeks ago about where you came from and your family, right?" He stopped rocking as he broke the silence.

Any light-heartedness she felt evaporated. "Yes sir."

"I'm confused by you."

"I'm sorry sir. I don't vant to confuse you." Her nervousness heightened her accent. "How am I confusing of you?"

"You are one of my smartest researchers." He reached out and set the half-empty mug on the small end table to the right of his rocker. "But you do some stupid things. Like a couple weeks ago, when you tried to interfere with the experiment just because the student was in mild distress."

"But sir..."

"No buts!" He leaped up from the chair, suddenly irate. The veins in his unshaven neck popped out, like earthworms straining against loose topsoil. He clenched his fists and bounded into the space in front of her, nearly stepping on her feet. She instinctively flinched and lurched backward.

"I make the rules! I'm the director of The Woodlands!" He screamed into her face. "Get this in your head. We are not here to coddle children. We are here to do real, hard scientific research. If we lose a subject, that's the cost of discovery!" Spittle bubbled on his lower lip and her nose filled with the stale aroma of tobacco. He pointed at her, his bony finger nearly tapping the bridge of her nose. "Your recent behavior is more than troublesome. I go to the file cabinet this morning" – he pointed to the other side of the room – "and I can't find Thirty-Nine's file. My hunch is that you have it. Do you?"

Her silent feeble nod confirmed his suspicion and intensified his anger. His small eyes popped open wide as he yanked his glasses off and waved them under her chin in a cutting motion.

"You've got one chance. If you break protocol again, if you try to comfort a subject, if you so much as look like you're going to grin, you're done."

He backed away and slid his tortoise-shell spectacles onto his prominent nose. Researcher-9 was nearly in the fetal position; her feet were drawn up to the seat of the small sofa, her hands occupied the space in front of her stomach and her head was turned down. She stared at his bare feet, noticing the wayward black hairs on his big toes. Her stomach told her throat it was time to vomit. Her mind said "no". And, somehow, her stomach obeyed.

Dr. Nampala turned his back on her and walked to the rocking chair. He sat down, grabbed his coffee and proceeded to direct her as though no threat to her life had been issued.

"Go get me the file. And get Eleven and Thirty-Nine up here."

"Yes sir," she mumbled. The tension from the confrontation had stiffened her joints so much she felt like she needed a pulley to extend her legs and arms. She slowly unfolded her body, comforted by the increased distance between her and Dr. Nampala. She haltingly exited the room without saying another word.

November Fourteen, Nineteen-**EIGHTY**-Eight

7:26 AM

"Let's get going!" Bruce announced to Corey as he banged on the bathroom door. "I want to get over to the mill and complete the inventory process today so we can get out of here by tomorrow afternoon."

Corey was in the shower, awakened an hour earlier than he preferred.

"I'm hurrying!" he shouted over the dripping water that barely enabled him to bring the soap to lather. "Better off taking a sponge bath." He grabbed the complimentary mini-bottle of shampoo and turned it to pour some into his hand. Simultaneously, he glanced at the pitiful stream of water tapping his chest. "Better not wash my hair – I could be here all day trying to rinse." He snapped the lid shut and tossed the miniature bottle into the back of the tub.

Bruce sat on the edge of the twin bed that had strained to hold his full frame during the night. The bedside phone rang as he was contorting over his stomach, trying to reach the laces on his boots. He twisted to his right and slapped the receiver off the base. He yanked on the receiver to wrestle the cord free from the lamp power cord. He sat up straight, took a breath, and answered.

"Hello, Bruce Newton here."

"Bruce! How ya doing out there in Port Mashton?" The jovial voice on the other end could only be one person – Jimmy McIntyre – founder and president of McIntyre Lumber and Corey's father. He was a gregarious man with a voice as big and booming as his presence in any room, or even outdoors. Bruce laughed every time he recalled their first handshake. No midget himself, Bruce's hand had nearly disappeared in the suffocating grip of Jimmy's paw.

"We're doing good, Jimmy, how are you?"

"We're busier than a costume salesman on Halloween morning! I got seven more prospective mills lined up for you boys to do some recon on!"

Bruce held the phone away from his ear in an effort to temper the blast. Jimmy's enthusiasm was on full-tilt, even for him. Jimmy had the passion of a campaigning politician (which he'd considered), the work ethic of a lumberjack (which he used to be), the determination of a wolverine (which he'd killed more than once), and the colloquialisms of a native Oklahoman (which he was).

"That's great, Jimmy." Bruce stood up, his unlaced boots loosely clucking at his feet as he took a few steps toward the nightstand. He was concerned about Corey's interest in the company. Jimmy loved giving surprises, but he hated receiving them.

"I think you might want to give Corey a little pep talk. He's got a disinterested tone to his voice and a faraway look in his eye."

"Again! Dadgumit! We've already been down this road and the bridge is washed out! Why don't you tell him to suck it up, Bruce?"

Bruce lowered his voice as he heard the water shut off in the bathroom. "It's not that easy, Jimmy." He whispered. "You know, I'm trying to build a good working relationship."

Jimmy backed off a little. "Well, I can see that but still..."

"I think you need to be careful with how much you push him, Jimmy. He's barely out of his teen years, you know."

"Is he there? Let me talk to him."

"Yea, hang on."

Bruce set the black plastic receiver on the magazine-sized phonebook and sloughed off to get Corey. He knocked on the door again.

"Hey Corey, your dad's on the phone for you."

A threadbare white towel covered Corey's head. He wasn't drying off so much as he was swiping water from his body with limited success.

"Corey!" Bruce called out more loudly.

The towel fell around Corey's neck like a horse collar as he responded. "I'm hurrying!"

"Your dad's on the phone for you."

"Can I call him back?"

Bruce leaned against the door. He hated being the man in the middle. He hated mentoring his future boss. He hated listening to them complain about each other. But he was paid well and had two kids in college with a third starting in a couple years. This was just part of the job.

"His schedule's pretty jammed, Corey. Better to take a couple minutes now and talk to him."

"Fine." Corey yanked the door open, causing Bruce to stumble into the bathroom entrance. Corey jumped back and Bruce caught himself on the cheap gold-colored doorknob.

"What are you doing?"

"Sorry, Corey." The moment was made all the more awkward by Corey's nakedness. Bruce stood up and tried to look Corey only in the eyes.

"Do you want a robe?"

"I'm fine." Corey squeezed by Bruce, reinforcing his annoyance by sliding his bare butt against Bruce's midsection. Bruce stepped into the bathroom and looked at his reflection in the mirror. His sagging chin and his hound dog eyes staring back at him only reminded him of his frustrations.

"I'm getting too old for this nonsense." He told the aged face in the mirror.

As Corey approached the phone, his rudeness to Bruce had already begun to make him feel foolish. He reached for the small quilt at the foot of his bed and wrapped it around his waist.

"Hello dad," he spoke into the phone.

"Corey! How ya doing, boy?"

"I'm doing pretty good. How's mom?"

"She's fine – she's off visiting your sister at Tech. What do you think of the mill there?"

"It seems pretty decent."

"Pretty decent? Ted Clements told me last year that it had a lot of potential."

"Well, we've only gotten about half the equipment inventoried. So, it's still hard to say. That's why we're here, right? To get a real answer?"

"You're right, son. How you feeling about going to check out some more mills next week? Maybe you and I could go on a trip together?"

"I don't know...It would be nice to work at the main office at least one week a month." Corey looked at the aging headboard and the dried paint drips scattered along the ledge that served as testimony to the lodge's informal management motto – "If it's broke, paint it." Corey could use a break from life on the road. He could use a couple days floating the river.

"Tell you what, dad. Why don't you go fly fishing with me when I get back and I'll go on a road trip with you the following week?"

"Fly fishing? Fly fishing?" Jimmy shrieked. He became nearly unhinged by the notion of lazily tossing bugs after fish while there was so much work to be done.

"I thought we covered this, Corey. The business needs you – and you need it!"

"I didn't say I wasn't going to work, dad." Corey shrunk down and sat on the floor as his father continued. He regretted it almost immediately as a massive cockroach scurried across his foot and back under the bed.

"Listen, Corey. I understand you like fly-fishing, and I'm glad it's your hobby. But that's all it is. A hobby! I don't want you doing it until you put together at least six solid months on the job. And I don't want to talk about it."

"I just wish –" Corey started.

"Wish, wish, wish." Jimmy interrupted. "Go ahead and wish in one hand and take a dump in the other and tell me which one fills up faster!"

"Ok, Dad, I think I better go." Corey stood up feeling like he did at the end of most conversations with his father – as small and useless as the dead batteries that rattled around the drawer in his mother's kitchen – unnecessary, but not thrown away because she cared about the environment.

"Ok. You and Bruce have a productive day." Jimmy answered.

The phone clicked on the other end and Corey nestled the receiver back into its space. He silently turned to his backpack that hung on the end of the bed and pulled out some underwear. As he got dressed, Bruce remained in the bathroom, regretting his suggestion that Jimmy encourage his son. The sound of birds chirping and the tic-tac of light rain on the roof filled the room. Bruce straightened the toiletries Corey had dumped on the sink, waiting for Corey to finish dressing before entering.

"Well, dad hasn't changed."

Bruce didn't respond. He had worked with the family most of his life and understood Corey's introspective nature. Jimmy and Corey responded to conflict very differently. Jimmy was like a porcupine, quills-a-quiver, ready to fire; Corey was like an armadillo, curled up tightly in his shell, waiting for the attack to end. Bruce knew any comments about Jimmy right now would just bounce off Corey.

"You want to get to work?" Bruce asked as he wiped down the sink counter with a washcloth.

"Let's go." Corey answered.

Bruce followed Corey out of the bathroom. They grabbed their packs, slipped on their raincoats and exited the room. Corey drove, staring straight ahead into the spitting mist, and Bruce obliged Corey's unspoken request for silence. After several miles of no noise except the intermittent squeal of the aged wipers against the windshield, they pulled up to the old mill parking lot.

"Here we are." Bruce announced, hoping the drive had helped Corey calm down.

Corey shoved the gear selector into park and yanked the keys out. He popped the door open and slammed it behind him. Bruce stared through the drops on the windshield as Corey walked toward the mill.

"Well," Bruce said to himself as he stepped out of the truck and walked up to the crooked doorway. "Hope this day ends better than it started."

November Fourteen, Nineteen-**NINETY**-Eight

7:27 AM

Until this morning, Seventeen had been complicit in the show if by no other means than the most essential, holding her tongue. Eleven's trust in her initially reluctant conspirator had recently increased. Her growing confidence in Seventeen was due in part to Seventeen's secret-keeping, but was mostly the result of Eleven's tremendous fatigue. Friends are found in foxholes, and the pod they shared felt like the only bunker of safety from Dr. Nampala's daily attacks.

As Eleven was summoned earlier than usual to go up yet again for a barrage of stressful analysis, she decided to ask for help. Seventeen was half awake, curled up in her light green sleep sheath. She was aware of movement in the pod, but equally aware of wild horses running across a field of poppies in her dream.

As she lay there dreaming, a strong full-maned appaloosa broke from the pack and galloped toward her. It was moving swiftly, and its muscles shimmered as it thundered into the side of the ridge upon which she reclined. Seventeen should have been afraid, but she wasn't. She stared into the horse's blazing eyes and its flaring nostrils, and she knew it was a friend. In fact, as it crested the side of the hill, it slowed down and knelt in front of her. She turned onto her stomach and looked up at its moist dark eyes.

"Seventeen," it said.

She looked at its narrow speckled face and smiled.

"Seventeen, Seventeen." It repeated, this time nudging her chin with its coarsely haired muzzle. It tickled.

"Stop," Seventeen giggled, reaching out to push it away. As she pushed against its face, it felt strangely smooth and round. Seventeen continued to trace it with her hand, reaching what felt like a hardened mushroom.

"Seventeen, get up," it insisted. "And quit twisting my ear!"

The horse morphed before her as she opened her eyes. Eleven was kneeling beside her bed, calling her name. She held Eleven's ear in her hand, caressing it as though she was petting the horse. As the reality of the moment registered in her still foggy brain, she released her podmate's ear and sat up.

"Sorry, Eleven. I was dreaming you were a horse."

Eleven stood up. "A horse, huh? Well, I'm glad you didn't try to ride me."

"Me too." Seventeen looked at the clock. It was only 7:30 AM. Breakfast collection was still thirty minutes away.

"Why are you waking me up so early?" She lay back down and wriggled into her sleep sheath. As she felt the comfortable warmth of the spot where her body had been sleeping, she started to close her eyes, only to be startled back to consciousness by her podmate.

"You can't go back to sleep. Get up!" Eleven stepped closer to the bed and pushed against it with her thigh. "Wake up, Seventeen."

"Ok. What is it?" She half-sat up, propping her body up with her hands against her mattress. Her eyes were fully open, her big dark brown pupils almost scolding Eleven for the interruption.

"Thirty-Nine and I have been summoned even earlier for testing. Researcher-9 just stopped by and woke me. I have ten minutes to be ready to go up there."

"Seems like you're practically living there."

"Yes, it's getting harder and harder to think clearly. We are back and forth between dream sequencing and consciousness so much, I'm beginning to forget which moments are real life and which moments are a dream." She sat down on her bed and folded her hands between her knees. As she sat hunched over, staring at the ground, she was the embodiment of near defeat.

Eleven lifted her hands and rubbed her freshly shorn scalp. Seventeen could see the cross-shaped scar that became synonymous with Eleven's attempted escape and a reminder of Fifteen's death. Now, it struck her as a symbol of the mental and emotional crucifixion that she was enduring at the hands of Dr. Nampala. Something about the pitiful sensation in the pod compelled her to speak.

"I'm sure the Chief will give you a break soon."

Eleven brushed her head a final time, slinging her hands back down to her knees as she snapped her head up to look at her confidant.

"He's not going to stop until he discovers what he wants. And if he breaks me, so be it." Her chin trembled as she continued. "I'm scared, Seventeen. For the first time, I'm scared I can't make it."

Seventeen had seen Eleven's spirit breaking down over the past week. Little things that Eleven would never have done before, like letting other students go ahead of her for a game, or losing to lesser skilled players in chess. She thought it was because of Thirty-Nine's promotion; that Eleven was really struggling to find her new place in The Woodlands' society.

"You can make it, Eleven. You're the strongest person I know. Everyone here knows you are the best."

"Used to be the best." Eleven stood up and walked over to the wardrobe to get her shoes. She had slept in her tunic from the day before and didn't appear interested in switching to clean clothes.

Seventeen exited her sleep sheath and stood between the beds. She placed her slim hands on her pointed hips and watched as Eleven slipped on her shoes.

"Thirty-Three went back yesterday." Eleven whispered as she turned to face Seventeen. "I need you to run interference for him today. If you hear any students talking about him, tell them you heard he was sick. Researcher-9 is going to sneak him out during morning classes. He's already had problems and got punished yesterday afternoon."

"What do you mean he went back? Was the book right?"

"Yes. It was..."

"Wow!" Seventeen interrupted. "Are we going to be able to get out of here? I can't believe it! I mean, it's unbelievable!"

"Yes, it is. But," Eleven tried to calm her young peer. "We are far from getting out." She stepped closer to Seventeen and grabbed her hands. "We are very far from getting out." She repeated, her stern expression tempering Seventeen's exuberance. "What I need you to do is keep quiet. Only tell other students that Thirty-Three is sick. And, only if they ask."

"I understand." Seventeen nodded.

Eleven let go of Seventeen's hands and whispered, "I'm counting on you. I can't do it alone anymore."

Seventeen embraced her, squeezing Eleven unexpectedly. She pressed her face into Eleven's chest as Eleven reluctantly reciprocated, placing her arms on Seventeen's back.

"I will make you proud." Seventeen whispered. Just then, the buzzer sounded, announcing Researcher-9's arrival. They quickly disengaged.

"I know you will." Eleven whispered. "I know you will."

November Fourteen, Nineteen-**EIGHTY**-Eight

8:23 AM

"Something's wrong, Aunt Rita." Nicole called from the cramped bathroom at the back of the camper. The water in the toilet was rust colored. It looked like someone had dropped small clumps of red clay into the bowl. Nicole was leaning against the sink, holding her enormous stomach with one hand. She looked at her reflection in the postcard-sized mirror. Her skin was pale, even for a white girl in the Pacific Northwest in November. Her face glistened with a thin layer of perspiration, which had formed as she struggled to stand.

"What is it, dear?" Aunt Rita called from the kitchenette, where she was whipping a half-dozen freshly stolen eggs from the coops on the Frazier Farm.

"I'm hurting. And there's blood in the toilet." Nicole stepped out from the bathroom and fell onto the bench seat. Her weight dropping against the slim cushions shook the camper. Aunt Rita dropped the bowl, its stolen contents splattering against the countertop and the window. She rushed to Nicole's side and pressed her weathered hand against Nicole's moist forehead.

"Goodness, Nicole, you're warm."

"I really think something's wrong with the baby. I'm scared, Rita."

"Have you had any contractions?"

"I don't know. I don't think so."

"It's probably just a little spotting. Nothing to get alarmed over." Rita tried to reassure Nicole. "Let's get you up and in a comfortable position."

Aunt Rita squeezed her arm between the vinyl padding and Nicole's back. She hooked her hand under Nicole's far shoulder and straightened her to an upright position. As Nicole shifted, she felt increased pain in her abdomen. Nicole reached down and held her stomach. Her head fell back onto the frame of the bench with a thud. The sharp twinge that shot through her head and neck caused her to sit up straighter.

"Can you stand up, Nicole?"

"Yes. I think so."

Aunt Rita was hardened by life in the elements but she was not as spry as she had been twenty years earlier, when she could have been seen dragging a stubborn cow into its pen with nothing more than a rope and lots of shouting. Age had done nothing to reduce Rita's stubborn ways, but the ways of nature had diminished her physical strength. As she stood there, bent over Nicole's weak frame, Aunt Rita realized she couldn't get Nicole up on her own.

"If you can slide to the edge, I'll help you stand and walk you over to the bed, ok?"

"Ok."

They moved upward in unison, Nicole pressing her body up, Aunt Rita tugging under Nicole's back. They wobbled the six steps from the bench to the bed and eased Nicole onto her back. Rita pulled the checkered afghan from the foot of the bed and draped it over Nicole's body. Nicole pulled it to her chin, exposing her shins and feet.

"I'm cold, Rita."

"I'm going to take care of you, dear. Like we planned." She bustled to the back of the camper and dragged the box of medical supplies until it bumped against the lip of the table that poked out into the walkway.

As Aunt Rita reached under the table to fold it up and out of her way, she began singing a song her mother had sung at least seventy years earlier, whenever Rita was sick.

"Come to the window, my baby with me,

And look at the stars, that shine on the sea,"

She pushed the table up and pulled the box the rest of the way until she reached the side of Nicole's bed. She rummaged through some gauze pads, a large bowl and tubes of various ointments before finding a bundle of cloths. She peeled the binding off, turned to the sink and moistened the cloth.

"There are two little stars, that play bo-peep,

With two little fish, far down in the deep,"

The sound of Aunt Rita's delicate voice softly singing comforted Nicole. She closed her eyes and listened as Rita approached the bedside, holding the cool wet cloth. She continued the song as she dabbed Nicole's forehead.

"There are two little dogs, that bark and leap,

With two little angels, who dance over the deep,

And two little frogs, cry 'Neap, neap, neap'

And I see a dear baby that should be asleep.

And I see a dear baby that should be asleep,

Yes, I see a dear baby who is falling asleep."

As Rita concluded her lullaby, Nicole's pain subsided. She drifted back to sleep as Aunt Rita continued softly humming and pressing the cloth against Nicole's cheeks and forehead.

November Fourteen, Nineteen-**NINETY**-Eight

8:50 AM

Thirty-Nine was strapped in, eyelids fluttering, almost an hour into the dream sequencing session. Researcher-9 obediently jotted notes in the various graphs and charts on her clipboard, wary of doing anything that might enrage Dr. Nampala. As she escorted Thirty-Nine up that morning, they had agreed that she would sneak Thirty-Three into the Yard during morning classes. Thirty-Three had reported at Illness Level 3 before breakfast. He had run around the pod, overheating his body, so that he was sweaty and had a low fever when The Woodlands nurse surveyed his vitals. The nurse ordered 24-hour bed rest. She would review his condition before dinner, which would allow Thirty-Three to have an extended visit back to try and make contact with the man in Thirty-Nine's dream. The man who also rescued Eleven from the bus. The man who could rescue them all from The Woodlands.

Eleven was struggling to keep up with the intensity of the sessions. Even in the dream sequencing her weariness could be seen. She followed Thirty-Nine into a secondary phase of his dream, a dark forest thick with branches and a pungent smell – like hot asphalt being poured.

"Wait up!" Eleven called to Thirty-Nine as she stumbled over a protruding root. Thirty-Nine was at least twenty feet ahead of her, and she could barely see him through the extremely dense brush that enveloped them.

He looked back at her. "Sorry, but we have to keep moving. Don't you get the feeling we're being watched?"

"Well, we are always being watched so it's hard to distinguish it from the feeling of simply being alive. It's a constant part of our condition. Like breathing. Which is not easy right now." She skipped over a fallen log and splattered mud and moss as she landed.

"Yes. But what's happening at The Woodlands is merely observation. My skin is crawling with the sensation that we're being hunted."

"Hunted?" She caught up with him. He took her arm and led her onward. They ignored the occasional arm scraping bush and most of the time ducked under the spider webs and low-hanging branches.

"Yes. I sense the presence of others. And they aren't friendly."

"If you say so." Eleven replied without conviction.

"Keep moving. We'll get through this forest eventually. We need space to see what this dream's all about."

Yes sir, She thought, her mouth too tired to continue discussing Thirty-Nine's premonitions.

"You're funny – it's not like that."

Whatever you say.

He turned to look at her as he pushed against a cluster of bushes. Eleven's energy was so drained, even her dream self had no strength for their usual competitive banter. He was saddened, especially because he couldn't give her any real reason for his insistence that they keep trudging forward.

"I'm following my instinct," was all he could mumble as he stepped back in front of her to lead.

Watch out! Eleven thought.

He whipped his head around just in time to see he was about to walk into an overhanging branch about as thick as a grown man's thigh.

"Whoa!" he exclaimed, ducking. "Thank you!"

You're welcome. I'm with you no matter how I feel.

Thirty-Nine paused. Her thought toward him was surprising. She had confirmed his leadership and her commitment to the plan in one sweet phrase. It turned his heart away from the danger he sensed and toward her condition.

"Do you need to rest a minute?" He whispered.

_____

"Did you see that?" Dr. Nampala called out from his station jammed with monitors and dials.

"What, sir?" Researcher-9 replied.

Researcher-4 was adjusting the IV drip clipped to the metal rod over Eleven's cot.

"See what?" Researcher-4 chimed in.

"That spike in the activity in Thirty-Nine's temporal lobes. It's enormous!" He stood up from his station and danced across the room, his excitement uncontainable. "If what I think is happening..." He clapped his hands together and rubbed them vigorously. Dr. Nampala nearly vaulted over the small table at the end of Eleven's cot and bounced on his toes, peering over Researcher-4's shoulder.

"If what I think is happening," he repeated. "Enlarge screen 3, take it back to a one-minute segment." As he studied the graph, his glasses slid down his long thin nose, and his lab coat sleeves' frayed edges trembled against his bony wrist.

"That's it!" His shout made Researcher-4's hand jerk the knob she was turning. "Go back, go back. Never mind! Get up! Let me do it!" His normally pushed back hair was now falling over his forehead and eyes. Researcher-4 stood up from her chair, though not as quickly as Dr. Nampala would have liked. "Move it! We're on the verge of history here!"

"Sorry." Researcher-4 shuffled out of the way, grabbing her notepad off the desktop as she did. Even though she was rattled by Dr. Nampala's animation, she was a professional. She stepped around him as he feverishly turned dials and pressed buttons. She stood to the right of Eleven, who appeared more peaceful than she had in at least a week, if not longer.

"She looks better, even better than when she came in this morning." Researcher-4 said lowly to herself.

Researcher-9 eyed her from the other side of Thirty-Nine's **bed**. *I thought she didn't care...* Her thought was interrupted by a terrific shout from Dr. Nampala.

"That's it! That's it! Yes!" He pressed a couple buttons and raced around the workstation to the printer on the backside. He stood over the waist high white plastic box, waiting for the printout. "Lamp warming! Come on, come on!" Finally, the machine kicked into gear and spit out the paper evidence he had been searching for since he was a teenage graduate student.

"We did it! Well, we did part one!" He waved two pieces of paper over his head and jumped up and down like a child on Christmas morning.

"What is it, Dr. Nampala?" Researcher-4 asked.

He skipped around the equipment and motioned for Researcher-4 and Researcher-9 to join him at the main table, on the other side of the room. Both researchers stared at Dr. Nampala, confused by his direction.

"But, sir, we are never to interrupt our monitoring of the students."

"This is different, Researcher-9. This is monitoring the students." He held the papers out toward them. "Come see this. The students will be fine."

They reluctantly left their post and stood on either side of Dr. Nampala. He aligned the pages horizontally before them, flattening them perfectly with his hands so that Thirty-Nine's chart was directly above Eleven's.

"See here." He pointed to a dramatic spike about one-eighth of the way across a page labeled Student Thirty-Nine Temporal Activity. "And see here." He pointed to the exact same spike, at the exact same time on a page with the title Active Communication Formation: Student Eleven.

"Do you see it?" He smugly asked as he looked at his top researchers like a proud teacher; hopeful they would connect the dots. They stared at it for half a minute. As they stood there Researcher-9 glanced at her leader's scrawny frame.

I wonder if I could beat him up if I had to, she thought.

"I see it, Dr. Nampala, but I confess I'm not sure I fully know the source of your excitement." Researcher-4 responded.

"Well, Researcher-4," he shot a disapproving look at Researcher-9, surprised by her lack of engagement, which immediately turned her focus to the charts. He continued explaining, "Eleven's Broca's Area is spiking – it's on fire really – at precisely the same moment that Thirty-Nine's temporal lobes are ablaze. Researcher-9, what are those areas responsible for?"

"Well, sir," she began, fighting the urge to avoid eye contact, "the Broca's area controls the formation of words."

"That's right. And Thirty-Nine's temporal lobes?"

"The temporal lobes process auditory sensory input – hearing."

"That's right. So, Researcher-4, if Eleven's word formation region is active at precisely the same moment as Thirty-Nine's hearing and word input processing region is hyperactive, do you think it's possible...?"

"That Thirty-Nine is *hearing* Eleven's tho –"

She was interrupted by a beeping sound from the students' machines. She looked over to the cots.

"Go on, check on them." Dr. Nampala sighed. They scurried over to the two unconscious subjects to determine the cause of the alarm. Dr. Nampala trailed behind, holding the pages. As they approached, it appeared as though both of the students' heart rates were elevated.

Researcher-9 began the assessment protocol on Thirty-Nine. Researcher-4 did the same on Eleven. After a couple of minutes, Researcher-4 announced, "preliminary evaluation doesn't point to any demonstrable stress."

"Can you at least turn off the infernal beeping while you're checking?" Dr. Nampala stepped away and found his rocking chair. He turned it to face the two researchers and watched as they continued their examination of the students.

"I could use a break." Eleven accepted Thirty-Nine's invitation. They sat scrunched together, side-by-side, on a mossy patch. A couple shafts of sunlight fought their way through the trees, warming Eleven's upper back.

"That feels good." She placed her hands on the damp earth behind her and leaned back, tipping her head into the sunlight. She closed her eyes. As she did, Thirty-Nine studied her, from tip to toes, his bright yellow orbs filled with her graceful beauty. Her chin was firm yet delicate, matching her button nose. Her collarbones peeked out like a fawn's antler buds as they met in the open space at the neck of her tunic. The coarse fabric couldn't prevent him from noticing the outline of her mature, athletic torso. He was observing the curve of her hips when her eyes opened.

"Now I do feel like I'm being watched," she scolded, drawing her arms away from the ground, smacking the dirt off her hands and clutching her thighs up to her chest. She rested her chin onto the top of her knees and scowled at him.

His face turned bright red, his cheeks aflame with embarrassment, yet he did not look away. His metamorphosis from reluctant hero to bold leader extended even – perhaps especially – to his interactions with his, and his podmate's, erstwhile fantasy girl.

"You know, Thirty-Three was right."

"Right about what?"

"What he said yesterday in the Yard. Before he ran off to the sentry."

Eleven blushed at the memory. She played as though she didn't remember. She wanted to hear Thirty-Nine say it. She looked at his golden eyes, and the corners of her lips started to curl up in anticipation.

I don't remember. What are you talking about? She thought.

He said you were beautiful, Thirty-Nine thought. He stared at her. He suddenly laughed, remembering that the thought hearing thing was one way. She hadn't heard his response.

"What's so funny? It's not nice to laugh at me."

"I'm sorry. I responded to your thought with my own."

She wobbled her chin on her knees and opened her eyes wide. "You know I can't hear thoughts. That's mean."

Thirty-Nine slid away from her, ignoring the damp sensation from the mud and moss on his butt. He turned to face her, standing up as he did. She reached for his hand, and joined him, pouting as she stood.

"I'm sorry to joke with you." He looked up at her.

"You should be." She looked down at his hand, still holding hers. He released her hand in response. She reached for his hand back.

"It's ok," she took his hand in hers and stepped closer. A single ray of sunlight split the inches between them, casting a shadow of their silhouettes against the broad tree trunk that held the canopy of green under which they stood.

"You were going to tell me what Thirty-Three said?"

Thirty-Nine felt the breath from her question against his forehead. Her height was intimidating and alluring all at once. He arched his back slightly so he could see her without craning his neck.

"Well, Thirty-Three did say it. But, now, I'm saying it."

"Saying what?"

"Saying that you are beauti – "

———————————————————————————

"Bring them out." Dr. Nampala ordered from his rocking chair. "I'm convinced Thirty-Nine can hear thoughts – time to put him to work for real."

"Researcher-4, please take Eleven to the recovery room. Thirty-Nine will remain with me."

"Dr. Nampala, shouldn't he also –"

"Don't, Researcher-9," Nampala stood up from his chair and stepped toward her. "What did we talk about this morning?"

"Yes sir." She replied, lowering her head.

Researcher-4 disconnected the students and slowly helped Eleven to her feet.

She does look better than she has lately; her spirit seems lighter, Researcher-9 thought, watching Eleven from the other side of Thirty-Nine's bed. She returned to removing the straps from Thirty-Nine's arms, legs and waist. She stepped back as he slowly returned to full consciousness. He usually responded quickly, as though he was excited to be back in the real world. This time, he lay on the cot for a few minutes and stared at the sky through the giant glass ceiling.

"How do you feel?" Dr. Nampala's face suddenly hovered over him, blocking his view of the sky and interrupting his thoughts of Eleven. He flinched, startled by the suddenness of Dr. Nampala's appearance.

"Oh, did I scare you?" Dr. Nampala laughed.

"A little bit."

"I need you to sit up. Now." Dr. Nampala stepped back and stood beside the cot. Thirty-Nine pushed up and swung his legs out over the edge.

Dr. Nampala folded the papers and stuffed them into his coat pocket. He reached out, wrapping his skinny fingers around Thirty-Nine's neck, probing the glands in his neck and pressing against the space behind his ears. He tucked his hands behind Thirty-Nine's ears, and rested his thumbs on Thirty-Nine's nervously clenched jaw. Their eyes met.

How do you do it? Dr. Nampala thought.

Thirty-Nine blinked but said nothing.

He knows but if I admit it, he'll never let me out of his sight, Thirty-Nine thought.

"Not going to say anything?" Dr. Nampala asked as he dug his fingernails into Thirty-Nine's neck. He flinched but did not give in.

"About what, sir?"

"About what? Ha! You are good, kid, but you aren't that good." Dr. Nampala looked skyward for a moment, releasing Thirty-Nine's neck and resting his hands on his hips. His lips flattened as he pressed them together. He lifted his hand and drummed his fingers on his cheek as he considered how to continue his pursuit of his Head Student's power.

"Researcher-9!" He lowered his head and stared angrily at Thirty-Nine as he yelled for his assistant.

"Yes sir, I'm right here," she replied. She was standing at the foot of Thirty-Nine's cot.

"Go get me the Mind Cocoon from Thirty-Nine's pod. There's an easier way to do this." Thirty-Nine sat still and rubbed his neck. Researcher-9 looked at Thirty-Nine, hoping he would look at her before she left.

"Yes, Dr. Nampala. Let me grab my sweater. It's a little chilly in the hall today."

"Hurry up."

"Yes sir." She moved around his back as he continued to stand in front of Thirty-Nine. As she circled behind Dr. Nampala, she stared at Thirty-Nine until he glanced at her.

I'm going to send Thirty-Three back now.

"Look at me!" Dr. Nampala ordered his Head Student. "There's no reason to look at her." He turned to Researcher-9. "I said hurry up. Get out of here. Now!"

Dr. Nampala paced along the side of the bed.

"As soon as she gets back I'll just use the recording device in the Mind Cocoon to more finely analyze the patterns. It's got all your brain activity from the last few nights. I can cross-reference with your detail during the past week in here but I already know what I'll find." He reached in his pocket and pulled out the papers.

"Because," Dr. Nampala waved the paper in Thirty-Nine's face, "I know you can hear thoughts. And all that's left is to figure out how to reverse the process. Once that's done, The Woodlands wins. I win!"

"What?" Thirty-Nine asked as the door shut behind Researcher-9.

"What? What?" Dr. Nampala replied, mocking his pupil.

"I don't know what you're talking about. I'm confused."

"The project will be complete, boy. Look, I don't expect you to understand. But, I don't for a minute believe that you can't hear thoughts." He moved closer to Thirty-Nine. They were eye-to-eye and once again Thirty-Nine could smell the constant funky cigarette and deli meat odor of the Chief.

"If you could appreciate what I've been through." His dark eyes stared into Thirty-Nine's bright, light-filled eyes. "But you can't." Dr. Nampala suddenly coughed, shattering the tension and filling the air with the smell of his nasty breath. Thirty-Nine leaned back, trying to escape the accosting presence of his leader.

Dr. Nampala cleared his throat. "Guess I need some rest. Next month I'll get some."

"I'm sorry you don't feel well." Thirty-Nine tried to deflect the attention on hearing thoughts by showing compassion. It didn't work.

"Oh, I'm fine boy. I don't need your sympathy. Save it for the government. The men who stole me and all the others who ridiculed my proposal fifteen years ago will be in for a rude awakening." He smirked at him through his thick glasses. "And, I have you to thank for it." He slapped Thirty-Nine on the thigh and laughed.

November Fourteen, Nineteen-**NINETY**-Eight

9:20 AM

There's no turning back now, Researcher-9 thought as she rode the elevator down to the student residence hallway. As she stepped out of the metal box, the corridor was full of students marching silently behind sentries, heading to their classes or chores.

She nodded at the sentries as she passed by. She glanced at the digital clock hanging from the ceiling as she turned the corner, six doors down from Thirty-Three's pod. I've got 5 minutes.

Sentry-1 was approaching from the other end of the hallway. She walked up to him.

"Sentry-1, I need access to Thirty-Three's pod. Dr. Nampala requested I draw some samples." She held up a small medical case.

"No problem." He grunted and followed her to the door.

He listlessly pressed the buttons and swiped the card to unlock the door. She looked at his large head and thick hands. His forehead was sweating and his hands were trembling.

"Are you ok?" She whispered.

"I don't know."

The door beeped and he pushed it open. "There you go, Research-er-9. See you later."

Sentry-1 trudged away. She watched him for a moment. He moved slowly, almost clumsily.

"Are you coming in?" she heard Thirty-Three's voice from inside the pod.

"Oh, right! Sorry!" She stepped through the doorway and closed it behind her.

Thirty-Three stood up from his bed. He was wearing his work over-alls and a big grin.

"Gonna redeem myself today."

"Just relax. In a minute, the hall will be clear and we'll get you out of here. Then, it's up to you. I have to get this first." She walked over to the desk and grabbed Thirty-Nine's Mind Cocoon. She put it in the bag and turned to Thirty-Three.

"Dr. Nampala knows your podmate can hear thoughts."

"No!" Thirty-Three exclaimed. "He won't be able to do anything now. The Chief will be all over him, all day long!"

"You're right. It's up to you now. You can do it." Researcher-9 en-couraged him as she looked at the would-be hero in front of her. His dark eyes shone with enthusiasm. His stocky body wobbled with anticipation.

"Let's do this." He said.

They made it down the hall and to the exit without incident. Re-searcher-9 held the Mind Cocoon bag in her hand, and pushed the door open for Thirty-Three.

"Just a second." She stopped him before he crossed the threshold.

"What?"

"Take this." She reached into her pocket with her free hand and pulled out a small black plastic rectangle. "Keep this in your pocket."

"What is it?" Thirty-Three huffed as he held it between his pudgy fingers, examining the implement.

"It's a tracking device I lifted from the lab. It's a prototype, so I don't know how well it works. Much less if it works through time...but, if it does, it will let me know how you're progressing."

"Progressing?" Thirty-Three pushed it into his pocket, still puzzled by the purpose of the cheap looking piece of plastic.

"I'm going to be here at 12:40 *sharp*. You have to be here as well. If I can track your progress, I will know how close you are to the tree, and therefore, how close you are to returning. Either way, you have to get back here then or we will all be in danger. Got it?" She tilted her head and stared hard at him.

"Got it."

"Go on now, and good luck!"

The door slammed shut as she turned back into the hallway. She had done her part and needed to hustle back with the Mind Cocoon. She gripped the bag a little tighter as she hustled down the hall.

Thirty-Three was on his own. He hurried across the Yard. The tree was standing as though it were waiting for him. A breeze blew through, lifting the willow's long arm-like branches. He depressed the wooden key and just as he had yesterday, stepped into the past.

November Fourteen, Nineteen-**EIGHTY**-Eight

9:23 AM

"There's a whole bunch of salvageable equipment down here." Bruce yelled from the farthest end of the mill. Corey was twenty feet above him, in the former general manager's office. The stained plywood walls used to hold a large glass window. Now, they only held a few shards of glass and a growing expanse of spider webs.

"Hang on Bruce!" Corey pulled open a few drawers in the old metal desk that sat just below the large opening. Most of them had papers and files. Purchase orders and customer feedback surveys were in the top drawer. The second drawer rattled with a few pens and dead bugs. The last drawer he opened held something interesting.

"Keys." Corey said as he slid the drawer open and saw several sets of vehicle keys pegged to a small corkboard. He lifted the board out and yelled.

"Bruce! Got some keys to some trucks or something up here! Do you see any trucks down there?"

"What?" Bruce yelled from deep in the bowels of the mill. He was in the middle of a pile of cutting and sanding tools.

"Trucks! Do you see any trucks?" Corey walked out of the office and down the rickety wooden staircase. He landed on the metal catwalk that connected the management area to the operations center.

"No!" Bruce yelled back, walking toward the wide metal staircase that Corey was descending.

"You don't have to yell anymore." Corey laughed as he saw Bruce approaching. The building was cool yet Bruce was sweating like he'd been running a marathon.

"Why are you so sweaty?"

"You'd be sweaty too if you'd been pushing that equipment." He pointed to the large pieces of faded rusty metal tools. He wiped his face with his sleeve. "But I guess you're too busy playing scavenger hunt!"

"No," Corey stepped onto the concrete floor and stood beside his mentor. He jingled the keys in front of Bruce's face. "But if we have some trucks around here, the mill's valuation might change a bit."

"True." Bruce begrudgingly allowed. "But I haven't seen any."

"Well, maybe we need to look harder." Corey slapped Bruce on the back.

"You're awful happy all of a sudden."

"I know." Corey replied. "I guess I just realized that I'm not going to let my dad make me feel bad. It's not my problem if he can't figure out how to have a nice conversation. I'm moving on."

"That's a mature response, Corey. But what do you mean about moving on?" Bruce eyed his young protégé with concern.

"I mean I'm just going to keep going. Starting now." He stomped his foot and began walking away from Bruce. "I'm starting with figuring out where the trucks are for these keys." Corey waved them over his head as he marched into the dusty expanse of woodpiles and old equipment in the space before him.

"Good luck!" Bruce yelled as Corey disappeared behind a row of old logs.

"Funny boy," Bruce told himself. "I'll give him a little time. But I need to get the real equipment inventoried now."

Ten minutes passed. Bruce was elbows-deep in a stack of hand-held sanders when he heard a rumbling sound echoing through the mill.

"Corey?" He turned his head and looked around. He had his clip-board in his hand and slapped it against his leg at the sight before him.

Headlights.

"He found a truck, all right!" Bruce shouted and laughed.

Corey drove down the center of the basement floor, honking the horn of a 1950's era box truck. He pulled up next to Bruce. The truck was sputtering and spitting puffs of black smoke everywhere.

"Turn it off!" Bruce shouted, coughing.

Corey pulled the emergency brake but kept the truck running. He tugged on the window crank, trying to roll the window down. It didn't budge. The rubber trim was dry rotted all around the thick glass. He opened the door and jumped down.

"I can't turn it off!" He yelled at Bruce. "I don't know if it will start again!"

"Well get it out of here! Those fumes are going to kill us both!" He pointed down the row of logs to the double doors that exited into the parking lot. Years ago, those doors would always be open, day and night, as truckloads of timber came to be processed and left to be sold.

"Yes sir!" Corey shouted and climbed back into the cab. He patted the stiff black vinyl seat with his hand as Bruce walked ahead to open the doors. The old AM radio dial with the little orange stick reminded him of sitting with his dad when he was little.

"Dad loves these old trucks. Maybe we can restore this one together. Maybe he'll understand I'm just not a logging man. Probably not." He shook his head and stomped on the clutch and grabbed the leather wrapped ball atop the floorboard gearshift.

He pressed the gas as the truck lurched into gear. Billows of filthy smoke poured out the dual exhaust as he rolled toward Bruce, who was standing to the side of the now opened double doors.

He pulled into the gravel parking lot outside the main building. Bruce walked out into the daylight. Though the clouds prevented direct sunlight, any sky was brighter than the dark abyss of the mill.

Corey left the truck running and hopped out. He rubbed the wheel fender and whispered to the truck, slowly walking around the front. He stopped to admire the open-faced grill. It looked like an old football player's helmet with just one beam separating the open gap where the air-cooled radiator sat. The iconic symbol of the lower case "i" in the center of the capital "H" got him even more energized.

"International Harvester!" Corey shouted. He ran around the side of the now faded but still beautiful candy apple red cab and passed the black bed that had likely hauled tons of wood for many years before being abandoned in the recesses of the mill.

Bruce was standing at the back of the truck, nodding knowingly as Corey ran up to him.

"International Harvester! Isn't that cool!"

"Yes, it is, Corey." Bruce smiled bigger and started to laugh, infected by his protégé's glee.

"Dad said these were the trucks everybody drove back when he was getting started!"

"He's right." Bruce replied, growing nostalgic. "I drove something just like this one when I first got hired in the business. I was not even your age. Boy, time sure flies."

The smoke thinned as the truck burned off years of dirt.

"I'm going to take it for a spin." Corey announced after they stood together looking at the antique.

"I don't know about that." Bruce replied. "That old hauler is bound to need oil, water, gas. Who knows how long it's been sitting?"

"Look up there." Corey pointed to the bed of the truck. Strapped to the old painted boards against the back of the cab was a large metal container with the word FUEL stenciled in white lettering.

"I don't know..." Bruce said. Corey was already scampering up into the bed.

"Check it out!" Corey yelled as he opened the container. Inside were quarts of oil, transmission fluid, a five-gallon plastic jug of gas, and other truck maintenance essentials.

Corey held a quart of oil over his head. "This will do the trick! Dad will think this is so cool!"

"That stuff's old." Bruce replied. "Your dad –" he paused and thought about the morning's telephone call.

"Ah, never mind, you could use a break. Go ahead. Have fun. How about two hours? I'm going back in to work." He looked at his watch. "Be ready to work at 11:30, ok?"

"Yes sir!" Corey saluted Bruce as he walked back into the mill.

He pushed the metal box to the end of the truck bed, snagging it on a couple loose bolts. He nearly tripped over a thick coil of rope resting along the side.

"Whoa! If you were a snake, you could have bit me!" he yelled at the ankle-thick strands of faded white rope. He kicked at it. "Guess I'll have to watch out for you."

He finished pushing the container to the edge and hopped down. Before moving on, he looked at the worn boards.

"You may be old, but you've got some life left in ya!"

As if to reply, the still-running truck coughed a big puff of smoke right into Corey's legs. He waved his arms feverishly and stepped back.

"Ok, ok, I'll get you some fresh oil!"

He walked around to the front of the truck and turned off the engine. As he went about filling the truck with fresh oil and fluids, he whistled. After twenty minutes of tinkering, he slammed the heavy hood shut and jumped in the cab. He turned the key and revved the engine. As he pulled reached the nearly deserted road, he paused.

"Left or right?" Both directions looked equally empty. A few small buildings and homes dotted the roadside for a bit before giving way to an endless stretch of mammoth evergreen trees. "Dad would say go right. Left it is!"

He turned onto the road just as the drizzling rain stopped.

"If I could roll down this window, it'd be perfect. Well, almost perfect. The window's not the only thing that's wrong. Could be better with a pretty girl sitting here." He reached out and patted the seat.

"I guess we'll have to work on that." He looked at the road as he sped up to the limit of 45 mph. The dotted yellow line blurred into a solid divider between his lane and the empty lane headed back toward the mill. The hill ahead split the trees like a football through goal posts. It was serene. The hour ahead looked as peaceful and relaxed as a day spent floating his favorite river.

November Fourteen, Nineteen-**NINETY**-Eight

9:30 AM

"What took you so long?" Dr. Nampala asked Researcher-9 as she stood in the doorway holding the Mind Cocoon bag. He glared angrily at her, the same way he had when he threatened her family on the couch a few days earlier.

"It took a few minutes to get a sentry to open the door."

"Well, you need to hurry. Every minute counts. Now, go get the girl."

"Girl? You mean Eleven?" She stuttered.

Dr. Nampala stomped over to her, his bare feet slapping against the hardwood floor. He snatched the bag from Researcher-9's shaky hand and rolled his eyes.

"Yes, Eleven, you idiot! What other girl could I possibly mean?" He grabbed her by the shoulder and shook her. His jarring movement caused his glasses to slide down his nose.

"Now go get her!" He released Researcher-9 and pushed his glasses back up. She briskly walked out of the room. The fear that had begun to seep into her heart was now flooding every part of her body.

"And now the fun begins." Dr. Nampala turned to Thirty-Nine, who was beginning to become genuinely scared for the safety of his new friend. The Chief no longer intimidated him, but even if he did overpower Dr. Nampala he wasn't sure how to overcome the brute sentries that patrolled the halls.

Dr. Nampala walked to his desk and pulled the Mind Cocoon out of the black case. He connected a couple wires to a computer screen and began typing on a keyboard. "This will confirm everything. I hope you are ready, young man."

"Ready for what?" Thirty-Nine pulled his feet up onto the cot. He wrapped his arms around his knees and looked down at the monitor at the foot of his bed. Five green lines started dancing across the screen. As the wavy lines blurred together, he thought about how remote the possibility of escaping The Woodlands was.

This was a really stupid idea. We're just kids. What did we think we were going to do against the Chief and the Sentries?

"Sentry-1, Sentry-5." Dr. Nampala called into the loudspeaker as the screen before him interpreted Thirty-Nine's overnight dream recordings stored on the Mind Cocoon. "Report to my office immediately."

Dr. Nampala turned from the loudspeaker microphone and looked toward the sky. A light patter of rain splashed on the glass ceiling. He smiled as if something humorous suddenly came to mind. He looked over at his Head Student.

"Thirty-Nine, it's clear now. You truly are the best. I suppose now that you can hear thoughts, I should tell you everything. You'll overhear it eventually anyway."

Dr. Nampala walked toward him. Thirty-Nine slid his feet back down to the floor and stood up.

"Don't get any ideas, boy." Dr. Nampala stopped at the small end table near a rocking chair a few feet away from the cots. He reached into the top drawer and pulled out a flat rectangular aluminum case. He spun the chambers of two dial combination locks near the handle, aligning the numbers so he could open the case.

"What is that?" Thirty-Nine asked.

Dr. Nampala turned his back and opened the lid. The case lifted slightly as he tugged at whatever was in it. As he turned to Thirty-Nine, the now empty case rattled on the polished wood, echoing off the steel walls, sounding louder than it was in contrast to the tense silence of the moment.

"Just some insurance." Dr. Nampala answered, pointing a chrome handgun at his top pupil.

Thirty-Nine froze. He clutched the edge of the mattress behind him. His fingers clawed the thin top sheet into a wrinkled wad in his trembling hands. He looked at Dr. Nampala.

This will settle you down. Just nod if you can hear me, Dr. Nampala thought.

The Chief is thinking at me, Thirty-Nine thought. *What do I do?*

Dr. Nampala stepped closer to Thirty-Nine. He pointed the gun at his flat chest.

"Look at me!" He ordered.

"Yes sir." Thirty-Nine blinked but did not budge.

I'm going to give you one more chance, Dr. Nampala thought. *Quit pretending you can't hear my thoughts. Just admit it.*

The office door burst open as Sentry-1 and Sentry-5 entered.

"You called sir?" Sentry-5 asked.

Dr. Nampala lowered the gun and turned to face the sentries.

"Yes, men. Thank you." He held the gun against his thigh as he looked at them.

The door had scarcely closed behind the sentries when it opened again. Researcher-9 walked in, her arm around Eleven's shoulder. She seemed to be supporting Eleven, whose slouched posture and trembling eyelids told everyone she was tired. Dead tired.

"Here she is, sir." Researcher-9 announced from behind the massive guards as she led Eleven into the room.

"Ha ha ha!" The Chief laughed maniacally, his head falling back as his mouth opened wide. After a moment of reveling, the Chief snapped his mouth shut. The scraping sound of his teeth clashing startled Thirty-Nine. The hair on his neck stood on end as Nampala snorted a few times before finally addressing the group.

"Well, this is fun, isn't it?" He waved the pistol over his head and used it to point to his audience as he spoke. Even the sentries were visibly shaken by his reckless action. Sentry-5 and Sentry-1 stepped back toward the door and stood on opposite sides of Researcher-9 and Eleven.

"Eleven," Dr. Nampala began, "Just a few days ago, you thought you were going to leave The Woodlands. You were prepared to risk it all..." he paused and stepped toward her. He flicked his wrist at her causing the gun to bob up and down.

"You. You. You." He repeated himself all the while keeping his dark stormy eyes focused on Eleven. Her eyes started to dampen with tears as she clenched her fists, trying as hard as she could not to be affected by the Chief's tactics.

Researcher-9 gripped Eleven's shoulder tightly. She looked around Dr. Nampala at Thirty-Nine.

We've got to get out of here. He's losing it. She thought.

Thirty-Nine nodded but remained still. He didn't know what to do. His inventory of the situation told him not to risk anything right now. A couple of kids and a petite lady, even though she grew up in a dangerous foreign country, were no match for two burly guards and a deranged man with a gun.

"You! You thought you were the top dog. The head honcho. The big deal." Dr. Nampala stepped next to Eleven. He tapped her forehead with the barrel of the gun. "Let go of her, Researcher-9." He ordered.

"You were the Head Student. But you're nothing now, girl." He grabbed her by the waist and pushed the cold steel into her neck. She flinched and turned her head away from his nasty breath.

"Stop!" Thirty-Nine called out, punching the mattress behind him.

"I thought so." Dr. Nampala marched over to the cots, pushing Eleven along. "She is nothing to me, but she means something to you, doesn't she?"

Answer me Thirty-Nine, Dr. Nampala thought.

"Yes sir." Thirty-Nine didn't comment further.

"I don't have time for small talk, Thirty-Nine. You can hear thoughts, can't you?"

He grabbed Eleven by the neck and pushed her head toward the ground. He lifted the gun to her temple as she trembled before him. A single tear fell from her eye, splattering the toe of Thirty-Nine's shoe. He looked down as her salty cry spread into a dark spot on the toe of his boot leather.

"Ok, it's true." Thirty-Nine admitted. "Please let her go?"

"I don't think so." Dr. Nampala lifted her head up and flung her into the other cot. "Sentries!"

"Yes sir." They answered in unison.

"Come strap them into their beds."

Sentry-5 walked straight to Eleven. He grabbed her waistband with one hand and grabbed her neck with the other. He chucked her onto the bed like he was throwing hay bales into a barn loft.

Sentry-1 strapped Thirty-Nine in without abuse. He followed orders but his hesitation as he secured Thirty-Nine displayed his uncertainty over Dr. Nampala's unwarranted hostility. As he buckled the last strap, Sentry-1 looked down at Thirty-Nine. The guard's eyes were moist. His face flashed pain. He seemed conflicted. They stared at each other for a moment.

This has got to stop. Sentry-1 thought.

Thirty-Nine gulped. *Is he turning against the Chief too?* A tiny bubble of hope popped up inside Thirty-Nine.

"Are you ready?" Dr. Nampala asked. He stood at his desk and pulled two small glass bottles filled with a thick amber fluid out of a wire crate. Six bottles remained in the crate. He Held a bottle in each hand. The gun was sitting next to a stack of papers just a few inches from the space where he was working.

Sentry-5 jerked the straps across Eleven's body. He tightened the wrist restraints until her hands began to turn purple from loss of blood circulation. She whimpered lowly.

"Got a problem?" He asked.

"No." Eleven mumbled.

"We're all ready here, Dr. Nampala." Sentry-5 declared.

"Great. Researcher-9." Dr. Nampala called out. "Please call Researcher-4 up here. I'm going to need you both to monitor the students."

"Yes sir." Researcher-9 walked to the loudspeaker microphone and announced, "Researcher-4, please report to Dr. Nampala's office immediately."

She released the button on the microphone and looked to her left. The pistol was within reach. Its matte black handle was nearly camouflaged by the Mind Cocoon case but there was no missing its finely milled gleaming metal barrel. She entertained the fantasy of rescuing everyone. Right there. Right now. She could snatch the gun, pop Dr. Nampala and Sentry-5 and then...

"What are you looking at?" Dr. Nampala's stern voice interrupted her heroic daydream. "Get over to Thirty-Nine's bed." He set one bottle down. He picked up the gun and tucked it into the deep pouch pocket on the lower right side of his lab coat.

"As soon as Researcher-4 arrives we'll begin." Dr. Nampala spoke slowly as if unveiling a great new invention. He held the bottles up for everyone to see; everyone except Eleven and Thirty-Nine, who were strapped in place, staring at the misty raindrops falling on the glass ceiling overhead.

"In my hands I hold the final element to achieving our goal. What we've worked on for nearly a decade is about to become a reality. This serum is the final piece to the puzzle. It has been waiting years for this moment. And the best part? Its development was financed by the government twelve years ago. Ha! They will be overthrown by their own research, and they won't have a clue."

"What is it sir?" Reasearcher-9 asked as she walked to Thirty-Nine's bed.

"This beautiful concoction," he shook the bottles, forming oblong orange bubbles that slowly gurgled to the top, "is the enhancement that will enable the thinker," he nodded to Thirty-Nine, "to speak through the speaker. In this first case, Eleven. After they drink it, it will do its work. And finally, we will have what The Future desires. We will have Ventriloquism Chaos!" Dr. Nampala finished his speech with a slight bow. Sentry-5 smacked his hands together twice then stopped, self-correcting his unprofessional applause.

Researcher-9 walked to Thirty-Nine's bedside and fidgeted with the straps on his legs.

Researcher-4 entered the room.

"Ok. Researchers, prepare the students as usual. Except –" he paused for dramatic effect, clearly feeling revitalized by what he thought was a successful end to a risky project. "This time, do not put them to sleep.

They will be awake and alert for this experiment. Do not connect their minds with the brain cable. This will be the first wireless brain-to-brain transmission, or should I say, brain-to-mouth, in history."

The researchers began their setup as Dr. Nampala beamed behind them. As Researcher-4 approached Eleven, she spotted her swelling purple hands. For once, she displayed a glimmer of humanity.

"Those are too tight." Researcher-4 whispered, undoing the straps a couple notches.

"Thank you." Eleven whispered. "I hope I survive."

Researcher-9 leaned over Thirty-Nine. She gently rubbed his fuzzy head. She looked in his bright eyes. *Thirty-Three is out there. Just be patient. Be ready*, she thought.

November Fourteen, Nineteen-**EIGHTY**-Eight

10:12 AM

"What am I going to say when I go back there? That I'm ready to drink my hot chocolate?" Thirty-Three mused aloud as he tramped through the woods. The plant debris and muck underfoot was squishier than the day before. A steady rain fell, though rarely did a drop land on his chunky body, thanks to the dense evergreen branches high above his sheared scalp.

He was taking a different route to Port Mashton. The scenery wasn't much different from yesterday's trip except for a creek he spotted under a crisscross of lightning-struck fallen trees. Its babbling effervescence enticed him. Thirty-Three specialized in spontaneity. This surprising stream enticed him so he decided to follow it.

"This creek probably runs to the Bay. I've got time today. Let's follow it all the way!" Thirty-Three laughed at his rhyme as he walked along the edge of the narrow band of dribbling water. He checked his timer.

Two and a half hours. That's like an eternity. He thought. He hummed. His energy was high, and his spirits even higher. Thirty-Three's belief that escape was possible had never wavered. Now, he was experiencing it and like everything in life, the second time was easier. The stress of facing a foreign world had diminished. He discovered the outside wasn't so different from the inside, at least in the way things looked. The air was different though. He didn't feel suffocated here. He didn't feel the constant invasion of watchful eyes. Most of all, he didn't feel like he was going to be beaten half to death for speaking his mind.

"That's it." He said as he paused and grabbed a few pebbles along the water's edge. "Speak my mind. That's what I'll do." He flung a few stones into the crook, causing a dark green bullfrog camouflaged in the rocks to belch its dissatisfaction.

"Sorry, Mr. Frog!" He laughed. "Didn't mean to scare you. Don't worry, I'm not Sentry-5!"

He dropped the rest of the pebbles and sat on the trunk of a fallen tree. A few tall jagged strips of wood rose from the perimeter of the trunk, giving it the appearance of a rustic throne. The water-soaked surface penetrated the seat of his overalls but he ignored the dampening of his underwear as his thoughts returned to the purpose of his mission. He pulled the pictures out of his pocket and studied the faces from Thirty-Nine's dream.

"That was her. No doubt about it." He looked at the image of Nicole and recalled the brief interaction at the coffee shop. He heard the bullfrog again, bellowing to the woods.

"I hear you Mr. Frog. I know how you feel!"

He stood up. "Well Mr. Frog, I better get going. This lady," he held the picture out toward the edge of the creek, "is my friend's mother. I met her yesterday. She's pregnant. With my friend. I know, it doesn't make any sense. And, there's also this guy." He switched Nicole's picture for the picture of the man in the dream and waved it around.

As if in response to his pronouncement, the woods came alive with a chorus of frog croaks, followed by a cluster of bird chirps overhead. Even a squirrel on a tree branch hanging over the stream started yammering like it was talking to him.

"Ok!" Thirty-Three shouted, arching his eyebrow. "You're right. This young guy would probably be more help than a pregnant lady. Of course he would. But I have no idea how to find him."

Animal sounds echoed all around him. Frogs and crickets below him, squirrels beside him and birds above him. A cascade of chirps and croaks and scampering claws assaulted his eardrums.

"I hear ya, I hear ya! I know it's the guy that I have to find." He looked around. A clap of thunder echoed overhead. "Weird. It never thunders. Maybe everything out here is trying to tell me something. Nah. That's stupid." He told himself. "I better get moving. I think I'm starting to lose my mind! Animals talking to me!" He snorted at his own foolishness.

The sounds of the forest subsided, and only the muttering of the trickling water beside him remained.

He tucked the pictures in his pocket and started marching once again. He barreled through the occasional bush. He hopped over fallen logs. His body was alert and his mind was resolved. Resolved to get back to the town. Resolved to stop the Chief and The Woodlands. Resolved, more than anything, to find the guy in the picture.

After ten minutes of steady progress, the trees began to thin. As the drops of rain began penetrating the forest floor and his clothes, he wished he had worn a jacket.

He paused and stared at the sky as if he was praying, then looked at the meadow with tall grasses and wildflowers spread out to the left and right as far as he could see. On the other side of the clearing, through a final patch of trees, he could see pavement.

"Just a few hundred yards left. There's the road. I'll follow it into town." He crossed his fingers and pulled out the picture once more. "With any luck, I'll run into this guy!"

November Fourteen, Nineteen-**EIGHTY**-Eight

10:17 AM

"Still got an hour before I got to get back to the mill." Corey said as he pulled onto the gravel shoulder near the intersection of State Route 71 and US Highway 13. He had passed two cars and a few delivery trucks during the half hour he'd been driving.

"Not much out here but trees. Which is good, I reckon, since that's what dad's company uses to make wood." The crunch of the gravel under the thick rubber tires, the squeal of the windshield wipers and the chug of the engine were the only sounds he could hear. He drove further into the triangle of gravel and hopped out of the truck. He didn't dare turn the engine off. He stood beside the front of the truck and stared out at the road. Open spaces always felt like home.

Drops of rain plinked against the warm metal hood of the truck. Corey didn't mind the rain today. It was refreshing to be out here, looking at the wide-open space and smelling the clean air.

As he stared down the road before him, he thought about the life before him. Figuring out how to talk with his father was a never-ending puzzle. As he stood there thinking about that morning's phone call, an old VW bus rolled by, its square windows clouded with years of dirt and its bumpers stained with stickers declaring "peace to the world". The driver slowed down as he approached the intersection. He rolled down the window and propped his elbow on the inside of the doorframe.

"Need any help brother?" A heavy-set, curly-haired kid younger than Corey asked.

Corey smiled. "No man. I'm just enjoying the view."

"All right then. Keep on trucking." He shot Corey a thumbs-up and shifted into gear. "Nice ride!" He shouted as he headed away from Port Mashton.

Corey looked at the old truck. "Yes, you are a nice ride. If nothing else, maybe Bruce will find out how we can buy you." Corey smacked the hood, spraying water across his chest. He looked down at his shirt.

"Oops! Allright," he squinted up at the sky, "enough already, huh? Let's get going, old girl." He yanked the driver's door open and jumped in the cab. The truck sputtered as he tugged the gearshift into reverse and backed in a semi-circle.

"Come on girl." Corey coaxed as he turned the truck. His right arm was pressed against the rear window as he looked over his shoulder, guiding the truck into position. He looked down State Road 71.

"Nobody coming. Time to head back to the mill." He shifted into first gear and grabbed the hard plastic steering wheel. "Let's go." He said as he pulled onto the asphalt.

As he rode along, Corey was already beginning to think of the truck as his own. He began creating an inventory in his head of the various improvements that could be made.

"Need to get you some new wipers. That's at the top of the list for sure." He laughed as he looked at the windshield. The old thick glass was streaked by dust and rain. On the passenger side, a patch the size of his hand remained un-swept by the wiper, as the rubber in the blade had crumbled away and no longer made contact with the windshield.

Through the blurry glass, he spotted a figure in the distance. It was a red blur of a person, nearly two hundred yards ahead on the side of the road.

"Definitely need to get these wipers replaced. I can barely tell what that is." As he drove closer, he could see it was an older woman. She was standing in the road, waving her arms frantically. Corey downshifted and stomped on the brakes, causing the truck to shudder and nearly conk out.

"Hold on, girl!" Corey shouted as he slowed the truck to a stop just before colliding with the lady in the road. She ran to the front of the truck and banged on the hood.

"Help! Help!" She screamed. She made her way to his door, which Corey was opening as she approached. "Help! Help!"

She grabbed the outside handle and pulled the door back, ripping it from Corey's hand. The rain fell harder as he tumbled out of the truck. Standing before him was an old woman wearing a red sweatshirt and gray work pants. Her silver hair was plastered to her head.

"What's wrong?" Corey asked. He placed his hands on her shoulders and tried to calm her down. Her body trembled as she reached up and grabbed his shirt. Several soaked strips of hair clung to her cheeks as she spoke. She was out of breath but between the gasps, she explained why she was in the middle of the road.

"You have to help us." She inhaled and exhaled, trying to gain composure.

"Sure. I'll help. Of course." Corey replied. He studied her eyes. They were clear and vivid, showing no sign of drug use or disorientation. She was clearly in an emergency situation but she was focused and direct.

"Nicole." She pointed down the road. "Nicole is in trouble." Her breathing steadied. "You have to take us to the clinic. Franklin is about four miles from here."

"Who's Nicole? Where is she?" Corey asked as he guided the old lady into the cab of the truck. "Let's go." He ordered. "You can tell me what's happening on the way."

Corey grabbed her by the back of the elbow and helped her step up into the cab. As she slid across the stiff vinyl bench, he scrambled into the driver's seat.

"Thank you so much!" She cried as Corey started driving.

He looked at her. She was wiping off the rain around her face. Or was it tears? The lines in her face were deep and filled with the cares of life. But her eyes were bright and filled with hope. Something about her presence was calming, even as Corey drove toward a possible tragedy.

"Nicole is in labor. It's not good. Our turn is just up the road a little bit."

"I'm sorry ma'am. What's your name?" Corey asked.

"Rita. Rita Ann Havens is my full name. But Nicole calls me Aunt Rita." She looked at Corey. "You're a young fella. You call me Aunt Rita too. Now turn up here, on your left, just passed mile marker forty-seven."

Corey could barely see the green and white sign but he could see a cut in the tree line. As he slowed to make the turn, Aunt Rita continued describing the situation.

"We're poor. Nicole don't have health insurance. But I'm pretty good with taking care of sickness. I've even helped calve a few cows in my time. I didn't think it would be any problem." She stared at the dusty cracked dashboard. "But I was wrong."

Corey turned onto a trail that wasn't meant for a big truck. Branches scraped the sides and top, screeching like dying owls as he slowly navigated the mushy dirt path.

"She is really hurting. Got a fever of one hundred four. The baby won't drop and she's having trouble breathing. It could be anything. I don't know. I guess I shouldn't have talked her into having the baby at home."

The dark sky only made the moment seem more ominous.

This joy ride sure changed in a hurry, Corey thought.

They pulled into a clearing. To his left, Corey could see a small pop-up camper. It was the kind of thing his family used for vacation when he was a little kid. It was not a home. He shifted into neutral and set the parking brake.

Aunt Rita tugged at the passenger door handle. It wouldn't open. She strained and tugged for a few seconds but it didn't budge.

"Great. Add that to the list." Corey muttered. "Come on, Rita, out this door.

He flung the driver's door open and waited for Rita to scoot across the seat. Her leg caught on the tall gearshift in the center console. It only delayed her for a moment. Her stiff body was surging with adrenaline. She was so desperate to save Nicole she barely noticed the bump already forming on her knee. She slid out of the truck and rushed to the door of the camper, Corey trailing right behind.

As Rita opened the screen door, Corey heard a sickening sound. His stomach churned. His mouth dried up so fast he choked on his own breath.

The camper rattled as they stomped through the door. Nicole was wrapped in a blanket, lying on the permanent bed next to the kitchenette. She struggled for each breath. Alternating between deep sobbing moans and harsh nasal screams, her cries pierced the room. This no longer seemed like a little camper in the woods.

"Feels like a war zone." Corey whispered.

It was a war. The battle to save Nicole's life, and the life of her baby, was being waged solely by her will. She needed reinforcements and the only place close was the clinic in Franklin, over four miles away.

"Quit standing there staring!" Aunt Rita shouted.

Corey realized he had not moved. He was standing, mouth open, eyes wide, just a foot inside the doorway. Rita had already knelt down and was grabbing Nicole under her armpits, trying to move her up. She was losing the wrestling match with Nicole's larger convulsing body.

"Sorry! I got her." Corey dove into action. He slid his head under Nicole's arm and wrapped his arm around her back. He felt sweat drop onto his neck as he tugged her up.

"Don't let me die." Nicole faintly whispered into his ear. The metallic scent of blood accompanied her plea.

"I've got you." Corey slid his left arm under her thighs. The underside of her sweaty legs tugged at his cotton shirtsleeve.

"Get the door!" He shouted at Aunt Rita.

He hoisted Nicole and staggered back, banging against the frame of the dining bench. He wobbled. As he turned to exit the camper, Nicole's body clenched. Her weight shifted toward the core of her body and she started to fall from his grip. Corey slid his knee under her low back, saving them both from tumbling to the ground. The spasm subsided and he regained his hold.

"I've got the door." Rita replied.

Corey prayed for strength as he stepped into the driving rain and gusting wind. "God, help me help her."

Rita ran to the open door of the truck and climbed to the far side.

She squished her body against the door and extended her hand as Corey approached, stumbling under Nicole's weight and convulsions.

"Lay her on the seat and I'll pull her head onto my lap."

"Ok, Rita." Corey huffed.

The rain pelted them with unusual fury. The Northwest was always damp but the rain typically drizzled. It rarely came in a deluge. Despite the torrent, Corey never slipped.

He shoved Nicole in the truck and bent her knees up so he could sit. He pumped the gas and shifted into first gear. He turned the steering wheel hard to the right and sprayed mud as he accelerated up the narrow lane.

Nicole's moans had turned into whimpers. She was losing strength. Rita rubbed Nicole's hair and held her hand. Corey glanced through the passenger window as he reached the highway. The pounding rain made him feel like he was staring through foggy goggles in a dirty swimming pool.

"Looks clear." Aunt Rita said.

As Corey turned his vision back to the road ahead, out of the corner of his eye, he caught sight of Rita's hand overtop Nicole's. Rita's wrinkled, brown-spotted thickness of her skin clenched Nicole's pale limp fingers as though trying to pump life back into her body.

"Let's go." Corey leaned into the steering wheel. He pressed the pedal and the truck exhaust popped but the old engine responded gamely to his request for speed.

"We're going to make it. Hang in there." Corey whispered. His knuckles tingled as the vibration of the truck rattled through his hands.

Nicole squirmed on the seat. Her breathing was stable but every thirty seconds she lurched as her contractions twisted her body like a contortionist.

"Got to hurry." Aunt Rita said, mostly to herself.

"I know. I'm trying." Corey replied. He turned his arm and gripped his cuff in his hand. He pressed it against the inside of the windshield, trying vainly to wipe away the fog that was creeping up the old glass.

"Man, this rain needs to stop." He said in exasperation.

"This rain is crazy!" Thirty-Three shouted as he crossed the clearing and reached the tree line. His overalls were clinging to his legs as he ran as fast as he could to get back under cover of the evergreens. Beads of water stuck to his eyelids and trickled down his nose and lips.

"Guess it doesn't matter now!" He sputtered. "I'm completely soaked." He ducked under a low hanging branch as he exited the clearing.

"I should have asked Researcher-9 to check the weather report before I left Nineteen-Ninety-Eight!" He shook his arms and wiped his head and face. He looked up at the trees. The tightly clustered branches were nearly impenetrable, even for the heavy rain. Thirty-Three gripped his knees and hung his head as he caught his breath.

He reached for the pictures. He felt a damp mush of paper as he slid his pudgy fingers into the pocket. He pulled out the folded pages. They were fused together by the rain. He couldn't even grip a corner or an edge to peel the pictures apart.

"Great! They're probably ruined!" He closed his eyes. "Maybe I can remember what he looks like." He searched his memory for an image. His mind flashed an image of himself holding the page out over the creek. "Good, I think I can picture him. Not going to find him here, though."

He shoved the paper back in his pocket and began walking toward the road just beyond the trees. As he moved steadily through the thick trunks, he encouraged himself.

"He's out there. Maybe he's closer than I think."

Corey shifted into third gear and glanced down at the cracked speedometer. The orange marker slowly climbed higher, passing the still bright white "35" as it neared "40". Corey pressed the clutch in to shift to fourth as Nicole drove her heel into his hip as a fierce contraction surged through her body.

"Oh my God! I'm going to die!" She wailed.

"No you're not." Corey called out, looking down at her. She was writing on the seat. He reached down to readjust her leg.

"Watch out!" Aunt Rita shouted.

Corey jerked his head up just in time for his brain to register a human figure on the edge of the road. The next few seconds crawled. Corey slammed on the brake pedal without pressing in the clutch. The clunk of the engine stalling was loud but the thud of impact was louder. Through the dreary windshield, Corey saw a small person collide with the front passenger side of the truck. The person's head smacked the top of the hood and caromed off the heavy steel. The figure flew several yards through the air. It flopped, doll-like, clearly rendered unconscious from the blow. Even through the clouded glass, Corey could see the figure bounce off the pavement and roll into the grass.

"Oh, my gosh!" Corey shouted. "No! No!" He repeated as the truck lurched to a stop. Its engine hissed and clunked as it stalled.

He ran from the truck to the side of the road where the body lay. Rita reached for the door handle to help but it didn't open. She banged on the vinyl ribbed black panel, hoping it would somehow work. It didn't. She was stuck. She couldn't climb over Nicole, who wailed once again and squeezed Rita's hand as her body stiffened from the current contraction. Aunt Rita grabbed the window crank and tugged until it dropped the window a few inches.

"What is it?" she called to Corey.

A young boy lay in the grass. His head was shaved and blood leaked from his nose. A rectangular welt was growing on his forehead. He was dressed like an old wheat farmer. He had work overalls and a white collared shirt that now had blood and mud on both sleeves.

"It's a boy!" Corey yelled back. He looked into the trees along the road. It looked like the rest of the area. Dense evergreens with no sign of a trail.

"Where did this kid come from?" Corey asked himself as he reached down to feel for a pulse.

Corey's hands felt the boy's neck. His heart was beating steadily. Corey stood up and clapped his hands atop his head. The rainfall was lighter. As he stared down the road, he could see a break in the clouds.

"What am I going to do?" Corey looked down at the boy. His arm was twisted like a carousel pole.

"Well, his arm is broken." Corey muttered.

"Let's go!" Aunt Rita shouted through the slit in the window. "Nicole is fading!"

Corey scooped the boy up in his arms. He lugged him toward the truck just as he had carried Nicole minutes before. Corey could see Rita's gray hair through the opening in the passenger **window.**

There's no room for him in the cab, he thought. He continued around to the back of the truck. The bed was virtually empty. There was the metal box where he had found the fuel.

The rope!

"Hurry!" Rita screamed.

He climbed into the truck bed and gently slid the unconscious boy toward the cab. The rope was easily thirty feet long, maybe longer. It was wrapped several times back and forth along the length of the truck bed.

This thing is heavy enough to keep him from rolling out, Corey thought. He dragged the rope into a barrier between the injured kid and the open tailgate. He jumped down and ran to the front of the truck.

He pressed the clutch in and threw the shifter into gear. He pressed the gas and nothing happened.

"The truck died when you hit him." Aunt Rita said.

Nicole arched her back off the seat and drove her shoulders into Rita's chest.

"I'm trying, I'm trying." Corey said. He turned the key and the engine sputtered but failed to engage.

"Come on! Dear God!" Corey shouted. He turned the key again and tapped the gas pedal, careful not to flood the engine. The thirty-year old machine rumbled to life, answering his prayer.

"Atta girl!" Corey yelled. "They sure don't make 'em like they used to. This baby's purring like a kitten. Let's go!"

"You can say that again." Aunt Rita yelled.

He wheeled back onto the road and floored it. The rain was sprinkling now, and the clear sky ahead promised a safe road. His focus was on the few miles remaining. Nothing, even another mule kick from Nicole, would distract him the rest of the way.

The rest of the trip was a blur. As they chugged through Port Mashton and on to Franklin, he got the old claptrap up to nearly eighty miles an hour. Every bump and jolt in the truck caused Nicole to shudder.

As they neared the clinic, Corey's mind drifted from the wet pavement before him to the boy behind him. He turned into the small parking lot under a blue sign with "Franklin Emergent Care" in white letters. He had one repetitive thought that he couldn't shake:

Where in the world did that kid come from?

November Fourteen, Nineteen-**NINETY**-Eight

10:55 AM

"Just another hour and the serum will finish its work." Dr. Nampala said. He sat in his rocking chair near the foot of Thirty-Nine's bed.

"Everything remains stable." Researcher-4 announced as she studied the bank of monitors lining the side of Eleven's bed.

"It won't be long now." Dr. Nampala looked at the scene before him as he crossed his feet, stretching his skinny legs.

Researcher-4 and Researcher-9 hovered over their respective students, checking charts and graphs on the various electric screens. Sentry-5 stood, arms folded, near Dr. Nampala's desk. Sentry-1 stood with his back to the group. He was on the other side of the room packing stacks of file folders into cardboard boxes.

"Good job, Sentry-1." Dr. Nampala said. "Leave those for now and do a floor perimeter sweep."

"Yes sir." Sentry-1 finished packing the box he was working on and folded its lid. He turned and walked past the beds and Dr. Nampala.

"Don't forget to check *all* the rooms." Sentry-5 added as Sentry-1 neared the door.

"I got it." Sentry-1 replied firmly, annoyed at Sentry-5's implication that he wouldn't do a thorough job.

"Settle down Sentry-5." Dr. Nampala turned his head and warned his most vicious guard. "We're almost there." He nodded toward the students in front of him. "Before lunch is served, he'll be transferring thoughts to her. She'll be speaking his thoughts. Voila! The first thought soldier. I think you can relax a little."

"Sir. I can't relax. It's my job to remain vigilant." Sentry-5 replied, uncrossing his arms and planting his hands on his hips.

"I suppose you're right. But it won't be long until we can all breathe a little easier." Dr. Nampala drew his legs under him and stood. "I'm going to the balcony for some fresh air."

Researcher-9 peeked up from the monitor and watched Dr. Nampala walk by. As he neared the sliding glass door, she cleared her throat.

"Umm, Dr. Nampala?" She stuttered.

He turned halfway and looked at her sideways. She felt like she was in his cross hairs as he peered at her over his glasses. She coughed a dry forced cough and thought of what she could say to get out of the room. Anything out of the ordinary would only raise his suspicions.

"What?" He asked.

"Umm. Is it possible? Err – would it be ok if I could be excused to use the restroom?" She lifted her head and maintained eye contact.

"The restroom? Aren't you supposed to go before the shift? How long have you been in here?" He completed his turn as he spoke and now faced her directly. His cluttered desk, the boxes Sentry-1 was filling and the equipment around Thirty-Nine's bed separated them but his penetrating stare made her feel as though they were inches apart.

"It's been over an hour and a half, sir. I'll be fast. I just don't want to interrupt the work once the serum takes effect." She pointed at Thirty-Nine and Eleven as she finished speaking.

Dr. Nampala looked up and rubbed the underside of his chin with his long fingernails. He turned his head from side to side, all the while stroking his wispy beard. Finally, he looked at Researcher-9.

"Ok. But hurry." He flicked his hand toward the door as if to shoo her away.

"Yes sir. Thank you. I'll be right back." She adjusted a knob on the monitor in front of her and stepped toward the door. Dr. Nampala watched her walk out. He waited until he heard the click of the door behind her then spoke to Sentry-5.

"Do you sense anything unusual with her?"

"I'm not sure, sir. Have you noticed something strange?"

"I don't know. Just seems like she has softened in the last week or so. She would never ask to leave before. She was reliable and strong. Like you." Dr. Nampala winked at Sentry-5.

"I'll keep an eye on her, sir." Sentry-5 kept his reply brief. He didn't know how to respond to Dr. Nampala's playful gesture.

"All right." Dr. Nampala turned back to the door and stepped outside. "Come get me in twenty minutes."

Researcher-9 slipped down the hall and entered the female restroom. It was empty. She opened the second stall door and latched it closed. She reached into her pocket and pulled out a small black plastic box. It was the size of a TV remote control. Instead of control buttons, it had a total of twenty tiny bulbs that formed a cross. Twelve bulbs ran from top to bottom, and eight bulbs ran from side to side. She clicked the on-off switch at the base of the device. The bulb on the far right glowed solid red.

"It's working. Even through time." She whispered. The box was a homing device. It was linked to the tracking mechanism she had given Thirty-Three before he went back. A yellow "N" "E" "S" "W", corresponding to the four points of a compass, was etched at the end of each row of bulbs.

It worked to guide whoever was holding the box. As they moved nearer to the tracking square, the bulbs glowed brighter. If the person with the tracking square, in this case Thirty-Three, moved, the lights blinked.

"He's not moving." Researcher-9 stared at the single lit bulb. It remained lit. It didn't flicker. "Well, its working. I think. If it is, he isn't going anywhere. Maybe he's talking with someone on the other side. Someone who can help shut this place down."

She turned it off and dropped it back into her pocket. She unlocked the door and stepped out of the stall. She looked at the cold bare concrete wall.

"I'm sure ready to shut this place down." She mumbled as she walked out into the hallway.

She had barely taken a step when the door opposite her opened. It was the door to the male restroom. Sentry-1 stepped through, holding something in his hand.

"Hello. You startled me." She clutched her hand to her chest and giggled. She looked at him directly. He was average sized, with a flat face and cleft chin. His face was dotted with dark stubble.

"Sorry." He turned and started walking toward Dr. Nampala's office. As he walked away from her, she could clearly see what he held in his hand.

The diary, She thought. Her heart raced. *We forgot to get it after Thirty-Nine hid it yesterday. I have to do something.*

"What is that?" She called out to Sentry-1. Her rapid steps to catch up with him made trying to sound nonchalant difficult.

"I found this book stuck up in the ceiling of the restroom. I don't know how long it's been there but my hunch is that one of our students is hiding something." Sentry-1 held up the beige canvas volume discovered by Eleven a week before.

Researcher-9 gulped. "It looks really old."

"It's probably some kind of propaganda. We've found things like this before. Now, if you're satisfied, I have to report it to Dr. Nampala." Sentry-1 tucked the book under his arm and turned on his heel.

"Can I hold it?" She pitifully asked.

"No. Just let me do my job." Sentry-1 replied without turning to look at her. He stepped to the door and entered the code. The door beeped twice and he pulled it open and stood, looking back at Researcher-9.

"Are you coming?" He asked.

Researcher-9 hesitated in the hallway.

If Dr. Nampala figures out what's happening, we're all dead. Of course, if we don't succeed, we're all dead anyway. Act natural. You can do this.

Sufficiently reassured by her own thoughts, Researcher-9 buttoned the top of her jacket and patted the sides of her hair. She cracked her knuckles.

"Let's go." She replied tersely.

They entered the room side by side. She was closer to the book under his arm than she had been to the gun on Dr. Nampala's desk earlier. The same impulse to become a hero – or die trying – rushed through her mind. She looked at his tight grip on the book.

Not only was he squeezing the book in his right hand, but he also had his hand and book tucked under his left arm. He was smaller than Sentry-5 but he outsized Researcher-9 by at least fifty pounds and eight inches.

"Dr. Nampala?" He called out as they walked into the center of the room.

"He's on the ledge." Sentry-5 responded. "What do you need?"

"I found something during my perimeter sweep. It might be nothing but he needs to look at it." Sentry-1 walked over to Sentry-5. Researcher-9 peeled off and turned to Thirty-Nine's bed.

Sentry-1 found the diary you hid in the bathroom, she thought.

Thirty-Nine's eyes bugged out in silent response. "No," he mouthed, careful not to attract attention from the guards or Researcher-4.

Yes. I don't know what's going to happen. I'm going to try and distract them. Be ready for anything.

Thirty-Nine nodded.

"Thirty-Three?" He whispered through clenched teeth.

Thirty-Three is back in 1988. The tracking device shows him due west of here but it showed no movement. I can't check it now but it does appear to be working.

"Researcher-9." Dr. Nampala's nasal voice called her name from the balcony.

She looked up to see him entering the room.

"Is Thirty-Nine ready?"

"Yes sir. I think so." She replied, looking down at her co-conspirator.

"Dr. Nampala," Sentry-5 said, "Sentry-1 has something to show you."

"Not now," Dr. Nampala replied. "Save it for after we test the serum."

"Yes sir."

The sentries looked at each other. Sentry-5 reached to grab the book from Sentry-1. He refused and stepped back from Sentry-5. A stare down between the alpha guards ensued.

"Give me the book." Sentry-5 ordered.

"No. I found it. I'll give it to Dr. Nampala." Sentry-1 replied, curling the book in half in his thick strong hands.

Sentry-5 inched closer and raised his voice. "Take your post at the door. I'll keep this until he's done with the experiment." He said as he tried to intimidate Sentry-1.

"Step away from me. Now." Sentry-1's surly reply took Dr. Nampala by surprise.

"Sentry-1. What is the problem?" Dr. Nampala asked.

"Sir. I will not be ordered around by him. By this," he pointed at Sentry-5's broad chest and fumbled for the right word. "By this...this...murderer."

As the word tumbled from his lips, Sentry-1 knew immediately he'd crossed the line.

"That's a strong accusation." Dr. Nampala said. He turned to Sentry-5, whose surprisingly smirking face looked at Sentry-1 condescendingly.

"I never murdered anyone. I just did my job. Unlike you, apparently." Sentry-5 said.

"That's enough. From both of you." Dr. Nampala said before Sentry-1 could reply. "Sentry-1, you go guard the door. And give me the book."

"Yes sir." Sentry-1 handed Wesley Kenton's diary to Dr. Nampala. He flipped it over in his hands and felt its weight. He traced the title with his pointed fingernail.

"**Notes in Time**." He read aloud. "Very interesting. Sentry-1, where did you find this?"

"In the male bathroom just outside your door." Sentry-1 answered from across the room.

"We'll need to get to the bottom of this." Dr. Nampala said. He glared at Sentry-5 as he handed him the book. "Hold on to this. After we're done here, you better figure out where it came from."

"Yes sir." Sentry-5 said. He looked over at Sentry-1 and smiled. He was nearly giddy over Dr. Nampala's implied elevation of himself over Sentry-1.

"Ok," Dr. Nampala said, turning to the researchers. "It's time to test the serum. I need the beds tilted and turned so the students are facing each other. Keep them strapped in."

The researchers adjusted the beds according to his orders. As Eleven came into Thirty-Nine's field of vision, he noticed her hollow stare and her droopy eyes.

"It's going to be all right." He whispered, hoping to rally his friend.

She stared at him. A faint twinkle in her eye caused him to grin. Fortunately, Dr. Nampala was still behind him.

I'm ok, she thought. *Just preserving my strength. Whatever happens with this thought transferring experiment, I'm glad it's you. You turned out to be way different than I thought.*

He smiled.

Don't worry, she thought. *If we get out of here, great. If not, we gave it our best shot.*

"All ready, Dr. Nampala." Researcher-4 said from behind Eleven's bed.

"Great! Thank you researchers." Dr. Nampala replied. He walked around to the square of floor that held his two students, now face to face, strapped to their beds.

"My star students. The time has come. We have been – well, I have been – waiting for this day for a very long time. There's not a research facility in the world that is capable of doing what we are about to do." He lifted his hand up as though he were holding a glass to propose a toast. "To The Future!" He yelled.

"Let the fun begin. Thirty-Nine," he instructed, "I want you to look at Eleven and think the words on this page." He held a yellow journal pad in front of Thirty-Nine's midsection.

Jotted on the page in difficult to read print were two simple sentences. "Dr. Nampala is a genius. The Woodlands forever."

Thirty-Nine looked at Eleven. He didn't feel any different. She didn't look any different. Yet he was now supposed to be able to control her speech just like a ventriloquist with a wooden dummy.

I'm tired of doing his bidding, he thought.

"I'm tired of doing..." Eleven uttered, startling herself.

"Ouch!" Thirty-Nine shouted to prevent Dr. Nampala from hearing the end of his thought.

Dr. Nampala looked at Eleven and back at Thirty-Nine. He shook the pad in front of Thirty-Nine.

"What are you whining about? There's nothing wrong with you! Think what's on the page. Now!" Dr. Nampala shouted.

November Fourteen, Nineteen-**EIGHTY**-Eight

12:12 PM

"Now! Hand me the forceps now!" The doctor demanded.

Corey paced in the small waiting area of the medical clinic. He could hear everything through the thin walls. This tiny medical center had one doctor on staff, two nurses and a receptionist. Pandemonium invaded the dingy building when Corey arrived shouting for help.

The receptionist was an elderly bookish lady wearing cat-eye spectacles. She nearly passed out when Corey rushed in with Nicole in his arms, and then returned a minute later with an unconscious boy in his arms. Aunt Rita went back in with Nicole, but Corey, as a non-family member, was restrained to the waiting room.

Fortunately, only routine cold and flu patients were in the waiting area and they were easily postponed for the triple life-threatening situation now facing the under-qualified staff. The doctor, a bearded gentleman in his mid fifties, approached the situation as calmly as possible.

Corey stood stressed in the waiting room, overhearing every sentence of the frightening conversation between the nurses and the doctor.

"Cut off the boy's clothes." Corey heard the doctor say. "I need to manipulate his torso for internal injuries. How's his brain stem? Spinal column? Call Seattle Children's Hospital. Tell them to be on standby for a possible brain trauma. We may need a helicopter."

The interchange between the doctor and the two nurses alternated between trying to save Thirty-Three and helping Nicole deliver the baby.

"The boy's heart rate is dropping!"

"The mother's blood pressure is strong. Get the oxygen mask on her."

"The boy shows minimal reflex response."

Listening to the tension of life-and-death medical directives without being able to do anything was more than Corey could take. He stepped outside into the cold November air just as Bruce pulled up in the rental car.

"Hey buddy." Bruce called out as he slammed the car door shut. "What the heck happened?"

"I'm so glad to see you." Corey sighed. "I was just driving the truck when I got flagged down by an old lady whose niece was in the middle of having a baby! Then I hit a kid who came out of the woods!" He kicked the gravel. "I mean, how crazy is this?"

"Try to calm down." Bruce said. He put his arm around Corey's shoulder and walked him back onto the small porch at the front of the clinic. The porch floorboards creaked as they stepped across the faded welcome mat's fraying edges.

"Sit down." Bruce said. He pushed Corey toward an old rocking chair near the doorway. Corey slumped into the seat and hid his face in his hands.

"What if the kid dies?" Corey asked. His shaky voice bounced off his cold palms.

"He won't," Bruce reassured. "And don't worry, I've called your father. He's on his way. Jumped on a flight thirty minutes ago."

"You called dad? Oh geez, just great!" Corey lifted his head and shot Bruce an angry look. "Forget if the boy lives, it won't matter, at least for me. Dad is going to kill me!"

"Nonsense." Bruce said. "Your father's not going to kill you. I don't know what you expect him to do, but he's not a monster." He knelt down in a catcher's position, wincing as his balky knee buckled and forced him to bend over at the waist. He steadied himself on the arm of Corey's chair.

"I know." Corey said, returning his hands to his face.

"Listen Corey." Bruce said. "Look at me."

Corey looked down at his boss, who was tipping back and forth on the balls of his feet, tugging at the arm of Corey's chair to stay balanced.

"Corey, don't worry. Your dad cares about you. And he's a problem solver. He'll get this sorted out and we'll all be home soon."

November Fourteen, Nineteen-**NINETY**-Eight

12:32 PM

"It worked." Dr. Nampala said. "Try this." He wrote on the pad and held it in front of Thirty-Nine.

"Look at Eleven! Think this!" He commanded.

Axiom 6, Thirty-Nine thought.

"Axiom 6." Eleven said.

Dr. Nampala giggled. He was overcome with excitement.

No mind exists without another, Thirty-Nine thought.

"No mind exists without another." Eleven said.

"That's it!" Dr. Nampala shouted. He turned his head toward Sentry-5. "It's working, it's working!"

The ultimate existence, Thirty-Nine thought.

"The ultimate existence." Eleven said.

"Ten million dollars." Dr. Nampala whispered. He rubbed his hands together like a homeless man standing over a rubbish fire.

"What sir?" Sentry-5 asked.

Is found when collective power is uncovered, Thirty-Nine thought.

"Is found when collective power is uncovered." Eleven said.

Dr. Nampala dropped the pad and looked at Sentry-5.

"What did you say sir?" Sentry-5 asked again.

"Did I speak to you?" Dr. Nampala asked.

"No sir." Sentry-5 replied.

"Then hold your tongue. Do something useful. Figure out where that book came from. Shouldn't be hard, not many students have ever been on this floor." Dr. Nampala said.

Researcher-9 slipped around the back of Dr. Nampala's desk while Sentry-5 and Dr. Nampala were talking. She held several folders in her hand and wrote on the outside cover of the top folder while she walked.

Dr. Nampala turned back and faced Thirty-Nine. Sentry-5 walked toward the doorway. He was still holding the book.

"I'll bag up the Mind Cocoon, sir?" Researcher-9 asked.

"That's fine." He said. "It's time for some celebration. Sentry-1, come over here and help Researcher-4 release our students."

Sentry-1 intentionally brushed against Sentry-5 as they crossed paths. Sentry-5 snickered. "You know who's really in charge now, shorty." He whispered.

"Sentry-5!" Dr. Nampala shouted. "Quit pestering Sentry-1. Go find out where that book came from. Find out who is trying to hide whatever is in that book from me!"

"Yes sir." Sentry-5 walked toward the door, thumbing through Wesley Kenton's diary.

Sentry-1 watched him walking away. He held his tongue and walked to the students' beds. Researcher-4 pressed the lever to lower their beds.

Researcher-9 looked around the room. Sentry-1 and Researcher-4 were focused on releasing Eleven and Thirty-Nine. Dr. Nampala's back was to her. She palmed one of the vials of serum that Dr. Nampala left on his desk. She placed it in the bottom of the bag and laid the Mind Cocoon in next. She velcroed the flap lid closed.

"I need a cigarette." Dr. Nampala said, turning to Researcher-9 just as she slid her head under the strap of the Mind Cocoon bag. "What a great day this has been!" Dr. Nampala continued. "Nothing like a good smoke to settle me down and enjoy the moment." He brushed against Researcher-9 as he walked to his desk. She clenched the top of the bag with her hand and pinned it to her side.

"Why so nervous Researcher-9?" Dr. Nampala asked as he fished in his desk drawer and pulled out a thin metal box.

"I'm not nervous. Just excited. Sir." Researcher-9 replied.

"Sir." Researcher-4 said. "I'll complete the report and finish the log book. Is there anything additional you'd like me to accomplish?"

"No. You've done well." He replied. He raised his eyebrows and looked at her from head to toe, and back again. "You know what, Researcher-4, you should celebrate too. You want a cigarette?"

She blushed a little at his offer. He was usually harsh. He was certainly never kind. She thought he might be offended if she said no.

"Yes sir." She answered.

"Let's go on the balcony, Rearcher-4. Don't want to get the smoke near this expensive equipment. Researcher-9, Sentry-1, you all can escort the students to their pods."

He tapped out a couple cigarettes. Researcher-4 slowly walked over to him.

Eleven and Thirty-Nine remained strapped to the beds. Sentry-1 undid the straps on Eleven. Researcher-9 released Thirty-Nine.

Dr. Nampala placed his arm over Researcher-4's shoulder. "Do you know that you're a good researcher?" he asked.

"Thank you sir." She replied.

"And you're a foxy lady too." His hard laugh turned into a brief hacking cough. He led her to the balcony and just before stepping outside, he turned to the group standing near the beds.

"Thirty-Nine. Get some rest. We'll reconvene this evening to replicate our session." He turned back to Researcher-4 and fished a lighter out of his pocket. "Need a light beautiful?" He asked.

Now we can check on Thirty-Three, Researcher-9 thought.

Thirty-Nine nodded.

Sentry-1 stood beside Eleven. She was wobbly. "Can I help you?" He asked, extending his hand to her upper arm. His thick fingers nearly covered her arm from shoulder to elbow.

Researcher-9 and Thirty-Nine raised their eyebrows at each other, surprised by Sentry-1's kindness.

"Maybe we should just get them back to their pods." She said.

"Ok. Let's go." Sentry-1 said.

They shuffled toward the door, led by Researcher-9. Thirty-Nine and Eleven were side-by-side, with Sentry-1 closely following.

They exited the room and silently returned to their pods.

November Fourteen, Nineteen-**NINETY**-Eight

12:45 PM

As they entered Thirty-Nine's pod, Researcher-9 dropped the Mind Cocoon bag on the floor next to her feet. She yanked the tracking box out of her pocket. Sentry-1 remained in the pod and pulled the door shut. The four of them stood near the closed door, all sensing the direfulness of the moment but none knowing what to say.

Thirty-Nine stood beside Researcher-9. His nerves were as frayed as the trim on the Chief's smelly threadbare robe. Eleven leaned her exhausted body against his. She placed her chin on his right shoulder and tossed her arm around the other. Her fuzzy scalp tickled his neck.

No one was sure why Sentry-1 remained in the pod but everyone was afraid to ask. Thirty-Nine had heard him grumbling about Dr. Nampala, but what if he was a spy for the Chief? Thirty-Nine glanced at Researcher-9. All he saw was the white zigzag separating her tightly parted hair. She was looking down at the single lit bulb on the far right of the tracking box in her hand. She shook it a couple times and tapped it against her hand like Dr. Nampala tapped his cigarette case against his palm before pulling out a nicotine stick.

Finally, Sentry-1 spoke. His deep voice felt like drum kick against their spirits. His matter-of-fact tone belied the deep pain he fought to bury under the routine work of each day since Fifteen died.

"I can't take it anymore. I know you all are up to something. I think I know what it is. I might die but..." He paused and looked at the trio as if he was sizing up a team about to take the field. He looked like a coach, too. Not one of those coaches who wore a suit and went to college. No, Sentry-1 looked like a former player who wasn't the smartest but could relate to the players because he'd been there. He knew the game would be tough. He knew his team was a bunch of long shots and misfits, yet he believed so compellingly in the potential victory that his words alone could move the players to believe just a little more. That extra belief that so often becomes the difference between winning and losing.

"I might die." He repeated. "But, I'm already dead inside. I died when they killed her. When *Sentry-5* killed her."

Thirty-Nine looked at Researcher-9. She shrugged her shoulders but held her tongue. She wasn't going to interrupt the gentle brute before them. He hadn't spoken to her since the day she arrived, over seven years ago. Whatever he had to say would be worth listening to. Eleven stiffened against Thirty-Nine but remained in contact. The crook of her elbow tightened against his collarbone as she tensed in anticipation.

"I followed the rules. I obeyed the commands. Just like you all. I've been a good soldier. The best. I know you are all trying to get out of here. I sense it. And I think you can do it. I've had enough of *him*. Enough of *The Woodlands*." He spit on the floor to emphasize his disgust.

Suddenly Thirty-Nine remembered Fifteen spitting on the ground that day in the Yard when she talked about leaving the earth. He looked at Sentry-1. He noticed the wide forehead. That thick jaw. Those same bushy eyebrows flanking those same dark deep-set eyes that resembled the cherry pits left on the ground after the crows were finished feasting.

"And, if you'll have me, I want in." Sentry-1 concluded, sounding more like he was asking permission than he was demanding acceptance.

No one replied for a few seconds. Thirty-Nine felt emboldened by another traitor joining the mutiny. Even Eleven strengthened. She stepped back from Thirty-Nine, breaking physical contact to his disappointment. She smiled. It was a weak, closed-lip smile, but a smile nonetheless.

No one replied to Sentry-1's request to join the show. They just knew he belonged. So did he.

I can't believe this, Thirty-Nine thought.

"I can't believe this," Eleven said.

He whirled around to look at her.

Sentry-1 and Researcher-9 looked at Thirty-Nine's lanky back as he looked at Eleven.

"You just said what I thought." He turned back to The Woodlands insiders. "She just said what I thought." He grabbed Researcher-9's arms and leaned toward her. "Do you know how long the serum lasts?"

"I believe it last between six and eight hours. It has to since it would have to be administered to the target before he spoke." She looked down at the dark plastic tracking console.

"But right now we have to figure out what's happened to Thirty-Three. All we know is he hasn't moved for an uncomfortably long time. He hasn't come back. What if he's in trouble? Or worse."

"What is that?" Sentry-1 asked, staring at the shining solitary bulb in Researcher-9's hand.

"It's a tracking device. It's supposed to track Thirty-Three." Researcher-9 answered. She looked over her shoulder at the clock. "We have ten minutes until students will be sent from lunch to the Yard for free time. We have to hurry."

"Maybe the device is broken?" Thirty-Nine asked.

"Maybe..." Her response trailed as she studied it cock-eyed. She squinted and looked at the seal along the outer edge of the case. "Don't think so..." she finished.

"Where is Thirty-Three?" Sentry-1 asked.

"He's out there. Well, I mean, he's back in time. I think. We don't really know because he's the only one who's gone back." Thirty-Nine struggled to answer. He could feel the ticking of the clock, urging him to take action.

"The book you found." He looked at Sentry-1. "The one I hid in the bathroom ceiling. It's a diary from a young boy who found a way to go back in time. We sent Thirty-Three back. The way through is the tree in the Yard. But, it ends today. At midnight tonight, it closes for good and it won't open up again for another ten years. Thirty-Three went back because me and her," he thumbed over his shoulder at Eleven, "were stuck doing dream sequencing with the Chief. I mean Dr. Nampala."

"I knew about that nickname." Sentry-1 interrupted, eager to connect.

Thirty-Nine nodded. He wasn't sure what to say in response. Though he was grateful for Sentry-1's assistance, the transition from ten-year-foe to fellow mutineer was going to take more than a couple minutes.

"Sorry. I interrupted." Sentry-1 said.

"That's ok."

"Go ahead, Thirty-Nine, you were saying?" Researcher-9 asked.

"I was about to say the problem is the tree takes you back exactly ten years. There wasn't anything happening here then. The Woodlands wasn't here, exactly. By her investigation," he pointed to Researcher-9, "we are pretty sure that Dr. Nampala got started out here about nine years, eleven months, and two weeks ago."

"I know exactly when he got started. I was here. You're pretty close, Researcher-9." Sentry-1 replied. He placed his fingers to his lips and closed his eyes.

He spoke without opening his eyes. "It's all there. I can see it all. The broken drywall. The smell of paint. The boxes and boxes of equipment and chemicals. I remember it all. How could I forget? It's burned in my memory like the smell of Nana's burnt pumpkin pie the weekend before I showed up. Like the stench of burning rubber later that same night. That despicable night when I couldn't rescue Clara from the burning car. When me and Denise showed up here the next week because we had no place else to go. It was Thanksgiving, Ninety-Eighty-Eight." Sentry-1 finished speaking and opened his eyes. A single plump tear hung on his lower eyelash before tumbling to his cheek and streaking down his stubble-covered chin.

Wow. That was unexpected. Thirty-Nine thought.

"Wow. That was unexpected." Eleven said.

"Ok. Ummm." Thirty-Nine said. He looked up at the clock and stepped through the space between Sentry-1 and Eleven. He turned and faced the group.

"There's no time. Thirty-Three is trying to find the guy in my dream. Or anyone who will help us get out by shutting this place down when it first started. A couple of weeks from now. Ten years ago."

Sentry-1 stared at him. His thick lips parted a little. A soft whistle slipped between his gappy teeth.

"So, we have to do something." Thirty-Nine said. He hammered his fist into the palm of his open hand. The clapping sound startled Eleven.

"Ok. What are we going to do?" She was alert now. Between Sentry-1's revelation and Thirty-Nine's loud clap, she gained focus. She was ready.

"Not we." Thirty-Nine replied. He looked at Researcher-9.

"Me. You were right in your letter, Researcher-9. I have been chosen. It's on me to do something. It's my mother out there. My podmate. My best friend. I'm going back."

"No, Thirty-Nine, you can't." Eleven replied. "We need you here." She bit her lower lip, squeezing two plump pink bubbles of flesh out either side of her mouth. She blinked several times then whispered as she stretched her hand toward his. "I need you here."

Researcher-9 cut her off. "No Eleven, he's right. We don't have a choice."

"Then I'll go with him." She pouted.

"No. You're too weak." Thirty-Nine replied. He took Eleven's hands in his. "You need rest. Researcher-9 will tell the Chief that we are sleeping. He said we could take a rest, right?"

Thirty-Nine glanced at Researcher-9. She nodded.

"So. You rest. I'm going back to rescue Thirty-Three. To rescue us." He turned to Sentry-1.

"Thank you for helping us. I don't know what you can do, but be ready to do whatever it takes."

"I will. I am." Sentry-1 moved to open the door. "You all need to get going."

Eleven held on to Thirty-Nine's hands as he stepped away.

"I have to go." He said.

"Not without this." She held up a little piece of etched wood.

"The key!" Thirty-Nine shouted. "I almost forgot."

"I know. Remember, I told you in our dream. I have the key." She pressed it into his hand and caressed his fingers as she slowly dragged her hand away.

"Be safe." She whispered. A red hue flooded the whites of her eyes as she reluctantly released him.

"I will. I promise. Let's go."

"Not before I get this." Researcher-9 said. She picked up the Mind Cocoon bag and wrestled with the shoulder strap folded across the top flap.

"Come on. Open up." She sighed dramatically and exhaled, overreacting to the delay.

"Let me help you." Sentry-1 knelt beside her and gently lifted the straps out of the way. He tugged at the Velcro and opened the case. He looked up at Researcher-9 and smiled.

He slipped his thick hand into the inside edge of the case and felt for the glass bottle holding the thought projecting serum. He pushed the Mind Cocoon to one side with his other hand and pulled the bottle out.

"Looking for this?" He held it up.

"Yes. Thank you." Researcher-9 replied.

Sentry-1 opened the door and they stepped into the quiet hall.

"Eight minutes until the cafeteria empties." Researcher-9 whispered.

"I'll take Eleven to her pod." Sentry-1 answered. "You get him to the Yard."

The foursome split two by two as they left the room. Researcher-9 accompanied Thirty-Nine to the same door where she had bid Thirty-Three goodbye that morning.

These kids are tough, she thought. *Tougher than I was at their age.* She held Thirty-Nine's arm as he opened the door.

"What?" He asked, looking at her.

"I'm proud of you." She smiled. "You can do this. But not without this." She reached in her left pocket and pulled out a folded slip of paper.

"What's that?" He asked.

"This is a note. We don't know what might happen. But if you make contact with your mother, or the guy in the dream, or anyone who seems to be helpful, give them this. It may just save our lives."

Thirty-Nine took the piece of paper and unfolded it. It was simple and direct, just like the note she'd written him:

We are hostages. We need rescue. We are from the future. This is the truth. We know you will find it hard to believe. But, does it hurt to take a hike in the woods? There are nearly 100 children and many adults whose lives can be saved.

One month from receiving this note, get law enforcement and come to the following coordinates: 48.1322° N, 122.6714° W.

You will find Dr. Leonard Nampala, an evil man, preparing to take over the abandoned Roschcraft Weather Research Center. You are our only hope. Please save us. Please come in one month.

Undoing one thing always does another. This is something that must be undone.

Thirty-Nine finished reading and folded the note. He slipped it into the same front pocket used by Thirty-Three to store the pictures and the homing device.

He turned to go, but Researcher-9's hand remained fixed to his arm.

"Be careful." She whispered.

"I will. I promise."

She released him and he sprinted into the Yard, straight for the tree. He lined up the key with the opening in the trunk and pressed it in. In an instant, the Yard disappeared and a dark path extended before him. He stepped through and entered the past. He was a little nervous, a lot excited, and mostly unprepared.

November Fourteen, Nineteen-**EIGHTY**-Eight

1:02 PM

"Ok, we're almost ready for you to push." The nurse said. She stood between Nicole's spread legs. "We've got the baby turned around. You're going to make it. You're *both* going to make it."

"Hear that honey?" Aunt Rita said. She leaned over Nicole's shoulder dabbing at her sweaty forehead with a cold sponge. "The nurse says you're going to make it."

Nicole's eyes fluttered. "That's great." She managed between deep breaths. She dug her nails into the mattress as she contracted again.

Aunt Rita stood up. She gently massaged Nicole upper chest. "Get ready Nicole." She whispered. "Nurse?"

The nurse was feeling Nicole's lower abdomen as she peeked under her tent-like gown. Her head popped up slightly but she kept working.

"Yes?"

"I was wondering. Do you think the young man in the other room is going to make it?"

"I can't discuss patient information. Unless you're family. Are you family?" She never looked up. "Nine centimeters. Everything's in place.

Whenever you're ready dear. Do you think you can give me a couple hard grunts?"

"Yes ma'am." Nicole replied. Her cracked voice sounded like dry leaves blowing across pavement. She summoned her strength. In a moment, every memory of the past year roared through her head like a bullet train. Brian. His trailer. His lies. The goodbye in the rain. Her father. His good riddance. The cold rain. Aunt Rita's embrace.

"You can do this honey." Aunt Rita whispered.

"I don't know if we can pull him out." The doctor said on the other side of the curtain drawn between Nicole and Thirty-Three. His overalls were clumped in the corner. His socks and boots were still on his naked body. The doctor and the other nurse were feeling his side.

"Did Linda call for the helicopter?" He asked, wiping beads of sweat from his face with the back of his gloved hand.

"Yes sir." His assisting nurse replied.

"His breathing is failing. He may have a collapsed lung. We can't wait for the copter. We have to intubate. Now!" The doctor turned away and fumbled through several metal drawers in a rolling cart behind the bed.

Thirty-Three moaned slightly. He was half-awake. His last memory was stepping onto the edge of the road. He ached. Everywhere.

Feels like there's a fiery boulder crushing my leg, he thought. He tried to reach but couldn't move his arms.

"Am I drowning?" he mumbled in a whisper so faint it wouldn't have been heard by the doctor even if his stethoscope were in front of Thirty-Three's bloody lips.

I can't breathe, he thought. *God, let me live.*

"Got it!" The doctor yelled, hoisting a light blue crinkled section of plastic tubing overhead. He ripped the plastic wrap off the tubing and reached for a grapefruit sized membrane pouch that was wedged between old patient folders and a jar of cotton balls on the wooden shelf along the back wall.

He screwed the tubing into the pouch and turned to the nurse. "We've not got much time."

I don't have any time, Thirty-Three thought. The fiery boulder had jumped from his leg and was now parked on his chest. He couldn't get air. Everything tightened and the room started to get darker. He couldn't open his eyes.

"We have to pop that hole!" the doctor ordered.

Corey could hear the shouting even though he was outside on the porch. "I'm going back in there. I have to do something!"

"Stay out here. Haven't you done enough?" Bruce asked.

"No. That's the problem! I haven't done enough. And I always do what I'm told. Not this time." He stormed through the screen door, flexing the undersized spring beyond its breaking point as he whipped the door against the outer wall of the clinic. The snapping spring ricocheted against the back of a chair, impaling a piece of rusted metal in the wooden handrail. The door creaked as it slowly drifted away from the wall. Bruce shook his head and kicked the top step.

Corey bolted past the counter and through the swinging doors. He ignored the receptionist's faint utter of "Sir, wait, you can't" and walked into a scene straight from the latest late-night television hospital drama.

In front of him, a nurse was crouched below Nicole while Aunt Rita comforted her at the top of the upright bed.

Through a drab curtain, he could see shadows bustling and hear sharp voices speaking medical lingo in shotgun bursts.

Everything moved in slow motion. He started to speak but realized he had nothing to offer. He folded his hands on his head and watched. More important than the watching, was the listening.

"I can see the head!" The nurse in front of him cried.

"Hold his head still!" The shadow beyond the curtain yelled.

"Push, Nicole, push." Aunt Rita said.

"Hang on son. Hang on!" The shadow pleaded.

"Almost there. Just one more push." The nurse said, smiling.

"Just shove it in there." A female shadow said.

A solid digital beep rose above all the noise. Its familiar sound eclipsed all the other noise. From the other side of the curtain, the female shadow cried, "Get the defibrillator. Pump his chest."

A moment later, the equally familiar shrill staccato cry of an infant pierced the confusion. The sharp bark of the newborn came in waves, followed by long breathless pauses before resuming.

"It's too late." The doctor mumbled through the curtain.

"Just in time." Aunt Rita said, smiling at Corey.

At precisely the same moment, at least as Corey perceived, two voices announced opposite results.

"He's gone."

"It's a boy!"

"Ouch!" Thirty-Nine yelled. He stopped and grabbed his chest. He looked at his clean overalls.

"Feels like something stung me." He looked around. He didn't see anything but trees. Same thing he'd seen for the last twenty minutes. He rubbed his upper chest and rolled his shoulders. The burning sensation faded.

"That's weird. Got to keep moving though." He looked down at the tracking box. He was headed due east, the same direction it had guided him since he stepped through the willow tree and into ten years before. Going back was so smooth and natural.

It sure was easier than I expected, he thought. *Something tells me that may have been the only easy part of this assignment.*

He bulldozed his way through the occasional cluster of ferns and the random patch of tall grass. Mostly, he just traipsed over dead branches and soggy earth. Once or twice, he slipped on a moss-covered rock. After nearly thirty minutes of slogging, he reached State Route 71.

He exited the dark evergreen awning that had covered him most of the way and blinked, adjusting to the relative brightness of the overcast sky.

He looked down at the asphalt stained rocks. He knelt for a second and grabbed a couple. He felt their smoothness through the gritty dust that stuck to his fingers as he rolled them in his fist like a pair of dice.

"Not much out here." He said. He looked down the endless row of trees lining the road. Like a long green alleyway, they pointed whichever direction he was going. The light shifted to the top of the box as he paused. "Guess I'm headed that way." He pointed due south and started jogging down the road.

The daze surrounding Corey was as impenetrable as the rain he had driven through when he ran into Thirty-Three. A flurry of white-coated people rushed about while he remained frozen just inside the doorway. He heard water running in the tub sink on the wall near him. He heard a baby crying. He could hear voices but understood none of the words.

"Thank you. Thank you." Aunt Rita was standing next to him.

He looked down but couldn't focus on her face. He saw a whitish ball with fuzz all around it, stacked on top of a dark clump of clothing.

"Thank you so much Corey. Thank you so much." She started crying and thrust her head into his chest. As she wrapped her arms around him and shook with sobs of joy, he began to gain focus.

"You saved her life. You saved his life." She cried.

He looked to his right. The room was clear now. The pale brightness of the fluorescent lighting washed the life out of the place. Except for the rosy glow emanating from the bed in the middle of the tiny space. Nicole was beaming, looking down at a shrieking reddish newborn in her arms.

"Shhh. Shhh. Don't cry." She repeated, gently rocking the baby.

She looked up at Corey as he stared, mouth open at her. Aunt Rita continued to whimper and hug him, though his hands remained at his side.

"Thank you." Nicole mouthed over the cries of her fussy baby.

Her eyes were so full of love, Corey practically melted. Her curly wet hair was sort of cute, pushed back from her round face. Her ears were small, almost elf-like.

She's pretty, he thought.

"Cancel the helicopter!" The doctor shouted through the room to the receptionist.

Corey's moment of admiring Nicole abruptly ended.

"The boy's gone." He heard the doctor say. "Time of death, 1:04 PM. Call Sherriff Woodley, call the coroner."

Aunt Rita released Corey and stepped back. "Thank you." She whispered.

The doctor walked around the curtain and looked at Corey. "Son, please exit this area. Come with me. I'll take you back to my office to wait for Sherriff Woodley."

"I'm sorry. Wait for Sherriff Woodley?" Corey sputtered.

"Yes. I know it was an accident. But, this boy died. There's going to have to be an investigation."

"But. But." Corey didn't know what to say. He understood the situation but he sure didn't want to be detained by some small-town cop. He was an out-of-towner. What if this boy was the mayor's son? His mind raced with worry over the possibilities.

"Come on son. Let's go." The doctor took Corey by the arm and started walking him back. Corey remained silent as they walked behind the curtain. A nurse unfolded a sheet and draped it over Thirty-Three's dead body. As she drew it up toward his face, Corey glanced at his tan skin and his shaved head.

They walked through a narrow doorway. The room was no bigger than the bed of the truck that had started this now horrible day. There was a single upholstered armchair buried under several small boxes of patient records. The wall above it held multiple framed certificates and diplomas, evidencing the doctor's bona fides for the community.

"Excuse me." The doctor pulled the boxes off one at a time, placing them on the thin rug between the chair and the floor-to-ceiling bookshelf.

"Have a seat. The sheriff will be here in about an hour. He was dealing with a domestic over in Prestonsburg when we called."

The doctor walked away and closed the door, leaving Corey alone with his thoughts and the endless stacks of books that seemed wedged into every spare inch of the room.

Corey stretched his legs out before him and stared at his dirt-caked shoes. He sighed. A deep long sigh that ended with a sputtering blow of air.

"Well," he told himself, "I don't think mighty McIntyre Lumber is going to help me out of this situation."

He looked at the crammed bookshelf beside him. Hardbound books with gold lettering on the spine blurred into one another. At last, his eyes focused on one light blue volume shoved between two black books. "High Speed Collisions: On-Scene Treatment & Increased Survival Rates."

Survival, he thought. *I sure wish that kid had survived. He's dead. Oh, my gosh! He's dead!*

The more he thought, the more frantic he became. *I just killed a kid! I just killed a kid!*

Corey thrust his face into his palms and began to wail. "*No, no, no, no.*" He cried. "*Oh my God, I killed him!*"

He stood up and slammed his fist into the wall, crumbling drywall into powder. He punched it over and over until blood trickled from his knuckles, creating a brownish paste as it blended with the drywall powder that coated his hand.

He gasped for air and looked through the hanging slat like blinds on the only window in the room.

"Out there." He whispered. "Somewhere out there, that boy has a mom and dad. Where did he come from? It was like he just appeared. What was his story? Was he running away? What could he be running from? There's nothing out there but forest for miles."

Corey tossed himself back into the chair. He stared at his wounded hand.

That was stupid, he thought as he looked up at the dinner plate sized hole in the wall. *Now they'll probably charge me with destruction of property, too.*

"Ha." He laughed a nervous laugh at the insanity of his situation. "This is crazy."

"There's got to be some reason why and how that kid ended up out there. If I don't end up in some backwoods prison for the rest of my life, I'm going to figure it out. I'm definitely going to figure it out."

He tilted his head back against the wall and stared at the tile ceiling until the emotional drain of the past few hours overcame him and he drifted to sleep.

November Fourteen, Nineteen-**NINETY**-Eight

1:31 PM

Eleven fell asleep. Finally. After sharing the details of all that had happened with Seventeen, she tossed for a quarter hour before wriggling into a snug position and drifting off to sleep.

Seventeen sat at the desk mulling over her afternoon assignment. She was required to write an essay titled "The Woodlands: A Great Family, A Great Mind".

A great family? She thought, her tongue sneaking out of the corner of her mouth. She clamped down on it, unconscious of her focusing habit. *What can I write? I don't even want to write. If Thirty-Nine saves us all to-night I won't even have to turn in this assignment.*

She kicked back in her chair and tossed her spindly legs up on the desktop. It felt good to relax. She clapped her hands together behind her small fuzzy dome and closed her eyes. Her imagination ignited, at first like a sputtering engine but in short order it was firing on all cylinders.

Like most of the students in these rare moments of quiet thought, she imagined all the things she'd seen in various books during her short life. The geography books in particular held her fascination. The mountains, the deserts, the oceans. Oh, the oceans. Seventeen whistled softly as she pictured rolling waves crashing into rocky shores, like the New England coast. She grinned as she envisioned gentle foam bubbling along the Gulf of Mexico's beaches.

"First thing I'm gonna do," she said, "is find the closest ocean. I think it's the Pacific." She opened her eyes and looked at her gangly feet wrapped in stiff dark leather, laced well past her ankles. "Well, I'll get some sandals first. Can't wear boots to the ocean!"

"Researcher-9 report to my office." Dr. Nampala's voice invaded her daydream. His demand echoed over the intercom. The sound of his slow cadence caused her to tense. She flipped her feet off the desk and sat up straight.

Just in case Thirty-Nine doesn't come through, she thought. She picked up her pencil and started to write on the blank page: "The Woodlands is a one of a kind family with many great minds. The greatest is Dr. Nampala."

What nonsense, she thought. *I sure hope Researcher-9 isn't in trouble.*

Researcher-9 was in her own pod when the order came for her to come to Dr. Nampala's office. She opened a small built-in cabinet at the foot of her bed. She dug through several small boxes until she pulled out a plastic IV bag. She held it up and peered through the light.

"No holes. This should work." She popped the lid on the bottle she had lifted from Nampala's desk. She sniffed the fluid. "Doesn't smell like anything, really. Maybe a little bit like ketchup. Interesting."

She pinched the bag open and poured in half the bottle. She put the lid back on the bottle and buried it under a stack of neatly folded examination robes.

"Time to go." She checked the buttons on her jacket and slipped the pouch of fluid into the deep outside pocket.

As she exited her room, she spotted a familiar beastly outline toward the end of the hallway.

Sentry-5, she thought. *Just act natural.*

She stuck out her chin and walked stiffly down the hall. She kept her hands in her pockets. She could feel the thought transference liquid sloshing in her pocket with each step.

"What are you doing?" Sentry-5 called out while they were still several doors apart.

"Dr. Nampala called me to his office." She replied.

As he drew nearer, she could see a sliver of the diary's edges. Most of the book was swallowed by his meat hook of a hand.

"What are you doing?" She asked.

He stepped through the last light between them. He stopped walking and stood in the shadow that fell between the light fixtures mounted on the wall. The outline of his body eclipsed all the light from the remaining section of hall before her. She stopped.

"I'm doing my job. Going to go to forensics and get the fingerprints off this book." He finally replied after a prolonged silence in which she imagined he was considering ending her life just for asking.

Oh no, she thought. *We're done for.*

She mustered a soft reply. "Ok."

She took a single step forward. They were nearly eye-to-chest now. He stood in the center of the hall, refusing to move out of her path.

He leaned closer and slowly pumped his fist near her eyes, as though he was about to draw back and pummel her. She trembled..

"I'm watching you. Now go on to your meeting. Ha ha!" He laughed as he finished speaking and dropped his hand to his side. "Another fearful weakling." He mumbled as he moved to the side of the hall.

She didn't reply. She looked down and walked toward the elevator at the end of the hall.

What are we going to do? He'll discover our prints on the book in just a few minutes.

"Researcher-9! Report to my office at once!" Dr. Nampala's voice roared over the loudspeaker.

She sped up, nearly jogging as she reached the elevator door. She pressed the up arrow and tapped her foot as she waited.

Great. Now Nampala's upset.

She looked at the floor. Its light tile was so sterile, so bland. The pleasures of life were nowhere to be found. Her mind drifted back to her life as a child in Belarus. Though poverty-stricken, she still found moments of delight in the forest. Not so here. There was no joy in the forest of The Woodlands.

The elevator door opened and she bolted in, nearly colliding with Researcher-4.

"Excuse me!" Researcher-4 exclaimed, dodging Researcher-9. "Watch where you're going!"

"I'm sorry." Researcher-9 replied without looking up. She turned to press the third floor button but Researcher-4 remained in the doorway, preventing the elevator from closing.

"What's happening with you?" Researcher-4 asked. She stared at her colleague. Her ocean blue eyes carried a glimmer of sincerity.

"I'm just in a hurry, that's all." Researcher-9 replied.

Researcher-4 persisted. She chicken-winged her elbows out, propping the door open against the will of the mechanical arms inside the frame and against the insistent dinging sound pleading to allow the doors to close.

"Don't tell me that's all. There's something more happening."

It was then that Researcher-9 noticed her co-worker's jacket.

"Your buttons aren't matched up. You've got two buttons unbuttoned at the top and only one buttonhole left." Now it was her turn to inquire.

"What happened up there?" Researcher-9 asked.

She blushed and drew her hand up close to her jacket top. As she covered her chest, the doors closed, forcing her into the hall.

"Nothing happened!" Researcher-9 heard her yell as the elevator purred and carried her up to Dr. Nampala's office.

No one was in the upstairs hall. What could he want? He was in a good mood. Celebrating, even. *Maybe I can get him to celebrate with a drink.* She tapped the pouch in her pocket and said a quick prayer as she approached the door.

"St. Nicholas, help me get these children out of here. Somehow." She whispered.

The usual sentry was gone. There was no one in the hall.

How am I going to get in? She thought.

She stood before the thick metal door for a moment. To her surprise, the door swung open and Dr. Namapala stood before her, grinning like he'd just won the lottery. In his mind, he had. In just a few days, he would contact The Future and collect his prize. Ten million dollars.

"Well, hello Researcher-9. I'm so glad you could make it."

"Yes sir. I came as soon as I heard your announcement."

"Come in. Come in. We need to discuss your future."

She followed him into the office. He had rearranged some of the furniture in the hour since she'd left. The cots where they'd held marathon dream sequencing sessions for the past week were shoved against the farthest wall to her left. The large dining table had been dragged into the center of the room.

Between the dining table and his desk sat his favorite rocking chair. He walked to it and sat down. He crossed his legs and flapped the end of his robe over his bare shins.

He rocked and stared at Researcher-9. She stood on the other side of the dark table. As he looked at her, she grew nervous and began clumsily tapping on the back of the closest chair. She drummed her fingers and peppered the room with glances, afraid to hold his stare.

"Researcher-9, it's been quite a week." He cleared his throat and continued. "I was worried we might lose you. You were behaving incorrectly." He coughed and wheezed. "But I've got a feeling you might be open to changing." He hacked. A dry rattling sound accompanied his cough.

"I've got a proposition for you." He couldn't stop coughing. "My throat." He grabbed at his neck with his bony hand then flicked his finger toward her while coughing.

"Are you ok, sir?"

"It's those cigarettes." He gasped. "Should stick with the pipe. Just not the same kick. Now my throat's irritated."

"Can I get you a drink sir?" She asked and started walking to the sideboard along the wall to her right.

"Yes." His faint scratched voice replied. "In the bottom cabinet."

She reached the cabinet and tugged on the ivory knob. Two glass shelves held several jugs of water.

That's no good, she thought. *I need a dark liquid.*

Dr. Nampala coughed again. "Hurry up." He said. He made a clucking sound as he repeatedly tried to clear his vexed throat.

"Yes sir. Just getting you something tasty."

She opened the next cabinet door. She reached in and grabbed a tall bottle of apple cider.

The left-over cider from the Halloween party, she thought. *Perfect.*

"How's this?" She held up the bottle.

"Fine. Just pour it." Dr. Nampala stood up.

"Just relax, sir. I'll be right there."

She grabbed a crystal tumbler etched with The Woodlands emblem. She turned her body, shielding her pour from Dr. Nampala's view. All she needed was the plastic bag in her pocket. She slid her hand into her pocket and felt its squishiness. She made a fist several times in her pocket without grabbing the pouch, trying to shake the nervousness out of her hand.

"Do I have to do it myself?" Dr. Nampala asked. He coughed and started walking toward her.

"I've got it." She answered without turning her head. In one motion, she grabbed and pinched open the pouch. She poured it into the glass and returned it to her pocket. She splashed a healthy amount of apple cider into the mix and swished it around gently.

"Well?" She heard from right behind her.

She jumped, startled by Dr. Nampala's voice. The dark liquid spilled onto the countertop. She quickly wiped it with her sleeve and turned to Dr. Nampala.

He coughed in her face. His ever-present bouquet of cigarette stench invaded her mouth as she started to speak. She choked.

"Here you go, sir." She spit out.

He grabbed the glass from her hand and gulped two-thirds of the drink before taking a breath. He held the glass out and stared at it.

"That tastes different. Let me see that bottle."

"Here's you go, sir." Researcher-9 said, handing him the bottle. "Does your throat feel better?"

He studied the bottle. He smelled its contents. "Hmmm. Smells like cider."

"Does your throat feel better?" She asked again.

"Yes." He handed the bottle back to her and finished the drink. "Still tastes funny. Maybe I need something stronger. You bring any booze?"

Dr. Nampala stared at Researcher-9, arching his eyebrows. His dark eyes seemed to twinkle.

"Uh. I don't -" she started to reply, only to be interrupted by his hysterical laughter. He slapped her on the shoulder and continued laughing, which caused him to start coughing again.

"I was just kidding. I can't have anything affecting my thoughts right now!" He hacked. "It's a joke!" He sneezed, spraying mucus droplets all over the side of her face and on her glasses. "Give me that bottle again!" He sputtered between racking coughs.

He took the almost empty bottle of cider and polished it off.

"Ok. Let's talk about why you're here." He turned around and walked toward his rocking chair. He waved his hand forward, motioning for her to follow.

She didn't see the motion. She was cleaning his sneeze off her glasses with a cocktail napkin from the sideboard.

He sat down in the rocking chair.

"Listen," he began. "I'm going to make this simple. I'm going to offer you the same deal as I offered Researcher-4." He looked across the room.

"What are you doing over there? I told you to follow me."

"Sorry, sir. Just cleaning my glasses." She held them up to the light.

"Well, get over here."

As she walked across the room, he shifted in the chair and placed his arms on the armrests.

"You look nice without your glasses. Why don't you leave them off for a minute?" He suggested.

"Because I can't see without them." She replied, quickly sliding them back onto her aquiline nose. She walked closer to him and stood near the end of the table.

"What's that?" Dr. Nampala asked, pointing at her lab coat.

She looked down. The thought transfer fluid! A dark brown stain lined the bottom edge of her pocket. It had seeped into the fabric and created several splotches near the midline of her coat.

"Must have spilled some cider." She shrugged.

"Well don't stain your coat. Take it off." He suggested. "I'll call for a sentry to take it to the laundry for you."

"Oh, that's ok."

"Nonsense. That's what it's for. I don't want you walking around in a dirty jacket." He insisted. "Go ahead, take it off. Besides, aren't you tired of wearing that boxy stiff thing? It's not very flattering."

"I didn't think appearance mattered. Sir." She replied.

"Let's not be naïve, Researcher-9." He smiled. "That's just propaganda for the students. Grown-ups know better. Don't we?" He tilted his head to the side and smiled with his lips pressed together. "Don't we?" He asked, pushing his hair back from his eyes. He reached in his pocket and pulled out a large rubberband. He scooped his hand over his forehead and tugged his hair back tightly, binding it in a ponytail.

She remained standing at the edge of the table. Her jacket buttoned. Fortunately, he had moved on from the stain in her pocket. Unfortunately, he was initiating some kind of romantic encounter between them.

"Sir?"

"You don't have to call me sir." He replied. "You can call me Leonard. Better yet," He stood up and smoothed the front of his cloak. "You can call me Leo." He winked through his thick lenses.

She shuddered.

"If it's all the same, sir, I'm more comfortable calling you Dr. Nampala. You are my boss, after all." She replied, stepping back.

"I am your boss. That's true. But, my dear, things are about to change in a very big way. And old Leo is about to have a whole lot of money, and a whole lot of time to figure out what's next." He stepped toward her and she scooted back. He dragged his raw-boned hand along the top of the table, rubbing its smoothness.

She kept walking backward. He kept walking along the table.

"Where you going?" He asked.

"Nowhere, sir." She replied.

"You keep moving back." He said just as she bumped into the apple cider cabinet.

"Ouch." She mumbled as she took a knock on the back of her head from the ornate trim along the bottom of the upper cabinets.

"Well, well." He smiled. "I guess you have to stop now."

His narrow eyes focused uncomfortably on her. She was trapped. He reached out for her arm. She pulled it behind her.

"What's the matter?" He whispered. The accosting stench of tobacco flooded her nostrils.

"Can we sit down, sir?"

"Oh, are you tired?" He replied. "If you are, we could always lay down. That might make you feel a lot more comfortable." He grinned and motioned to the cots across the room.

"Oh I'm not tired." She quickly answered. "I'm sorry, sir, I just don't understand why you're so cheerful."

"You don't?" He took a half step back. "Really? Well," he rubbed his sparse beard with his long dirty fingernails. "Thanks to your student, Thirty-Nine, we are about to be richly rewarded. Well, I should say, I am about to be richly rewarded." He stepped even closer and slid his foot between hers. Their chests touched. She drew her head back until it touched the cabinet behind her.

"But," he continued, "that rich reward could be for we. If you know what I mean. All thanks to Thirty-Nine."

Thirty-Nine, she thought. *I don't know how I'm getting out of this, but I sure hope Thirty-Nine is doing better than me.*

November Fourteen, Nineteen-**EIGHTY**-Eight

1:45 PM

Thirty-Nine reached a four-way intersection. Several cars stopped and then rolled on by him as he stood in the gravel. The passengers in a station wagon stared at him. He stared at them. They all had hair. Lots of hair. Their curious eyes pushed him to step further away from the road. The rumble of the engine as the driver accelerated startled him.

"People." He whispered. "Cars. It's real. It's real. Everything we've read about." He looked at the sky. He had been completely focused on the black box in his hand. The interaction with humans reminded him of the immense truth of the mission. The imperative of rescuing the other students. Of finding his mother. Of finding Thirty-Three.

Thirty-Three, he thought and looked down at the tracking box. The east-facing bulb lit up on the tracking device.

"Time to go that way." He pointed to his left and turned to cross the street. He looked down the road. There was a vacant fruit stand in a dirt lot across the way. Beyond that, along the right side of the road, stood several older single-story buildings. On the other side of the street an abandoned gas station, decorated with two rusty pumps and a plastic sign full of bullet holes, served as a silent testimony to better days.

He crossed the street and walked by the fruit stand. "Bennie's Berries" was stenciled on faded plywood, titled up against the simple wood awning.

As he walked, a second bulb lit up. He was getting closer. He picked up his pace, ignoring the scenery. As he neared another intersection, a third bulb glowed. He looked to his right and saw a white Victorian two-story building with a green portico. "Douglas Dry Goods and General Store" was painted in bright red on the side of the building.

As he looked across the street for traffic, an old man came barreling out of the general store, shouting at him.

"Thirt! Thirt!"

Thirty-Nine looked at him. *What kind of language do they speak here?* As their eyes met, Mr. Douglas realized this was not the same boy who'd run from his hot chocolate the day before. But he was dressed the same. His head was shaved.

"Hey young fella." He greeted Thirty-Nine as he stepped down the creaking stairs. "Where's your friend?'

They speak English. That's good, Thirty-Nine thought. *But how does he know about Thirty-Three?*

They stood a few feet apart, on the corner of the street.

"Aren't you cold?" The old man finally asked, rubbing his bare arms.

Thirty-Nine studied him. *The hot chocolate guy!* He thought. The man's pudgy face reminded him of Thirty-Three. His floppy ears and his slicked-back hair combined to give Thirty-Nine the impression he was talking to a human hound dog. His eyes twinkled. He seemed kind. Jolly.

"Do you know how to speak, son?" He stepped closer to Thirty-Nine.

Thirty-Nine stepped back. He didn't know whether to trust him. *Maybe this guy did something to Thirty-Three.* Thirty-Nine held up the tracking device. *If he was here, all five bulbs would light up. Still just three. Got to keep moving.* All these thoughts rushed through Thirty-Nine's mind in a second.

"I got to go!" He blurted out and started running down the street.

"Wait!" Mr. Douglas yelled after him. He started running but within ten steps realized he couldn't catch the boy. He bent over, wheezing, and waited to catch his breath.

He looked up to see Thirty-Nine's figure getting smaller down the road. "Where are these kids coming from? And why are they in such a hurry? I'm going to find out." He walked back to his store and went to the side garage. He opened the door and got in his classic Buick. "Let's go girl." He said as he started the engine. "We're going to find that kid and figure out what in the heck is going on!"

Corey woke up with a start, hot and sweaty. He lurched up in his chair. Had it all been a dream? He wiped drool from his mouth and instantly tasted blood and drywall dust. Nope! He spit, shoving his tongue out of his mouth as he did.

"Not a dream." He muttered. "How long was I asleep? Man it's hot in here!" He stood up and walked to the door. He peered through the narrow glass rectangle into the patient treatment area. The doctor was standing, with his back to Corey, talking to Aunt Rita. He opened the door and felt the coolness of the well-ventilated space. It calmed him as it refreshed his body.

"Excuse me?" He said.

The doctor turned around. Aunt Rita moved beside him. Her eyes were red but happy.

"How are you doing Corey?" She spoke before the doctor could utter a word.

"I'm hot. Sir, would it be possible for me to wait for the sheriff on the porch?"

The doctor stared at him for a moment, as though he was weighing whether Corey was a flight risk. Aunt Rita spoke again, deciding for him.

"He's fine, Doc. He ain't going nowhere. He's a good kid. Saved Nicole and little Jake, he did."

Jake, Corey thought. *Jake's a cool name.*

"Please, sir? I'll wait on the porch. I could use the fresh air."

"I suppose –" the doctor cut himself short as he looked at Corey's right fist. "What is that?"

Corey looked down. He brushed his hand against his leg, grimacing as it scratched the cuts. "Oh, I'm sorry. I kind of punched your wall."

"You punched my wall?" The doctor looked at Aunt Rita.

"He's been through a lot, Doc. I'll fix your wall. Let the boy get some fresh air. Besides, his friend's been pacing out there. Probably be good to have some company."

"Fine. Go ahead." The doctor stepped aside and motioned for Corey to walk out. "But, you're going to fix my wall." He scolded as Corey walked by.

"Yes sir." Corey answered, lowering his head.

"Oh, stop!" Aunt Rita slapped the doctor on the shoulder. "Come on, Corey."

She grabbed his clean hand and led him through the room. They paused as they approached Nicole's bed. She was quietly stroking baby Jake, now silent and sleeping.

"Just beautiful, aren't they?" Rita asked.

"Yes." Corey replied.

Nicole looked up, her green eyes dancing with joy. "I guess I have a lot to be thankful for." She smiled at Corey. "And I guess I have you to thank. At least that's what she tells me."

"I just did what any guy would do." Corey said.

"Not any guy." Nicole replied, her eyes reddening with tears. "Not a lot of guys." She added.

"Well, it was worth it." He smiled as he looked at her. Even in the turmoil of the day, he couldn't help noticing her dimple when she smiled. The spirit in her eyes. Full of life. He couldn't help noticing her natural beauty.

"You look great." He added. "And so does he."

She blushed. Aunt Rita smiled as she watched. "Your cheeks are glowing, Nicole." Rita laughed.

"Must be the glow of having a baby." She replied smartly. She held him up. "This is my little Jake. Say hello Jake." Jake yawned and curled his tiny fists up to his tightly shut eyes.

"He likes you." Aunt Rita said, nudging Corey.

"I like him, too. Jake. That's a good name."

"Thank you." Nicole replied, turning him back into her body.

Corey stared at them. *So peaceful. So content*, he thought of his own family. He thought of his mother. His father. Which made him think of Bruce.

"Well, I better get outside. Bruce is probably worried sick."

"Ok." Nicole looked up. "Thank you Corey. Thank you so much."

"You're welcome." He walked to the door and opened it. "I'll see you around, huh?" He said.

"Yes. For sure." Nicole replied.

Corey smiled as he walked through the waiting room and onto the porch.

Bruce nearly crashed into him. He was pacing, head down, as Corey stepped into the solemn grayness of the Northwest afternoon.

"Sorry Bruce!" Corey said, jumping back into the doorway.

"Oh Corey!" Bruce grabbed him. "Don't be sorry. I'm sorry. This is all my fault. I should have never let you take that truck!"

"Relax." Corey said. His interaction with Nicole had brightened his day and lifted his spirits. "It's going to work out. I didn't do anything wrong. Everything will be ok."

"Corey." Bruce slowly replied. "You may not have done anything wrong. But everything is not ok."

Corey put his arm around Bruce's thick hunched shoulder. "I know, Bruce." He walked him to the edge of the porch. "But, we have to just keep the faith." He looked at the cloud-packed sky. "Even when it seems dark and gloomy."

They plopped down on the top step and stared at the gravel parking lot.

"I don't know Corey. I just don't know." Bruce said. He looked at his young associate. "It's good to stay upbeat. I guess I should be an example, instead of having you be the example for me. You're doing pretty good thinking for yourself."

Corey tossed his head back and straightened his hair with his hands.

"You think so?"

"I do."

"Even if it means I quit the lumber business?"

"Corey," Bruce looked at him and smiled, "Even it means you're a fly fishing guide in the middle of nowhere. Just remember, though. Life is full of challenges. And jumping from a hard spot to something else doesn't change that." Bruce chuckled.

"What's funny?" Corey asked.

"Just something my old Uncle Louis used to say. He used to say, 'Be careful kids. Undoing one thing always does another'."

"Undoing one thing always does another." Corey repeated. "That sounds about right."

———————————————————————————————————

Thirty-Nine sprinted up the sidewalk, glancing over his shoulder at the yellow Buick trailing him. He looked down at the tracker.

"All five lights!" He shouted. He slid to a stop and looked to his right. He could see a narrow wooden building through a sparse row of newly planted maple trees. Most of the leaves were on the ground, and the few remaining were as brown as Thirty-Three's eyes.

As he stood staring at the property, he grew excited to see Thirty-Three. He never thought he'd miss his podmate as much as he did. Thirty-Three's rambunctious relentless drive actually helped him do more. To be more.

"Hey son." A voice called from behind him.

Thirty-Nine spun around to see the old man leaning his arm and head out the window of his antique car. He had driven up to the edge of the sidewalk. The motor was still rumbling. Even in the dreariness, the chrome trim around the window and the side mirror gleamed.

"Yes sir." Thirty-Nine said.

"What's going on? Why are you here?" He looked at Thirty-Nine's hand. "What you got there?" He threw the steering wheel gearshift into park.

Thirty-Nine looked back and forth at the building and the old man. He noticed the man's overalls. He looked down at his own. He decided to trust him. Thirty-Three had.

"I'm here to see my friend. He's in there." He held up the tracking box. "This helped me find him.

"Is he hurt?"

"I'm not sure." Thirty-Nine slowly replied.

"Is he sick?"

"I don't know."

"Well, there's no other reason to visit the Franklin Clinic."

Thirty-Nine turned and looked at the building. His eyes traced the loose and dented gutter along the roof edge and for the first time noticed the sign on the other side of the building. Its top half jutted above the roof, declaring to passers-by that this was the place for medical treatment.

Thirty-Nine's heart sank. "I've got to see what's wrong with him." He told the man in the car. "Thanks for caring." He jogged through the trees and stood at the back of the building.

"Hang on, son." Mr. Douglas called out. He turned off his car. "Let me help you."

Thirty-Nine ignored his request and walked around the side of the building. Four old eight-pane windows at eye level alternated with weather-worn siding. Bare wood showed through the cracking paint along the wood trim between the panels of glass. The windows looked like they'd spent more than several hard winters since a brush had been lifted to tend to their maintenance.

Mr. Douglas slammed his door shut and walked across the damp grass. He ducked under the low hanging branches of the young maple trees and walked into the small yard that separated the clinic from the street.

Thirty-Nine crept along the side of the building. The first two windows had blinds drawn. He reached the third window, encouraged by its absence of shade.

He slowly edged his face to the base of the window, rising until his eyes could see inside. He blinked. The layers of dirt on the window made the room appear smoke-filled. He squinted and saw her through the smudges. No mistake about it. It was her.

The woman in his dream. Mom. She was lying on her side in a small bed. Her eyes were closed. She was so beautiful. He fought hard but lost the battle with the welling tears in his eyes. Huge drops tumbled onto the windowsill, splashing and splattering his grimy hands as they gripped the termite-eaten wood.

It's real. She's real, he thought. He stared at her curly hair. Her long slender nose. Her dark eyelashes pressed together, concealing the sparkling green eyes he had only seen in his dreams. Her chest rose and fell under the thin blanket as she breathed the contented breath of peaceful sleep.

He followed the line of the bed to a small crib. Through the dirt, through his tears, and through the rails of the tiny bed, he saw a baby sleeping.

If that's her, he thought, glancing at sleeping Nicole. *Then that's me.* He looked back at the baby.

"That's me!" he yelled.

The baby flinched at his shout.

Nicole's eyes popped open. She looked at the window. Thirty-Nine slapped his hand over his mouth as his yellow eyes opened even wider.

Their eyes met. For a moment, he saw everything he had been missing his entire life. Love, admiration, wonder, mystery. Mom. Nicole's eyes answered every question he ever had about who he was and where he came from. And where he belonged.

"Everything ok?" Mr. Douglas limped toward Thirty-Nine. He looked at the old man approaching and dropped to the ground.

Nicole blinked, unsure of what she had seen. She looked at sleeping baby Jake.

Must have been dreaming, she thought. She closed her eyes and nestled into her pillow.

"No. It's not ok." Thirty-Nine replied. He turned his back on the old man and walked to the front of the building, wiping tears from his eyes as hard and as fast as he could.

He reached the front corner of the building. The parking lot contained a few cars and an old red truck. As he turned the corner of the porch, he saw two men seated in the middle of the top step.

That's him, Thirty-Nine thought. *That's him*!

He reached in his pocket and fingered the note.

"Wait a second, young man." Mr. Douglas called from the side of the clinic.

He couldn't wait. Thirty-Nine got halfway to the steps of the porch when Bruce saw him. He nudged Corey and pointed at Thirty-Nine.

"Look at this kid. I tell you, there's some strange folks out in these isolated towns."

Corey jumped from the porch. "Strange kids?" He swatted Bruce on the chest with the back of his hand. "This kid looks just like the boy in the clinic."

Thirty-Nine approached as the men stood. As he drew within earshot, he overheard Corey say, "The boy in the clinic. The boy who just died."

"Did, did you say died?" Thirty-Nine asked, his heart pounding. He began to tremble. His head flooded with liquids – tears, snot and saliva – everything rushing out as he grabbed the banister along the steps to steady himself.

"No – he didn't die!" He screamed into his sleeve as he dropped his head onto his arm.

He can't be dead, Thirty-Nine thought. *He can't be dead. He just can't.*

Corey hesitated with his arms extended, unsure whether to hold the sobbing boy.

Mr. Douglas turned the corner to see and hear everything.

"That boy, the one named Thirt. Did you say he died?"

Corey looked over at Mr. Douglas. "Who are you? What did you call him?"

Thirty-Nine's shoulders shook as he gasped for air. "No, no, no, no, no, no."

"Do you know him?" Corey asked Thirty-Nine. "Are you brothers?"

Thirty-Nine crumbled on the porch steps and looked at the three men – a twenty-something, a fifty-something, and a seventy-something. His eyes were gushing. His nose was dripping. His heart was breaking.

They all stood in silence looking at Thirty-Nine.

He sucked in a deep breath and blew his nose into his sleeve. He sniffed hard. Finally, he answered Corey's question.

"We aren't brothers. But we are family. He's the only family I ever had."

Ninety
November Fourteen, Nineteen-~~Eighty~~ Eight

2:05 PM

"My dear, we can build a family together. So that's the proposi-tion." Dr. Nampala said. "You can run away with me and have the life of your dreams. Your family will be taken care of. For the rest of their lives. And we will be together for the rest of ours."

At least he had given her space as he talked. He had waved about the room, declaring his affection for her and his ambition for the world. They could have it all. Except she'd be stuck with him. Nothing was worth that. No amount of money could compensate for a life with the vile, homely, repul-sive Dr. Nampala.

"Pretty amazing, eh?" He asked. "You're speechless. I suppose that's only natural. It's not every day a woman is granted a kingdom. It's certainly not every day a woman is offered to share her life with a soon-to-be world renowned genius."

"Yes sir. I suppose you're right." She replied.

"Please, I told you. Not sir, call me Leo." He walked to his desk and rummaged through stacks of folders. "And your given name..." He thumbed through the labels, searching.

"Is..."

"Vera." She answered. "Vera Panchivski."

"Yes." He held up a small folder. "Here it is. Vera Panshivski. Well, Vera Panshivski, what do you say? Are you ready to run away with me?"

She gulped.

"Is it really that hard a decision?" He raised his voice. "Let's see," he mocked, "a life of luxury with a brilliant man or poverty and misery for the rest of your life. Which will be much shorter than you hope if your answer is incorrect."

"I understand, sir." She stammered. "But, don't you think it takes a little time for me to think? You have always been my boss. I've never thought of you in this way."

"Well." He walked toward her once again. On his way, he pulled his glasses off. They dangled in his hand as he moved closer. "Maybe you've never thought of *me* this way. But, I've been thinking of *you*. For quite some time." He smiled. "What do you say, Vera?"

The beeping of his office door opening interrupted them.

"Don't say anything!" Sentry-5 shouted as he crashed through the doors. He was dragging two students behind him. Their bodies followed him like wet mops, picking up dust and dead bugs as he tugged on their tiny wrists.

"What's going on?" Dr. Nampala shouted. His face turned bright red as he faced Sentry-5.

Sentry-5 dropped the students and reached in his pocket. He dug out the book.

Oh no. This is it, Researcher-9 thought. She looked around for the case holding Dr. Nampala's pistol. Her eyes scanned the desk. All she could see were papers and pencils, a coffee mug. No gun.

"This book," Sentry-5 replied, "had the fingerprints of these students," he pointed at the floor.

"Eleven? Seventeen?" Dr. Nampala asked. He looked down at the girls on the floor. They were quietly moaning. Seventeen was curled into the fetal position. Both of them had blood dribbling from their nose and mouth.

"Did you hurt them badly?" Dr. Nampala asked.

"No. I just knocked them around a bit. We are not finished punishing them, though. They deserve The Wheel. Or death. Or both."

"What's in the book?" Dr. Nampala asked.

"They are trying to escape. But I'm not even finished with the list of traitors. This book also has Thirty-Nine's prints. And," he paused and stood as tall as he could. His hulking frame seemed to stretch to the sky.

"It also had her prints." He pointed his lumber-like finger at Re-searcher-9, who was leaning against the cabinet.

"What are you talking about?" Researcher-9 asked. "That's non-sense. He's out of his mind!" She stood up straight and took a step toward them. She looked down at Seventeen and Eleven.

"I can't believe you beat them. For what reason?"

"Easy Researcher-9." Dr. Nampala said. "Where's Thirty-Nine, then Sentry-5? Why isn't he here?"

"He's gone." Sentry-5 replied.

"What do you mean, he's gone?"

"I mean he's gone. Vanished. Nowhere to be found." Sentry-5 leaned down to Dr. Nampala and slowly finished. "He. Is. Not. Here."

"That's crazy. Where the heck is he then?" Dr. Nampala put his glass-es back on and undid his ponytail. As his hair fell down around his face and neck, his demeanor darkened.

"Where is he?" He shouted. He looked at Researcher-9. "Where is he?"

Sentry-5 waved the book in Dr. Nampala's face. "This book tells about a way to go back in time. It's some kind of doorway that opens through the willow tree in the Yard."

"The tree in the Yard!" Researcher-9 laughed. "That's preposterous!"

"It's all here, sir." Sentry-5 said, handing Dr. Nampala the book with the page open where Eleven had written the message that first gave Re-searcher-9 and Thirty-Nine hope.

This is the answer. This is our way home.

"Not only is Thirty-Nine not here." Sentry-5 said as Dr. Nampala began reading. "But neither is Thirty-Three. He was supposed to be sick but none of the nurses saw him today. They just assumed he'd gone to his regular class. Thirty-Three and Thirty-Nine are gone. I think they both went back in time."

Dr. Nampala glared at Researcher-9 as he flipped the pages.

"Grab her." He ordered Sentry-5.

"With pleasure, sir."

Escape was impossible. She didn't fight Sentry-5 as he manhandled her. He shoved her into the cabinet, banging her spine against the hard decorative shelving. He grabbed her by her hair and tossed her toward the dining room. She slammed into the back of a chair and grabbed the table to steady herself.

"Take her and tie the three of them together." Dr. Nampala said over the grunts of Sentry-5 and the smack of Researcher-9's bones and flesh against the furniture.

Dr. Nampala paced as he read the two hundred year old entries of Wesley Kenton.

Sentry-5 bound the wounded girls to Researcher-9 with insulated electrical wire. He stood them in a triangle, back to back to back. Seventeen could barely stand. Eleven's head hung and her mouth never closed. A trickle of bloody saliva oozed from her lips. He pulled the wire tight around their waists and wrists, making sure it dug into their skin until drops of blood popped to the surface and trickled down their hands.

"It says here that it takes a key to go back in time." Dr. Nampala announced. "Is there a key, ladies?"

No one replied. Researcher-9 was in the best shape. Dr. Nampala approached her. "You could have had everything. Now, tell me, what are you going to do?"

"I don't know what you're talking about, sir." She replied. She looked at him. A bruise was forming on her cheek from Sentry-5's assault. Dr. Nampala pushed on it. She winced.

"Does that hurt? That's nothing. You're going to hurt a lot worse unless you tell me the truth." He grabbed her chin and shook her head. A shock went down her neck as he twisted her face back and forth.

"Now." He released her face. "Tell me. Is there a key?"

"I don't know what you're talking about." She answered. She felt dizzy. She stuck her foot out to keep from falling. Her sudden movement caused the weight of Seventeen and Eleven to shift. She could see the floor rapidly rising to meet her face as they tumbled forward. She closed her eyes and turned her head to the side.

She banged to the ground with the full weight of the two girls against her body. She felt her ear pop and heard the loud thud of her own skull whacking against the floor.

I hope Thirty-Nine finds help, she thought as the room went black.

November Fourteen, Nineteen-**EIGHTY**-Eight

2:17 PM

Corey looked at the sky. Dark clouds had gathered as the afternoon passed.

This sure fits, he thought as he looked down at the crying boy on the steps.

Thirty-Nine looked at him. "What fits?" He asked, sniffling.

"I'm sorry?" Corey asked.

He looked at Corey, standing there before him with frightened eyes, his hands shoved into his pockets.

My pocket, Thirty-Nine remembered.

He stood up. The tears slowed as he responded to Corey. "Nothing. I mean. I need to talk to you." He glanced at Bruce and the old man. "In private."

Corey looked at Bruce.

Bruce chuckled an awkward quick burst of nervous laughter.

"I guess so. It's not like this situation can get much weirder."

Thirty-Nine walked to the side of the building.

What have I gotten myself into? Corey thought as he followed.

They turned the corner and Thirty-Nine spun around to face Corey. He looked around the side of the building to make sure Bruce and the old man weren't following them.

He looked at Corey. All those nights, all those dreams. He had never been able to see the face of the man who saved him from falling. The man who walked his mom down the aisle.

Could the dream come true? He thought. He looked at Corey's strong features. His firm jaw, his strong eyes, though clouded by concern and a little bit of fear, were bright and intense.

Maybe this kid – these kids – have mental problems, Corey thought as he returned Thirty-Nine's inquisitive stare.

"We don't have mental problems." Thirty-Nine said. "Well, not the kind that insane people have, if that's what you're thinking."

Corey jumped back. "What? What did you say?"

"Don't worry." Thirty-Nine said. "Yes I can hear thoughts. I don't have time to explain."

This can't be happening, Corey thought.

"This is happening." Thirty-Nine said. "I can hear thoughts. I hope it helps you believe what I have to tell you."

"Ok." Corey gulped. He rubbed his hands together. The friction re-opened the freshly formed scabs on his knuckles. "Ouch!"

"What'd you do?"

"I punched a wall. It's not good to lose your temper." Corey smiled. "Listen to me. Giving you advice. You can read minds. I should be asking you for help."

"No. I need your help. We need your help." Thirty-Nine furrowed his brow and lowered his voice. "This is serious. This is life or death. Do you understand?"

"Yes." Corey replied.

"We, me and my best friend, Thirty-Three, who you said is dead..." Thirty-Nine felt the sting of tears forming again. He breathed a deep breath and shut his eyes tight.

Stay focused, he thought.

"Did you say your best friend's name is Thirty-Three?"

"Yes. We don't have names. We are numbers. We," he continued, "are from the future. From ten years from now. We thought we were orphans but we found out we're not. My mother is in there." He pointed to the clinic.

"Your mother is Nicole? The woman in there?" Corey asked.

"Yes."

"How old are you?"

"Yes, what you're thinking is true. I was just born in there. In your time. Today's my tenth birthday. In my time."

"That's impossible." Corey said.

"Is it? I just heard your thoughts. I bet you thought that was impossible up until five minutes ago."

Corey shrugged. "Yes, I guess you're right."

"She's cute isn't she?" Thirty-Nine asked.

Corey blushed. "Yes."

He seems really nice. He could be a great dad, Thirty-Nine thought.

"We need help. If someone doesn't come save us in a few weeks – your time – we will all be dead."

"I don't understand. You're already out here. Safe. Why do you need to be saved?" Corey scratched the top of his head.

"It's not about me. There are nearly a hundred of us kids. And some workers."

The sound of a siren wailing interrupted their conversation.

"What's that?" Thirty-Nine asked, spinning his head around. The sound seemed to be coming from all directions.

Corey looked at his watch. "I'm guessing that's the sheriff. He's coming to ask me questions about how the boy died."

"What do you mean?"

Corey sucked in and exhaled. "I'm not sure how to tell you this." He ran his hands through his hair. His eyes started to tear up, which caused Thirty-Nine to start crying.

"I ran into him." Corey finally said. He began to speak rapidly, tears tumbling down both of their faces. "I was rushing to get Nicole to the clinic, it was pouring rain. He just appeared on the road. On the side of the road I don't know where he came from. I looked up and then he was in the road and then –" Corey broke down. He couldn't talk, he spluttered and wailed as the loss of the boy hit him in full.

"Where's the young man who was driving?" A deep voice echoed in the parking lot.

"Over here, Sheriff." Corey heard Bruce's voice answer.

Thirty-Nine heard it too.

I got to get back before the Chief discovers I'm gone, he thought.

He reached in his pocket for the note just as two men in brown uniforms appeared a few yards behind Corey.

"Take this." Thirty-Nine whispered. He pressed the note into Corey's bloody hand. Corey looked down at the scrap of paper.

"Come and save us." Thirty-Nine whispered. He took off running as fast as he could down the side of the clinic. As he reached the end of the building, he felt like he couldn't breathe but he couldn't stop. He had to get back. For the rest of the students. For Thirty-Three.

"Wait!" Corey shouted.

"Are you Corey McIntyre?" The deep voice called out.

Corey thrust the note into his pocket. He turned to see a white-haired man with a wide-brimmed hat, a thick moustache and a thin waist walking toward him. Just behind the moustache man stood a blonde haired, middle-aged man with plump cheeks and a gut that didn't stop until halfway down the zipper of his polyester pants. Bruce and Mr. Douglas stood on either side of the lawmen.

"Yes sir."

"I'm Sheriff Woodley. This is Deputy Dawson."

"Yes sir." Corey replied.

"Mind if we talk for a bit?"

"No sir."

"Who was that?" Sheriff Woodley asked, pointing at Thirty-Nine as he crossed the trees and stood in front of Mr. Douglas's car.

"I'm not sure." Corey answered.

This will get me back fast, Thirty-Nine thought as he felt the metal trim along the edge of the windowsill. He looked inside the still-running car. Its brown vinyl seat was shiny from weekly polishing.

"That's my car!" Mr. Douglas yelled.

I read about these. Just press the right pedal, and off it goes, Thirty-Nine thought.

"Thirty-Three would do it." Thirty-Nine told himself as he pulled the door open and slipped in.

"Deputy Dawson!" Sheriff Woodley barked. "Go get him."

Thirty-Nine slid behind the steering wheel. He pressed the gas pedal. The engine howled but he didn't move. He scanned the dashboard.

All these big knobs, he thought. He looked out the window. Deputy Dawson was huffing toward him, trudging across the grass. The extra eighty pounds hanging from the obese deputy's midsection gave Thirty-Nine the extra time he needed.

Thirty-Nine looked at the white "P R N D 2" in the rectangular glass between the steering column and the dash.

"That's it!" He yanked on the handle sticking out from behind the steering wheel. "D for drive!" Nothing happened. "I know this is it. Come on!"

"Stop kid!" Deputy Dawson yelled. He was on the other side of the young maple trees. He would be at the car in seconds.

"Think, think, think." Thirty-Nine told himself. "Come on. Just give me a break!"

Deputy Dawson tumbled into the saplings and onto the sidewalk.

A break! That's it, Thirty-Nine thought. He mashed the brake pedal and tugged the gearshift down until the needle split the "D".

Deputy Dawson planted his fat hands on the side of the car.

He held up his hand and bent over to catch his breath. He wheezed. He tried to speak but couldn't get air.

Thirty-Nine glanced at the top of his head. Sweat was beading and dripping down the back of his neck from under his stiff hat.

Sorry, sir. I can't wait, Thirty-Nine thought. He punched the gas and squealed the tires, dragging the cop a couple feet before his hands slid off the car and he fell to the ground.

"If I can go back in time, I guess I can drive a car." Thirty-Nine said. He steadied the steering wheel. It felt loose. The car drifted back and forth in the street. He had to turn it around to go back the way he came. There was plenty of open grass on either side of the street. He gunned it and jumped the curb, bouncing up and down as he rolled onto the grass.

Deputy Dawson stood and dusted himself off.

"Come get your car!" Sheriff Woodley shouted from the front of the clinic.

"Yes sir." Dawson started walking back just as Thirty-Nine spun the car around and jumped the old Buick back onto the street. He pressed the gas as hard as he could. He could feel the back of the car surging and the air rushing through the window. As he passed by the spot where he had just sent Dawson to the ground, he looked over.

The deputy was marching back to the group of men standing where he had just told Corey everything he could. They all were staring at him as he drove by.

"Come on, Corey. We're counting on you." Thirty-Nine said. He motored on past the old run-down buildings, past Bennie's Berries, and turned onto Route 71.

As he reached the spot where he exited the woods, he heard the same wailing siren he had heard just before the Sheriff arrived. He pulled the car to the side of the road and looked through the back window. Flashing blue and red lights were approaching quickly.

"Time to go!" Thirty-Nine shouted. He pressed the brakes to the floor. As he opened the door, the car started rolling. He pressed the brakes again. The car stopped. He lifted his foot and the car started moving again. The siren grew louder. It was so loud he could feel it.

"Forget this." He jumped out of the slowly rolling car and sprinted into the woods. As he disappeared into the evergreens, Deputy Dawson jumped out of his car, gun drawn.

"Stop!" He shouted. "Stop!"

Thirty-Nine ignored him as he crashed through the thick ferns. He pulled out the tracking device and flipped the reversal switch. In a second, the bulb lit up to guide him back to the tree.

Back to The Woodlands.

November Fourteen, Nineteen-**NINETY**-Eight

2:34 PM

Researcher-9 woke up with the taste of mud on her tongue. She felt the ground under her body, damp and cold. She turned to lift her head but couldn't move. She was trapped, face down. Her wrists and ankles were shackled.

I'm tied to the horseshoe stakes in the Yard, she thought.

She tried to look but could only open her left eye a crack. Her right side remained dark. Her right eye was swollen shut and throbbed like it was stuck in a blood pressure cuff.

Through her left eye, and through two pairs of boots just a few feet in front of her, she could see the Yard.

This has gone from bad to worse, she thought. *Where's Eleven and Seventeen?* She felt thirst overtake her throat, like fire crackling through August hay.

She closed her eye. There was nothing she could do. *If we're going to survive*, she thought. *It was up to Thirty-Nine. And maybe Sentry-1.*

"How's that feel?" Sentry-5 asked as he whipped Eleven. She crashed to the ground. "Second Run of Penance in a week!" He yelled.

"Didn't learn from the last one, huh?"

Every student except Thirty-Three and Thirty-Nine were assembled in the Yard. Almost every guard, including Sentry-1, surrounded them. Sentry-5 stood alone along the dirt trail, whipping Eleven. The students sat on their knees in the mushy turf. They were silent as death watching Eleven and Seventeen endure endless torture. The violence they observed exceeded anything previously seen at The Woodlands.

Dr. Nampala stood at the front of the group, screaming as he stomped back and forth. "We will be answered! We are family! No one betrays the family!"

He held the diary in his hand and waved it over his head. "Students." He looked down at the cluster of frightened children. He glared at their prickly heads beaded with the misty rain. "How many times do we have to explain this? No one leaves The Woodlands!"

"But they did." Seventeen's squeaked, her voice cracking. She was strapped to The Wheel. Sentry-5 had pummeled her unconscious and as she woke, she remained obstinate. Though she couldn't muster the strength to lift her head, she remained resolute.

Eleven heard her voice as she lay on the ground at the end of the Run of Penance. Eleven's voice was nearly gone either from fatigue or from shouting "no" at Dr. Nampala as he repeatedly asked her if she had the key to the willow tree.

"That's it!" Nampala shouted. He turned to face Seventeen. "Sentry-5, finish her. I've had enough!" As Dr. Nampala gave the execution order, Sentry-1 walked from the back of the students.

Sentry-5 whipped Eleven one last time. She flinched and cried as she lay on the ground, a ball of barely breathing skin and bone.

"Yes sir." He replied. He coiled his whip around his fist and shoved it under his belt.

Dr. Nampala flipped the book around. He looked at it closely. His skinny fingers traced the binding, tickling the spine and wrapping around the bottom edge. As he moved his hand across the old canvas, he felt a puffed out section. He rubbed his finger on it and turned the book over. He saw the outline of a key.

"There is a key!" He passed the front row of students, walking quickly toward the tree, staring at the book. As he neared the edge of the students, he nearly bumped into Sentry-1, who was making his way toward The Wheel.

"Excuse me, sir." Sentry-1 said.

Dr. Nampala looked up. He pressed the book into his chest. "What are you doing?" He asked. He peered over the rim of his glasses at his longest serving guard.

"Going to the front, sir." Sentry-1 balled both hands in a fist and held them tightly against his legs.

"What for? Did I order you to come up here?" Dr. Nampala asked. He stepped back from Sentry-1. "Go on back to your spot."

"No sir." Sentry-1 stood firm. He stared at the evil scientist.

"No sir?! What do you mean, 'No sir'?!" Dr. Nampala shouted, sputtering. He jerked his glasses off his broad nose and shook his head. His hair flapped across his face as he became exasperated.

"What I said, sir. I have an idea."

"You have an idea?"

"Yes sir."

"An idea for what?" Dr. Nampala said as he returned his glasses to his face.

"It's obvious the students aren't going to give you the key. Why don't you just chop the tree down? Then no one else will be able to escape?" Sentry-1 crossed his arms as he finished speaking.

"Interesting thought." Dr. Nampala replied. He tucked the book under his armpit as he twisted his forearms across his chest, mirroring Sentry-1's posture.

"Sentry-5, come here!" He yelled.

Sentry-5 had just reached Seventeen and was unclasping the metal brackets around her feet.

"Yes sir." He replied. He snarled at Seventeen. "I'll be back to finish you." He slammed the brackets back in place against her thin ankles and laughed. He walked to Sentry-1 and Dr. Nampala.

"Sentry-1 says we should just cut down the tree. What do you think?" Dr. Nampala asked.

"That would shut down the escape hatch. But how are we going to get Thirty-Nine and Thirty-Three? They must be punished. They should be executed." Sentry-5 replied.

"We can't chop the tree down!" Dr. Nampala suddenly realized. "I have to get Thirty-Nine back – he's my thought soldier. He's the realization of my vision."

He squinted at Sentry-1. "What are you trying to do? You trying to save Thirty-Nine by shutting down the escape hatch?"

"No sir." Sentry-1 uncrossed his arms and held up his empty hands, palms out. "I didn't even think of that. Why would he come back anyway? He's free."

"He'll come back." Dr. Nampala replied. "It's in his nature. Thirty-Three, I'm not so sure. But, he doesn't matter. I don't really care what happens to him. Or any of them." He flipped his hand toward the students.

"Except Thirty-Nine." Sentry-5 added.

"Yes. Except Thirty-Nine." Dr. Nampala echoed.

November Fourteen, Nineteen-**EIGHTY**-Eight

2:41 PM

Thirty-Nine looked down at the tracking device. Four lights were lit. He had made it through the forest without interruption. He guessed the cop had quit trying to chase him. Probably, he never started.

He jumped over a log and splashed in a trickling creek.

"I could use a drink." He squatted and scooped a handful of clear cool water. He sipped it slowly. It tasted great. He cupped both hands in and splashed the refreshing water against his face and neck.

"That feels good." He smiled and continued to drink and splash.

"It's been a long time since I just sat still. Since I wasn't running." He looked at the trees all around him. The air was calm. A little cold, but its briskness was welcome. Thirty-Nine slid onto the log and swung one leg over. He straddled the fallen pine and watched the water gurgling through the rocks below.

He thought of Thirty-Three, that chubby boisterous soul who repeatedly pushed him, who laughed in the face of danger. His podmate who had those "emotional parts." Thirty-Nine peeled a strip of bark from the log between his legs.

He tossed it into the creek and watched it bump along, pushed by the water, knocking against a rock, stalling until a surge in the creek flow pushed it forward again. As it drifted away, he whispered, as if Thirty-Three were beside him.

"I guess you were right all along about those emotional parts, Thirty-Three. Those emotional parts make life worth living. But they sure hurt during the dying."

He slid off the log and splashed into the creek. He looked at the tracking device.

"I better get back to The Woodlands." He walked a few steps and stopped. He looked back at the creek.

"I hope I did enough. Thirty-Three did more than enough. I sure hope Corey does enough. It's all up to him now to stop anyone else – all of us – from dying."

November Fourteen, Nineteen-**EIGHTY**-Eight

2:49 PM

"Corey, come here." Sheriff Woodley said as he poked his head into the doctor's back office. The Sheriff had asked him to wait there while he interviewed the doctor and the nurses.

Corey stood up, glanced at the hole he'd put in the drywall, and rubbed his sore hand.

"Could I wash my hands?" He asked.

"Sure, son. Right there's the sink."

Corey stepped into the treatment area. Several men in black long-sleeve t-shirts with "CORONER" printed in white across the shoulder stood near the draped body of the boy. Aunt Rita was sitting in a small wooden chair next to the crib. Bruce was there, also, leaning against the wall behind Aunt Rita.

Nicole was awake, propped up with a stack of pillows, sipping a mug of something steamy. She smiled as she spotted Corey.

Corey grinned stiffly and stepped to the sink. He turned on the water and closed his eyes as it poured over his hands. He softly rubbed the drywall powder away, careful not to pull any more skin off his raw knuckles.

"Corey, you said the boy just appeared on the side of the road?" Sheriff Woodley asked. He was holding a steno pad and pen.

Corey reached for a paper towel from the stack against the side of the sink counter. He wiped his hands slowly as he turned to face the policeman.

"Yes sir. I was driving. It was raining hard, like I said. And she was in the middle of major labor pains or something." He blushed as he glanced at Nicole.

"That's right, officer." Nicole said.

Sheriff Woodley looked over at Nicole. "I didn't know you were awake young lady. I'll want to take your statement also, in a bit, if that's ok."

"Yes sir. That's fine." She set the mug on the table tray next to her bed and shuffled herself up taller in the bed. "Everything's fine now. Thanks to him." She pointed at Corey.

"Ok, thank you." Sheriff Woodley replied.

"I couldn't catch him!" Deputy Dawson burst into the room. He banged against the narrow doorframe.

"What do you mean you couldn't catch him?" Sheriff Woodley replied, slamming his pad on the counter by the sink.

Corey eyed his notes, hopeful to see if there was anything written on the page that would help. The scrawled half-words and weird squiggly lines were of no assistance. Corey huffed.

"I'm sorry sir." The obese junior lawman replied. "The kid had a good head start. He only went a couple miles up Route 71 and then he ran into the woods." He dug his pudgy hands between his pants and his leather belt, which was already strained by his huge belly.

"I even had to stop the car for him. He just jumped out with it still in gear and dove into the trees. I saw Mr. Douglas outside. I told him his car was parked up there a mile past the fruit stand."

"Well, you could at least give old Mr. Douglas a ride to his car! Come on Dawson!"

"Yes sir, Sheriff Woodley." Dawson turned to leave.

"And Dawson?"

"Yes Sheriff." He replied from the now empty waiting room.

"Let's get some off-duty men from over in Manatuk to come down and do some tracking with us this weekend. That's two boys – one dead – who've jumped out of the woods. Something's out there. And we need to find it."

"Yes sir."

Corey pushed his clean hand into his pants pocket. He felt the note from Thirty-Nine. He looked at the sleeping baby. Maybe this whole thing is true.

As if agreeing with Corey's thought, the baby started to cry. His piercing wail quickly ended the Sheriff's impromptu interview.

"Well, Corey." Sheriff Woodley said. "I'm going to need to ask you to come with me to finish our questions." He looked at Bruce. "You can go with him if you like."

Bruce nodded. "Good. I would like that. His dad'll be here by night-fall. I just need to be able to let him know where we'll be."

"No problem. You can call him from the station."

Sheriff Woodley turned to Corey. "All right son. Let's go." He grabbed his note pad and pen and stuffed them into his extra wide shirt pocket.

Bruce stepped out into the waiting room.

"Go ahead." Sheriff Woodley motioned for Corey to walk out.

Rita picked up the baby as Corey walked past. She bounced the baby in her arms, shushing him. He kept crying.

"Just bring him to me." Nicole said.

Rita turned to carry the baby to Nicole. She lifted his head against her shoulder and tucked her arm under his butt.

Corey paused and stared.

The baby suddenly stopped crying.

Nicole looked around Rita.

"He likes you." She said.

"I feel like I've met him before." Corey replied, rubbing the note in his pocket. He blushed. "That was really stupid. Sorry." He rushed into the waiting room.

"He's cute." Aunt Rita whispered as she handed the baby to Nicole.

"Yes, he's my cute boy." Nicole said lovingly as she kissed baby Jake's forehead.

"I wasn't talking about him." Aunt Rita whispered. "I was talking about him." She thumbed toward the waiting room.

Nicole blushed.

"Ok, ma'am. I'll come back tomorrow to get your details of the accident," Sheriff Woodley said as he walked to the end of Nicole's bed.

"Yes sir."

"You all have a good evening." Sheriff Woodley turned to walk out.

"Just a minute, Sheriff." A coroner called out. "Don't you need these for evidence?" The coroner, a slender lady with delicate features and thick eyeglasses, held out Thirty-Three's clothes.

"Yes ma'am. We do. Thank you."

As she extended her latex-gloved hand, the overalls slipped. Sheriff Woodley reached to grab them but he missed. The dark fabric dropped to the floor. As he bent over to grab the clothes, Sheriff Woodley spotted a wrinkled corner sticking out from the center pocket. "Looks like a handkerchief." He said.

He picked up the overalls and reached inside the pocket.

"That's paper." He said as he pulled it out. "Wet paper. Of course."

Corey and Bruce looked in from the waiting room.

Sheriff Woodley unfolded the paper and held it up to the light. He looked at Nicole. He stared at Nicole. He stared at the paper. He turned the page over. He stared at Corey through the doorway. His eyebrows nearly popped off his face as he looked at Nicole. At Corey. At the paper.

After about two minutes of staring at Nicole, Corey, and the paper, he finally spoke.

"Corey, you say you never saw that boy before today?"

Corey stepped to the doorway. "Yes sir, never."

Sheriff Woodley looked at Nicole and Aunt Rita. "And you've never seen him before either?"

"No sir." They replied in unison.

"Well, well, we got ourselves a real mystery here." He squinted at them and stuck out the corner of his lower lip.

"I don't know if you've never seen him before or not." He held up their pictures for Nicole and Corey to see. "But it sure looks like he's seen you."

November Fourteen, Nineteen-**EIGHTY**-Eight

3:04 PM

Thirty-Nine looked at the tree.

This is it, he thought. *I'm going back. I sure hope Corey comes to find us in a couple weeks. Ten years ago.*

He put the tracking device back in his pocket and pulled out the wooden key. He pressed it into place and the dark path opened before him, obscuring the forest that had been his companion for the last half hour.

He stepped in. He was ready, or so he thought, to return to The Woodlands.

November Fourteen, Nineteen-**NINETY**-Eight

3:01 PM

"Finish her off!" Dr. Nampala shouted. Researcher-9 was jolted awake by his shout. She tugged on the chains that still held her pinned to the ground.

"Settle down." A faceless sentry told her. She looked at the back of his boot. She still couldn't open her right eye and the pulsing pain throbbing in her head made it nearly impossible to open her left eye. She finally pried it open through sheer willpower.

As the Yard came into focus, she could see Seventeen and Eleven lying on the ground. They were barely recognizable. Several sentries were taking turns clubbing them across all parts of their bodies.

"Nice hit!" Sentry-5 yelled.

Researcher-9 could hear crying from the gathered students. Each cry was followed by the dull whap of a club from one of the sentries stationed around the group.

"No!" Researcher-9 shouted. "Put me in their place!"

The sentry standing over her laughed. "Hey Sentry-5!" he shouted. "Researcher-9 says she wants to take the punishment!"

"Halt!" Sentry-5 yelled to the guards.

"What did you say?" he shouted across the Yard.

"I said, Researcher-9 wants to take their place!"

"Why didn't I think of that!" Dr. Nampala interjected. "Go get her Sentry-5!"

Sentry-1 remained near the back of the students. His tree-cutting idea nearly blew his cover. He wanted to do something but he was dramatically outnumbered. He reluctantly watched the abuse.

Where's Thirty-Nine? He thought.

"So you want to take their place?" Sentry-5 said as he unlocked the shackles from Researcher-9. He dragged her to her feet. Only then did she realize she couldn't stand. A searing pain rocked her to her knees. Her right leg was numb.

"You're weak." Sentry-5 grabbed her by the collar and tossed her toward the edge of the students. Squeals rose from the younger ones.

"Shut up!" Dr. Nampala yelled. "Stand her up."

Two sentries lifted Researcher-9 to her feet. They held her up as he approached her.

"What is that on the ground? Under her?"

Her head was already hanging. She fluttered her eyelash, trying to look. A brown rectangular shape was near her feet.

"What is that?" Dr. Nampala scooped it up. "This is an IV bag. Are you taking medicine? Drugs?" He held it close to his face. "That color is unusual. Reminds me of..." He smelled it. He sniffed several times. "That's the serum. My serum!" He shook as he recalled their encounter in his office. He looked at her jacket. Though stained with mud, the stain around the edges of the pocket was still visible.

"You! You traitor!" Dr. Nampala screamed. He grabbed his throat. "The apple cider!" He threw the IV bag at her.

"Sentry-5! Do it. Take her and kill her!" He ordered. "No! Don't kill her!" He yelled. "Kill her!" He looked at Sentry-5 who paused, his club lifted overhead.

"Don't kill her!" Dr. Nampala shouted.

"Sir?" Sentry-5 asked. "Which is it? Kill her or don't kill her?"

"Of course, kill her. Don't!" He shouted.

"I think I'll just do it." Sentry-5 said

What is going on? Dr. Nampala thought. *The serum*. He gulped. *Thirty-Nine*. He looked across the fuzzy topped students.

Thirty-Nine was standing next to Sentry-1. They began walking toward Dr. Nampala.

I've got you now, Thirty-Nine thought.

"I've got you now." Dr. Nampala said.

"What?" Sentry-5 replied, holding a fistful of Researcher-9's hair.

Dr. Nampala held his hands over his mouth. He suddenly felt like a rat in a cage. A very small cage.

Let her go, Thirty-Nine thought.

"Lemhurgo." Dr. Nampala said through his hands.

"Sir, I think you are having a major problem. I believe we've reached the point –" Sentry-5 began, interrupted by Dr. Nampala's frantic pointing.

He looked across the Yard and saw Thirty-Nine and Sentry-1. They were in front of The Wheel, and Sentry-1 was unleashing Seventeen.

"Thirty-Nine! Welcome home!" Sentry-5 shouted.

He drug Researcher-9 by her hair, pulling clumps out as she stumbled and dropped to the ground repeatedly. Each time she fell, he yanked her back up by a wad of hair. He laughed as he marched.

"Go ahead, release Seventeen! I don't need her anyway."

"Sentry-5!" Dr. Nampala shouted from behind him. "What are you doing?"

Thirty-Nine stared past Sentry-5.

Let go of Researcher-9, he thought.

"Let go of Researcher-9!" Dr. Nampala ordered.

Sentry-5 paused. He shoved Researcher-9 to the ground. As he did, he lifted his knee into her temple, knocking her unconscious. She flopped to the earth.

He turned to Nampala. "Sir. I am afraid it is time for me to relieve you of your command." As Sentry-5 stepped on Researcher-9's back, her vertebrae snapped like firecrackers. Multiple pops echoed through the Yard as he walked across her body. He stood facing Nampala.

"I represent The Future."

"What?" Dr. Nampala cowered before him.

"You didn't think they'd risk all this money and not have someone looking out for their interests did you? You're more naïve than I imagined!"

Sentry-5 waved his arms toward the sky. "This place is under surveillance. Every night a new satellite image of activity in the Yard and the facilities is uploaded to headquarters. I was sent here to observe and report. And," He held up his club, "if necessary, to take command. Dr. Nampala, you are hereby relieved."

The other sentries surrounding the students stared at Sentry-5. Whispers from the students went uncorrected as the collective group processed Sentry-5's announcement.

"No, I don't think so." Dr. Nampala said.

"You'll still get paid. You've done your job. Don't make me kill you." Sentry-5 said, stepping towards Dr. Nampala.

Sentry-1 dragged Seventeen from The Wheel and laid her next to Eleven. He assessed their injuries while Sentry-5 threatened Dr. Nampala. They were in need of serious medical attention, but were not in critical condition.

"I'll be back for you." He whispered.

You can't kill me, Thirty-Nine thought.

"You can't kill me." Dr. Nampala said. Once again, he clapped his hand over his mouth.

Sentry-5 laughed. He looked over his shoulder at Thirty-Nine. "Well, Dr. Nampala, how does it feel to have your invention work against you?"

It feels great, Thirty-Nine thought.

"It feels great." Dr. Nampala said. He realized he was outmatched. He turned and sprinted toward the doors.

"Detain him!" Sentry-5 yelled at the sentries.

"Don't go anywhere!" A voice shouted.

The sentries froze.

Sentry 5 slowly turned around and saw his nemesis.

"Sentry-1." He grinned. His eyes flashed with a darkness that matched the sky. "I've been waiting for this."

"Not as badly as I have!" Sentry-1 replied. The years of pent-up grief, the week of pent-up rage flooded Sentry-1 with adrenaline and anger. He was as explosive as a forest after a ten-year drought. Every fiber of his being burned with fury. He ran toward Sentry-5.

Sentry-5 crouched and cupped his hands. "Come on big fella. Bring it on!"

"You'll never kill anyone again!" Sentry-1 yelled as he ran to meet his daughter's killer.

Sentry-1 tunneled into Sentry-5's midsection. They tumbled to the ground, a jumble of violent limbs, flailing at each other with all of their energy.

The students stood. The sentries did not correct them.

Only Thirty-Nine noticed out of the corner of his eye, Dr. Nampala moving slowly toward the door.

Where's he going? He thought.

"Where's he going?" Dr. Nampala said as he reached the entry to the main building. He turned and looked at Thirty-Nine. The expression on Nampala's face gave Thirty-Nine a touch of pity.

He looked lost. Confused. But more than anything, the frantic rapid blinking of his eyes and the nervous tremor in his hands made the Chief, the lord of The Woodlands, look desperate.

He opened the door and sprinted into the building.

Thirty-Nine looked back at the fight.

Sentry-1 landed multiple punches to Sentry-5's midsection. Sentry-1 had gotten on top of Sentry-5 and was battering his thick ribs with all his might. As Sentry-1 punched, Sentry-5 flexed his leg and kneed Sentry-1 in the back of the head. It was enough to knock him off and now Sentry-5 had the upper hand.

"I've got to do something." Thirty-Nine said. He looked around the Yard. The students and the sentries were glued to the action between the two alpha guards. Eleven, Seventeen and Researcher-9 lay in the dirt clinging to life.

He looked back at the fight. Sentry-5 was pummeling Sentry-1 in the face. His knuckles like jackhammers, pounding and shattering Sentry-1's jaw and cheek like sidewalk being chipped to pieces in a work zone.

"Come on Sentry-1!" He shouted. The students, the sentries and researchers looked at him. No one moved.

Researcher-4 stepped out from the crowd. "Come on Sentry-1!" she shouted. She looked at the rest of the guards and workers. Her big blue eyes were lively and determined.

One by one, the other sentries joined the shout. The students, for the first time, felt truly liberated. With one voice and one heart, every person in the Yard began to chant.

"Sentry-1! Sentry-1! Sentry-1!"

Dr. Nampala exited the elevator, carrying the pistol he had retrieved from his office. He could hear the noise through the closed doors, echoing down the hallway.

Sentry-1 heard the cheer and began to gain strength. He closed his eyes and pictured the moment that Sentry-5 had kicked him off Fifteen. His daughter had died and he couldn't stop it. She died because he couldn't stand up to this man. The man who was now on top of him, pounding him with blow after devastating blow.

From deep within him, a force rose. Through his legs, into his abdomen, from the bottom of his heart and out of his lungs came a warrior cry.

"ENOUGH!" He shouted with all his might, flinging Sentry-5 to the ground.

The cheer from the students, the other sentries, and the researchers shook the building. Dr. Nampala walked to the glass door and stared at the scene. Everything he had worked so hard to build. His life's dream. His life's work. His first thought soldier used against him. Everything was disintegrating before him just moments before he would collect his prize.

Sentry-1 leapt onto Sentry-5. Blood poured from his face, dripping onto Sentry-1's eyes and mouth. He spit as Sentry-1 drove his fist into his throat. Over and over again, Sentry-1 sledgehammered Sentry-5 in the throat and mouth. Each punch flashed a memory of Fifteen's crash to the ground.

The death punch dislodged Sentry-5's nose and fractured his orbital cavity, spraying slivers of bone into his brain. As Sentry-5 slipped from life to death, Sentry-1 continued the assault.

Dr. Nampala watched through the glass doors. He stared silently as Sentry-1 continued to pummel Sentry-5's lifeless body. As the students and workers of The Woodlands realized Sentry-5 was dead, they stopped cheering and looked away. Though no one liked Sentry-5, no one could bear to see his corpse being mauled. Sentry-1 was in a frenzy. He thought only of avenging his daughter's death. The mashing sound of his fist on broken bone splatted through the Yard.

"Sentry-1!" Thirty-Nine said.

"Sentry-1!" Several guards yelled.

"Sentry-1! Stop!" The crowd of children and researchers and sentries shouted.

He looked up. His fists hung heavy at his sides. His glazed eyes looked out at a blur of faces. He stood over his daughter's killer. He felt no joy. No excitement. He wore the stoic expression of a man who did his job; nothing more, nothing less.

Thirty-Nine looked over at Dr. Nampala. The Chief opened the door and staggered into the Yard.

It's time to surrender, Thirty-Nine thought.

"It's time to surrender." Dr. Nampala said. He raised the silver gun in his hand.

I don't want to hurt anyone, Thirty-Nine thought.

"I don't want to hurt anyone." Dr. Namapala said. He stopped just a few feet inside the Yard. Everyone stared at him. Sentry-1 took a few steps toward him.

"Stop!" Dr. Nampala shouted, his voice quivering. He pointed the gun at Sentry-1. It shook like a falling leaf. He clutched the handle with both hands, trying to steady his aim.

"Don't do it." Researcher-4 cried. She walked to the three broken bodies on the ground between the students and Dr. Nampala. "There's been enough suffering today." She pleaded.

I won't shoot you, Thirty-Nine thought. He inched toward Dr. Nampala, slowly moving closer and slowly commanding his thoughts by controlling his speech.

"I won't shoot you." Dr. Nampala said. "I can't take this. I can't take having you in my head." He looked at Thirty-Nine, who was now a few feet away.

Sentry-1 took a step, cracking a pinecone.

"Don't move!" Dr. Nampala ordered. He waved the gun at Thirty-Nine, then back at Sentry-1. Back and forth, he alternated his target, all the while lamenting the end of his decade of research.

"I can't live like this. I can't bear to see this...The Woodlands. Like this. We were going to see breakthroughs."

We did see breakthroughs, Thirty-Nine thought.

"We did see breakthroughs." Dr. Nampala said. "That!" he shouted. "That right there! I thought it would be the most amazing thing. It's horrible. It's wretched! I'm losing my mind to a – a – a child!"

He pointed the gun at Thirty-Nine. The barrel bounced as he trembled.

"It's ok, Dr. Nampala." Thirty-Nine whispered. "No one else has to die."

"Yes. One more person has to die." Dr. Nampala replied. "And there's nothing you can do to stop it."

The next few seconds seemed to pass more slowly than the previous ten years. Sentry-1 ran toward the Chief. Researcher-4 yelled.

The crowd of students screamed and The Woodlands staff gasped.

Thirty-Nine ducked as Dr. Nampala lifted the pistol higher. And pressed it firmly against his temple. As the end of the barrel dug into the side of his head, he thought a message to Thirty-Nine.

Bet you didn't see this coming. Goodbye Thirty-Nine. At least I lived to see my vision realized. Do better than I did with your powers. Goodbye.

Thirty-Nine heard the Chief's thoughts. Everyone heard the explosion of his gun firing, driving a bullet deep into his brain. Dr. Nampala crumpled to the ground, dead.

The world fell silent. No one moved. No one spoke. Finally, Sentry-1 walked to Thirty-Nine's side. Together, they stared at the once fierce leader, their nemesis.

"What now?" Researcher-4 asked from in front of the crowd of on-lookers.

"Yes, what now?" Several voices echoed.

Thirty-Nine dug in his pocket and fished out the wooden key. He held it up to Sentry-1.

"This is the way out."

Sentry-1 took it and studied it for a moment. He was in charge now. After all these years taking orders, it was his turn to give one.

He turned to face the crowd and held up his hand for silence. The students and sentries obliged. The researchers huddled together to listen.

He looked down at Thirty-Nine. "Did you make contact on the other side?"

"Yes. I gave Corey, I mean, the man, a note. I think he's going to come here in a month. Ten years ago."

"Ok." Sentry-1 looked at the group. All the children he had watched grow up. All the guards he had worked with. He held their fate in his hands.

"Researcher-4, Sentry-13, Sentry-7, some of you other guys. Help get Researcher-9, Seventeen and Eleven into the recovery room. Get the nurses working on them."

The workers jumped to work, carefully carrying the wounded from the Yard.

"The rest of us." He tucked the key into his pocket. "We will continue to function normally. And we will wait. Sentry-5 said The Future monitors this place. They take satellite imagery. If they don't see the normal activities happening, they'll invade this place. My hope," he looked down at Thirty-Nine, "our hope, is that in a few weeks we will be rescued. This young man has gone at great risk and enlisted the help of a strong man, who will come for us. It's just a matter of time." He squeezed Thirty-Nine around the shoulders and pulled him close.

"We can't go back in time. One hundred fifty people. It would just cause way more harm than good." He whispered as the students began chattering about the possibility of rescue.

Thirty-Nine thought for a moment. "I guess you're right. I guess Wesley Kenton was right. Undoing one thing always does another."

"Yes it does." Sentry-1 answered. He looked at the students. "Hush! I know you're excited. And so am I. So are we." He smiled at his fellow guards. "But we all have to be faithful to our routine. We can't do anything out of the ordinary. Does everyone understand?"

The students calmed as he repeated his request.

"Does everyone understand?"

"I don't understand, sir." A small voice meekly said. It was Seventeen. She was lying on the ground, battered but not broken.

"Oh Seventeen. You've been so brave." Sentry-1 felt fatherly as he knelt down. "You see, everyone. Seventeen has kept a secret and has endured punishment. She has been so brave."

The students clapped.

"There is an organization that wants to do you harm – wants to do great harm to the world – through you. They are watching us with occasional photographs taken by satellites high up in the sky. We must go through our normal routines. We are waiting for a rescue to happen. In the past. That part is impossible for me to explain. I just need you to trust me. Do you trust me?"

"Do you trust me?" Thirty-Nine added, kneeling down over Seventeen.

"Yes."

"Good. So let's go back to our stations. Back to our classes. Back to our pods. We will wait. And we will be saved."

The students started to mill about and the sentries watched unsure of what to do. The researchers began slowly walking back into the main building.

"Students!" Sentry-1 bellowed. "Please line up behind Thirty-Nine." He smiled as he looked at the skinny shaved head boy with the bright yellow eyes.

"After all, he is our Head Student."

The students formed a line behind Thirty-Nine. Two by two they filled the space between him and the tree. He looked to his right, at the space normally occupied by Thirty-Three. He looked back at the tree. He looked up at the clouds. As he led the students back into the routine of nearly a decade, his single thought was of the single hope they all had.

Undoing one thing always does another. Corey, please undo all of this. He thought of Thirty-Three, his pudgy podmate, one last time.

Please undo ALL of this...

Turn the page for a preview

-BOY 33-

the sequel to BOY 39

Available Christmas 2013
@derekholser.com

August Twenty-Eight, **Two Thousand**

7:30 AM

"Jake! It's time to go. Your bus is going to be here any minute!" Nicole called from the kitchen.

"He's never late." Corey said through a mouth full of oatmeal.

"I know. But it's his first day at the new school. He must have spent an hour washing and conditioning his hair this morning." Nicole grabbed her mug of coffee and stirred in two scoops of sugar as she stared through toile drapes at the yard behind them.

"He's obsessed with his hair. He still won't let anyone cut it, will he?" Corey asked, standing from the maple colored round table. He picked up the red plastic bowl of almost finished oatmeal and walked to Nicole.

"Yes, he does love his hair." She sighed.

Corey slid next to her and dropped his bowl into the sink. The bowl landed with a thud and the spoon rattled against the stainless steel.

Nicole turned to him. He slid his arm around her trim waist and flicked her long curly hair from her face as she smiled. Her cheeks reddened.

"After nearly twelve years, you still make me blush." She said, placing her slender fingers on his chest.

"Not again! C'mon mom and dad!" Jake burst into the kitchen, interrupting their cuddle.

They separated and looked at their son.

"What?" Corey laughed. "You jealous? Come here son." He held his arms out wide. Jake stared at his dad's arms, draped in flannel.

"No thanks! I got to run." He rushed past Corey and snatched his backpack off the granite countertop. "See you guys after school! Love ya, mom!" He yelled as he swung the door between the kitchen and the garage open wide.

"Love you too honey!" Nicole replied. They both stared at the open door and Jake's backside disappearing down the driveway.

"Shut the door." Corey said. "When is he going to start shutting the door?"

"Quit complaining. And rinse out your oatmeal bowl." Nicole scolded her husband.

"Yes ma'am."

As Corey turned on the water to clean his dish, Nicole lingered at the doorway, watching Jake board the big yellow bus next to their rainbow trout silhouetted mailbox.

"Think he'll be ok?" She mumbled, not expecting an answer.

"He'll be fine. He's a good kid." Corey placed the bowl and spoon in the dishwasher. "He's got a great mother, too."

"Thanks babe. I just worry about him, you know." Nicole closed the door as the bus pulled away leaving a puff of black smoke in its wake.

"Find your seat son." The heavy-set bus driver ordered Jake as he stood at the front of the bus.

He glanced down at the seats before him. A pimply-faced girl with stringy hair slid her backpack across the first seat. No vacancy.

His bright golden yellow eyes scanned the dark pleather benches before him. Most seats were full and those that weren't had students responding like pimple girl.

"Hurry up!" the driver shouted. "I got to get moving, your highness!"

"Yes sir." Jake replied and started walking down the aisle. He felt the bottom of his shoe sticking with nearly every step on the black rubber flooring.

"Disgusting." He whispered.

"Sit here, buddy. I'm not disgusting." A voice on his right said.

He turned to see a chubby brown face with dark hair nearly as long as his own smiling at him. The kid pulled his navy blue and yellow backpack into his lap and motioned for Jake to sit.

Jake slid into the bench, clutching his own backpack.

"My name's Henry. What's yours?"

"I'm Jake."

Jake, the lanky pale kid with the bright eyes stared at Henry, the pudgy tan boy with dark eyes. Henry stared back until they both began to feel uncomfortable.

"You seem familiar." Henry said as Jake stared down the row of heads in front of them. "Where'd you go to elementary school?"

"Not around here. We just moved here from Washington this summer. My dad's the new fly fishing guide over at Swampy's River Tours."

"Oh. Well, I've been here in Idaho my whole life. I'll show you around." Henry tapped Jake's bare leg. He was wearing shorts since it'd only be another few weeks before the cold weather started.

Jake looked at Henry. "What?"

Henry winked, his dark brown eyes glistening. "You like adventure? I can show you some fun stuff around here."

"Umm. I like adventure, I guess. You always this friendly?"

"Why not? I mean, we're going to be in school together. Gonna be on this bus every day. Might as well make the best of it. Though I've never been good at following the rules, you know what I mean?" Henry nudged Jake in the ribs.

Jake flinched then smiled. "You know, Henry, I feel like I do know what you mean."

"Everybody out!" The bus driver yelled.

Jake looked out the window at the long, low brick building. It looked ominous but his parents assured him it was the best school in the county. Change is never easy.

"We're here." He said.

"We sure are." Henry replied. He looked at Jake who was fidgeting with his backpack handles. "You nervous?"

"Not really." Jake replied.

"Good." Henry stood up, bumping Jake into the aisle. "Go on. Don't be shy. Let's go in there and give 'em a show!" Henry laughed an abrupt loud guffaw.

This kid seems so familiar, Jake thought.

Too familiar.

Derek Holser